SCIPIO'S DREAM

BOOK THREE OF THE SCIPIO AFRICANUS SAGA

MARTIN TESSMER

Copyright © 2015

All rights reserved

Dedication

To Cheri, my Sophonisba.

Table of Contents

I. Victory's Price 1
II. Astapa 32
III. Rebellion 48
IV. Coming Home 82
V. Departure 142
VI. Sicily 221
VII. Locri 257
VIII. Judgment 288
IX. Scipio's Dream 319

About the Author 349
End Notes 350

ACKNOWLEDGMENTS

Among 20th and 21st century historians, I am primarily indebted to Professor Richard Gabriel for his informative and readable *Scipio Africanus: Rome's Greatest General,* and *Ancient Arms and Armies of Antiquity.* H. Liddell Hart's *Scipio Africanus: Greater Than Napoleon* provided many valuable insights into Scipio the general and Scipio the man. John Peddle's *Hannibal's War* helped flesh out the personality, tactics, and motivations of Hannibal the Great. Nigel Bagnall's *The Punic Wars* provided confirmatory evidence for information I drew from Gabriel, Livy, Polybius, Mommsen, and others. Thanks to you all.

Among classic historians, I owe a deep debt of gratitude to Titus Livius (Livy) for *Hannibal's War: Books 21-30* (translated by J.C. Yardley) and Polybius for *The Histories* (translated by Robin Waterfield). Cassius Dio's *Roman History* provided additional details and confirmed some of Livy's and Polybius' assertions. Appian, Dodge, and Mommsen, thanks to you all for the many tidbits and corrections your works provided.

Cato the Elder's *De Agri Cultura* and Plutarch's *Roman Lives* provided insight into Cato, this simple but ruthless and powerful man that so influenced the course of Western History.

Ross Lecke has written two fine historical novels about Scipio and Hannibal: they are *Scipio Africanus: The Man Who Defeated Hanniba*l, and *Hannibal*. Ross showed me that a writer can spin a good yarn and still stick to the facts, where there are facts to stick to.

Finally, I must give a tip of the hat to Wikipedia. Wikimedia, and the scores of websites about the people and countries of 200 BCE. The scholarship of our 21st century digital community is amazing.

Susan Sernau, your copyediting of my humble manuscript helped to evolve it from report to story. You are a wonder.

A Note on Historical Accuracy

This is a work of historical fiction, meaning it combines elements of historical fact (such as it is) and fiction. It is not a history textbook.

The book's major characters, places, events, battles, and timelines are real, meaning they are noted by at least one of our acknowledged historians such as Livy, Polybius, Gabriel, Mommsen, Appian, or Peddle. You will see footnotes scattered throughout the text to document various aspects of the book. I have included several quotes of Scipio's and Hannibal's actual words, as described by Livy or Polybius. You will find a source footnote to those at the end of the quote.

The story's Hellenic Party and Latin Party factions were created to capture the mood of the times, when there was real enmity between those favoring a more "decadent" Hellenic lifestyle and those of agrarian sympathies who disparaged it.

Similarly, the creation of hobnailed sandals, the cohort formation, cavalry formations, lighter packs, rudimentary steel, and the falcata sword seem to have occurred during this era, but it is difficult to know who invented them versus who popularized them. In this book Scipio Africanus is given attribution for them to help illustrate the military inventiveness that took place during the Punic wars. A hundred years later, the redoubtable Gaius Marius institutionalized the cohort formation, lighter packs, and reduced baggage trains.

CREDITS

- Cover design by pro_ebookcovers at Fiverr.com

- Battle maps created by renflowergrapx at Fiverr.com

- Terrain maps created by wesdsd at Fiverr.com

- Scipio sculpture portrait "Ritratto di Scipione" by Mino da Fiesole, courtesy of Wikimedia Commons at commons.Wikimedia.org

- Iberian falcata provided by Wikimedia Commons, courtesy of Luis Garcia

- Roman gladius provided by Wikimedia Commons, courtesy of Purmont.

Italia, Second Punic War, 205 BCE
ALPS
LIGURIA
Genova
APPENNINES
Metauro River
Rome
Ostia
APULIA
LUCANIA
BRUTTIUM
Kroton
Locri
Rhegium
Sicily
Lilybaeum
Syracuse
Hippo Regius
Carthage

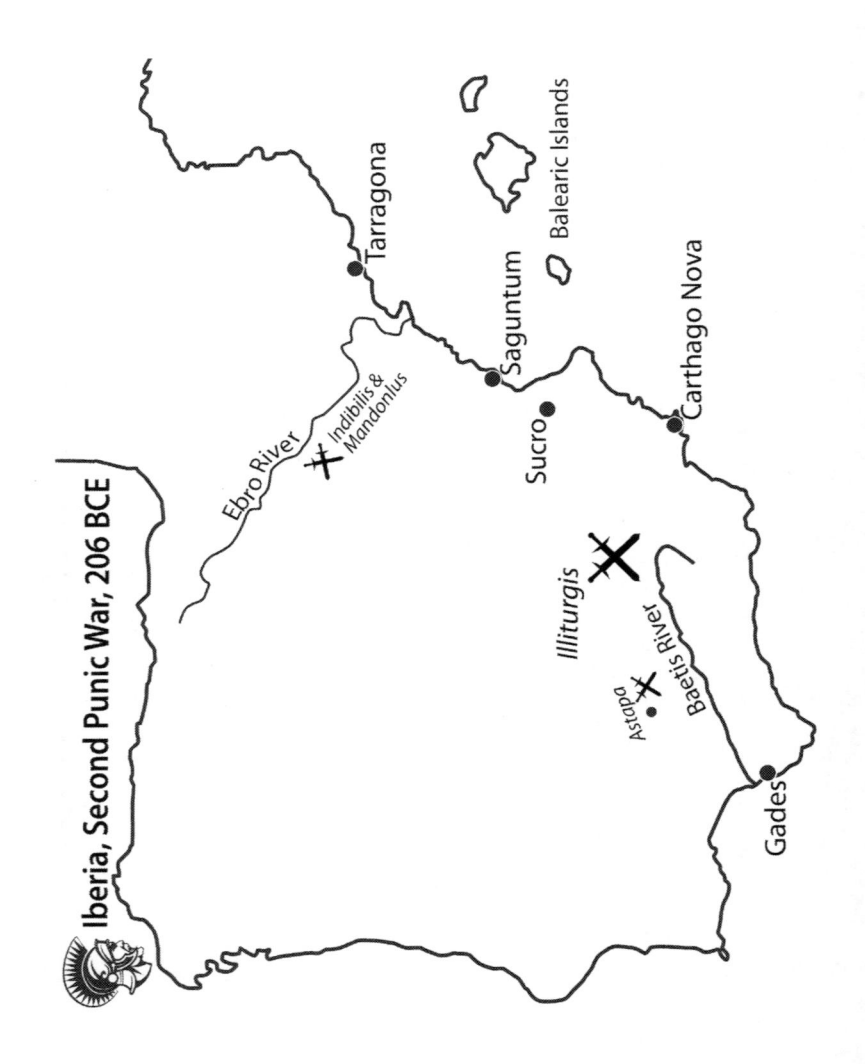

Second Punic War Theatre, 218-201 BCE

Iberian Falcata

Röm. Gladius.

I. VICTORY'S PRICE

SIGA, NORTH AFRICAN COAST, 206 BCE. "I wish I had an animal to sacrifice," grouses Scipio. "That might get this crate going." He stomps across the deck of his hundred and fifty foot warship, kicking an empty amphora jar into the railing. *I will give you an ox when we land,* he prays to Jupiter, *just bless us with some breeze!*

The winter winds have deserted the Roman fleet, leaving its oarsmen to stroke the five quinqueremes toward the faint outline of the hilly African coast. Scipio paces nervously across the planked deck of his slow-moving craft, anxious to reach the safety of Siga before nightfall. He leans over the railing of his trim ship, peering into the dusky gray veils of the Mediterranean sunset, searching for Carthaginian patrols.

General Scipio is a sturdily built young man with curling black hair and a jutting double chin. His green eyes flash with the determination that has become part of his persona as he has grown from a quiet and scholarly youth to a relentless Roman conqueror. Though still in the flower of his youth at twenty-nine, his face is lined with the wrinkles of an older man, a record of the many fateful decisions he has made in his six years of command.

For the hundredth time, Scipio glares at the linen sails draped stiffly about the quinquereme's two broad beams, as if willing them to fill. He wipes his sweaty brow. "These pissy wind gods abandon you just when you need them most," he exclaims, spreading out his hands. "What am I supposed to do, drag sacrificial animals along, just to please them? I sacrificed a chicken to Fortuna before we left. Wasn't that enough?"

"Perhaps you should pray to Zephyrus, the Greek god of wind," replies Admiral Laelius, Scipio's best friend. Tall, supple, and handsome, Laelius is perpetually good humored, but on this short trip from Iberia he has already become irritated at Scipio's impatience with the vagaries of sea voyages. He decides to jostle Scipio out of his petulant mood. "I would wager the Roman gods know you are a

I. Victory's Price

Hellenic sympathizer. They are likely to be Latin Party members, being so powerful and wealthy. They will surely not support you. Seek the Greeks deities, I say. They'll be happy with a chicken!"

"Your humor does little to cheer me, Admiral," Scipio growls, prompting Laelius to laugh.

"You are certainly of a mood today, old friend," he chuckles. "You should not have come out sea. Sailing is best left to sailors!"

Scipio shoves Laelius on the shoulder. "And what choice did I have? Syphax refused to sign the treaty you brought him, unless I was there to sign it with him." [i] He looks out towards Africa, watching for signs of wind. "I know this might be a Carthaginian trap, but Syphax commands at least fifty thousand warriors. Think what it would mean to have him as an ally when we land in Africa. We could march on Carthage itself!"

"*If* we go to Africa," says Laelius. "You must still gain the Senate's approval. Flaccus and Fabius will oppose you, of course, along with the rest of the Latin Party. They will not take kindly to your dragging an army over there."

"I am prepared to argue for our cause," Scipio retorts. He flaps his hands in frustration, staring at the dormant sails. "I just don't want to bob along out here in the middle of the sea, easy prey for the Carthaginians."

Laelius nods, his mouth a tight line. *There isn't a ship in sight. He's letting this Imperator title go to his head.* He nods, and bows theatrically. "As you wish, oh conqueror of Iberia. I will double the oarsmen's pace. If we get wind, they can ease off."

Laelius barks an order to his captain. The ship's five banks of oars quicken their swinging strokes into the deep blue waters, and the quinquereme gradually speeds up. Scipio hears the waves lap faster against the hull timbers, and says no more. But Laelius notices that Scipio still looks anxiously about the empty seas, still searching for Carthaginian patrols, even though Rome has controlled these seas since Scipio's conquest of Iberia. *He worries about every eventuality, every*

I. Victory's Price

little detail, Laelius muses. *I have never seen the like.*

After several uneventful hours of watching the glimmering Mediterranean waves, Laelius sees a most welcome sight. Flocks of seabirds slowly circle on the air swells above the ship, their presence a sign that land is near. He spies the outline of Rachgoun Harbor's sheltering bluffs, the gateway to Syphax's inland citadel at Siga.

Laelius grins with relief. *We're here. Now maybe he'll stop fussing about Carthaginian patrols.* The young admiral trots to the ship's sharply curved prow and leans over the front railing, searching for any treacherous rocks and shallows. Finding the seas clear, Laelius leans back and admires the immaculate stone harbor, its wide timbered piers reaching far into the lapping turquoise waters of the encircling port.

"Prepare to dock," Laelius shouts to his captain. The crew scrambles to lower the sails, as the oars beat a slow pace into the placid waters. Scipio stands at middeck, arms crossed, carefully watching the sailors tie up the sails.

Laelius scans the harbor's four long piers, looking for open spaces to dock his small fleet. He notices seven trim warships that are tied up to the front pillars of the pier to his right.[ii] He peers in at the purple bird that decorates each ship's curved prow, trying to make out the characters carved beneath them. *Are those Syphax's ships? The Numidians have leopard heads, don't they?*

His eyes widen. "Scipio!" he shouts. "Over here!"

Scipio strides over to Laelius' side, his lips pursed. "What is it now? I was watching your men sheath the sails. They seem a bit disorganized, if I may say."

Laelius stabs his finger at the docked vessels. "I swear, those look like Carthaginian triremes."

The words no sooner leave his mouth than the faint sounds of battle horns drift across the sea. The two friends gape at each other as hordes of ant-sized men swarm about the docked ships, rushing to set sail. Scipio pounds his fist on the railing. "By Jupiter's cock, those are

3

I. Victory's Price

Carthaginians. And they're coming out for us!"

Laelius curses. "We're the flagship, they'll come for us first. If we can get into Syphax's harbor, we'll be under his protection."

Laelius waves over his captain. "Ram speed!" Laelius bawls, "Straight toward the docks!" The captain yanks open the middeck hatch and clambers down the rope ladder, screaming orders to quicken the pace. The flagship's weary oarsmen surge to their task, their oars threshing frantically into the waves. Laelius and Scipio stare anxiously at the docks, watching the triremes push off from their moorings and hoist up their sails.

Laelius grimaces. "We are moving too slow. We won't reach the harbor in time."

"We cannot surrender. Arm the marines and the oarsmen," says Scipio. "We have to get to Syphax and make that treaty." He pounds his fist onto the mast. "We were so close!"

The ship's cornicen blows the call to battle. A hundred tunic-clad marines line up along the ship's stout oak railings, clenching their javelins and shields.

Laelius is strapping on his greaves when he feels his hair stir. He looks behind him and a broad grin splits his face. "The wind! The wind is coming!"

Scipio licks his finger and raises it to feel the air. He wrinkles his nose. "It is but a strong breeze, but it may be enough."

"Hoist all the sails!" Laelius shouts. "Hoist them now!"

The quinquereme's sails billow out shallowly. The ship's pace quickens, impelled by wind and oar. The four trim ships turn away from the Carthaginians, racing to the far side of the mile-wide harbor, its sailors frantically angling the sails to capture every scrap of breeze.

By now the Carthaginian triremes have backed away from the pier and are stroking out from the docks, knifing through the shallow harbor

I. Victory's Price

waves. They head broadside for Scipio's flagship, their decks lined with armored warriors. The Carthaginians' intentions are clear to Scipio: they will storm his ship, knowing it must hold him and the rest of the officers, then demand the fleet's surrender. *I hate to disappoint you, but I will be no man's prisoner*, he thinks as he straps on his sword belt.

Laelius' face flushes with excitement. "It's going to be close! They are faster, but we have the wind behind us. I'll see what I can do to eke out more speed from the oarsmen."

As Laelius dashes off, Scipio fingers the hilt of his gladius, the cleaver-like sword he has created for his army. He watches helplessly as the triremes close the distance between them. For the first time since he became general, he cannot think of any stratagem or tactic that would turn the tide in his favor. *I can at least take some of them with me.* He grabs several javelins from a wicker casket of them.

Scipio watches the triremes pass the far end of the pier, pushing through the stiffening wind that fronts them. He raises his eyes to the skies. "I pray you, Zephyrus. Get behind us with all your strength. I promise you three oxen at the next new moon!"

He moves to the center of the deck as the Carthaginian force closes in on them, preparing to lead the defense. The marines crowd into the railings, ready to hurl their javelins. The sailors tug at the sail ropes to capture more wind, even as the oarsmen push frantically with the last of their strength. Scipio's four other ships follow suit, desperately thrashing the water.

The Carthaginians' battle horns blare out across the sea, followed by the battle shouts of the triremes' eager warriors. A grim-faced Laelius stalks among his men, telling them of Scipio's final order: there will be no surrender, only victory or death.

Scipio hears the gusts before he feels them. The wind begins to blow so strongly it howls in his ears. The Roman ships surge ahead, slapping through the emerging whitecaps, their two large sails rigid with wind. The enemy triremes struggle to maintain their bearing in the wind that

I. Victory's Price

fronts them, and Scipio's ship angles past them.

Even as the first Carthaginian spears clatter onto the quinquereme's deck, the flagship noses its way into rocky borders of the calm harbor waters, under the protection of Syphax's realm. A chorus of Numidian horns bellow out from the landside docks, sounding their recognition of the Roman fleet's arrival – and a warning to their Carthaginian guests.

Slowly, reluctantly, the triremes turn about and head back to their docking places. Scipio can see the Carthaginian commanders aft of his ships, hurling futile imprecations and warnings in their foreign tongue.

So close to losing all, Scipio thinks. *After all these years, a capricious wind decides my fate. Zephyrus, Fortuna, I give you thanks. And fitting sacrifice, I swear.*

The quinqueremes tie up at an empty dock, far from the returning enemy ships. Laelius is the first to debark, leaping over the railing and onto the walkway, grinning like a man who has just cheated death. "I think I'll go over and say hello to those Carthaginian bastards," he shouts over at Scipio.

"You will not tempt Fortuna, fool," says Scipio with a smile. "I need you to die for a greater purpose than mocking an armed enemy."

A lean and hawk-faced man shuffles out along the wide-planked dock walkway. He wears an indigo robe edged in silver. A thin gold diadem rests across his craggy brow. The man is surrounded by a score of tall Numidian warriors armed with oblong black shields and gleaming curved swords, their white linen tunics resplendent against their light brown skin. Looking at the shields' leopard-head insignia, Scipio knows this sharp-featured older man must be Syphax, lord of the powerful Masaesyli tribe of western Numidia—the sworn enemies of Scipio's Massylii ally, Prince Masinissa.

"Hail, King Syphax," Scipio says, bowing his head slightly. The Numidian smiles beatifically and raises his leathery right hand. He beckons for Scipio and Laelius to approach.

Scipio's eyes widen at the sight of the sturdy little man standing next

I. Victory's Price

to Syphax. Commander Hasdrubal Gisgo, Scipio's mortal enemy in the Iberian war, is glaring back at him. Gisgo grimaces as he looks at Scipio, his face evidencing his disappointment at Scipio's escape. *What is Gisgo doing here? This is an odd turn of affairs*, Scipio thinks, as he musters an awkward smile for King Syphax.

"The esteemed General Gisgo did favor us with his presence on his way to Carthage," Syphax exclaims anxiously, his eyes searching Scipio's face. "Most unexpected. But, uh, most welcome, of course."

Gisgo nods briefly at Scipio. He favors Syphax with an ingratiating smile. "Thank you, King Syphax. I thought I should pay a visit to Carthage's old ally. To celebrate your lifelong friendship with our empire."

"Ah yes, friendship. That is important," declares Scipio theatrically. "If I remember my military history aright, King Syphax, you were our ally in the first Carthaginian war. We even sent a praefectus castrorum here to help train your troops."

Syphax shifts about awkwardly. "Well, yes, you are both correct. Changing times beget changing alliances, you know... But let us be off to my palace, that you may refresh yourselves before we dine. I have much to talk about with the both of you."

Laelius rolls his eyes. "Oh, of that I am sure!"

Gisgo eyes Scipio resentfully, and slowly extends his right arm, as if he were putting it into the mouth of a lion.

Scipio takes a deep breath, steps forward, and grasps Gisgo's forearm. "At least tonight, Gisgo, let us be comrades in arms. We can always talk about our common enemy—the politicians back home!"

At that comment both Gisgo and Syphax laugh, Syphax loudest of all. Gisgo touches his hand to his forehead by way of a salute. "Your point is well met, General Scipio. Tonight we are but fellow soldiers, sharing bread and wine."

A relieved smile covers Syphax's face. "Nobly spoken, General

I. Victory's Price

Scipio! And nobly accepted, Gisgo. Now, let us proceed to my palace. I have prepared a feast that will be the stuff of songs!" The Numidian king shuffles down the dock, his wood-soled shoes clacking noisily. Scipio and Gisgo walk on each side of the king, glancing speculatively at one another.

True to their word, Scipio and Gisgo spend the night peacefully feasting, drinking wine, and sharing war stories. They tactfully avoid talking about their battles against each other at Baecula and Iberia. Both endure Syphax's rants about his rival Masinissa, the rebel prince of eastern Numidia, and bear up to his endless brags about how he defeated Gala, Masinissa's father, and took over Gala's eastern Numidian kingdom.

Syphax presses Scipio and Gisgo to commit troops to his war against Masinissa, gloating that he has taken much of eastern Numidia while Masinissa was fighting against Scipio in Iberia.[iii]

Gisgo drains his wine up and gestures for more. "King, I promise to send troops to you as soon as Carthage takes back control of Iberia from the Romans."

Syphax cocks a doubtful eye at him. "I need men now, Gisgo. Thousands of men. Then, when I have disposed of the last of Masinissa's rebels, my army is free to join my ally." His eyes dart from Scipio to Gisgo. "Whoever that may be."

Scipio fingers his wine cup, still half full. "I will not dishonor you with false promises, King. For now, I can only promise to help end the war peacefully between the Masaesyli and the Massylii—to help you build a united nation."

Syphax nods gravely. "So be it, I appreciate your peaceful sympathies. I hope you will say the same to Masinissa, should he approach you."

Scipio sighs, relieved at Syphax' words. *He does not know that Masinissa has allied himself with me. I can still arrange a peace with him.*

I. Victory's Price

Ever cordial and entertaining, Laelius regales the party with stories of his roughshod childhood on the docks of Ostia and the back streets of Rome. After several more cups of the Syphax's strong red wine, Scipio and Gisgo commiserate about a general's common complaint; having military decisions made by businessmen and officials who have never laid hand to sword.

Scipio dutifully listens to Gisgo declaim the sheltered merchants who dominate Carthage's Senate and Council of Elders. As Gisgo pours out his frustrations about his business-driven country, Scipio begins to feel sorry for him. Then it comes to Scipio—*Cato was wrong. We do not have to destroy Carthage to protect Rome from this merchant nation. We just have to make peace more profitable than war. We can coexist.*

The next morning there is a final meeting between the three woozy leaders. Gisgo and Scipio walk together toward the docks. The two have agreed to leave at the same time, so neither gains a diplomatic advantage with Syphax by lingering behind. Even so, Scipio leaves with a most powerful advantage. In his right hand, Scipio carries a signed treaty between himself and Syphax, a declaration that there will be no war between Rome and Syphax' kingdom.[iv]

As he rubs the weariness from his eyes, Scipio smiles. *Now I have an alliance with the second most powerful nation in Africa. Syphax can supply me with troops and food during an African campaign. I won't have to worry about the Latin Party cutting off my resources.*

Gisgo stumbles back to his triremes. He is downcast, for he carries no such treaty. Gisgo refused to commit troops immediately to Syphax's cause, and the offended king informed Gisgo that Carthage, Numidia's rival for control of Africa, will lose the war to Rome. And Syphax will be waiting to take over when they do.

The Roman quinquereme pushes off from the dock and opens its sails to the welcoming wind. Scipio calls Laelius to his side, and points in the general direction of Iberia. "On to Carthago Nova," he orders.

"Why go back to Carthago Nova?" blurts Laelius. "That's way south of Tarraco. Weren't we going to sail to Rome after we landed at

I. Victory's Price

Tarraco and turned control of Iberia over to the garrison?" Laelius puts his hand on Scipio's shoulder. "Look, I know you are committed to protecting Rome, but Amelia grievously misses you. And your mother, too, I am sure." He throws up his hands in frustration. "For the gods sake, you can take a bit of time away. Carthage is afraid to fight you, they won't try anything!"

Scipio only stares out at the glistening whitecaps, his face impassive. "We must eliminate the last traces of rebellion in Iberia before I leave it for someone else to manage. Rome and home will have to wait. "He looks at Laelius, his eyes filled with a distant stare. "And Africa awaits our conquest. Hannibal is still out there."

Laelius is silent for several long moments, then he shrugs. "I don't think I know you any more, double-chin. But you are the General." He calls over his captain. "Set sail for Carthago Nova, full sail until we get there." The sailors leap to adjust the sails and turn the rudder. Within minutes the quinquereme slowly heels to the west, and its four fellows follow.

As Scipio's ships ease away, Gisgo steps on board his trireme. "Let us be off, Altos" Gisgo says to his captain.

"What news from the meet with Syphax?" the grizzled old sailor inquires. "Did you learn anything new about the Romans' weaknesses, or how to drive that Scipio boy out of Iberia?"

Gisgo laughs derisively, and shakes his head. "Now that I have met this Scipio, I have greater admiration for him than I had for his many military victories." [v]

He shakes his head forlornly. "Syphax and his kingdom will soon be in the power of Rome. Now let me be." Gisgo repairs to the prow of the ship, watching Scipio's five quinqueremes ease out toward the open sea. *No, Altos, the question is not how we can retake Iberia, it is lost to us. It is how we can hold on to Africa.*[vi]

Gisgo leans out and spits over the railing, aiming it at the Roman fleet that is fading from sight. *By Baal's balls, I'll have to face Scipio in*

10

I. Victory's Price

Africa, Gisgo realizes, as he slumps over the side rail, scratching his head in perplexity. *If Syphax joins forces with him, their combined might could be too much to overcome. We'll lose the war.*

Gisgo looks east toward the Atlas Mountains that border eastern Numidia, the domain of Prince Masinissa's Massylii. *My daughter is betrothed to Masinissa, so he would have to join me in the fight against Scipio. But he only commands a few hundred men, he would be no match for their allied force.* Gisgo pushes himself from the railing and paces about the trireme, waving away his officers so that he can think. *I must have Syphax at my side, whatever the cost.*

The Carthaginian general racks his brain to think of something he can offer Syphax, something that will sway his loyalty. *I can promise him all of Numidia, but he thinks Rome is more likely to give it to him. A wagon of gold? He is already rich beyond want or need. I have to give him something beyond compare, something he truly desires.*

The Carthaginian triremes ease east along the coast, passing by the craggy Atlas Mountains. Watching its cloud-clawing peaks come into view, Gisgo smiles with the dawn of an idea. *Masinissa be cursed, this is no time for sentiment or honor. I will give Syphax my most prized possession, the one treasure he truly desires.*

Sophonisba.

* * * *

DOMUS OF AMELIA PAULLUS, ROME, 206 BCE. "It defies belief," Pomponia exclaims, wringing her hands together. "They extended Consul Livius' dictatorship! After he *promised* he would not accept it!"

Amelia quietly studies the wall frescoes while Pomponia stalks about, livid with disappointment. Wise to her future mother-in-law's ways, Amelia knows Pomponia's anger is but a prelude to a scheme, and that she will soon calm down and develop it. When Pomponia finally plops onto one of the atrium couches, Amelia seizes her opportunity to speak.

"It amazes me that noble Nero did not make himself available to

11

I. Victory's Price

become dictator," she says. "He would have been readily elected, he was clearly the people's choice!"

"Ah yes, but not the Latin Party's choice!" replies Pomponia, flinging up her hands in frustration. "And they made sure he would not get elected! Nero finally admitted to me what happened. Livius threatened to expose Nero's illicit contributions to the Hellenic Party unless Nero nominated Livius to be dictator."

Pomponia laughs bitterly. "Can you imagine? That old bastard Livius was convicted of embezzling war spoils for himself,[vii] and he would presume to indict Nero of immorality!" She grabs a peach from a table basket and bites into it, chewing furiously. "This must be Cato's doing. Livius has not the wit or courage for such a plan."

"Then Cato has declared war on the Hellenic Party," observes Amelia, "Striking at all who support it!"

Pomponia shakes her head. "Cato would not do it out of pure vindictiveness. It's likely because he regarded Nero's actions as immoral." She leans over and spits the peach pit into a basket. "The little bastard may be callous and short-sighted, but his character is beyond reproach. Still, you are in the right. We must strike back at the Latins. Particularly at Livius."

Amelia rubs the back of her head. "Hmm. The best way would be to gain Senate approval for the land reform proposal. Livius would not dare oppose the Senate on it, he would be afraid they might indict him again."

"Perhaps," says Pomponia, "but Flaccus and Fabius have spoken out against the reform before. And they would certainly do it again. They are war veterans, their words carry much weight with the Senate conservatives."

Amelia paces about, mulling Pomponia's words. She snaps her fingers and smiles. "Your comment about war veterans has given me an idea. Why not bring Rome's biggest war hero to our side; our own Publius Cornelius Scipio! Remember the letter your son sent to the Senate after

I. Victory's Price

his victory at Ilipa? He said he has conquered Iberia, and he is busy establishing a colony there for all the war veterans.[viii] Everybody loved that idea, including most of the Latin Party. He is very popular right now."

Pomponia plays with a strand of her hair. "Hmm, yes, the idea has merit. That colony would give land to all the plebs who are veterans; they could have their own farms over there. With my son's endorsement, we could create a provision for that each veteran be granted some Iberian acreage, and add it to the land reform bill. The Senate would *have* to fund his community, because he has reclaimed Iberia for them!" Pomponia smirks. "And fattened their coffers with plunder."

"Exactly," says Amelia excitedly. "And Nero could speak up for it in the Senate. That new consul used to be Nero's second in command; he would support it, too. They would outweigh Flaccus' and Fabius' dissenters."

"Well," counters Pomponia, "I think it's still not enough. We need some popular support." She rises and gestures for her attendant. "Send a messenger to Fabricus. Tell him I want to meet tomorrow." She turns back to Amelia, eyes glowing with excitement. "It is time for me to visit the new Tribune of the Plebs," she says. "I will gain his support for this measure, or I will not come home."

"Wonderful. But the Senate will not approve spending without a new source of funds," says Amelia. "We must still think that through."

Pomponia chortles. "I already have a plan, and it will bring some delicious revenge. Our Senate allies will propose the one thing that enrages any Latin Party member—raising taxes. We will resurrect the salt tax proposal that was narrowly defeated two years ago. Those rich salt merchants can pay for the veterans' homes."

Amelia nods. "Livius is a salt merchant, is he not?"

Pomponia smiles gleefully. "Oh yes! Romans have good reason to call him 'The Salinator.' That is his principal source of wealth."

I. Victory's Price

"But Livius is still the dictator," says Amelia. "He can use his imperium to veto the tax increase."

Pomponia merely grins. "Will he veto it if General Publius Cornelius Scipio proposes it? And Nero and Consul Lucius Veturius speak out for it in the Senate? I think not."

"Veturius will certainly support Nero, his former general," says Amelia. "But can we be sure about Nero?"

"Nero feels that Livius has betrayed him." Pomponia says. "He truly hates him. Wait until he learns has a chance to hit Livius in his money pouch!"

"Then I will gladly help with the propaganda for it, Mother-to-be. It will be worth it just to see the look on Livius' face. And on Flaccus' simpering visage!"

Pomponia's green eyes flash angrily. "Flaccus! Do not think I have forgotten he tried to have me killed. I have reserved something special for him." She smiles to herself. "But I will wait until my son Scipio returns and settles in. Then we shall see..."

"I so miss him," says Amelia wistfully. "Will he be returning soon?"

"In his last letter he said that he still has to take over three towns that have resisted him," says Pomponia. "From what I gather, it will be a routine matter. Then he will return to Rome and be given a proper triumph!"

A cloud of worry crosses her face. "All will be well, I am certain. But perhaps we should visit the temple tomorrow, and sacrifice a pig for his safety."

"Of course he will be fine," Amelia says. She smiles at her future mother in law, but her eyes are troubled. *He is not back yet, Mother.*

* * * *

ILLITURGIS, SOUTHEASTERN IBERIA, 206 BCE. Scipio stamps

I. Victory's Price

about the hard ground outside his command tent, slapping his arms about his chest for warmth. *I ought to storm the walls of this place and get the Hades out of here*, he fumes. He is irritated that he is out besieging this hilltop fortress in the gloomy winter cold, when he could be reading military history scrolls before a warm fire in his Carthago Nova headquarters, planning his African campaign. He is even more irritated that he feels a sense of urgency to complete his final mission and return to Rome. He knows urgency is the enemy of deliberation, and this assault will require careful planning if it to be successful.

Scipio's victory at Ilipa destroyed the power of the Three Generals, and mighty Carthage is no longer a factor in Iberia. But Scipio knows that he cannot leave there until he subdues the last of the native tribes that resisted Rome, so that his successors are not facing rebellions as soon as they arrive.

He is especially angry with the Oretani tribesmen who populate the citadel of Illiturgis, a redoubtable town built into the side of a cliff. Once a longstanding ally of his father and uncle—Generals Publius and Gnaeus Scipio—Illiturgis deserted to Carthage as soon as the Three Generals killed Scipio's father and uncle. Even worse, when the remnants of his father's army came to Illiturgis seeking shelter, the townspeople welcomed them inside and summarily massacred them.

Now, rightfully fearing a dire retribution, the Oretani refuse to surrender to Rome. *They'll fight to the death*, Scipio muses, as he stares up at the redoubtable citadel. *And death is what they will get. They will be a warning to all.*

With Laelius at his side, Scipio has led seven thousand legionnaires and auxiliaries on the four days' march from Carthago Nova to this mountain town, to remain until Illiturgis is subdued. At the same time, he has sent out Marcius and his legion from Tarraco toward the rebel town of Castulo, where Scipio will join him when Illiturgis is vanquished. They will then move on to the last rebel stronghold at Astapa. But Illiturgis is first in the way, and he is anxious to dispose of it.

Scipio hears footsteps crunch into the frosted ground behind him. He

I. Victory's Price

grabs for his dagger. "Any ideas how to get in there?" comes a familiar voice, and he withdraws his hand. "No, Laelius. Right now it looks as formidable as Rome."

Laelius grimaces at the fortress. "Short of catapulting our men in there, I can think of nothing that would not cost us thousands of casualties. We will have to lay siege to it."

"No siege, we have not the time!" barks Scipio angrily. "Lucius Lentulus and Lucius Manlius will arrive at the next full moon to replace me. If I have not taken these three towns by then, my conquest of Iberia will be incomplete. I will lose my chance to be given a triumph at Rome. If I don't get a triumph, we could lose our chance to attack Africa!"

"You sound impatient," Laelius says, "and hasty. Did you not tell me that haste felled the consuls who fought Hannibal at Trebia, Trasimene, and Cannae, all of whom played into Hannibal's hands? This attack requires much consideration."

Laelius scrapes the thin snow into a snowball and hurls it toward Illiturgis. "Look at that place, will you? It has long remained unconquered for good reason: those thirty-foot stone walls encircle an inner citadel that is built into the cliff at the rear of the town. We can't sneak around the back like we have before."

Scipio takes a deep breath, then another. "It is not amenable to a hasty conquest by sheer force of numbers, I give you that. But there is always a way, we just have to figure it out. No one sleeps until we have an answer."

That night, Scipio calls his senior tribunes and allied commanders to his command tent. The officers huddle around a large rectangular table containing a terrain map of Illiturgis and its environs. The men point their fingers at the map, arguing vehemently over various assault tactics. Scipio stands silently behind his men. He listens carefully to their arguments and proposals, weighing their ideas.

"It is a formidable city," observes a gray-haired tribune. "It is like a

I. Victory's Price

smaller version of Carthago Nova."

Laelius nods. "Then perhaps we should try an attack from the front and rear, as we did there. Keep everyone busy at the front while we sneak toward the back walls."

Scipio stares at Laelius. "Really? The 'back walls' are sheer cliffs, a bit more of a challenge than Carthago's shortened walls, wouldn't you say? It would take a mountain goat to get up them. And even the goat would need a rope!"

"Hah! Those cliffs are nothing," says Roltis, the brawny commander of the Italia allies.

"They are very high, Roltis," replies Scipio.

"You think that is high?" Roltis laughs heartily, arms crossed over his wolfskin vest. "Back home, we climb that for fun. Take the women and children with us! I take that wall easy."

Scipio looks curiously at the older man, trying to figure out if he is serious.

Laelius bends to his ear. "Roltis is from an Umbrian tribe near the Appenninus Mountains." He raises his eyebrows. "He brought his own climbing equipment with him."

The roughshod Umbrian grins confidently at Scipio, and holds his thickly calloused palms in front of him. He turns them around, exposing his thick, cracked fingernails. "You see? I have hands like feet, climb rocks all my life."

Scipio waves Roltis' hands away, sighing. "I believe you could, Roltis. But we need more than one man."

The Umbrian stamps his feet impatiently. "Phah! You give me those naked little dark men I see in camp. They climb the rocks like monkeys, I see them!"

Laelius laughs. "He means the Masaesyli who deserted Syphax to join

I. Victory's Price

us." He grabs Scipio's shoulder playfully. "It is not such a bad idea, you know. I have seen them here, they climb up the mountains as if they were spiders. They laugh at our use of ladders. They call our escaladers 'women-men.' "

Scipio looks at the map, then back at a waiting Roltis. *It would be totally unexpected,* he considers, *with minimal loss of men.* Scipio chuckles. "I may be touched by the moon, but let us do it. If I have learned anything in my five years of war, it has been to trust those who believe in themselves, for they will find a way." He turns to his guard. "Bring me the leader of the Numidians, he can talk this over with Roltis."

At these words, Roltis' gap-toothed grin widens. "Now I be like you, play big trick on the enemy!"

Scipio stares at the unkempt, grinning, barbarian and shakes his head. *Truly, I must be crazy.*

The next morning, after the soldiers have eaten and donned their battle armor, Scipio calls them to a final convocation. He stands atop a wooden platform supported by four large pottery urns. Laelius stands proudly on his right, his carefully polished armor gleaming like the sun.

Scipio starts by recounting the Illiturgians' betrayal, angrily reminding the men that they are assaulting the town because the Illiturgians have murdered their comrades, and would have done the same to them had they ventured there for safety. His voice quakes with anger as he recounts the slaughter of his father's legionnaires after he was slain. He points at the fortress looming in front of them.

"There it is, men," he shouts. "The time has come for us to set an example for any who would contemplate perpetrating such mischief on a Roman soldier or citizen." [ix] He pauses for a moment, composing himself, and his voice becomes deadly calm. "Today we destroy Illiturgis. Not just to revenge the past, but to protect our future. Should any Iberian ever think of rebelling against the men who follow us, let the destruction of Illiturgis leap to their minds and daunt their spirit. Now, we march forward to conquest and glory!"

I. Victory's Price

Scipio takes an e-shaped cornu from the centurion next to him. He trumpets the call to battle, his face purpling with the effort to make it as loud as possible. The battle horn's strident notes echo over the cheers of his army. The tribunes shout out a call to formation, and the men march toward their officers.

The army immediately separates into two sections and tramps toward the stone walls of Illiturgis. Laelius leads thousands of battle-hardened socii on a quick march toward the left wall, while Scipio gallops to the front lines of his legionnaires and leads them toward the front gates. The townspeople fling rocks, pottery, and manure at the oncoming Romans, even though they are well beyond range.

Hundreds of lightly armored escaladers rush past the soldiers, each pair carrying a ladder. The escaladers halt in a line before the town walls, just out of reach of the stream of projectiles that rains down in front of them. The tribunes order the escaladers to wait. The men stand at attention, gripping their tall ladders on top of their shoulders, looking at the hordes of Oretani who are intent on killing them.

When the rain of projectiles begins to lessen, the senior tribune looks over at the trumpeters and chops his hand down. The cornicenes sound the charge. The escaladers stream forward toward the walls, holding their ladders on their shoulders and their small round shields over their heads.

The ladder men race across the littered plain. The townspeople begin a fresh onslaught of missiles, but this time the Oretani warriors fling spears and stones. Four Romans fall screaming to the ground, pierced by spears. The Oretani yell with triumph and concentrate their throws on the fallen legionnaires, stoning and spearing them until they lie still. The surviving Romans rush even faster, fear giving wings to their feet. Within minutes, hundreds of escaladers are scrambling up the thirty-foot walls.

Inside Illiturgis, the entire town mobilizes to combat the hated Romans, and all but the infants have now become warriors. Men of all ages crowd the town walls. Grim adults hurl spears and rocks at the Romans. Wide-eyed boys fling garbage, sticks, old furniture—anything

I. Victory's Price

they can lay their hands on—echoing the taunts and insults of their elders.

The speediest Oretani rush about the walkway and push ladders away from the walls as the climbers reach the top, plummeting their enemy to the ground. The women and girls run back and forth to supply the wall defenders, carrying any missile or weapon they can find. Many a Roman scales to the top of the wall and cuts down the men there, only to be driven back by knots of screaming women wielding hoes and pointed sticks, wearing naught but robes and gowns to protect themselves.

Illiturgis fights with the desperate fury of a people who know they are doomed, but who burn to destroy their oppressors in their passing. Thrice the Romans assay the walls, and thrice they are beaten back by the suicidal frenzy of the defenders.

Scipio gnashes his teeth. The relentless fighters who have conquered all of Iberia are being repelled by an outnumbered contingent of townspeople and militia. Watching his army's determination wane, Scipio's right hand begins to twitch uncontrollably. He feels the loathsome inklings of doubt and realizes must do something to spur his men on, or the attack will quickly fail. [x]

A duo of escaladers marches by Scipio, carrying their ladder toward the walls. "Stop!" he shouts. The men halt in their tracks. "I'll take the damn walls myself!" Scipio grabs the front of the ladder and pulls its two escaladers along with him, rushing toward the walls of Illiturgis.

Seeing their general take up the attack, the surrounding laddermen yell in dismay and hurry to catch up to him. "Gods above, let me have that, General!" spits a gruff little veteran as he wrests the ladder from Scipio's hands. "We shall not come back until the gates are open, I promise you!"

Scipio relinquishes the ladder and waves over a nearby tribune. "Send the velites to cover them. Tell them to throw every rock and spear they can find at those walls!" Within minutes the light infantry trots forward to follow the escaladers into the deadly shower from the walls of

I. Victory's Price

Illiturgis.

Laelius is calmly regrouping his own ladder men when he sees Scipio's escaladers renewing their assault, with his rash general in the forefront. "My gods, Scippy!" murmurs Laelius to himself. "You'll lose this war for us yet!"

Laelius screams for his Italia escaladers to catch up to the others. "I promise a gold corona muralis for the first one to make it to the top of the wall!" he shouts to his men, "And a purse of silver to the second!"

The promise spreads like wildfire among the wolfskin-clad socii, and they roar their enthusiasm. The Italia allies dash forward, rabid to attain the glory and wealth of a gold battle crown. They throw their ladders onto the walls and clamber up as if Hades was at their backs, racing their fellows to the top.

Scores of new ladders encircle the front walls of Illiturgis, and This time Scipio's army will not be gainsaid. The velites rain their javelins up onto the parapets, suppressing the townspeople's retaliation. When the javelins are gone, they hurl back the spears and stones the Illiturgians had thrown at them. Scores of wounded Illiturgians plunge screaming from the wall, and many more grovel along the walkways.

The townspeople's missile assault lessens, and the Romans scramble up the walls during the lull. Dozens of Scipio's men mount the walls. The vengeful legionnaires hack into their tormentors, stabbing down the defenders, beating the Illiturgians back. More escaladers join them on the walkway. Soon the legionnaires and socii are fighting their way down the stairs inside the fortress. They battle their way toward the main gates, slowed only by the occasional group of soldiers that rushes to confront them—and dies.

As the main army assaults the front walls, Roltis leads a contingent of Numidians to Illiturgis' back wall, the rear of the town's interior citadel. The "wall" is a two hundred foot cliff so sheer that no defenders have stayed to guard it, electing to either join the battle or defend the citadel's front doorways.

I. Victory's Price

Roltis stands before his Numidians, wearing only a homespun tunic. He reaches into his belt pouch and rubs chalk dust into his hoary hands. "You savages, you follow me!" Roltis shouts to the uncomprehending Numidians. He begins to climb the rock face. "I show you how to be a real climber!"

The wiry Africans loop their shields and swords over their backs and clamber up the rocky face. Where there is no handhold they drive iron spikes into the precipice, creating handholds for the men behind them.[xi] Scores of Numidians follow the leaders. They grab each outcropping and spike, firmly planting their feet before reaching for the next. The ascent is quiet, save for the occasional scraping of flesh upon rock, mingled with the grunts of men pulling themselves ever higher.

Long minutes later, Roltis crawls across the top of the cliff and into one of the citadel's tower windows. He plops into an empty room, his dagger at the ready. *No guards,* he exults. *They think no one could get in here.*

Roltis scrambles back to the clifftop and waves a white rag at the ascending Numidians. The Africans clamber up and join him inside. When all of the climbers are in the room, Roltis motions for them to follow him down the winding stone steps. The fortress echoes with a brief clash of blades—several voices cry out in anguish, death cries lost in the din of battle below. Then all is quiet.

The front doors of the citadel fly open. The climbers dash across the town square and crash into the Illiturgians defending the city gates. The Africans whirl about their heavily armored opponents, jabbing and slicing from every angle, doubling and tripling up on a solitary opponent. Soon the last of the gate men fall to the earth, bleeding out their lives. Roltis' head lies a yard from his body, severed by an Iberian's ax blow.

The Numidians shove aside the two timbers that bar the city gates, and crack them open. "Inside, inside!" shouts the oldest African. The massive doors spring open and Scipio's soldiers flood into the city.

Scores of escaladers fight their way across the square and rejoin the

I. Victory's Price

army. Scipio's men quickly encircle the hundreds of defenders that remain in the town square. They close in upon the warriors and townspeople, cutting them down with quick jabs and slashes. Soon, none remain to oppose them.

The bloodlust is upon the Romans, however. They rage into the town streets and cut down every living being they can find: women, elders, and children—even livestock. They are no longer men, they are maddened beasts.[xii] Scipio's words of Illiturgis' betrayal are fresh on their minds, and their centurions' cease-and-desist orders fall upon deaf ears. The vengeful Romans ignore the money and plunder about them, lusting to put a sword into anything they associate with the town that murdered their comrades.

Scipio and his guards fight on horseback in the town square. He rides about the front, slashing down any Oretani warrior who confronts him, cutting into the necks and shoulders of unwary defenders. When the square has been cleared of enemy, Scipio halts his horse. He watches in horrified resignation as his men slaughter their way through the town, steeling himself not to intervene.

Laelius rides up to join him. He slides his shield onto his back, his grim work finished for the day. "You could call them back," Laelius says. "The town is ours."

Scipio looks straight ahead, his face a stone. "The legend is not yet made," he murmurs. "The story of what Rome does to those who betray them. A mercy now would kill thousands later."

"Are you justifying or rationalizing?" asks Laelius, looking closely into Scipio's face. "You were ever skilled at both."

"Mercy seems right, but this time it would be wrong," replies Scipio doggedly, as if talking to himself. "There is no profit in me becoming weak about it."

"You have destroyed an entire fortress. Saving a few of them will not damage your reputation," Laelius says quietly.

Laelius sees Scipio's face soften.

I. Victory's Price

"Well, perhaps we should save a few," Scipio says. "Why don't you capture a dozen of the Illiturgis men, and twice that of women and children? We can use them to pass along the story." Scipio's eyes turn cold and he looks back toward the massacre. "But no more than that."

Laelius' begins to say something, then his mouth tightens into a line. He nudges his horse forward. "As you say, General," he replies tonelessly. "Let me oversee the rest of this grim task. If death must be done, it is best done quickly."

By late afternoon all the defenders are dead or captured, with few casualties to the Romans. The town's plunder is piled in the square and loaded into the town's wagons.

When the last of Illiturgis' treasures, livestock, and supplies are carted out onto the plains, hundreds of the young velites rush back inside, brandishing torches. They dash to the back of the town, jumping over scattered mounds of corpses, running as if they were in an Olympian race. Once at the back of the town, they turn around and run back toward the entrance. They torch each house, stable, and shop they can reach, racing ahead of the pursuing conflagration.

Scipio's army watches the inferno burn through the night, the fires lighting the legions' night-long victory celebration. There is much singing and drinking throughout the army, but a somber Laelius does not partake. And Scipio remains in his tent, alone.

The next day, when the embers have cooled to a smoldering mass, the army assaults Illiturgis again. The soldiers cast hooks and ropes into the charred remains, leveling every building and wall, leaving no stone upon stone. By sundown the once-proud fortress is a blackened spot upon the plain. Only the stench of burnt flesh testifies that people once lived there.

Six days after the destruction of Illiturgis, Scipio's army joins Marcius' force at the town of Castulo, one of the last refuges for Carthaginians. Scipio has no desire to repeat the horror of Illiturgis, believing it will serve no further purpose. He sends one of his native speculatores into the city under cover of darkness, and the spy quietly

I. Victory's Price

confers with Cerdubelus, the commander of the Oretani tribe that dwells inside Castulo.

The news about Illiturgis has already reached Castulo, and has taken its desired effect. The speculatore returns with a secret agreement from Cerdubelus: in exchange for the safety of his people, he will subdue the Carthaginians inside and open the town gates. Scipio quickly signs the agreement and sends it back with his spy. And he waits.

Two days later, as the cocks inside Castulo welcome the dawn, there is a loud clash of weapons. Men scream and beg for mercy, but the clash continues. Scipio summons Marius to his side. "It is time to take the town," he tells him.

The commanders lead two cohorts to Castulo's front gates and station them at the entrance. A thousand soldiers wait patiently, listening to the fading sounds of conflict. Two hours later, the gates open and hundreds of unarmed Carthaginians march out in chains, led along by Cerdubelus and his brothers. As the Carthaginians march out, Scipio and Marcius lead their men into the city and occupy the town, rejoicing that no men were lost.

Scipio passes by Cerdubelus. "Good work," he shouts over to the Oretani leader. "The town will be yours."

Cerdubelus touches his sword to his brow. "We got them at breakfast," he yells in his pidgin Latin. "Kill a bunch, rest quit."

Scipio returns the salute and trots inside Castulo.

The Oretani sign an agreement to ally themselves with Rome, and Castulo is left to the governance of the town's citizens. Scipio takes his army back to New Carthage, towing along his Carthaginian captives.

His mission completed, Scipio leaves Marcius to negotiate the surrenders of the surrounding cities. Dozens of Bastetani and Carpetani towns surrender without a fight, and the Romans' control of Iberia spreads wider. Soon Marcius' task is almost finished. The legate has only one fortress town remaining to subdue: Astapa.

I. Victory's Price

The town of Astapa is known for its irrational and longstanding hatred of Romans. It is not a large town, nor is it strategically placed for defense, but it is the last pocket of resistance. Marcius confidently leads his legion toward it, little suspecting that he is heading for a conflict that will go down in history—and infamy.

* * * * *

GADES, IBERIA, 206 BCE. *What in the name of Mot is he doing here?* Mago asks himself as he stands on the Gades Wharf, watching the richly caparisoned trireme pull into the aquamarine waters of the port. Mago had received a message that Durro, the chief emissary of the Council of Elders, would soon be calling on him. The message did not state the reason for Durro's arrival, and Mago is anxious about why he has come. Durro would only sail this far on a matter of gravest importance, one that cannot be trusted to his underlings.

Mago knows his army's defeat at Ilipa was mourned for days in Carthage, with some notables in the Council arguing to withdraw Hannibal from Italia and sue Rome for peace. *If Hannibal is recalled*, he worries, *would I be next? Does the cross await me?*

With the loss of Iberia to Scipio, Mago suspects that he will be sent to a far outpost to finish his term as general, living in disgrace. Or worse, he will be taken back to Carthage and crucified in the town square, as happened with the last two failed generals. *Hasdrubal and I owned Iberia but a few years ago. What happened?* Mago shakes his head. *You know what happened. Scipio happened.*

As Mago watches, Durro's ship glides into the timbered dock. A tall, thin, figure in a flowing purple robe debarks onto the plank walkway, shuffling unsteadily towards Mago. The aged emissary is flanked by a large retinue of guards and attendants, as befits a wealthy merchant of such high political status.

Mago summons his best smile and walks out to welcome his political nemesis, knowing that this old man holds Mago's fate in his well-manicured hands. "Welcome, Durro!" Mago says. "May Baal smile upon you."

I. Victory's Price

The saturnine elder gives the barest of nods. "The same, the same to you," he mutters, looking critically at the dozen transports about him. "This is all of the fleet you have?" he asks, his lips pursed.

"Well," blusters Mago, "I have some out on patrol, searching for Roman ships. Keeping the coast safe, you know."

Durro smiles thinly. "More like the Romans are searching for you, from what I have heard."

Gods below, the man is a pain in the ass! Mago rubs the back of his neck and musters an encouraging smile. "So, Durro, what news from Carthage?"

Durro merely blinks his icy blue eyes at Mago, and looks at the guards. "May we repair to your quarters?"

"Certainly," says Mago anxiously. "We can go there now, if you wish."

Mago leads Durro to a sumptuous litter at the end of the dock. Eight richly dressed slaves carry Durro's litter while Mago rides alongside, up the hill and through Gades' iron-and-timber gates.

When they arrive at Mago's headquarters, Durro eases himself off the litter and walks into the spacious meeting room. A welcoming committee of town officials awaits him, smiling hopefully.

Durro bows to the party and turns to Mago. "We need to talk alone. Completely alone. Now." Mago looks at Durro for a long moment, saying nothing. "As you wish," he growls, and waves the officials out of the room.

The two sit opposite one another at a large table filled with food-laden platters, their voices booming off the thick stone walls. Mago offers Durro some wine and food but the emissary refuses both. He sits rigidly across from the general, his face blank.

"Everyone has left, Durro. What sits on your mind, that would inspire such rudeness?"

I. Victory's Price

As is his manner, the rich old merchant immediately broaches his topic. "Iberia is lost; your defeat at Ilipa was its ending. Scipio controls our towns and allies." Durro grimaces. "And worse, he controls all our mines." He breaks off a finger-sized crust of bread from a loaf the size of his head, and nibbles it. "He will take this city next, that is a certainty."

Red-faced Mago vaults from his chair to object but Durro pushes his palm at Mago's face. "The time for argument is past, General. Your time here is over."

Mago shakes his head vigorously. "No! We can recover Iberia! I only need the coin to recruit ten thousand mercenaries. In spring we will retake Carthago Nova from Scipio, I swear upon my life!"

The emissary sits silently for several heartbeats, his eyes wandering across the food-laden table as if he had not heard Mago's words. Mago shifts his feet about uneasily, his hands clenched together. The Elder pulls out a sealed lambskin scroll from his sleeve and lays it in Mago's hand. The general stares at it as if it were a death sentence.

"What is this?" Mago blurts.

"Your orders," Durro replies. "Open it."

Mago carefully unrolls the three-foot roll and sees a lengthy itemized list. The list details the money, ships, armament, and food that Durro has brought to Mago, with a following section on what he is to do with them. Mago blinks at Durro, amazed at what he sees. "You want me to go to Italia? To join my brother Hannibal?" he sputters.

"You will first go to the Balearic Islands," says Durro. "You have said before that the Balearics are staunch allies. Go there and recruit them to our cause, you have the funds now. Then sail to North Italia and recruit the Ligurians and Gauls. They fought well for your brother Hasdrubal. They should fight well for you, with the proper monetary persuasion."

Durro picks out an olive and nibbles on it. "When you have accrued a sizable force, you will march toward Rome. There you will ally yourself with Hannibal. Then you destroy Rome." Durro leans forward,

I. Victory's Price

flipping the olive to the floor. "And then you will end this expensive folly of a war."

Anger and relief fight inside Mago. Anger wins. "All this time, you have talked about making peace because it is more profitable than this war, and now you want to continue fighting?" Mago crosses his arms like a stubborn child. "I go nowhere until I know why."

Durro studies Mago's flushed face for several long moments. He smiles wanly, adding to Mago's confusion. "I think I will have that wine you proffered," he says.

Mago rolls his eyes and pours Durro a goblet of dark red Rioja wine. He grabs a larger bronze chalice and fills it for himself. Durro sips his drink, smacks his lips in approval, and looks back at Mago.

"After Cannae, we sent secret emissaries to Rome to discuss peace terms with them, negotiations that would allow us to weigh the costs of peace versus war." He throws up his hands. "Ah, we were so close to a peace resolution, because Rome had suffered so many defeats at the hands of Hannibal! With the terms we offered, both nations would have access to the shipping lanes, and we would keep Iberia."

The old man takes a longer drink, and sighs. "We almost had it done. Only a few of Rome's senators needed to be bribed to get the votes." Durro grimaces, and drains his goblet. "But Scipio's victories revived Rome's confidence and renewed their resolve."

The emissary stands up and paces about, suddenly animated, as Mago stares in surprise. "Now, the Romans insist on disarming our fleet and relegating us to a few merchant ships. And they want to take over all the mines and ports of Iberia." He flaps his thin arms, looking like a gaunt purple bird. "Can you see what would happen? Carthage would be bankrupt within two generations!"

General Mago laughs, enjoying the politician's discomfiture. "What about all that Senate talk about peace, Durro? What about all the peace-loving Elders that chirped about Carthage being destroyed if we fought Rome? Where are they now?"

I. Victory's Price

"Rome's peace would be as sure a way to destroy us as if they had burnt Carthage itself. So we must destroy them."

Mago nods mutely, still absorbing his incredible luck. *Hannibal and I will take down Rome! I owe you much, Scipio.*

Durro folds his fingers together and looks at them. "We will send a fleet of men and supplies to Hannibal, too. Enough to supply him for his campaign to Rome."

"So now the politicians want total war instead of total peace," Mago snipes. "And we say the gods are capricious!"

Durro merely shrugs. "Do you refuse the resources I brought?"

Mago snorts. "Of course not, no more than I would refuse food after starving for weeks! Would this sustenance would have come earlier, when we contested with Scipio." Mago tucks the scroll into his robe. "But I am a Barca. We never accept defeat. I will go."

Two weeks later, Mago sails out for the Balearic Islands. His new fleet is adorned with glittering white sails ablaze with Carthage's purple phoenix. His ships carry every capable soldier that remains from the Three Generals' surviving armies: Libyans, Iberians, Celtiberians, and Carthaginians, all with purses lined with Durro's silver.

Scores of heavy transports follow Mago's quinqueremes and triremes. They are laden with the vast wealth of Gades, Mago's erstwhile base in Iberia. Not trusting the Elders' guarantee of more money, Mago has plundered Gades' treasuries, temples, and citizens,[xiii] leaving behind a despoiled city that is more than ready to surrender to the Romans.

Mago stands in the prow of his new Carthaginian quinquereme, a trim blade of a warship laden with his finest Sacred Band fighters. Its sails blooming with wind, the warship's polished oak hull cuts effortlessly through the northern Mediterranean waters, as it leads Mago's mighty fleet toward Lucania.

Mago leans over the prow and stares north through the gray blue mist, eagerly searching for the first signs of land. *I swear to you, my brother*

I. Victory's Price

Hasdrubal; Rome will pay for your death. I will throw their generals' heads over the walls of Rome. And I will put that cursed Scipio on the cross.

II. ASTAPA

ITALICA, BAETIS VALLEY, SOUTH IBERIA. Scipio hobbles along the bank of the milky green Baetis River, his leg and chest swathed in bandages. He surveys the verdant grainfields that undulate across the expansive river valley and grins with satisfaction, despite his pain. Laelius walks beside him, his face drawn with worry.

"Over there," points Scipio. "That is where we build the settlement. See the two streams? Perfect for water and sanitation. We can take in thousands of veterans here."

Laelius hardly hears Scipio's words. "Look, don't you think you should go back to camp and get some help from your new medicus? You brought him from all the way from Greece to attend to your health. But here you are, tramping about in winter's chill, and burning with fever! You are a bit crazy, I must say."

Scipio coughs violently, doubling over with convulsions "No, no, this is too important. This will be the first Roman colony outside of Italy. I have to do it right, or the Senate may not approve any others."

Laelius shakes his head. "Your vanity afflicts your health, and your reputation. The men have seen you, they think you are near death, with all this wheezing and limping about."

Scipio sweeps his arm across the valley. "This is my medicine, Laelius. The chance to build something permanent, where people can live in peace." He sighs heavily. "It seems like every day I make a decision that kills someone. Now I can make one that gives our people new lives. I want this to be a paradise for our soldiers. They have earned that."

Laelius squeezes Scipio's shoulder. "You have saved many lives already, though it is not so evident when you murder entire towns. Fear

II. Astapa

of you has saved us from having more battles, that much I have learned from these horrors."

"Ah, let us hope it puts the fear into them," replies Scipio, his mood brightening. "Perhaps this little town of Astapa will see the futility of its resistance, and capitulate peacefully. That would be the best medicine for me."

* * * * *

ASTAPA, SOUTH IBERIA, 206 BCE. *Shlunk, shlunk, shlunk, shlunk.* The machinelike tramping crescendos as the four thousand legionnaires descend into the bushy flatlands south of the jagged Sierra del Becerro. The infantry marches four abreast along the narrow road, striding past carefully tended wheat fields and olive groves, all empty of their owners.

The local farmers have fled before the onset of Legate Marcius' army, shouting the alarm as they trundled their wagons laden with family and belongings toward the hillside fortress of Astapa. The refugees pour through Astapa's gates, seeking safety inside its massive limestone walls.

The legion continues past the fertile farms and croplands, ignoring the easy bounty that surrounds them. Scipio has told Marcius that the Astapans' land must be preserved as a gesture of reconciliation. Scipio has had enough of killing townspeople, he has directed his legate to seek peace whenever possible.

Marcius also hopes that the townspeople will peacefully capitulate to his army, as other towns have done since the brutal fall of Illiturgis. Fear and terror have been able negotiators on this campaign, and he trusts they will sway the obstinate Astapans.

Inside Astapa, town commander Bernat peers out from one of the squat stone towers that flank the log gates, watching the farmers pour into the inner courtyards of his town. As people and livestock fill the square he looks to the fields beyond the gate, trying to count how many more will be coming.

II. Astapa

Bernat draws back, startled. He sticks his head out of the tower window, peering down at a lithe teen who is loading rocks onto front wall's walkway. "Ciro!" he shouts, summoning his younger brother. "Come look at this."

Ciro lays his boulder into the pile and trots up the tower steps to join his brother.

"You see that?" Bernat says to Clio. "Those are Roman standards in the distance! Run down and tell the men to close the gates."

Ciro nods enthusiastically. "It is time anyway. The inner yard is filled with farmers. There are cattle everywhere, and they're getting into that big wood pile you put down there." He turns to his brother. "What is all that wood for, anyway?"

"Ah yes, the wood pile," says Bernat dolefully, avoiding Ciro's eyes. "We may need to use that very soon, for a big fire."

Ciro looks expectantly at him. "Are we going to have a bonfire, to celebrate our victory?"

Bernat closes his eyes tightly. He manages a sad smile. "Why yes, if we defeat them we would certainly have a big fire to celebrate." He bites his lower lip. "If not, we will still have a use for it."

For the rest of morning, Bernat and Ciro watch the Romans march in and surround the front of Astapa, setting up camp a quarter mile from its walls. Bernat sends his warriors out from the gates, to hurry in the last of the farmers. The soldiers whip and curse the refugees like they were cattle, herding them inside. Dozens of people are too late, however. The pitiless gates boom shut in front of them, leaving them to scatter into the hills and fields.

Bernat watches them flee, and heaves a heavy sigh. The Astapan commander turns around and looks at the hundreds milling about the courtyard. *Just as well we don't have too many down there. We may need room for the fire, gods help me.*

Rafa, Bernat's older brother, clambers onto the catwalk to join his

II. Astapa

siblings, clenching a knobby war club in his thick fist. "Look at that!" the blocky man says disgustedly. "There must be five thousand of those goat-fuckers out there, staking out their womanish little tents."

"Every one of them is a well-trained soldier, brother." Bernat says. "They won't leave until Astapa is theirs." He gazes across the rolling plains about him. "Until all of Iberia is theirs."

Rafa spits over the wall at the Romans. He turns to look back inside, his face grim. "I see people are still throwing on wood and furniture down there. That pile's becoming a mountain! You still intend to follow your plan?"

Bernat glares at him. "We all agreed on it, did we not?" He watches two young girls chattering happily as they throw an armload of branches onto the enormous woodpile. His heart constricts.

"If we do not overcome the Romans, our way of life ends. We can but choose its ending." He squeezes his brother's broad shoulder. "I will need you to command the Final Fifty inside here."

"Me?" Rafa asks, incredulous. "I have to get out there and fight the Romans, I give us our best chance to beat them!"

Bernat smiles. "You are the strongest warrior I have ever met," he says, nodding his head toward the town below them. "But I need that strength down there. I have a family, I could not do it." He rumples Ciro's hair, looking sorrowfully at him. "But I will take Ciro with me."

Rafa fingers his bushy beard, and nods. "Hmm. That is good. You can give him a warrior's death, if it comes to that."

Bernat leans over and kisses Rafa on the cheek. "Very well, brother. I swear by Cariociecus' heavenly ax, I will follow our plan. The horns will tell you if you have to start the fire. Now let us bend to our tasks, delaying only strengthens our enemy."

The three brothers trot down the walkway stairs and march into the courtyard. The Astapa militia waits for them there, a thousand armed townsmen milling around in front of the gates. They stamp their feet

35

II. Astapa

restlessly, eager to commence their assault upon the hated Romans. Most look wistfully down the streets toward their homes, blinking back tears.

Many of the Astapan militia are barely out of boyhood. Still more are of declining years, but all are ready to fight to the death. All wear the bronze cap helmets and dark red tunics of the feared Astapa warrior, with their hearts protected by a circular wolf's-head breastplate. Each carries a round shield, an iron javelin and a falcata, the curved sword clenched in their trembling fists.

Rafa stands in front of the warriors, watching his two brothers walk to the front of the gates. Behind the attack force looms the towering pyramid of wood, piled up with all of the citizen's valuables: money, silver, gold, jewels, carvings, and furniture. Fifty soldiers ring mighty tower, all carrying swords and unlit torches.

Astapa's women and children sit in the brushwood and tinder piled inside the ring.[xiv] The women fearfully watch the armed men standing about them. Their children play among the pile's belongings, and the women occasionally rush out to snatch a wayward child back to them. The ring guardians look mournfully at their loved ones' faces as they throw more wood into the pile, widening its base. When their task is finished they draw their swords and turn back toward the gate, unable to bear the women's imploring looks.

Bernat leads Ciro to the front lines by the gates. He reaches over to tousle his brother's soft curly hair and smiles encouragingly at him. "Today you will become a great warrior, I promise you. Your name will go down in history." The youth smiles bravely at his beloved older brother. He raises his head, sets his downy chin, and faces the gates.

Bernat looks behind him to assure that all his soldiers and militia are ready. He sees his raven haired young wife looking at him from her chair inside the pile. Her eyes are as large as saucers, her look pleading with him. His son Aldobo toddles near his mother and pitches handfuls of twigs into the pile. His cherubic face is as serious as the men he emulates. *Oh, dearest hearts, I will try to save you.* Bernat feels his eyes cloud, and he forces himself to face the gates. "Commence!" he

II. Astapa

screams, his voice quaking.

The gates swing wide. The Astapans stampede down the road toward the Roman camp, screaming like the lost souls they have become.

The Roman signal horns bray frantically, followed by the tribunes' calls to battle. A squadron of half-dressed equites thunders out from the disorganized camp, desperate to stop the Astapans before they reach it. Two hundred tunic clad velites run behind the equites, lugging braces of javelins on their backs.

The Astapans barely break stride as they storm into the oncoming cavalry, roaring curses at the riders. The youngest and oldest militiamen dash in recklessly, impaling themselves on the equites' blades and spears, enabling the veteran warriors to pull the encumbered Romans off their horses. Scores of equites fall to the ground, to be stabbed to death by their vengeful enemy. The blood-maddened warriors chop off the Romans' heads and fling them at the cavalry, bouncing them off of the equites' shields and armor.

Daunted by the fury of the suicidal attack, the cavalry retreat behind the ranks of the oncoming velites. Bernat's eyes gleam with pride at his men's momentary triumph, but he knows they cannot pause to enjoy it. *We have to keep them off balance, it is our only chance.* He runs out ahead of his men. "Onward! Don't stop! Kill them all!" he screams, waving his blood stained falcata over his head. The Astapans stampede toward the light infantry, voices raised in exultation.

"Close ranks," the First Tribunes shouts at his young charges, "Shield to shield." The velites pause and regroup into double lines, standing with their three-foot shields touching.

"Loose!" the First Tribune shouts. The young Romans rain hundreds of javelins into the oncoming Iberians. Scores of Astapans crumble to the earth, but the staunch barbarians only run faster, jumping over their fallen brethren. "No retreat!" Bernat screams, dodging a spear that hisses by his head. With a mighty shout, the Astapans crash into the velites' front line.

II. Astapa

The Iberian warriors fight furiously, hacking and thrusting like madmen. The Roman light infantry are young but battle-hardened. They maintain their shield to shield line, jabbing their javelins into any enemy body part they can reach. The velites slow the murderous charge but the Astapans' overwhelming numbers eventually drive them backwards, leaving serried rows of the dead youths behind.

Legate Marcius now approaches the battle, leading out thousands of his ablest legionnaires. The buccinae sound the light infantry retreat and the velites run back between Marcius' oncoming cohorts, dragging their wounded with them. The heavy infantry threshes into the onrushing mob. They drive the Astapans back a spear's throw, and then another.

But the Roman advance slowly grinds to a halt, stalled by the onslaught of men who have decided to die where they stand rather than retreat any farther. Scores of older men run forward and leap into the Romans with a suicidal frenzy, windmilling their falcatas with their gaunt bony hands.

The Romans quickly stab the elders down, but the Astapan veterans thrust into the Romans before they can withdraw their blades from their fragile, valiant, victims, felling dozens of legionnaires. The battle rages on, with no victor apparent.

Bernat is at the center of the Astapan assault, leading his seasoned warriors into a wedge attack at the Roman center. They cut through the first lines of hastati and principes, and close in on the palisades of the Roman camp. "Burn the camp!" Bernat shouts, driving his men forward. Several strong-armed Astapans manage to hurl their torches into the front of the timbered walls. Fires spring up among the timbers, provoking cheers from the Astapans. They lunge ahead with renewed fury, sensing victory.

As the Astapans approach the smoldering camp palisade, hundreds of the redoubtable triarii march out and line up along the front of the camp. The fearless veterans bend to one knee, plant their seven-foot spears into the earth, and pull their shields down in front of them.

II. Astapa

"Retreat!" Marcius shouts to his front line fighters. The hastati and principes march in between the triarii's shields, pursued by hundreds of screaming Astapans.

The Astapans charge the triarii three times. Each time they are repelled, as the Romans stab down scores of Astapa's best warriors.

The Roman hastati and principes regroup into cohort formation and march out to relieve the triarii. They push the Astapans back to their original conflict point, but the Iberians will move no farther. The front line Astapans are tested warriors, and they die where they stand rather than give an inch more, each one replaced by another determined to sell his life as dearly as possible.

Marcius is directing his men from behind his first line of infantry, alternately venturing out to fight with the legionnaires and withdrawing to confer with his officers. When the Astapans refuse to bend any farther, Marius looks over to his trumpeters. He lifts his sword once to the right and once to the left. The battle horns sound, and the rear lines of legionnaires quickly march out to attack the Astapans' flanks. The Iberians in the rear rush out to engage the flanking Romans, but they are more mob than army, and their lines are easily penetrated by the Romans' lockstep charge.

Soon the flanking maneuver becomes encirclement, and the circle closes ever tighter. Hundreds more Astapans fall, slashing at Roman legs and feet even as they writhe on the ground in their death agonies. The Astapan dead are so dense that the Romans must step over mounds of corpses to engage their remaining enemy, carefully planting their sandaled feet so they do not slip on the blood and gore.

Bernat is at the center of an island of survivors, hurling the javelins of his dead comrades, trying to muster his men for a final charge. He hears a scream to his right, and looks to see Clio lying on his back. A centurion straddles the boy, pulling his sword from Clio's chest. The boy turns his anguished face to Bernat. "Brother?" is all he can say before the blood floods his mouth.

"Clio! Oh gods help me!" Bernat leaps upon the centurion and cleaves

II. Astapa

his throat with a single thrust, heedless of the man's counterthrust that severs his shoulder. The centurion doubles over, trying to staunch his gouting throat with his hands.

Bernat bends over Clio. He lifts his dying brother up and eases him into his lap, slowly stroking his blood matted hair. "Easy, my beloved. Be not afraid, you are going to paradise. And I am coming with you."

The dying centurion surges forward and plunges his gladius deep into Bernat's stomach before he collapses at the Astapan's feet. With a grunt of agonized effort, Bernat pulls the sword from his vitals. He feels his life's blood pumping out of him, but he sits and cradles his dying brother's head in the blood pool that is his lap, even as his men fall about him. Bernat strokes the boy's head until Clio's eyes stare into eternity.

After a final kiss, Bernat totters to his feet, holding his bowels inside him. "Give me the horn!" he shouts at his trumpeter, yanking the curled bronze trumpet from his grasp. Bernat blows the horn thrice then repeats the sequence, facing the town gates.

Bernat casts the trumpet aside. "I need a weapon," he shouts. "I must die fighting!" A gut-stabbed older man tosses him a javelin. "Here, it is no good to me," the man replies, as he falls to one knee and rolls onto his back. "Kill a Roman for me."

Bernat summons the last of his strength and casts the spear into the back of a fur-capped Roman standard bearer, watching him fall. With a grunt of satisfaction, Bernat crumples to his knees. As two Romans close on him Bernat sees a bright light flicker behind the town gates, followed by rolling plumes of dark smoke. "Gods be with you, Rafa," he murmurs, as the gladius cuts into his chest.

Inside Astapa, Rafa hears the trumpet call. He prays he has misheard, but then he hears it sound again. The bearish warrior stares hopefully at the two remaining sentries overlooking the gates, but they shake their heads. Rafa takes a deep breath and swallows. He kisses two of his fingers and points them at the ground. *May I see you both in paradise below.*

II. Astapa

The Iberian spins about and strides quickly to his circle of men. "Our people have chosen death by honor instead of inglorious servitude. I call upon you to do your sworn duty to them. May the gods curse any who stay their hand from hope or squeamishness!" [xv] His eyes shine with tears. "Now!" he blurts.

One by one, the fifty guardians kindle their torches from each other, their hands trembling. "Turn," orders Rafa. They men face the women and children in the woodpile. Several warriors bend over and vomit, their peers grabbing their torch, holding it until their compatriots have recovered. Many of the women begin to weep, and their children's tears follow theirs.

"Silence!" several warriors shout, their words more plea than command.

Rafa points for his two chieftains to move to each side of the ring. He steps into the center of the pile and throws his torch into it, igniting the flames. As the fires flicker to life, dozens of women scream out in despair. *Act now! You have to set the example*, he tells himself.

With a moan only he can hear, Rafa steps back and shoves his falcata into the breast of a young woman who stands before him, her head high with resigned pride. As she wails out her life, Rafa hurls her onto the tower of flame. He bends over and cuts the throat of an unresisting man too old to stand. The people who escaped into Astapa watch in horror.

Once Rafa begins killing the townspeople, the rest of the Final Fifty follow suit, although some must be slapped by their compatriots to awake them from their horrified daze. No Astapan is spared, and the still-breathing bodies are tossed to the conflagration. The warriors move quickly and mechanically through their monstrous task, choking and sobbing. The bodies in the pyre become so numerous that the dazed warriors must pause to throw more wood onto the fire, as their victims' blood begins to douse it.[xvi]

When all their townspeople are gone, the warriors turn to face the outsiders. Many flee into the houses and stables about the town, only to be killed and dragged back to the fire.

II. Astapa

An eternity later, the horrific task is finished. The sobbing Oretani line up along the edge of the stinking fire and face Rafa. "Now yourselves," he commands. "May the gods bless you all for what you have done."

A dozen of the Fifty turn their swords upon themselves, shoving the blade up under their ribs and into their heart, gratefully embracing death's surcease from horror. The final cluster of warriors throw their comrades' bodies upon the fire and face each other in pairs. One stabs the other through the heart, drags him into the fire, and faces another for his death. Soon, only Rafa and his chief are left.

Rafa closes in on his old friend. "You first, dear comrade. I must finish my duty..."

Having dispatched the last of his enemies, Marcius marches his men toward the town. From a distance they hear so many screams and wails that the staid legionnaires look anxiously at one another, fearing there are malevolent spirits inside. But as they approach the sounds diminish, and then disappear. The Romans hear only the tramping of their caligae—and the caws of carrion crows.

The escaladers throw up their ladders and disappear over the town battlements. The gates are slowly pushed open, and the escaladers walk out to Marcius and salute him, their eyes glazed.

"General, you will want to see this," one says absently, waving Marcius to the center courtyard. Marcius stares at the leathery old warrior. His dust-grimed face is threaded with tear tracks.

Marcius rides through the gates, coming face to face with a towering bonfire of blue-black smoke, a fire fueled by wood, gold, silver, flesh and bones. A bear of a man stands in front of the enormous pyre, the oily smoke of burnt flesh curling about him. The bloodied warrior holds his red-streaked falcata high over his head, challenging the Romans to battle.

Marcius dismounts and walks toward the demonic soldier, halting just out of sword's reach. When Rafa sees Marcius standing before him, a defiant smile gleams from his smoke blackened face. He lowers his

II. Astapa

sword.

"We are all gone, Roman puke. All our treasures are gone," Rafa shouts exultantly. He steps nearer to the conflagration, his halo of wild hair crackling and withering. "We die free! You conquer nothing! Nothing!"

Marcius' guards move toward Rafa, but the Astapan's raised sword warns them to halt. Marcius can see the madness in Rafa's eyes. "Let him be, men," Marcius says. "It will not be long."

"Carthage will never conquer Iberia," shouts Rafa. "Rome will never conquer Iberia! None of you have the courage or will. Iberia will be free forever! We live free or die!"

Rafa leaps into the flames, shouting the Astapan battle cry. The shout quickly changes to a soul-ripped scream that mercifully dwindles. Marcius stands before the flame, watching Astapa's last warrior fall as a flaming skeleton. When the skeleton crumples to pieces, Marcius turns back to his men.

"We will take no plunder from this evil place," he says. "Each soldier will receive seven denarii by way of recompense." He looks at the blaze behind him, and waves over his first tribune. "Leave a cohort to occupy the town, they can salvage the molten metals. But we depart this cursed land on the morrow."

Marcius walks out the town gates and into the sweet fresh air of the countryside, breathing deeply. *Praise gods all the Iberians are not like them. We'd never conquer it.*

As Marcius and his army return to Carthago Nova, town after town sends out a delegation to meet them on the road and surrender to them, hoping to keep the Romans away from their city. A rumor has spread that the Romans captured the Astapans and threw them into the fire. The remaining rebel fortresses tremble at the thought they could meet the same fate.

Marcius does not correct the delegations that tell him what they heard. The lie blesses him with a dozen bloodless victories, and he is so very

II. Astapa

weary of the alternative.

* * * * *

CARTHAGO NOVA. Six days after Astapa, Marcius' army marches into Carthago Nova. It is the final day of the gladiatorial games being held in Scipio's honor. A robustly healthy Scipio embraces his victorious legate and leads him to Scipio's booth in the amphitheater, where Marcius joins Laelius and Marcus Silenus.

Dozens of tribes have provided warriors for the deadly contests, and most of the fighters have come voluntarily, seeking glory or justice through force of arms. Scipio watches two cousins, Corbis and Orsua, duel to the death for the chieftainship of a local community.[xvii]

The battle pits a smaller older man against a larger and younger opponent. The older man's experience serves him well—Corbis bides his time until Orsua tires and lowers his shield, allowing him to shove his long sword into the side of his skull. Corbis bows before an applauding Scipio. The army priest concludes the games by sacrificing an ox.

That evening, Marcius and the other legion officers gather in Scipio's council chambers, where the legate reports on each of his town conquests. Sitting in his throne-like council chair, Scipio smiles when Marcius tells of the ready surrenders that so many of the towns gave after learning about Illiturgis. *Mars be praised, their deaths were not in vain.*

Marcius concludes by giving a detailed report about Astapa, from the initial attack to the final bonfire. The room becomes very silent as he speaks, his words echoing off the stone walls. Several tribunes wipe at their eyes, but Scipio's face is impassive. Only his right arm betrays his feelings, as it trembles and twitches beneath his restraining left hand.

"Thanks for your report, Marcius. You need say no more," Scipio interjects, suddenly waving the legate silent. "This council is over."

Scipio rises and paces quickly to his chambers. As soon as he closes the door he rushes to an empty wine urn and retches into it, vomiting so

II. Astapa

violently it brings tears to his eyes. After his convulsions cease, he wobbles to his map table and pours a goblet of wine. He takes a deep drink, rinses his mouth, and spits it out, choking. He downs the rest in one swallow, and pours another.

There is a knock at the door. Laelius peers inside. Scipio shakes his head. "Tonight, I must be by myself," he says glumly.

Laelius studies Scipio's face, waiting for further words. When his friend says nothing more, Laelius softly closes the door. Then he reopens it. "The massacre at Astapa was truly abhorrent, but it was not your doing. In no way."

Scipio nods mutely, and stares at the floor. Laelius sighs, and pulls the door shut.

"Ah, gods!" Scipio moans. He walks over to sit at his map table, looking at the town figurine placed on the Astapa location. He reaches out and flicks the figurine off the table, listening to it clatter as it rolls across the stone floor. Scipio laughs briefly, deliriously, then sobs into his hands. He pours another wine.

That night, Febris visits Scipio. The goddess again brings him the fevered dreams that have plagued him since childhood. But tonight there are no clear visions, only a formless parade of screaming women and children, shapes echoing the dying voices of Carthago Nova, Illiturgis, and Astapa. Dawn brings no surcease, as a weary and sweaty Scipio pushes himself from his sleeping pallet.

Scipio shrugs on his purple-bordered tunic of consular office. He pushes himself out into the hallway, determined to fulfill his commander's duties and complete his campaign planning, knowing time still flows against him.

He walks into the feasting room and finds his officers arrayed about the twenty foot table, waiting for Scipio to appear. He shuffles to the head of the table, easing into its broad oak chair. Marius sits on his immediate right as the guest of honor, clad in a snow white tunic and silver studded belt. Marcus Silenus sits next to Marius, in his simple

II. Astapa

gray tunic. Laelius sits on his left, clad in the gold-embroidered black Greek tunic that he favors for special occasions.

Scipio stands, raises his wine goblet, and sniffs it. He wrinkles his nose. "More water," he says. "This wine is too strong for me today." The officers look at one another.

"You are well?" asks Marcius.

"As well as I will ever be," Scipio replies.

An attendant pours more water into his goblet. Scipio stands and raises his glass. "To the health of our Iberian Conqueror," he says woodenly and takes a draft from his glass. The officers heartily echo Scipio's toast, for the unassuming Marius is a favorite with the men.

Scipio smiles wanly, and starts to sit down. He grabs the edge of the table and begins to weave sideways. As Marius and Laelius jump from their seats Scipio collapses to the floor, his eyes rolled up in his head.

"Get out of the way!" Marcus Silenus bowls Laelius and Marius aside and picks Scipio up as if he were a child. "To his chambers," Marcus orders, and marches off with his general in his arms. Crying and cursing, Scipio's senior officers follow Marcus back to Scipio's chambers.

Laelius waits until all of the officers have left the meeting room, then he waves over the room's attendants. "If any of you mention what you have just seen to anyone, even your tent-mates, I will scourge all of you myself." The terrified young soldiers can only nod their assent.

In the coming days, Laelius and the other officers work assiduously to conceal Scipio's illness, joking publicly about his excesses of drink and women. But in the absence of truth, a worse lie is born. Rumors spread across Iberia that mighty Scipio has taken to his deathbed.[xviii]

And with that rumor, those who have lain in wait for such a weakness now emerge to seize their opportunity. Scipio's erstwhile Illergete allies, Indibilis and Mandonius, rise up to stir their tribes into revolt, pillaging the Roman allies' lands. But the fierce tribesmen will prove to

II. Astapa

be a lesser concern for the forces of Rome.

In a quiet garrison north of Carthago Nova, Scipio's greatest threat emerges.

Mutiny.

III. REBELLION

SUCRO GARRISON, EASTERN IBERIAN COAST 206 BCE. "What the fuck are we doing here?" grouses Gaius Albius, as he looks out from the garrison walls. The shrewish older man paces impatiently about the walkway, pausing to pitch a stone at the farmers who are dutifully tending to their olive groves. "We've won the war. It's time to go home and tend to our crops, like those lucky bastards down there!"

"It is true," muses his companion, a rangy Umbrian named Gaius Atrius, an angular man with a cavernous face and flinty eyes. "The Three Generals are gone and the rebel tribes are beaten. But here we sit, with no one to fight and nothing to plunder. And we still haven't been paid all that back pay we earned! We'd be better off joining the Iberians. At least we'd have women and wine!"

"Aye, and we are not the only ones," replies Albius. "At the dice games I met some legionnaires who are more dissatisfied than we are, they have already served thrice the normal period of duty. And some of my fellow Campanians, they are so broke they are ready to steal a ship and sail for Capua!"

"Idle boasts," sniffs Atrius. "There is nothing to be done. I don't even have enough coin to get drunk and forget about this crap!"

Albius looks around for eavesdroppers, then leans toward Atrius. "There is something that can be done, my friend. Remember the stories about the Campania mutiny?" [xix]

Atrius shrugs. "Of course. My grandfather told me about it, how the legionnaires rebelled over their pay and marched on Rome itself."

"That's exactly what they did," says Albius eagerly. "Dictator Corvus granted them amnesty, and the Senate gave them their pay! That is the only way we can get what we deserve!"

III. Rebellion

Atrius looks a long time at Albius, then shakes his head. "Forget that nonsense. Two men cannot accomplish such a thing."

Albius grabs Atrius' bicep and squeezes it so hard that Atrius winces. "True, but two dozen might, if they were organized. I know at least that many who would join us. Don't you?"

"Well," muses Atrius. "I know ten or twelve infantrymen who are so bored they would do anything for action. I could talk to them."

Albius shakes Atrius' arm. "We need to do more than talk, Atrius, we need to act. Four nights hence, at the granary. Bring all who are committed to a better life."

Atrius swallows hard, staring at Albius. "You are a clever man, all who know you say that. Do you think such a thing is truly possible?"

Albius counts the reasons on his fingers. "General Marcius is away south at Carthago Nova, taking thousands of the army. Scipio is dying, and only the gods know who will replace him. All is turmoil, it is the perfect time to take control of the garrison. Just think, you and I could become the commanders, the ones giving the orders." Albius heads down the steps, pausing to cast a final remark. "Four nights hence, or never whine to me again!"

Four days later, thirty five soldiers weave through the fort's darkened pathways, heading for the granary. They come from different ranks and regions, these legionnaires and allies, but when they meet they discover that they all want to take control of the Sucro garrison. The conspirators talk long into the night, airing grievances and arguing over possibilities to resolve them. As dawn creeps over the garrison walls, a plan is born.

A fortnight later, the plan's effects reach Carthago Nova...

* * * * *

CARTHAGO NOVA. Quintus, Scipio's chief aide, interrupts Scipio's strategy meeting with his officers. "There are some tribunes to see you," he says evenly, his eyes betraying his concern. "They have come from Sucro."

III. Rebellion

Scipio looks up from a map of southern Iberia. "Tribunes from the north are here? They cannot wait until we are done with this?"

Quintus raises the stump of his left arm. "On my honor, sir, it is important." Scipio shrugs resignedly. "Very well, bring them in."

Quintus walks over and opens the chamber door. Six armored legionnaires file into the room and stand along the wall, arranged as if for battle. Scipio glances over at Marcus Silenus and Laelius, but both look as mystified as he is.

"What are you doing here?" is all Scipio can think to ask.

A large, gray-haired man steps to the fore. "I am Tribune Tiberius Geminus. I was in charge of the Sucro garrison."

"Was?" asks Laelius.

Tiberius bows his head. "There has been a mutiny, Admiral. The soldiers have established their own army—a rebel army. They have replaced the eagle standard with the fasces, the symbol of death. They evicted all officers who stayed loyal to Rome."

"What?" Scipio blurts. "Are you saying there's been a munity?" Scipio's men stare at each other across the meeting table. None have encountered a mutiny, and they are unsure of what to do. Hearing no comments from them, Scipio quells his nervousness and clears his throat. "You, uh, say eight thousand men have rebelled against us?"

Tiberius gives the briefest of nods, avoiding Scipio's eyes. "It is so. All of the soldiers at Sucro, both Romans and allies. They want their back pay, they want to go home. They want all sorts of things..." Tiberius' brows furrow. "And the leaders, they just want power."

Scipio can feel his right hand twitching, and he becomes fearful of a seizure. *Steady, boy. You can't show weakness again.* He raises his head and pulls back his shoulders. "Gratitude for coming to me yourself, Tiberius. And for your loyalty. You all are dismissed for now." As one man, the six tribunes march out of the room. As soon as the door closes Scipio jumps up and stalks about the room, his hands

III. Rebellion

clenched behind his back.

"Mutiny! Can you believe it? Our own troops, our family, they rebel against us! Against me! We must act on this, before our men get the same idea."

"We could give them their back pay," offers one of the tribunes. "That should satisfy most of them."

Scipio glares at the officer, his pale face stern. "After they have mutinied to get it? Do you know what that makes us look like? The ram has touched the wall on that matter, Tribune. There will be no compensation without retribution."

"Agreed. The act cannot go unpunished," says Marcus Silenus. "To do so would abet future rebellions."

Laelius frowns at Marcus Silenus. "These are trained troops, not some wild band of Ilergetes that can be quelled with a single charge! Would you put Roman against Roman, Italian against Italian?" He shakes his head. "Think of the thousands of dead veterans. Think of the families who would seek revenge on us. It cannot be done!"

Marcus Silenus looks directly at Scipio. He speaks softly but decisively. "If you allow these cowards to go unpunished, you will undo all we have suffered – you have suffered – in our battles and sieges. And thousands of innocents will have died in vain."

Scipio recoils as if he has been struck a blow. His face whitens. Laelius watches him anxiously, fearing a fever attack will take him. But after a moment, Scipio's face becomes strangely calm.

"You are both right, in some measure. Iberia is watching us, we must punish them or we will look weak—we will *be* weak. But we cannot let thousands of our countrymen die in some incestuous battle between the Sucro and Carthago Nova garrisons."

"Quintus, bring wine and food!" Scipio commands. "We have a long night ahead of us." As Quintus leaves, Scipio turns back to his officers. "The punishment must fit the crime, and the instigators are the worst

III. Rebellion

criminals. We must figure out how we may punish them without fomenting a war."

Days later, seven Carthago Nova tribunes ride into the Sucro garrison. They announce themselves as emissaries of General Publius Cornelius Scipio. The leader explains that have come to negotiate a resolution to the soldiers' grievances as soon as possible.

The news of the tribunes' arrival spreads like wildfire throughout the fort, and the rebels grow excited about receiving resolution to their complaints. They become alarmed when the emissaries inform them that Scipio is alive and well, because they were recently told he was dying.

The tribunes move from tent to tent, recording each soldier's grievances – and quietly soliciting the names of those who led the mutiny. After days of polite inquiries and conversations, the tribunes meet with ringleaders Atrius and Albius. The emissaries tell the two conspirators that the rebels' major grievance is a lack of back pay from years past. Atrius and Albius heartily agree that the mutiny could be called off if that grievance were resolved.

The seven tribunes return to Carthago Nova, bringing three mutineers selected by Atrius and Albius to act as their representatives. The rebel emissaries watch Scipio issue a proclamation that the army will set forth to gather taxes on the allied Iberian towns, and that the money collected will be used for the mutineers' back pay.

The mutineers note that the Carthago Nova legions are packing to leave for a campaign against Gades, the Carthaginians' last refuge. The rebels are greatly pleased with the arrangement. That night they celebrate their victory with ample wine and meat.

The mutineers quickly return to the Sucro garrison, eager to give the news to their fellows. They inform the thirty-five ringleaders that all who come to Carthago Nova will be paid their wages without punishment. They add that the Sucro garrison will greatly outnumber Scipio's men after Marcus Silenus takes the legions to Gades, ensuring they will be free from retribution. The rebel leaders argue the issue

III. Rebellion

among themselves and decide that the garrison will go to Carthago Nova en masse, so their followers can protect them from being singled out for retribution.

Eight thousand legionnaires and allies set out from Sucro, marching south to claim their pay and voice their other complaints. Their advance scouts meet them on the march, informing them that Marcus Silenus will take the city's army to Gades within two days. Reassured that the Roman army will not be in force at Carthago Nova, the rebels pick up their pace, timing their arrival for the day when Marcus Silenus departs.

Days later, the mutinous horde marches into Carthago Nova at sunset. As soon as the first lines enter the gates, they see Laelius waiting for them, resplendent in his battle armor and blood-red cape. The seven tribunes who visited their camp accompany him. They are similarly armed and armored.

"Well, looks like we have a proper welcoming party!" exclaims Atrius as they lead their men inside the gates. He slaps Albius on the back. "Now we'll get some respect!"

"We are most glad to see you all here, fellow soldiers," says Laelius with a wry smile, emphasizing the word 'fellow.' "Now we can settle this petty affair and march upon Indibilis and Mandonius. Those two are naught but troublemakers—I hate troublemakers, don't you? Once we've disposed of them we can all go home with our pay. That is what you wanted, isn't it?"

The Sucro soldiers nod and grin at one another, eager to put the matter behind them.

Albius and Atrius listen somberly. "We will make our demands tomorrow," whispers Albius. "When Silenus leaves, Scipio cannot deny us."

Atrius grins smugly. "We should request a private audience with him. Get that patrician spawn to sign a treaty that gives us a legate's rank. If he won't, we take over the city."

Laelius' voice interrupts them. "Come, loyal soldiers, we have

III. Rebellion

prepared food and drink for you," says Laelius expansively, his eyes merrily agleam. "And for you Sucro commanders—Atrius, Albius, and the rest of the thirty-five—you will have a private little feast with the seven tribunes that visited you!"

Laelius grins. "Our tribunes were most impressed with your leadership. They said your men were quick to point you out as the organizers of the resistance."

The seven tribunes step forward. Each tribune reads the names of five rebel leaders that are to join him, beckoning for the traitors to step forward. Because they are called out in front of their men, the rebels have no choice but to join the tribunes. The officers lead the Sucro men toward the meeting halls in the city center, chatting and joking with them as if they were old friends, talking about Scipio's plans to combat Indibilis and Mandonius.

Laelius leads the seven groups into a side street. "We will feast at the temple of Justitia, it is just a few blocks this way," he says merrily as he marches on. "I thought it appropriate that you meet the goddess of justice." He stops and faces the group. "In fact, you can meet justice right now."

Laelius whistles sharply. Two centuries of legionnaires appear from the alleyways in the front and rear of the group. "Bind them," Laelius growls, "They are under arrest." The legionnaires surround the stunned rebels and rope their hands behind their backs. Several rebels grab for their swords, only to be smacked down with the broadside of a legionnaire's blade.

"What are you doing, fool?" barks Atrius, as a centurion yanks his arms behind him. "We have an army at our hands!"

Laelius glares at him. "Tomorrow we will see how loyal they are to you, traitor! They will have the opportunity to come to your rescue. And oh, you will need rescuing!"

While the instigators are being surreptitiously captured, the main body of mutineers feasts in the city's spacious marketplace. As the men

III. Rebellion

laugh and drink, they see Marcus Silenus' troops marching past them toward the distant city gates.[xx] His departure only adds to their festive mood.

When Marcus Silenus arrives at the gates he calls forward his officers. "You know what to do," he states. "Do it now." The tribunes rush back to their cohorts. Nine thousand soldiers dissolve into the perimeter streets of Carthago Nova. Within an hour the city is sealed. No one can leave – or escape.

Late the next morning the buccinae sound out, calling the Sucro garrison to assemble in the city forum and meet with Scipio. The woozy mutineers shamble into the spacious grounds, blinking and scratching. They see Scipio sitting upon a throne-like marble seat on a high dais, looking down at them with ill-concealed anger.

Marcus Silenus and Laelius flank him, their arms crossed beneath their stony visages. Many of the Sucro men are struck dumb at Scipio's powerful prospect. Expecting a sickly and weakened young man, they find a general in the full bloom of health and strength, his eyes burning with rage. When Scipio sees that all have crowded into the forum he nods at Laelius, who whirls off from the dais.

Scipio rises to face the mutineers, nightfall on his face. His eyes flare as he stares reprovingly into his errant legionnaires' faces. His gaze seems to bore into each man's eyes. One by one, the mutineers look away from him. When Scipio decides that they are sufficiently abashed, he speaks.

"Evidently you were displeased with me because I did not pay what was due to you. But that was no fault of mine, for since I myself have been in command, you have been always paid in full. But if you have a grievance against Rome because your old arrears were not made good, was it the proper method of complaint to revolt against your country and take up arms against her who nourished you? Should you not rather have come and spoken to me about the matter, and begged your friends to take up your cause and help you? Yes, that, I think, would have been far better." [xxi]

III. Rebellion

"We want to go home," blurts someone from the crowd. "Fight or leave!" shouts another. The rebels begin to mutter among themselves, a tide of dissent rising.

Scipio raises his fists over his head. "SILENCE!" he thunders. "On pain of life, you will be silent!" His command booms off the stone walls around him, and all is quiet.

"I am at a loss on how to address you," Scipio continues. "Shall I call you countrymen, who have revolted from your country? Or soldiers, who have rejected the command and authority of your general and violated your solemn oath? Can I call you enemies? I recognize the persons, faces, and dress, and mien of fellow countrymen!"

The general's cheeks grow flushed. He throws up his hands in frustration as he stalks across the dais. Finally he pauses, hands on hips, and spits at the rebels' feet.

"Mercenary troops may, indeed, sometimes be pardoned for revolting against their employers," Scipio chides. "But no pardon can be extended to those who are fighting for themselves and their wives and children. For that is just as if a man who said he had been wronged by his own father over money matters were to take up arms to kill him who was the author of his life!" [xxii]

Scipio falls silent. The mutineers detect a tramping sound behind them, growing ever louder. They turn to see Marcus Silenus' men pouring into the forum, enclosing the unarmed soldiers. The legionnaires link their shields into a wall and stick out their spears.

When the encirclement is complete. Scipio again speaks. "So far as you, as a whole, are concerned, I shall have satisfaction enough, more than enough, if you regret your wrongdoing."

The men start to murmur their relief when Scipio's voice knifes through them. "The Caledonian Albius, and the Umbrian Atrius, and all the other ringleaders of this foul insurrection – they shall pay for their acts with their blood!" [xxiii]

Several of the Sucro soldiers muster the nerve to yell out protests, but

III. Rebellion

Scipio glares them into silence. "Bring them out," Scipio intones, and resumes his seat on the dais.

The thirty five ringleaders are dragged in from behind the dais, each bound and naked. They are tugged over to the five scourging posts that Scipio has installed below. The general rises and stares down at the rebels. "Gaius Albius and Gaius Atrius!" he shouts.

The two men are dragged out from the group and placed before him. "You were the first to foment rebellion, so you will be the first to receive its due."

Atrius and Albius scream for mercy, even as they are tied face-first to the posts. Two army blacksmiths step forward, their thick muscular torsos bare. They each heft a three-thonged short whip laced with iron balls and sharpened sheep bones, a whip designed to both pound and cut its victims. The blacksmiths take a few practice strikes on the empty scourging posts, the impact clapping like a thunderbolt. They turn to face their commander, eager and expectant.

"Begin," is all Scipio says. The scourgers rear back their brawny arms and flash out their whips. The wet slap of thongs hewing flesh is drowned by the victims' screams, which soon turn to despairing shrieks.

Atrius and Albius are flogged until they are senseless. When the two no longer scream when the whip strikes, Scipio raises his hand. The victims are cut down and left to sprawl into the blooded earth beneath the post. Scipio watches the dazed ringleaders crawl about, moaning in pain. He looks up to see if the horror has set in on the Sucro rebels.

"Enough!" shouts a voice from the stunned crowd. "They have had enough!" echoes another.

Scipio's icy stare bores into the crowd. "Enough, indeed!" he declares. Scipio draws his hand across his throat.

The two floggers withdraw their razored swords from their belts. In one quick motion they bend over and slice off the rebels' heads, jerking the skulls back to break them from their spines.

III. Rebellion

Five more leaders are dragged forward screaming and protesting. The brutal process is repeated until thirty-five decapitated corpses are clustered about the posts. Throughout this parade of death, the mutineers watch in terrified silence, with barely a moan to be heard. [xxiv]

"Remove them," Scipio says. The bodies are dragged from the yard, and Scipio gestures for the mutineers in the front to ascend the dais. The men refuse to move. Marcus Silenus steps out and stands in front of them, slapping his sword onto his hoary palm. His men edge behind the front line, blades at the ready, and push the rebels forward.

Twenty-six terrified men stumble up the steps, glancing anxiously at their compatriots. When they attain the platform the guards push them toward one of four large tables on the side of the dais. Each table holds a thick log book. Two triarii stand at each table, holding their naked falcatas point-first into the ground.

The rebels stand about the tables, looking around with wide eyes. A young man on the far left table doubles over and vomits, prompting five others to follow him. Others merely stand in frozen shock, urine dribbling down their legs.

"Mercy!" a voice cries.

Scipio's head pivots to the source. "Mercy? Mercy is given to those who deserve it. You will get what you deserve, and no more." With a disgusted look on his face, Scipio leans back toward Quintus. "Bring them out!" he shouts.

Four quaestors march out from behind the dais, each with a pair of slaves toting two large and heavy sacks. The two guards at each table pick up their cleaver like swords and march up to their first man in line. They push their terrified charges toward the quaestors, bending over to pull up those that have fallen to their knees with fear.

"Give me your name," command the accountants to each rebel as he arrives. They write the rebel's name in a book, then push a stylus into their trembling hands. "Make your mark here," they demand.

As the Sucro rebels look on, their brethren make their mark and

III. Rebellion

receive a handful of silver coins. Scipio stands up and faces the bewildered crowd. "Hear me, traitors. You told my seven tribunes that you wanted your back pay. I was not the source of that problem, but I will be its solution. You will be given what you deserve." The men shuffle back down the steps, staring at the denarii they cradle in their hands. The guards push more to the tables, and the process continues.

Scipio and his commanders watch expressionlessly, making sure each man receives his due. Now the rebels rush to the tables, eager to receive their money—eager to escape the soldiers that stand by the flogging posts, as if they might grab more victims for Scipio's justice.

The payment ceremony continues into dusk. Scipio finally rises and walks down the back of the dais, followed by Marcus and Laelius. When they arrive at Scipio's quarters, Quintus pours them each a half goblet of wine. He returns to add river water to the cups, but Scipio waves it away. "Add more wine," he says dully. Scipio starts to raise his cup, but his hand is shaking so badly he quickly puts it down. *Be calm. It is over. You don't have to watch it any more.*

Laelius walks up behind him and grips his shoulder. "You have fully regained your health now, friend. Don't let dreams of this haunt you and make you sick again."

Scipio looks at Laelius. "The mutineers? Those bastards will not haunt me," he snarls. "They would have destroyed all that we have gained here, just for a few fucking coins." He glares into the distance. "I'd kill them all twice, were it possible. But we need them to secure the land."

"I thought I would never say this, but I am glad to see your heart has hardened," Laelius says softly. "You have let the consequences of your decisions cut too deeply into your spirit. Perhaps you will survive this war now, after all."

Scipio blinks at Laelius. "Survive the war? I will win it, all of it! In my dreams I have seen Africa burning, I have seen myself marching in triumph through Rome!" He smiles faintly and bends to sniff his wine, flipping a piece of toast into it. He raises his cup. "A toast to my

III. Rebellion

dreams. Not all of them are terrifying, you know."

Marcus jerks his thumb toward the town forum. "Now that we have captured all that scum, what do we do with them? Send them back to Sucro?"

"Not all," Scipio replies. "We have one final task before we depart, is that not correct?"

Marcus grimaces. "Ah yes, Indibilis and Mandonius, our former allies. You go to smash them."

"Do I have a choice? The two praetors will soon arrive to take my place," Scipio says, chewing on his soggy toast. "I cannot leave with those bandits rampaging about. We will take our men and the ones from Sucro, that will give us three legions and nine hundred Roman and Italia cavalry."

"You're going to take those criminals?" blurts Laelius. "First you kill their leaders and now you take them to battle as if nothing has happened?"

Scipio shrugs. "Rome watches us. We gave the mutineers what they were due; to do otherwise would be to act without honor. Besides, most of those 'criminals' are veterans of three campaigns. We need them."

"You will take nothing but Italians?" queries Marcus. "You mistrust our Iberian allies but trust the mutineers?"

"The Iberians are too close to the rebel tribes. I don't want them sneaking out the night before battle, as happened with my father. I doubt the Sucro men will mutiny when surrounded by my army. And the mutineers have other value..."

Scipio grasps his goblet with steady hand, grinning slyly. "The Sucro Romans can vote in the upcoming consular elections in Rome. And they would favor me, I think, were I run for consul. Especially if I provide them with victory and plunder before they go home. I will gain thousands of votes."

III. Rebellion

Hearing this, Marcus Silenus grins. "I swear to Jupiter, boy, you are finally learning how to win this war. Scheme like a politician, fight like a soldier."

Laelius shakes his head. "Run for consul? That way lies folly. You said you wanted to be a scholar, a teacher. Now you can go back and do it. We have won the war here, double-chin. You have fulfilled your vow to your father, to protect Rome. For Jupiter's sake, give it up!"

Scipio smiles wearily. "If only that were true. We have not won the war, we have moved its theatre to Africa. But we will cast the play on that stage."

Laelius looks at Marcus Silenus, who stares at the ceiling.

Scipio frowns at them as if they are slow school children. "Don't you see? Up to now the Carthaginians have been making war on the Romans, but now chance has given the Romans the opportunity of making war on the Carthaginians." [xxv]

Laelius nods. "So we will go after Hannibal in South Italia?"

Scipio shakes his head and smiles, amused at the enormity of his own vision. "No, we go to Africa. And make Hannibal come after us. But first, there is the matter of Indibilis and Mandonius."

*   *   *   *   *

EBRO RIVER, NORTH IBERIA, 206 BCE. "They are camped in the river valley, on top of a hill, General," says Scipio's interpreter. "Two days' march from here." The interpreter turns back to the barbarian who has given Scipio this treasured information.

The Celtiberian scout stands inside Scipio's tent, anxiously twisting his bearskin cap with his knotty fingers, waiting for Scipio to ask him more questions. Scipio has sent a dozen of his best Roman scouts in search of Indibiblis' and Mandonius' army, but this unkempt local huntsman has been the first to find the rebel army, tucked away in a protective valley near the Iberian border. The aged little man is nervous but eager, knowing Scipio has promised a purse of silver to the first

III. Rebellion

man to find them. A purse of silver means a strong young ox for his farm, and perhaps a glass bead necklace for his wife.

"How many?" asks Marcus Silenus.

The barbarian rolls his eyes, trying to express the amount. "As many as yours out there. And half again at least."

"Mmmm," says Laelius. "Given our Celtiberian friend here is no threat to the genius mathematician Archimedes, we should still assume they have about eighteen thousand to our twelve thousand. Or more."

Scipio shrugs. "We must take them on regardless, I cannot leave Iberia in the midst of a rebellion."

Marcus nods. "Then we had best move on them soon, before it gets any colder. Or it snows."

"We need a map before we do anything," says Scipio. "Send out four of our scouts. I want a map of their emplacement by tomorrow evening. We'll march toward it tomorrow."

The next night finds Scipio and his two commanders huddled over a freshly drawn map of Indibilis' and Mandonius' camp. The map indicates the rebel army is atop a flat hill at the rear of a narrow valley surrounded by steep hills, with a narrow valley entrance to their emplacement.

"It looks like they are in a strong location," observes Marcus, running his finger across the map. "Camped on the high ground and surrounded by hills. It could be very difficult to charge uphill on them."

"We may have no choice," replies Laelius. "If they disappear into the mountains, we could spend years trying to root them out. We do not have years."

"And they outnumber us greatly, so we don't want an open battle with them," says Scipio. He puts his hand on the sketch of the valley's mouth. "We can use the valley entrance to protect our men from being outflanked and surrounded, its narrow terrain will be our ally."

III. Rebellion

Marcus shakes his head. "Perhaps, but that means we have to draw them down from the top of that hill, or they will have the strategic advantage of making us fight uphill."

Scipio scratches his ear and smiles mischievously. Laelius and Marcus look at each other, knowing he has come up with a new trick. "I think we can draw them out by using one of Hannibal's old tricks, the one he played on Montanus and Fabius." [xxvi] His grin widens. "We'll use the Iberian allies we brought with us!"

Laelius rolls his eyes. "Very well, Scippy, I will play your game. We brought no Iberians from Sucro. You didn't want them."

Scipio laughs. "Oh yes we did. We brought Iberian cattle in the supply train!" His careworn eyes twinkle. "We'll recruit them tomorrow."

Two days later, the Illergete rebels notice that scores of cattle are wandering untended about the valley floor, grazing in the tall grass near its entrance. With thousands of men to feed during these winter months, Indibilis and Mandonius are delighted to find them there. They are pleased, but they are not fools.

The Iberan commanders send three hundred light infantry to round up the cattle and bring them back to camp. Six scouts ride ahead of the foraging party and investigate the environs for ambushes, but they find nothing and return to camp.

The Illergetes disperse and begin to rope up the cattle for towing back up the hill, pushing them into a herd. After two hours they have collected almost all of the beasts. The Illergetes trot toward the trees to retrieve the last of the herd. When they near the trees they hear the alarming blast of a Roman battle horn.

The Iberians drop their ropes and rush back to seize their swords and shields. The warriors look south toward the valley entrance, and see hundreds of Roman velites trotting toward them. Seeing that their enemy is lightly armed and few in number, the Iberian infantrymen immediately organize into two lines and tramp forward to drive the Romans away from their precious herd.

III. Rebellion

The velites dash in and hurl their first two javelins, but they keep one for battle, as per Scipio's orders. The youths dash about and jab at the Iberian infantry, wounding scores of them. The two sides fight in a free form skirmish, with men running about to clash with each other and then retreat.

Three turmae of Roman cavalry enter the skirmish. The ninety horsemen ride through the enemy's light infantry, trampling them down and hurling javelins into their backs. Within an hour less than half the Illergetes are standing. The equites leap from their mounts, draw their blades, and join the velites, slowly encircling their enemy.

The Illergete cavalry eventually rush down from the Illergete camp but it is too late, the Romans have abandoned the field, leaving a fresh crop of dead Iberians.

Indibilis and Mandonius are furious. "They think they can sneak in here and kill our tribesmen!" fumes Mandonius.

"That Scipio, he thinks he can fool us," adds Indibilis. "He thinks we are stupid savages. We will show him how stupid we are."

Mandonius shoves his finger toward Scipio's camp. "He is there at the mouth of the valley. He does not have as many men as we do.

III. Rebellion

**INDIBILIS'
AND
MANDONIUS'
CAMP**

ILLERGETE LIGHT INFANTRY

ILLERGETE INFANTRY

ILLERGETE CAVALRY

ROMAN CAVALRY

COHORTS

SCIPIO'S CAMP

BATTLE OF THE EBRO RIVER, 206 BCE

We can catch him on level ground, where he can't use any of his ambushes."

Indibilis grunts. "Tomorrow we'll go after his camp."

The next day the Illergete warriors breakfast heavily on meat and

III. Rebellion

grain, knowing they will not eat until dusk—if they are still alive. After their meal the rebel army musters along the top of the hill. The barbarians begin to march down the hill towards the Roman camp. Thousands flow onto the narrow plain inside the valley, an army so large that three thousand of them remain near the camp, waiting to descend. Indibilis and Mandonius ride along the top of the hill. They direct the descent from a distance, the better to watch their army's progress.

The Illergetes fill the valley and march toward its mouth. Following Indibilis' and Mandonius' orders, the tribal chieftains will pause once they are past the valley mouth and wait until the rest of the troops descend into the valley. The army commander orders a quicker pace, eager to get through the valley and destroy the Roman camp.

Four Roman cohorts suddenly march into the valley mouth, entering from each side of the hills. The cohorts are followed by four more behind them, and then four more.

The front cohorts march through the valley passage and halt near its mouth, filling the passage from side to side, preventing the Illergetes from outflanking them—or escaping. The rear cohorts follow suit, and soon the entire valley passage is filled with the serried ranks of Scipio's veterans. All are well protected by the steep hillsides.

Indibilis gapes in dismay at the sight of the Romans. "Where did they come from?"

Mandonius shrugs. "Last night there was no one out there, they were all in camp!"

Indibilis grits his teeth. "Now what do we do, brother?"

Mandonius laughs sarcastically. "What do we do? Look down there. You can see we outnumber them by thousands. We attack!"

Within moments, the valley echoes with the battle cry of a dozen trumpets. Ten thousand heavy infantry head directly for the Roman cohorts, marching more as a mob than an army. The chieftains direct their light infantry to the hillside of one flank and send their cavalry to

III. Rebellion

the other. The massed troops soon fill the remaining space between the valley floor and the steep hillsides around it, preventing any flanking maneuvers by the Romans.

But Scipio has no intention of outflanking his opponent. His four front cohorts dig in at the valley mouth, guarded by the steep hills on either side of them. The legionnaires watch the sea of Illergetes coming towards them; tall warriors with long oblong shields and razor edged falcatas, their stern faces evidencing their lack of fear.

Scipio rides to the front of his waiting lines, looking back at the oncoming barbarians. "Will of iron, men, will of iron!" he shouts. He trots his stallion across the front line, his blood red cape unfurling in the wind, brandishing his gleaming sword over his head, the blade he painstakingly polished that morning so it would catch the valley sun.

"They will twice try to break our lines, men. If you hold, we have them!" The Romans dig their feet into the ground, preparing for the impact.

The barbarians hurtle into the Roman lines, crashing into the Romans' stout shield wall. The Iberians scream with battle lust as they hammer at the Romans' shields and helmets.

The cohort lines remain steadfast, their shields held high in front of them. The tribunes bark an order to their centurions, who immediately blow a charge upon their battle whistles. As one, the hastati take a step forward and shove their bossed shields into their opponents, following with practiced sword thrusts that cut into to their enemies' legs, abdomens, and necks. As Iberians fall dead and screaming about them, the hastati take another step forward, and then another, firmly planting their caligae with each step.

Marcus Silenus rages along the front line, shouting encouragement to his troops. He shoves laggards into the fight, and searches for Iberian captains to kill. Marcus spies a large barbarian wearing a bearskin cape and shouting commands. With a grim smile, he stalks toward his prey, pushing aside an attacking Iberian as if he were a child.

III. Rebellion

The Iberian captain spies Marcus' approach and steps out from his men. The Romans and Iberians pause in their battle and step back apace, eager to watch the looming confrontation.

"Roman shit-face, come to me!" yells the Iberian, grinning at the small man marching toward him. "Little chicken-man captain, I take you home and fuck you!"

The Illergete captain stands with feet akimbo, his sword arm cocked back. Marcus says nothing, his feral eyes fixed on his foe, noting his stance and weapon positioning. When Marcus is within a yard of his boasting enemy, he sprints forward, his head aimed at his opponent's broad chest.

The Iberian swoops his sword down for a helmet-splitting blow, but Marcus is already inside his guard. His shield shoves aside the barbarian's oblong shield, leaving just enough of a gap for Marcus to push in sideways. His gladius leaps upward and blocks the fatal blow at his head. Marcus rams his red-plumed helmet up into the Iberian's chin and the Iberian sprawls backward, knocked out with a single blow. Deliberately, almost casually, the blocky ex-centurion straddles his foe.

Marcus Silenus shoves his sword through the captain's larynx. "Now, give me some more of your fucking insults," Marcus growls in Iberian. He yanks out his blade and steps away from the convulsing body before the first gouts of blood can fountain upon the arid plain. Marcus wheels about, his sword ready, looking for any who would assault him. No one steps forward.

Daunted by Marcus' victory, the Iberian captains call for their front line to retreat a pace and regroup. The barbarians step back from the Romans, dragging their wounded with them. When the Iberians back off from the front line, the centurions sound another call. The rear line hastati and principes rain their javelins upon the retreating Illergetes. The three volleys fell scores of men along the front, especially those who are dragging their wounded and have left their backs vulnerable.

The fallen Iberians are quickly replaced by more young warriors eager to take a Roman head and achieve lifelong glory. Shouting and

III. Rebellion

whooping, the tribesmen dash to the front, slashing energetically at their tiring opponents. After minutes of frenzied fighting, many of the hastati begin to hold their shields low, and their sword arms tire. Dozens of legionnaires fall with dismembered limbs, while others crumble to the ground from telling thrusts into their torsos. The centurions signal for a line replacement, and the second row hastati push between their front line fellows. The fresh legionnaires vigorously thrust into the Iberians, halting the Illergete assault.

The fight continues for hours. The Romans methodically exchange lines within their cohorts and then replace the cohorts, filing in fresh troops against their less organized foe. Their barbarians' superior numbers are constrained by the narrower space in which they must fight, so much of their army cannot get in to fight the legionnaires.

Scipio rides about in the space between the front and rear cohorts, learning the temper of the battle. He can see that the Iberians grow ever denser along the front lines, and he suspects that the entire army of Illergetes is packed into the narrow valley. Looking to his left, he can see thousands of their infantry lining the hillside slopes by their camp, with no room to descend. [xxvii] *It's time for Laelius,* he decides.

Scipio waves over one of his battle scouts. "Gnaeus, tell Laelius to start down the slopes."

The scout gallops into the forested hills to the right of Scipio, and abruptly turns east into the inner valley. The scout wends his way along the upper side hills, moving steadily through the concealing trees. He finds Laelius' cavalry scattered along the top of a spur mountain behind the Iberian lines,[xxviii] almost invisible among the trees.

Laelius is perched on a rock promontory overlooking the battle below, scrutinizing the Iberian cavalry who are wedged between the Iberian infantry and the hillside.

When he sees Gnaeus, Laelius' eyes light up. "May Orcus take you to Hades, I have been waiting since dawn for you to get here! Their scouts almost stumbled upon us. Thanks the gods they didn't go any higher up the trail."

III. Rebellion

Gnaeus looks down below. "You do not have to wait any longer. Scipio orders you to attack."

Laelius grins and turns in his saddle to face his men. "Follow me, down, my boys. Ride through them until you're kissing the legionnaires' asses on the front lines!" With a snap of his rope bridle, Laelius plunges down the hill. Nine hundred Roman and Italia cavalry follow him, switchbacking between the trees and rocks.

Soon the Illergete cavalry hear the rumblings of thousands of hooves. They look up and see that the terrain above them is filled with enemy riders dodging down between the trees and boulders. The rebel horns blare an attack warning but the Illergete cavalry are locked between their men and a hillside blanketed with enemy, giving them little room to maneuver. Or escape.

"Send our socii at their cavalry!" Laelius screams to his Master of Horse. The allied riders head for the enemy cavalry, while Laelius' Romans veer off to loop around them.

The outnumbered Illergetes trot into a two-deep protective circle, to best cover each other's backs. The Iberians hurl their spears at the oncoming socii, who respond with their own volley, and then another. Then the cavalry battle turns into a milling sword duel. The riders clash into and circle about each other, chopping at each other's heads and shoulders, fending off the thrusts of those who still carry lances.

With the enemy cavalry occupied with the socii, Laelius and his equites rush into the rear of the rebel infantry. Many a staunch barbarian falls with a javelin in his back, unaware of the Romans' presence until the lance pierces their flesh. With hundreds of men falling from the front and rear, the Illergetes mill about in confusion, easy prey for the methodical cohorts.

The front-line legionnaires fight their way farther into the valley, moving directly into their enemy. The rear cohorts march out from behind them and arrange themselves along the flanks, filling the widening valley floor. The Illergetes charge recklessly into the hastati and principes but they are pushed farther back, and farther into each

III. Rebellion

other.

The right flank cohorts beat back the Illergete ground fighters and move into the encircled enemy cavalry. The tribunes direct the legionnaires to break ranks and pursue any Illergete riders still fighting with the cavalry. The foot soldiers stab their swords into the legs and lower backs of the occupied enemy riders. Every time a rider falls, a Roman foot soldier dispatches him with a sword to the face or throat, and rushes to team up on the next one. The unyielding Illergetes fight on, even as they are pulled from their horses, and are killed to a man.[xxix]

With the cavalry threat eliminated, the legionnaires march into the rebel infantry on the right flank, pressing the Iberians closer together.

"All riders, follow me," Laelius screams and plunges his black stallion toward the rear. The Italian cavalry rejoin Laelius' men and thunder past the milling Iberian infantry along the right flank, circling into their rear. The Roman and allied riders trample into the backs of the Iberians, lancing down scores, and then hundreds of them.

The Illergete infantry fight fiercely for another hour, killing scores of Romans as they fight with the desperation of doomed men. Then the front-line Illergetes hear a shout from their fellows, and look behind them. They see Mandonius and Indibilis riding up to the top of the camp hill, leading their remaining troops on a retreat into the mountains behind their camp.

Cursing their cowardly leaders, the Iberians throw down their arms. The Romans immediately lower their weapons, relieved they no longer have to fight these unrelenting warriors.

Marcus Silenus strides out into the narrow clearing between the two armies. He sheathes his sword and lays down his shield. "You have fought well, Iberians." He shouts in their tongue. "But now your time is done. Take off your armor, strip down to your tunics and sandals. Anyone who wears more will be killed."

The glum warriors slowly remove their helmets and breast plates, many disdainfully flinging their armor near Marcus' feet. The legate

III. Rebellion

motions for his front line soldiers to move closer to him. No more armor is thrown.

Scipio rides about the battlefield, overseeing his men as they herd the prisoners together and gather the plunder. Marcus Silenus rides up to him, his eyes agleam from the excitement of battle.

"It was a good fight, General. We have lost about twelve hundred men. It looks like ten thousand of theirs are lying out there."

Scipio nods. "Gratitude, legate. It is twelve hundred more than I desire, but the rebellion is broken. For now."

"For now? We can send Laelius and his men after Indibilis and Mandonius," Marcus urges. "My men are fresh enough to catch them, if Laelius can ride ahead and detain them."

Scipio looks up the steep hillsides, and shakes his head. "They are hiding in their native terrain, among its precipices and caves. Pursuit would be a costly folly."

He pats Marcus' shoulder. "I think the rebels only want to go home, and we shall let them do it. Indibilis and Mandonius cannot form another army for years, and my replacements will be watching them." He looks at the mounds of dead lining the floor of the paradisiacal little valley, where his legionnaires are putting the last of the enemy wounded to the sword. "Enough have died today."

Days later, as Scipio's army prepares their prisoners and treasure for transport, Indibilis and Mandonius ride into his camp. They throw themselves and his feet and plead for a treaty—and their lives. Scipio drapes them with chains and confines them to a hastily constructed wooden cell.

That night, Scipio weighs the costs of executing them versus pardoning them, arguing the points with Laelius and Marcus. He decides that beneficence will best help him maintain peace with the other tribes. But peace is not his only concern. His mind still dwells on the Sucro rebellion against him for back pay, and he worries another uprising may happen again, effectively ending his consular campaign.

III. Rebellion

The next morning Scipio orders Indibilis and Mandonius brought before him. The two rebels are led to a nearby stream, where camp slaves bathe and anoint them. They are given fresh Roman tunics to wear and are brought unchained into Scipio's command tent. The two chieftains march in, heads held high, ready for their fate.

When they enter they find Scipio dressed his best purple bordered tunic, a slender gold wreath upon his head. He sits on a throne-like chair, plucking grapes from a vine that rests among a platter of olives, bread, cheese, and wine. Scipio's two blacksmith floggers stand on each side of him, their barbed whips in their hands. They gaze at the two rebels as though they are ready to flay them to death.

"Sit down, sit down," says Scipio, motioning to the two stools that rest near him. "Would you like some refreshment? You must be starved after your night in the cage."

A slave brings the platter over to them. The brothers look suspiciously at one another. They shrug, and begin stuffing their faces with food.

Scipio watches them eat for a moment, then motions to bring them a cup of unwatered wine. The Iberians gulp it down and place the cups onto the platter. They stare expectantly at Scipio.

"Gratitude," Mandonius mumbles reluctantly, in Latin. Scipio steeples his hands together, a slight smile upon his face, and looks at his former allies.

"Let me be brief. You have two choices. You can ransom yourself and return unharmed to your tribes, provided you swear not to rebel against Rome." The two chieftains start to smile with relief. Scipio raises his hand. "But there is one condition for your release. Quintus, bring it here!"

Scipio's attendant shuffles in with a small scroll of papyrus. He gives it to Indibilis. The Iberian unrolls it and stares at the figures writ on it in Iberian and Latin. "There it is," Scipio says. "Your ransom. The amount of silver you will order brought here within four days."

The two brother's eyes widen when they read the figure. "That is a

III. Rebellion

monstrous fortune! We are poor tribes."

Scipio barks out a laugh. "Poor? I know about your silver mines in the mountains. Would you rather I killed you both and took them over? Would that be a more profitable alternative to you?" He points at the scroll. "That is enough money to pay my army's salary for a year, and no more."

Indibilis looks at Mandonius and shakes his head. *No.* "You mentioned another choice," Mandonius says.

Scipio laughs. "Oh yes, I had almost forgotten. If you don't pay the ransom you shall receive the same punishment as the rebel leaders from Sucro. Surely you heard about that? You will be flogged senseless and then your heads will be wrung from your necks. And your tribes, why, your tribes will suffer the same fate as Astapa. Surely you have heard about Astapa?"

Indibilis swallows hard and stares at the ground, his face a mask of anger. Mandonius reaches out and pokes his shoulder, and pokes it harder when he does not respond. Indibilis raises his head and looks shamefacedly at his brother. He nods his head. *Yes.*

Within the hour, two Iberian captives gallop from camp, acting as messengers for Indibilis and Mandonius. Scipio orders the army to prepare for departure, and he waits. Three days later, a quartet of tribal elders arrives with two wagons of coins and silver. Scipio shows the ransom to his soldiers. He promises they will be paid immediately when the army returns to home base. The cheers drown out the rest of his words.

After they have taken an oath to never raise arms against Rome, Scipio releases Indibilis and Mandonius. He embraces his former allies and follows them outside his tent headquarters, watching them mount their horses and ride out the gates. When the two leaders have departed, Scipio turns to his lead tribune.

"We march back to Carthago Nova tomorrow, as soon as dawn arises." Scipio rubs the back of his neck, looking at the forested

III. Rebellion

mountains about him. He smiles wearily, feeling the relief of a vast weight being lifted from his shoulders.

"Iberia is ours. Finally. The campaign is over." He looks eastward and rubs his eyes, looking away from his men. "It is time to go home."

When the sun breaks the horizon, Scipio is already upon his horse. He is eager to return to Carthago Nova and begin his preparations for departure. He rides about restlessly as his men finish their final camp tasks: cooking their breakfast, rolling up their tents, and loading up their packs.

Knowing it will be a while before the men are ready to leave, he trots out from camp and heads toward the hillside stream near the mouth of the trampled valley floor, where so many men died those few days ago. As his guards follow him, he walks his horse along the Ebro River that feeds the lush valley. He savors the stream's crystalline beauty and searches for fish in the shallows, delighting at the darting brown trout. *Life is still here,* he exults.

A waving patch of bright red catches his eye. He sees a wide swath of flowers carpeting the far side of the stream, a blanket of life in the stinking blackened fields. Scipio gallops over to the flowers. He smiles as he looks at their long-stemmed beauty. *At last. A fitting present.* He immediately jumps off his horse.

Pulling out his dagger, Scipio digs out a large clump of the bright blooms, being careful to preserve the roots. He reaches to another clump and cuts off one papery red bloom. Scipio waves over one of his guards and carefully hands the plant to him. "I want you to ask our captives what this flower is, and I want it kept alive for the trip back to Rome." He looks sternly at the bewildered guard. "Treat it as you would any treasure, for it is precious to me."

The guard salutes and cradles the plant in his cape, tying the ends together into an improvised bag. Scipio watches him carefully until he is satisfied with the man's attention to his prize.

Scipio trots back to camp. He can see his men form up into marching

III. Rebellion

columns as the camp trumpeters blare their orders to prepare for the march. Scipio twirls the flower under his nose, sniffing its peppery scent. He smiles. *I have something to bring back to her. Now my mission is truly complete.*

* * * * *

BRUTTIUM REGION, SOUTH ITALIA, 205 BCE. Peace. Here in the sands below the fortress of Kroton, the destroyer of armies is finally at peace. Wearing only a ragged tunic, Hannibal gazes out across the emerald infinity of the Adriatic Sea, thinking about.... nothing. He sits with chin in hand, savoring the susurrus of lapping waves and the happy sounds of children playing in the surf, their voices like bright birds chirping into his ears.

Hannibal knows his respite is only momentary, but he does not complain. He realizes he would become bored if it were not. His mission to win the war still calls him, even after all these years of fighting. But how to do win it, he wonders, now that tragedy has thrice struck, and the gods seemingly oppose him at every turn.

Hannibal breathes deeply of the tangy sea air and exhales it slowly, as though reluctant to let it escape his body. He thinks about his recent year in south Italia. It is not a pleasing reflection.

By all accounts it has been a season of setbacks, enough to daunt a lesser man. Just when it seemed his brother Hasdrubal would join armies with him and conquer Rome, the Romans threw his head into Hannibal's camp. Then a messenger ship arrived from Macedonia, with a letter from his erstwhile friend and ally King Philip V, informing him that Phillip was making peace with Rome. Within the span of a week, Hannibal had lost forty thousand potential allies to his quest.

Then came news that Scipio had taken Iberia, eliminating Hannibal's last remaining hope for money or troops. *I should have stayed in Iberia with Mago and Hasdrubal*, he curses himself. *We'd still have the mines and tribes.* But he knows that he promised his father that he would save Carthage from Rome, and the only way to do that was to bring Rome itself to its knees. Italia was, and is, his destiny.

III. Rebellion

By Mot's breath, I destroyed their armies three times. Who would think that they would not seek a treaty after that? Who would think they would find peace so abhorrent? He shakes his head and casts a pebble at a shorebird skittering about for food, taking care to miss it.

Hannibal reminds himself that all is not lost. He is here in Bruttium, safe among his staunchest allies, with ample time to regroup, recruit, and plan. Though his army is half its full force, he knows no general will dare attack him, fearing his tactical genius. And so he sits, planning and pondering, trying to rescue the work of thirteen years of war. He is weary, so very weary, of conflict. But his vow to his father chains him to this land, until death or victory frees him.

Pitching pebbles out to sea, Hannibal notices the approach of a shining new trireme, its gleaming white sail vivid with the purple Phoenix of Carthage, its top deck glowing with polished ivory railings. Hannibal watches the ship stroke around a rocky outcropping, doubtless headed into Kroton's harbor. *That ship's too luxurious to be a common warship*, he muses. *It's from the Council.* Hannibal jumps up and trots off toward Kroton, eager to see what fate the gods have brought him.

By the time Hannibal reaches the docks the trireme has already debarked. He sees a tall elderly Carthaginian in a flowing purple robe leading a procession of guards toward the town. Hannibal runs to intercept the retinue, breathless and sweaty from his miles of running. As he nears the men, he recognizes the aged leader, one of the most powerful men in the Carthaginian Empire.

"Hail, Durro," says Hannibal, raising his right arm.

The emissary from the Council of Elders looks at Hannibal's unsavory appearance with ill-concealed distaste. He eyes the dark sweat stain under Hannibal's armpit. He sniffs audibly. "Hail, Hannibal the Great. I take it you have been exercising?"

Hannibal laughs, and wipes some sweat from his eye. "A sound body for a sound mind, eh? Keeps my wits sharp while I plan our next foray at the Romans."

III. Rebellion

Durro slowly bows his head, showing the trace of a smile. "Well, then, perhaps my news will help your planning. Your brother Mago is on his way to Genova, with money to recruit thousands of Ligurians and Gauls." Seeing Hannibal's look of surprise, Durro's grin widens. "He is to join forces with you in an assault on Rome, as your brother Hasdrubal had intended."

Hannibal stares at Durro, his eye unblinking. "That is welcome news," he says warily. "But why this push for war? When last we talked you spoke of peace, of war being bad for business."

"I tell you as I have told Mago," Durro retorts. "Rome spurns our peace offerings by setting untenable conditions. They refuse our attempts at compromise. There is no other choice."

Durro sweeps his arm towards Kroton's towering stone walls. "Come, let us discuss the details in more private surroundings." He wrinkles his nose at Hannibal's sweaty tunic. "When you are more comfortably dressed."

"Just so," replies Hannibal. As they walk toward town the two men are silent, each lost in his own thoughts. When they enter the back gates, Hannibal turns to Durro.

"Your words about Rome's recalcitrance sadden me, but they do ring true. When I began this war thirteen years ago, all I wanted to do was destroy Rome. Then, as their armies fell before me and so many men died, all I sought was a secure peace—which they rejected, even though they teetered on the edge of doom." He shakes his head. "Once again, all I can see is that I must pursue their destruction."

"I have prayed to Baal that one of their generals would argue for peace," says Durro. "But that is a futile hope. That Fabius and Flaccus, and their dog Cato, they rant for our destruction."

Hannibal rubs his chin. "Not all are so insane. My brothers told me that the Scipio prodigy is somewhat reasonable. They say Scipio won away their Iberian allies with his fairness, though oft backed by acts of murderous ruthlessness. He might listen to peace terms. I regret I will

III. Rebellion

never meet him to find out."

"Be not so assured," says Durro. "Our Senate spies say Scipio is returning to Italia. You might meet him sooner than you think. For better or worse."

Hannibal chuckles dryly. "Better or worse I can tolerate, as long as it is once and for all."

* * * * *

CARTHAGO NOVA, 205 BCE. "You say that Indibilis and Mandonius are well in hand?" queries Lucius Lentulus, the lanky propraetor who is replacing Scipio. Scipio grins.

"Aye, I do believe they are. My men caught their rebel force by the Ebro River and wiped it out. The brothers have sworn allegiance to Rome—again—but their rebellious fires still burn. Keep an eye on them, Praetor."

"And Mago is gone?" asks Lucius Manlius, a stocky older patrician who is the other new propraetor. At thirty years of age, Scipio is a decade younger than either of them, but his responses have a touch of parental condescension, as if he were reassuring young children.

"I told you last night, Mago sailed to the Balearic Islands, Gisgo fled to Africa, and Hasdrubal is dead. The Three Generals are gone." He looks levelly at the two anxious commanders. "But the Illergete chieftains, Indibilis and Mandonius, they bear watching. That is the task I leave you. You do not have to win a war, you simply have to keep the peace."

Scipio turns to go. He snaps his fingers and turns around. "Oh yes, I almost forgot. You should visit the Illergetes and Carpetani before the next new moon."

"Why so soon?" asks Lucius Manlius peevishly. "We just landed."

Scipio grins. "Because I told them you would! These barbarians are like neglected children. They can get into mischief if left unattended.

III. Rebellion

Diplomacy, my brothers—diplomacy will save you many battles. Go shake some arms and sacrifice some bulls."

"And that is the end of our Iberian affairs," comes Laelius' voice behind him. Scipio turns and sees Laelius leaning against the door, picking lint off his blood-red cape. "The ships are ready whenever you are, General," he declares, his voice tinged with impatience.

Scipio holds up a finger, ordering Laelius to wait. *I swear to Juno, he is always fussing about something. He's getting to be another Cato.*

Scipio faces his replacements. "If there are no other questions ..." he says, his tone indicating there will not be any.

The propraetors exchange a look, agreeing not to anger the legendary Publius Cornelius Scipio. "No, honored Scipio. You attended to every detail last night. We just wanted to be sure."

Scipio smirks. "Ah, to be 'sure,' that is a rare gift indeed. I have spent this war unsure of my decisions or what their outcome would be. But one thing I am sure of: you will not have to worry about fighting against the Carthaginians to win Iberia, you have to worry about fighting the Iberians so as not to lose it. The soul of Astapa's defiance dwells in many tribes, and resistance against us will rise. Heed my words and tend to diplomacy, my brothers. It is your best weapon."

With a final nod, General Publius Cornelius Scipio walks for the door, and Admiral Laelius joins him as he exits. The two friends head to the docks and board their waiting trireme. Laelius signals for his captain to begin departure.

"Let's get the Hades out of here!" Laelius shouts up to him.

Scipio laughs. "That is the best command I have heard since we came here!"

The flagship eases from the harbor. Scipio stands in the rear, watching Iberia fade from sight. He reaches into his pouch and gently extracts the bronze icon of Nike that Amelia gave to him. He picks off a few flecks of dried blood and kisses it, rubbing his thumb across it for good luck.

III. Rebellion

Goddess of Victory, do not yet desert me. We have purged the wolves, but the bear yet remains.

Scipio returns the icon to his pouch. He takes a last look at the mighty city of Carthago Nova, his first conquest those long years ago. He watches the legionnaires patrolling the garrison's parapets and the cohorts marching as one beneath its walls. The young general nods a final goodbye. He walks across the deck and up to the prow of the ship, staring out across the shoreless sea.

Looking out towards Rome.

IV. COMING HOME

PORT OF OSTIA, 205 BCE. The sailors swarm up and down the transport's gangplank. They rush to complete their unloading tasks, eager to visit their loved ones back in Rome. The men trundle down scores of two-wheeled carts laden with the silver, jewels, ivory, and gold that are the spoils of Scipio's Iberian conquest.

"Careful with that statue," shouts Admiral Laelius, overseeing his busy men. "That's worth more than a senator's ransom—as if anyone would want to pay for one of those bastards!"

Laelius pays special attention to a small cart that is heavily guarded, for its wealth is worth more than all the others together. The cart is piled with small bags of Carthage's Tyrian Purple dye, a tint so rare it has twenty times the value of gold. *At least those Carthaginians are good for something*, he smirks as he tucks a small dye bag inside his belt purse. *I'll make a purple tunic that will be the envy of all.*

The Admiral monitors each laden cartload that rumbles down the pier, ensuring that it is unloaded into a pile on the main dock street, inside a ring of protective marines. He scans the dock walkway for fallen treasures, eyeing the dock orphans who watch the carts with greedy eyes, their legs cocked to dash in and grab anything that falls.

When any of them draw too near the carts Laelius chases them away by waving his falcata at them. *I was once one of you, boys. I know what you are up to.* He gropes inside his purse and flings out a fat handful of silver sestertii. The boys scuttle about, worming between people's legs to grab the tiny coins.

"Throw a tent over that coin wagon, before they start to fall out," Laelius shouts to a marine. "Those statues, wrap them before you load them!" Laelius carefully attends to everything. While serving under

IV. Coming Home

Scipio he has learned the inestimable value of attention to detail in all aspects of war, from quality of grain to the edge of a sword. Laelius wants every bit of wealth to reach the Senate chambers, in hopes that the riches will promote Scipio's campaign to become consul of Rome.

Eight middle-aged Iberians tramp behind a pier wagon loaded with red-figured amphorae of the finest Rioja wine, large vases of drink that will be gifted to whichever Senators need a bribe. A centurion leads the barbarians toward the legionnaires amassing in Ostia's town square. The Iberians gape at the towering statue of Poseidon that stands in the welcoming bay waters. They blink at the walls of colonnaded buildings that fence in the port's circular border.

"The gods must live here," says one to his friend.

"If not, they are fools," replies the other.

The eight Iberians are the metalsmiths that Scipio has brought from Carthago Nova, craftsmen skilled in the art of making steel swords. Scipio has hired them to teach his army smiths how to forge the gladius hispaniesis that he has developed, a double-edged, wasp-waisted sword that is descended from the curved Iberian falcata that he has come to respect. He admires the flexibility of the falcata, a sword whose keen edge can be wielded to chop and slash as well as to stab and thrust. A sword known for leaving piles mutilated dead in the wake of its skilled users. Now his men will fight with a similar weapon, forged with flexible Iberian steel instead of brittle Roman iron.

Two dozen young men accompany the metalsmiths, wearing only unmarked light gray tunics. The youths might be taken as captive slaves, were it not for their upright bearing and inquisitive eyes. The men study all the people and buildings around them without appearing to look at anything. They are Scipio's Carthaginian speculatores, the African deserters he has recruited to plumb the secrets of Carthage and its armies. They will join his burgeoning group of Roman speculatores and exploratores to become the Roman army's first intelligence network; a group as deadly in their effects as any legion.

The triremes, transports, and quadriremes are all docked now.

IV. Coming Home

Hundreds of ships' marines and legionnaires march past the business temples and flow into Ostia's capacious forum. They will all sleep there tonight, preparatory to tomorrow's jaunt into Rome.

The soldiers enter the forum to the wild cheers of the Ostians and Romans who line the steps of the buildings around them. The people throw flower petals about their heads. Women and men rush up to kiss the war-worn veterans as their ranks file into the square.

The plebians are delirious with excitement and hope. They believe Scipio has brought Rome back from the brink of defeat, that he will soon defeat Hannibal and end this war. No Latin Party rhetoric, no whisper campaigns of theft, no innuendos of homosexuality can sway their adulation of the young conqueror. He is their god come to earth.

Legate Marcus Silenus leads the legionnaires. The stern army commander can barely repress a smile at coming home, at having a chance to rest his aching bones. Marcus has long been Rome's greatest warrior, but the years have begun to weigh upon him, though he would die before he would show it. *Now I can spend a couple of days at the baths. And then I'll tend to my farm.*

The doughty little ex-centurion looks at the music and cheering about him and sniffs theatrically, grinning at the grizzled First Tribune by his side. "Would have been better we had come under cover of night," he growls. "I should ask General Scipio if I can pitch my tent outside of town, away from all this foolishness!"

But Scipio is not there to answer him. He has quietly docked at one of the outer quays, his small ship nestled between two gigantic grain transports from Sardinia. When his fleet neared land hours ago, Scipio transferred from his flagship onto a smaller bireme, that he might enter the Port of Ostia inconspicuously and not be detained. He has to attend to matters of the utmost urgency.

As soon as his bireme is secured, Scipio trots down the narrow gangplank, even as his guards rush to catch up to him. Scipio is covered by a worn forest-green cloak, a lengthy garment that masks his gray silk breeches and purple-bordered tunic. A dagger and a worn goatskin

IV. Coming Home

pouch are all that hang from his frayed leather belt, with a bulging leather satchel slung over his shoulder. From Scipio's appearance you would think him a messenger or a wanderer, not the most famous man in Rome.

Scipio stands by the gangplank as his men unload the few stores inside the small ship. He watches the ship's captain direct the unloading of money, foodstuffs, and soldiers' belongings. *Come on, men, get to it. Rome waits for us.*

Two sailors come to the top of the gangplank with a long narrow trunk that is beautifully wrought of teak and brass. "Careful with that!" Scipio barks, suddenly very anxious. "That goes directly to the Scipio domus. And it must be unscathed!"

The captain looks quizzically at him. "Are there breakable things in there, General? Glass or precious art? We can pack them with linen." Scipio shakes his head. "My history scrolls are in there, and the records of our campaign in Iberia. The knowledge is worth an army!"

The captain shrugs, mystified at his general's words. "We will put them in the vanguard of Marcus Silenus' legionnaires," he says. "They will be safe from Pluto himself!"

Satisfied his books will be safe, Scipio walks down the short pier to the dockside main street. As per his orders, a horse is waiting for him, a scruffy-looking brown mare that is deceptively fast. Scipio prepares to vault onto the horse, but the centurion of the guards grabs his arm.

"Apologies, General." says the veteran warrior. "Where are our horses?"

"You don't need horses, I go alone. Go back to the ship," Scipio orders, shrugging off the centurion's grasp.

"You should wait for us," says the centurion. "We are your guards!" The other men anxiously close about Scipio, conflicted about following Scipio's orders versus doing their sworn duty.

Scipio whirls to face them. "Get away from me and do as I

IV. Coming Home

command!" he bristles, his voice imperious. The guards blink in surprise, taken aback by his uncharacteristic anger.

The guards step back from their general, but their grizzled centurion is not so easily daunted. "We are simply trying to protect you, my General," he mutters, his eyes flashing the cold fire of forced cordiality. "We would take our own lives if something happens to you."

Laelius rides up on his stallion. "Easy, Scippy," he says as he dismounts. "These men worship you, they are not the enemy."

Scipio rubs his eyes, then faces his men. "Apologies, legionnaires. I am a bit too eager to reach home."

The guards shift about uneasily, still not certain what to do. Laelius faces them, a reassuring smile on his face. "I will accompany him myself, men. And I bear witness that you did try to guard him but were ordered away by General Scipio," Laelius says. He leans to Scipio's ear. "You arrogant shit," he mutters.

The mollified centurion turns back to his men. "On to the town square," he orders, with an ill-concealed glare at Scipio. "Marcus Silenus will find purpose for us."

When Scipio's guards are out of earshot, Laelius turns on him, an accusing look in his eyes. "You're riding to Rome, aren't you?" He picks up a corner of Scipio's tatty old cloak and drops it as if it burned his fingers. "There's no other reason for you to dress like this, unless you're seeking to add to the treasury by taking alms!"

Scipio shrugs. "It's the only way to get in unnoticed. You know I'm forbidden to enter the city until I give up my imperium as commander of Iberia."

"I know you could be arrested as a fomenting criminal if you're caught," Laelius counters, his anger rising. "Hardly a good start for a man campaigning to be consul."

"I don't give a piss in the underworld about my image," Scipio replies petulantly. "I have to see Amelia. I'm not going to wait until all those

IV. Coming Home

silly proprieties are met. Would you?"

Laelius laughs. "If the love of my life were waiting, I would club you cold to get to him," he declares. "What is that saying—where the heart leads, the mind but follows? Just be careful. Latin Party eyes are all about us here, though the Senate be back in Rome."

As Scipio mounts his horse Laelius raises his nose into the air, loudly sniffing. "Is that lavender I smell, dread Imperator? Where's that coming from, have the dock harlots already arrived?"

Scipio grins sheepishly "I am learning to present myself properly for the proper audiences. In this case a woman," he replies. "Let it never be said that you didn't teach me at least *one* valuable skill."

With a snap of his reins, Scipio canters down the short pier and gallops along the port's cobblestoned main road. He goes through the town forum and passes by the necropolis that lines both sides of the road. *I have seen enough of the dead*, he thinks, as he hurries on.

Scipio turns onto a side trail, following the peridot waters of the Tiber as it winds twenty miles east towards the heart of Rome. With every mile he covers, Scipio feels the weight of his command lifting from his shoulders. He spurs his horse faster.

Hours later, Scipio trots up to the massive front gates of Rome's Porta Trigemena. A squadron of armed guards straddles the entryway, inspecting wagons and interrogating entrants. Scipio eases off his careworn mount and shuffles forward, head bent to the ground. Two guards step forward to question the hooded figure before them. "Halt, peasant! State your business!" barks one of them.

Scipio raises his head and pulls back his hood. "Do you know who I am?" he says in his best commander's tone. The leader takes one look into the penetrating eyes that transfix his own and steps to the side, waving Scipio in with a bow. The other guards look at their leader but he merely shakes his head and points them back to their post. When they turn their backs he grins broadly and shakes his head, wondering who would believe he met General Scipio in disguise.

IV. Coming Home

Scipio trots his humble mare through the squalid insulae that populate the back streets, negotiating narrow side passages until he approaches the Paullus family domus. Trotting the horse through an alleyway, he emerges into a wide street lined with city mansions.

Scipio pauses at the blue front doors of Amelia's home. An aged Thracian slave is sweeping the pebbled concrete sidewalk in front of the entry. A little boy carrying a twig broom follows him. Both of them sport tufted heads of rusty red hair.

"Hail, Rufus!" says Scipio, sliding down from his horse. "I am so pleased to see you again!" The man draws back, pushing the boy behind him. "Good afternoon, good master," he says cautiously. "How may I serve you?"

Scipio's welcoming smile fades. "Do you not know me? Remember when you gave me a wooden sword, telling me to quit reading and start fighting?"

Rufus stares at the weathered face in front of him. Recognition dawns in his eyes—recognition tinged with dismay. "Gods be kind, is that you, Master Scipio?" he averts his eyes, momentarily embarrassed. "You were but a boy when you left. You look so ... different." He summons himself. "So grand and official!" He frowns. "And, uh, very mature!"

Scipio manages a bittersweet grin. "Yes, Rufus, win or lose, war takes its toll on us." Scipio glances at the wide-eyed youth peering around Rufus' spindly legs, and he brightens. "Tell me it is not so! Is that your grandson?"

Rufus' spine straightens noticeably. "It is, for truth! We call him Mus, because he is quiet as a mouse. My son has joined the slave legions in the north, and I am blessed to tend to him. Mus is so smart. He will buy his freedom someday, I am sure!"

Scipio's careworn face suddenly transforms, and a lost boyish gleam returns to it. He fumbles inside his bulging satchel, and pulls out a small alabaster carving of an elephant with upraised trunk, exquisitely

IV. Coming Home

detailed. He bends deeply and hands it out to the child, shaking it as if it were bait for a fish.

Mus sucks his thumb while he looks up at his grandfather. Rufus smiles down at him, and nods. The boy dashes out and snatches the toy from Scipio, rushing back to hide behind his grinning grandfather. The child delicately fingers the carving, turning it this way and that, wonder filling his eyes.

Rufus looks at his smiling grandson and looks back at Scipio, smiling. "Yes, it is you," he says. "You were always so generous."

Scipio knots his satchel closed and starts to enter the manse. Rufus eagerly scrambles ahead of him. "Mistress Amelia will die with joy when she sees you!" he exclaims. "Let me announce you!" The slave opens his mouth to shout his news but Scipio places two fingers on Rufus' lips and shakes his head. "I want to surprise her. Is she in?" The slave bobs his head, pointing toward the interior gardens.

Scipio slides off his sandals and tiptoes into the busy manse. Several members of the house staff see him and start to shout a welcome, but he signals for them to be quiet. He is just entering the sunny atrium when he hears the loud scrabbling of clawed feet behind him. Scipio turns to see a gigantic mastiff-like dog hurtling at him, barking as if it has lost its mind. The molossus leaps into the air and rams into Scipio with its 250-pound body. Scipio crashes to the earth and the dog straddles him, happily laving his face with his enormous red tongue.

Laughing, Scipio pushes the dog's pot-sized head back from him. "Easy, Ursus. I'm glad to see you, too." He lifts the molossus' gray-tinged muzzle higher, so he can scramble out from under him. The aged dog spins about in circles, so ecstatic Scipio begins to fear for its health. "Easy, boy, eaaassy," Scipio croons, stroking the dog's wide back. The molossus calms, and suddenly wanders out toward the kitchen, lured away by food smells.

Scipio is brushing off his tunic when a woman's voice comes from the adjoining garden. "Rufus, is that you? See what's disturbing Ursus."

IV. Coming Home

Scipio's heart lurches at the sound. The conqueror of nations feels his legs weaken as he quietly steps into the sunny garden, easing in between the massive palms at the entrance. There, in a short green gown, stands Amelia. Her back is to him as she spades into a bed of roses, planting an offshoot beneath a tall stone statue of Minerva.

Scipio gently pulls the satchel strap over his head and eases the valise onto the ground. Amelia's head rises slightly with the sound, but she does not turn around. "Is Ursus well, Rufus?" she asks, patting down the soil about the root.

Scipio grins. "Is he well? I should be so strong and happy!"

Amelia drops her garden spade. She slowly looks over her shoulder, pushing back her tousled auburn hair, fearful of what she may not see. Her green eyes stare unbelievingly at the sight of Scipio, waggling his fingers at her in an awkward hello. Within seconds she is within Scipio's arms, burying her face in his shoulder, raising it to rain kisses upon him, crying with unbridled happiness. Scipio clasps her to him, gently rocking her back and forth. "I am here now, I am here. All is well."

"Oh, Carissimus! Thank the gods you are safe!"

"Finally, finally..." he croons, over and over, holding her tightly.

Long minutes later she breaks from his embrace to step back and inspects him, wiping the tears from her eyes. She runs her long fingers about his lined face, studying every inch of it. She touches the tufts of gray hair around his ears. "Oh my dear, you have changed! You look so ... you are such a man now!"

In turn, Scipio cannot help but notice that the girl he left six years ago is gone. Amelia's voice has lost its high girlish lilt, her voice is deeper and more decisive. Her eyes have sadness in their corners, as if she has done or seen things of great tragedy. *My gods, she has become so handsome!* His kisses become deeper, more passionate. His hands wander over her buttocks and clasp the back of her thighs.

Amelia can feel Scipio rise against her. She steps back and smiles at

IV. Coming Home

him. "We should go to see your mother first, dear."

Scipio reaches up to cup her breast, feeling its nipple harden against his palm. "Soon, soon enough. But I must first feel you."

Her breath quickens and she breaks from his grasp, taking his hand and pulling him toward her sleeping quarters. One look from her and the house slaves dissolve from sight. She parts the bedroom curtains and leads him inside, where she turns him roughly about and begins undressing him, much to Scipio's surprise. "I would not break my vow to preserve my virginity until we are married, love. But we have our ways, do we not?"

When Scipio is nude she bends down and begins to run her hands down his body, caressing every inch.

Scipio gently pulls her upright. Hands trembling, he lifts her green dress over her head and pitches it to the floor, and removes her linen breast band and loincloth. Scipio's breath catches at the sight of her. Amelia's hips and breasts are rounder and fuller now, her waist a little thicker. She is a woman, in the fullness of her beauty. And he burns for her. "You are a vision, my love. I have missed you so."

Amelia pulls him quickly to her sleeping pallet and sits him on the side. She reaches to a table and uncorks a bottle of olive oil, rubbing it into her hands. "This day, I shall not need the oil for myself, it is all for you," she croons. She bends over and lovingly strokes the oil onto Scipio's rigid phallus.

He arcs his head back and gasps. "Ah, I feel like Vesuvius, building to erupt already!"

Amelia stands back. "Not yet, love. I would have you passionate when you kiss me ... down there." Amelia lies on her back and strokes some oil onto her nether lips. She looks invitingly at her betrothed. "Taste me," she says. "Taste my love for you." Scipio crawls onto the pallet and eases his head between her legs. "The gods should feast so well," he says, as he eases his head downward.

The manse is quiet that afternoon, save for the chirping of the

IV. Coming Home

garden's captive finches. Amelia cries out, screaming so loudly that Ursus barks with excitement. Then the house falls still.

Amelia lies on her back, her breath slowing. She wraps her sweaty arms around Scipio and pulls him to her. Both lay silently, hands on hearts, listening to the random noises of resumed household activity. She leans over her lover and strokes his face, smiling tenderly. "Gratitude for letting me go first, beloved. My need was strong." She suddenly kneels above him, breasts swaying over him. "You need not wait any longer."

Amelia turns and crouches upon her hands and knees. She hands Scipio the vial of olive oil. "My virginity I would keep until marriage. But we can still enjoy the lion on the knife position ... my lion." She gently tugs Scipio over to kneel behind her, and lays her face into her pillow. Soon, Ursus is barking.

As the house staff begin to stir outside their chamber, Scipio stands up. "I have to return to my men," he declares. Scipio and Amelia dress quietly and walk into the sunny afternoon atrium, hand in hand. Scipio halts in mid-step. "Gods above, I almost forgot my present!"

He dashes back to her bedroom and returns carrying his worn leather satchel. Scipio puts the satchel on the floor and unties the rope clasp about it. He pulls out a clay-potted flower with three papery crimson blooms branching from its long, wiry stem. Scipio holds it out to Amelia. She gingerly touches the delicate, densely interleaved petals.

"It's called a 'carnation'," he says excitedly. "They grow wild in Iberia, in pinks and purples, all over the valleys and plains. And there are some red ones too, such as this. The Iberians worship the plant because it is so durable, though it has such a delicate beauty and fragrance. They call it the Flower of God."

Amelia kisses his cheek. "It's beautiful. Its flowers look like they are made of folded papyrus. Where did you get it?"

"I found it growing at the edge our battlefield by the Ebro River, flourishing in a place where life was all too rare. The red ones

IV. Coming Home

symbolize deep love and affection, which I do bear for you beyond all bounds of time and space. I brought this one back, that it may flourish as a symbol of our love."

Amelia brushes her fingertips across the flowers. She flashes a smile of inspiration. "I know! I will plant it next to my statue of Priapus over there by the garden entrance. Surely the god of fertility will help it grow strong."

Scipio looks sideways at her, feigning irritation. "Priapus? I am not sure I like you having a statue with a twelve inch phallus, it might inspire you to seek someone more, uh, gifted to be your husband!"

Amelia punches him in the arm. "And what would I do with such a man? You almost split me in two!" She touches his mouth and grins. "Besides, you have other tools at your disposal, and you wield them well."

Her playful smile suddenly disappears. "Oh, I don't have anything to give you! Pomponia and I were planning to welcome you at the Temple of Bellona, along with the senators. I would have brought something then."

Scipio bites his lower lip. "Hm. Perhaps it is best you wait until I walk into the city. Mother might not contain herself if she hears what the Latins will say to me at the Temple!"

He pulls her toward the door. "I have to go. I must return to Ostia before Laelius runs out of excuses for my absence. Please explain my wishes to my mother. But do not be sad, you did give me a wonderful present before I left..."

Scipio reaches into his bloodstained little purse and gingerly pulls out a figurine of a slender robed woman with wings flying from her back, arms outstretched in a v-shaped pose. He cradles it in his palm. "You gave this to me when I left for Iberia, remember? I was an ignorant boy with a small army of raw recruits, not knowing what to do next. You told me then, 'this is Nike, the Grecian goddess of victory. She blesses those with strength, speed, or guile. And you, my love, have all three.

IV. Coming Home

Use them and she will surely bless you.' "

Scipio kisses the figurine and holds it before Amelia's face. "I have kept it near my heart ever since. There were times before that I did doubt we would prevail, times when I doubted my wild new ideas would work. Then I would take out the goddess and remember your words, and I was restored." He curls his palm about his treasure and pulls Amelia close. "No other gift could have been as valuable."

They turn to leave, but Scipio tugs at her arm, a mischievous smile on his face. "I forgot. I have one more present for you." He reaches into the satchel and pulls out a short piece of rope, studded with knots. He holds it before Amelia and her eyes grow wide.

Scipio takes her hands in his. "Amelia, I ask you to share the water and fire of life with me, to live with me, to become my wife. And bear our children."

Amelia can only nod her head, time and again. She stands with her fist pressed to her mouth, watching as Scipio pulls the rope out straight, loops it around her waist, and carefully knots it in front.

"I tie the knot with you, I am tied to you for life. Mine is yours and yours is mine, queen of my heart."

She steps into his arms and they cling together as Ursus pads into the room. Sensing the mood, he nuzzles into Amelia's dress, his brown eyes alight with happiness.

As the afternoon sun edges behind the Paullus manse, Amelia and Scipio walk out to the street. Rufus and his grandson await them, the boy solemnly grasping the horse's reins in his chubby little fists.

Amelia and Scipio cling together in silent embrace. Finally, he summons the strength to push away from her. He takes the reins from the little boy and pats him on the head. "Well done," Scipio says, as the boy darts back behind his grandfather. Scipio pulls himself atop the mare and starts to ride off, but after a few steps he turns about.

"I almost forgot," he shouts. "I want to marry you very soon! Even

IV. Coming Home

tomorrow!" He points at the boy. "We need to have some of our own!"

Amelia clasps her hands together and laughs, tears clouding her eyes. "Soon, yes, soon!" she shouts.

Scipio grins. He gives her a mock salute and gallops back to Ostia.

* * * * *

CASSIUS' POPINA, CENTRAL ROME. "Well, he's back," grouses Flaccus. "The Scipio boy beat down the Three Generals and now he is the plebs' new hero!"

Fabius pulls off another chunk of flat bread and dips it into his wine, chewing busily with the few teeth remaining to him. "He will want to run for consul, I wager, so he can drag our legions south into Africa. Africa!" The old man slips another chunk of bread into a small clay pot of herbed honey, and points the dripping bread at Cato. "With Hannibal on our homeland shores, he wants to take our best men to another land. Can you imagine such nonsense?"

"In truth, I can imagine him defeating Hannibal, General." replies Cato evenly. "He may be an effete Hellenic, but he has proven his military worth. But I do not think he has to go to Africa to help Rome, when Hannibal is only seven days' march from us."

"He must not go there," interjects Fabius, as he fills his cup with honeyed wine. "If he loses, as doubtless he will, we would lose our best legions. He needs to stay here and avoid confrontation. Scipio could use my delaying tactics to drain Hannibal's resources." [xxx] Fabius slams down his cup, much to his partners' amusement. "Starve the bear, by Jupiter, that is what he should do!"

"It were best he didn't defeat the Carthaginian," growls Flaccus. "If Scipio brings down Hannibal, the Hellenics could carry the consular elections for years!"

Cato stares at the wily senator. "Years? You had best worry about them carrying this next election. Scipio will likely run for consul next month."

IV. Coming Home

"That makes sense, that is what I would do!" Fabius grins proudly at his young prodigy. "I can see why you are called Cato, the wise one!"

Cato shrugs. "It was not a great insight. The time is propitious for him. He is a war hero. There will doubtless be festivities held in his honor that he can exploit." Cato grimaces. "Expensive, wasteful festivities."

"Ah, but that is not the worst. He will want his triumph now," says Fabius, waggling his finger. "I know, I demanded the honor when I took back Tarentum, and they gave it to me." [xxxi]

Fabius pops an olive in his mouth and chews slowly, as Flaccus drums his fingers on the stone table, waiting for the elder senator to elaborate. When Fabius follows the olive with a large chunk of bread, Flaccus rolls his eyes and turns to Cato. "We cannot allow that to happen, do you hear me? Scipio would certainly win a consular seat."

Fabius nods, crumbs dribbling as he chews. "And if he does, he will press to go to Africa," the old man says, "And take our legions with him!"

"Tomorrow is the day of decision," says Flaccus. "By tradition, a triumph must be granted or denied before he enters the city. We have a few hours left to stop it." He turns to Fabius. "What senators can we buy to vote against him getting a triumph? Who has broken the law and not been caught by the censor?"

Cato's lips wrinkle in disgust. "You will use bribery and coercion?" he asks. Then he grins ruefully, waving his hand at Flaccus. "Do not bother to reply, I know the answer."

Flaccus bristles. "The Scipios have fouled my life. That bitch Pomponia got the land reform proposal approved." He points northeast, as if they could see farm fields there. "I was going to buy a farmer's property next to me for taxes owed, and now I cannot." He rubs his backside and shifts about in his seat. "And there are other debts I owe her."

Cato sneers. "You wanted to take land owned by a working farmer

IV. Coming Home

who went off to war, that is what you mean. Well enough you didn't get it."

Fabius plucks out a shriveled olive and pitches it at a passing mongrel. "The Party is the issue here, not land. If Scipio prevails we may have two Hellenics as consuls. The Latin Party would be powerless."

"Gods above and below," Flaccus says, banging his wine cup on the table. "Can you not see it? If he wins, there will be another round of debates about education for the plebs and land parcels for the veterans. And then, new taxes to pay for the lot of it!" He leans forward, eyes feral and voice low. "I know a man, an old Etruscan who is skilled with all sorts of herbs. He could mix ..."

Cato interrupts. "Go no further, Senator, lest you prompt me to act as a citizen of Rome." Flaccus' face flushes, but Cato continues. "We are the Latin Party, we espouse disciplined morality. I will not allow our actions to violate our words." He looks derisively at Flaccus. "Besides, there is a legal way to accomplish our ends."

Flaccus looks at Fabius, who shrugs in bewilderment. Cato sighs. "As a senator, you should know about the Law of Triumphs."

"I have not had to adjudicate any of them, boy," replies Flaccus airily.

For the first time since the trio sat down, Cato reaches for a piece of bread and dips it into his wine. He chews furiously, glaring at Flaccus. *I should get up from this table and leave this life of moral compromises. Just return to my farm in Sabina. If I explain the Law of Triumphs, they will exploit it for their own purposes.*

Flaccus sees ill-disguised glint of anger in his follower's gray eyes. *The boy looks like he's ready tell the both of us to go to Hades and walk out. The people like him too much, we have to keep him here.* He toys with a peach slice, turning it idly in his fingers.

"You know, Cato, these elections may be more important than you think. Fabius and I have planned to get you elected quaestor. If Scipio were elected consul, you could be to be the accountant for his campaign. You could keep an eye on him."

IV. Coming Home

"My duty would be to keep an eye on expenditures, not people. That I would do to the fullest of my abilities, regardless of who was general," Cato huffs.

Flaccus closes his eyes and takes a deep breath. "So you do not want to be quaestor?" he says slowly. "It is an important step to becoming a senator. And a consul..."

Cato looks down at the table, fists clenched. He thinks of the vow he made to his dead father, that he would bring the Porcius name to prominence in Rome. He takes another bite of bread. Flaccus looks over at Fabius, and winks.

"I would be glad to be of service," Cato finally says.

"Excellent," crows Fabius. "You will make an able auditor! Now, what do you have to tell us about this law?"

Cato spreads his hands, as if giving a speech. "Tomorrow, as is the custom, Scipio will meet us at the Temple of Bellona outside the city, to relinquish his command. If he asks for a triumph, the Senate can legally refuse him."

Flaccus shakes his head. "Nonsense! Scipio was proconsul of Iberia." Fabius nods his agreement.

Cato stares reprovingly at them. "Scipio is *privatus cum imperio*. Not *magistratus cum imperio*," he says. Seeing the recognition dawn in Flaccus' eyes, he stands up. "I have said my piece, you know what I mean. I go to my farm." He pushes himself from the table and tramps away, his worn leather sandals slapping against the cobblestone street.

Fabius and Flaccus exchange sheepish glances. "Of course!" blurts Fabius. "Cato has the right of it. "

Flaccus catches the eye of the serving slave. "Another pitcher of wine here!" he shouts triumphantly. "We must celebrate a defeat!"

* * * * *

IV. Coming Home

TEMPLE OF BELLONA, OUTSKIRTS OF ROME. Flaccus sprawls out on the steps encircling the domed little Temple of Bellona, his head under the statue of the goddess of war. He waits impatiently for Scipio to arrive, as tense as someone preparing for battle. Fabius stands in a sacred grove of lobe-leafed fig trees at the side of the temple, sharing a laugh with several other senators who are former generals.

Scattered groups of Hellenic and Latin senators have wandered down the meadow path that leads to the Temple of Apollo, conversing conspiratorially about party politics. Occasionally they cast an expectant eye for Scipio's arrival.

Fabius leaves his group and joins Flaccus on the temple steps, looking southwest down the road to Ostia. The roadway is empty, save for a garum merchant pulling his oxcart of fish sauce to market at Rome. The bored Senators watch the cart trundle past as if it were a triumphal chariot, arguing about the taberna that offers the best concoction of that heady sauce.

Flaccus smirks at Fabius. "Listen to that idle chatter, you'd think they were here for a feast, not an inquiry."

Too bad Cato is not here," muses Fabius. "He would take Scipio's measure, knowing he might serve as his quaestor." He grins. "He is not afraid to ask a rude question. Half these soft-assed patricians would never do so, they would fear Pomponia's wrath."

"Cato can come here when he becomes a senator," replies Flaccus moodily. "*If* such an event ever transpires."

Fabius glances suspiciously at Flaccus. He says nothing, but Flaccus' sharp eyes read his expression. "Why do I doubt he will be one? Because he is becoming ever more disputatious. And more self-righteous. I wonder if he will become more obstacle than asset."

For just a moment, aged Fabius becomes the stern general that fought the Carthaginians for years. His rheumy eyes flare with anger. "Have a care, Flaccus. That is all I will say. Have a care…"

The raucous temple magpies have been chattering all morning, but

IV. Coming Home

they suddenly fall silent. The Senators look down the road, expectant. The younger politicians are the first to hear the faint rumble of a thousand feet tramping in unison.

The Senators hurry over from the Temple of Mars and join the others on the Temple of Bellona steps, a small army of toga-clad patricians. Glabius hobbles to the bottom of the steps. The aged Senate leader, motions for them to arrange themselves in a semicircle. The tramping grows louder, and the first plumes of dust pinnacle up from the distance.

Now a figure on horseback can be seen, blazing like a sun in the midmorning light. Even at that distance he appears imperious and proud, his red plumed crest angled toward the heavens. He is followed by two figures on horseback, a tall graceful young man with mirrored bronze armor, and a stolid smaller figure that wears the simple protections of an infantry soldier, his only adornment the flowing red cape that marks him as a legate. Behind them tramps a four-wide column of marines and legionnaires, their faces stern and proud.

The small army draws near. The Senators can see it is Scipio who leads them, flanked by Laelius and Marcus Silenus. Many Senators who knew Scipio as a boy are amazed at who they see. The slim and studious son of Publius Scipio left them five years ago, brashly promising to avenge his father and conquer Iberia. The man Scipio has returned, a muscular and dignified commander, his curled raven locks framing a chiseled face marked with the distant cold eyes of absolute command—and ruthlessness. A man with eyes that do not blink or waver as he studies the armada of powerful men arrayed before him.

"Hail, mighty Scipio, former proconsul and governor to Iberia," shouts Glabius. "We do welcome you home!"

"Hail, Senator." Scipio replies. He sits quietly on his horse and stares at Glabius, an unspoken question on his face. Glabius nods, and looks back at the temple. "Yes, we have made a sacrifice to the gods before the meeting, and taken the auspices. The signs were good for us to meet." Scipio nods, satisfied. He slides from his mount and marches forward, as Laelius and Marcus Silenus follow. The trio approaches the

IV. Coming Home

ring of senators

"Salve, honored colleagues," says Scipio. His voice is solemn and heavy. "Today I bring you the gift of Iberia. It now belongs to Rome."

Scattered cheers erupt from the Hellenic side of the gathering, with others coming from those with no party affiliation. The Latins mutely nod their assent.

Glabius bows his head. "Your words are well met, son of Publius, and your achievements have certainly preceded you. But the law demands an accounting of them."

Scipio removes his helmet and bows, when his head raises he is smiling. "It will be my pleasure."

The young general walks to the top temple step and sits down. He stretches out his battle-scarred legs and motions for Laelius and Marcus to join him. They plop down beside him as though they are joining him for lunch instead of facing an inquiry. For the next hour Scipio details the battles he has won, the towns he has taken, and the tribes that he brought under the sway of the Roman people. [xxxii]

The senators pepper him with questions. Several veterans ask him about his battle tactics. The Hellenics ask him about the plunder and allies gained for Rome.

The Latins challenge him on the expenditures for his intelligence network. They criticize his perversion of the traditional Roman sword and his changes to the traditional maniple formation. Scipio calmly answers each query in turn. Laelius adds some elaborations to Scipio's replies, and Marcus provides some curt corrections to Scipio's explanations of battle tactics. But there are no apologies from any of them.

Scipio eventually grows impatient with the Latin's challenges. He raises his right hand high, signaling that he is concluding and will not be interrupted. "I went to Iberia and confronted four generals and four victorious armies, those of the Three Generals and Hanno," he says imperiously, his chin high. "When I left, there was not a single

IV. Coming Home

Carthaginian in the land." [xxxiii]

Several senators mutter their skepticism at Scipio's boast, but Glabius stamps his leader's staff and they soon quiet. "All praise and glory to you, General Scipio. You have done what no general has done before you." He looks accusingly at several veteran generals. "And did what no other would step forward to do; you ventured forth to defeat the undefeated."

Scipio glances at Laelius and Marcus, takes a deep breath, and continues. "I deserve a triumph. You have heard all my reasons for deserving it. Under my command our army has won numerous battles where over five thousand of the enemy were slain, with minimal loss of Roman life. That is the condition for a triumph." [xxxiv]

He runs his eyes across the assembled senators, staring down those who challenge his gaze. "For the sake of Rome and my men, give me the honor my army has earned."

Scores of senators cheer Scipio's words, and even more chant "Triumph, Triumph!" over the protests of a few. Scipio's mouth tightens in a faint smile. *By the gods, they may give it to me, after all. Fortuna smiles on us today.*

Flaccus struts down the temple steps and stands next to Glabius. He turns to his fellow senators and raises his hands. "Certainly, young General Scipio has brought much honor and wealth to Rome." He looks over his shoulder at the impassive Scipio, and grins unctuously. "And I would be the first to commend you, and recommend a triumph."

Scipio merely blinks at Flaccus, his face a stone. Laelius barks a sarcastic laugh, which he turns into a feigned cough. Flaccus glares at Laelius before he turns back to the senators, his long face etched with regret.

"Ah, such a tragedy! We cannot give Imperator Scipio his triumph," Flaccus says, waving his hands to quiet the protesting shouts of the senators. "By law, we cannot give it to him." He turns to Glabius. "This is a case of *Privatus cum imperio*. Not *magistratus cum imperio*. Am I

IV. Coming Home

correct, Glabius?"

The old lawyer purses his lips, thinking. Then he ruefully nods his head, and looks up at his fellows. "Senator Flaccus has the right of it. Only an elected magistrate or consul, someone given the imperium by virtue of their office, may be given a triumph. Noble Scipio volunteered for Iberia, and was made proconsul to purse his mission. He was not elected, making him a 'privatus cum imperio,' a private citizen with imperium."

Glabius' head falls. "The law is clear on that issue."

The ring of senators is silent, although many smile at the decision. Glabius frowns at Scipio. "I am sorry, General. Were it my choice, I would carry you through the streets on my own back." He glances briefly at Fabius. "We have given it to others, for less. But the law is the law."

"Fools," rings a voice behind Scipio. "You break laws daily to line your purses, but you will not make exception for the man who saved Rome!" Marcus Silenus stalks forward, his iron fist clutching the pommel of his sword, looking as if he is ready to execute them all.

Even at a distance, many senators involuntarily draw back in alarm, frightened at the righteous anger that burns on his face.

Scipio dashes after his legate. He places his hand on Marcus' rock-hard shoulder. "Enough, friend," he says softly. "It serves no profit." With a final glare at the alarmed senators, Marcus strides back from the steps. He stations himself behind his general, still fingering his weapon.

"The law is the law, as you say," replies Scipio. "Above all, true Romans respect the law," he adds, looking at Flaccus. He inclines his head slightly toward the senators. "I do accept your decision. And hereby relinquish my command of Iberia."

Glabius nods. "Then you may now enter Rome, *Citizen* Scipio. May Jupiter smile upon you."

The senators dissolve into chatting groups, and Scipio walks back

IV. Coming Home

toward his, men preparing to dismiss them. Laelius joins him, and the two make short speeches to the legionnaires about their pride in commanding them. The soldiers stand rigidly at attention during the speeches, but many eyes glisten with tears.

The two call for their stallions and leap onto their backs. Laelius pats Scipio's shoulder. "Regrets, my friend," he says. "I truly hoped you could march through Rome in glory." His voice breaks. "You have given so much of yourself, sometimes I am not sure you are still here anymore."

A gleam comes to Scipio's eyes, a pleased slyness that dismays Laelius as soon as he sees it. "I did not truly expect they would give me a triumph," he says.[xxxv] "But pleading my cause has served its purpose. I have gained sympathy for my election as consul."

"So your outrage was a sham?" says Laelius, studying Scipio's face.

Scipio returns the salute of several passing centurions. "As Marcus recently reminded me, I must win on the political as well as the military front, if I am to win this war."

"I am for Rome," says Laelius, turning his horse toward the road. "For all our sakes, I hope you win both battles." He puts his heels to his mount. "Just do not lose yourself in the process, friend. Old Hannibal's head isn't worth it."

* * * * *

GENOVA, NORTHWEST ITALIA COAST. *The gods have been bountiful to us this year,* muses Odhran, the diminutive Ligurian fisherman. He shakes out the bream and snapper from his knotted-rope net and piles his catch onto the floor of his worn little sailboat, already six inches deep with wriggling fish.

Satisfied with his day's work, Odhran unties his head cord and lets his greasy auburn hair fall to his shoulders, pulling out several stray fish scales. He grabs his wineskin and takes a deep drink, staring into the sunset that shimmers across the indigo waves of the Ligurian Sea. A breeze stirs his face, and he peers at the cloud lines to windward. *A*

IV. Coming Home

good breeze to grab before the weather comes in. I'd best get to it.

The fisherman pulls in his heavily-patched linen sail and begins to come about, reversing direction to catch the wind and head for home. As he crouches aft with the wooden tiller in his hand, he reflects on his past month's fruitful catches. *The portents are beneficent. This will be a good year for the tribe.*

The little fisherman pushes the wooden tiller further sideways, slowly turning the ship towards the faint outlines of the coast. Looking back out to sea, he can see curtains of rain hanging from the low-slung clouds. *It's coming my way, better go full sail back to shore.* He notices that the rain lines seem to be separating and thickening, forming into a spindly forest. Then he notices the dark bulges at the bottom of the lines, and his breath catches. *Those are ships! Many, many ships! Are they coming to destroy our city again?*

Odhran's curiosity overwhelms his trepidation. He pitches out his anchor and watches the flotilla approach. Soon the ships fill the horizon as the fisherman watches in terrified fascination. He stands in the bow near his anchor, hand on its rope, ready to flee when he can distinguish the mark on their sails. Minutes later, he discerns the Carthaginian Phoenix sprawling its red-purple wings across every sail.

Odhran yanks up the anchor and spreads his sail to its fullest, bucking across the waves until he skids to shore beneath the high cliffs of Genova. He ties into a small pier and scrambles from his boat.

The fisherman trots up the steep winding path that leads to the king's palace, a grand affair being built on an overlook above the harbor. Breathless, Odhran stops at the gates and explains what he has seen to the guards. A guard rushes into the palace. Soon King Baelon is staring out from a tower in one of his recently completed fortress walls, watching the Carthaginian armada sail towards his harbor. The guards count ships and report that there are at least sixty quinqeremes and even more transports, an entire army under sail.

Baelon views the Carthaginians' arrival with mixed emotions. When his men fought for Hannibal some thirteen years ago, they returned

IV. Coming Home

with loads of Roman plunder from their victories at Trebia and Trasimene. But Hannibal's brother Hasdrubal arrived five years later and burned most of the city to the ground, enraged that the local Ligurians had allied themselves with Rome. Now another Carthaginian army has arrived, with unknown purpose or sympathies. All Baelon knows is his city is largely defenseless against an onslaught, having no troops along the coastline.[xxxvi] *I must make the best arrangement I can with them*, he decides. *Or Genova may burn again.* He summons six messengers to his throne room.

"Stalia is in danger," he says, using the Ligurian name for his city. "Our tribe is in danger. Tell the chieftains to get here as soon as possible. The Carthaginians have come again." Baelon gathers his retinue and rides down to the harbor, eager to determine if enemy or ally has come to him.

The Carthaginian fleet flows into Genova's expansive bay. Baelon counts thirty quinqeremes already occupying his harbor environs, with twice as many transports stretching out behind them. Baelon is angry that these strangers would so brashly commandeer his city's port, but fearful at the number of men these many ships must hold. He decides that patience and dignity will serve him best against their superior power, as it has served him against the neighboring Gauls. The king waits at the foot of the harbor as the Carthaginian flagship docks in front of him.

Mago debarks from his shining new oarship. He pauses when he stands at the dock, looking about for a welcoming party. A score of his Sacred Band guards surround him; elite warriors in white linen tunics with purple borders, each with a heavy round shield and seven-foot spear. The Band guards are Carthaginian noblemen who serve Mago for the pure glory of fighting for Carthage. Each has been trained at birth to fight with hand, horse, sword, and spear. Each is prepared to fight to the death for their famous commander.

A dozen Balearic Island infantrymen crowd in behind Mago. The rangy brown men are brutal savages who were selected as the best fighters by their Balearic brothers in arms, as skilled with a blade as they are with a sling. The mercenaries wear padded vests over their

IV. Coming Home

simple gray tunics and a leather cap on their heads. They each heft a small wooden shield that bears the nicks and slivers of many sword blows. The Balearics would be altogether an unprepossessing lot were it not for the gleaming falcatas that they dangle naked from their belts, their belligerent expressions indicating they would eagerly deploy them at the slightest threat.

Wearing his polished bronze armor, Baelon strides down the wide dock walkway with his guards, his eyes sizing up this wiry man who stares hostilely at him. Baelon signals for his guards to draw closer to him. He strides stiffly toward Mago, drawing his hand up in greeting.

"Give me room!" bellows a voice behind the Balearics, halting Baelon in his tracks. The Balearic warriors are shoved aside by a gigantic bear of a man. He stalks down the gangplank to stand next to Mago, topping him by a head.

"You could be a little more discreet, Korbis," Baelon hears Mago mutter.

Korbis laughs. "Discreet for pussies. I meet this King now."

Korbis is the leader of the Balearics, a position he earned by battering down his rivals in hand-to-hand combat. The black bearded giant is clad in silver scale armor, a feathered blue plume sprouting from his silver domed helmet. His falcata is sheathed in silver-studded leather, signifying his high place among his savage brethren. Korbis' sword has been specially forged by the Iberian metalsmiths. It is a thick-backed cleaver blade that is half sword and half ax, capable of splitting a shield with a single blow from Korbis' ham-like fist.

"Is all safe?" he bellows in his pidgin Carthaginian. He glares at King Baelon's guards. "You want we cut them up, General?"

Mago shakes his head, irritated. "That will not be necessary, Korbis. But stay near me anyway."

Baelon studies Mago and Korbis, trying to determine which one is the leader. Korbis' onyx eyes glare fixedly at him, as if to establish dominance. When Baelon sees the haughty indifference in Mago's

IV. Coming Home

green eyes he knows he is the true commander, a man assured of his power over those he faces.

Mago walks toward Baelon, his palm raised in greeting. He growls an order to his guards and the Sacred Band split in front of him and halt. Mago signals for Korbis to wait and motions for his interpreter to follow him. He walks in to face Baelon and his armed retinue, unarmed and unperturbed.

"I am General Mago Barca, Commander of the Carthaginian army," Mago says through his interpreter.

Baelon nods. "I knew your brothers, Hannibal and Hasdrubal," he says, his voice cautious. "What is your purpose here, General Mago?"

Mago grins sardonically and waves his arm toward the armada that fills the Ligurian Sea behind him. "Within those hundred ships are eleven thousand soldiers and two thousand cavalry." He stares into Baelon's eyes. "I am here to either destroy an enemy of Carthage or gain an ally for Rome's conquest. Which I do, depends on you."

Baelon gulps down his fear. *Remember, you are the king here.* He knows Mago's army could easily destroy Genova—again—with scant opposition from the few Ligurians soldiers that are in the city. But pride will not allow him to simply capitulate, and his own people would flay him alive for cowardice if he did so. Baelon must bargain for some concessions and make it seem like there is an agreed alliance between their nations.

"If you are a Barca, you know we Ligurians are fierce fighters, the last to leave a battle, win or lose," blusters Baelon. "We would make formidable enemies."

Mago looks back at his guards and winks, indicating he is aware of the game being played. But he knows that Baelon speaks true. Like their Gallic neighbors, the Ligurians will fearlessly storm into the staunchest Roman lines, exhilarated with death and the fury of battle.

"My brother Hasdrubal speaks—spoke—of the might of your army." Mago replies. He grins. "And he regretted having to kill so many of

IV. Coming Home

you. It was a waste of noble warriors, I would say." At these words Baelon's guards stir restlessly and clench their sword pommels. Baelon raises his hand to calm them.

King Baelon nods slowly. "True, but we have learned much from our encounter with Hasdrubal. Anyone who tried would not find it an easy task."

Mago's lips tighten. He does not want to back the king into a place where he must fight to defend his honor. He needs to gain thousands of allies before he marches on Rome, not lose hundreds of his own men in a conflict of pride.

"For those who ally themselves with us, there is a measure of silver every month, without fail." Mago says. He casts a nod back at the Balearics. "Or pay in women, if you are some such as these."

Then it dawns upon Baelon. *The Carthaginians are not here for conquest or plunder, they are here to build an army against Rome. They will fight any who would try to stop them. I could set them against our enemies.* Baelon grows excited, but keeps his voice calm.

"Money we have in plentitude, though more is always welcome." Baelon stares accusingly at Mago. "We can use it to rebuild what your brother destroyed. But there is another matter, General."

Baelon motions for his guard to withdraw from him, and he waves for Mago and his interpreter to follow. They walk to a spot on the pier where they cannot be overheard.

"There is unrest and warfare among our tribes. Our friends the Inguani, they fight with the powerful Epanterii Montanii,[xxxvii] and there are other disputes," says Baelon. He looks pointedly at Mago. "Many of my fellow chieftains are besieged. As am I."

"The enemy of our allies is our enemy," says Mago expansively, reaching out to clasp Baelon's arm. "And we would destroy them with you." Mago sees no reaction to his words, so he adds. "And give you their lands."

IV. Coming Home

For the first time Baelon smiles. "Those are welcome words, General. If you would propose those conditions for other Ligurian tribes, you will bring many chieftains to your side."

Now it is Mago's turn to grin. "Bring them to me, and let us build an alliance as soon as possible." He gestures toward the southeast, across the waters. "Rome waits for us, with more plunder than you could ever imagine..."

* * * * *

KROTON, CALABRIA PROVINCE, ITALIA, 205 BCE. "Auugh!" the tribune yells, grasping at his leg as the spear plunges into it. "You godless bastard!"

Manius Fabius grunts with pain as the spear blade pops out from the back of his thigh. He drops his scutum and falls to one knee, using his left hand to prop himself upright. He screams again as the swarthy Bruttian yanks out his weapon and shoves it toward the Roman's face.

Manius pivots around and swings his short sword at the plummeting spear. The weapons clang together, and the spear hisses past his neck, leaving a shallow bloody gash. Unbalanced by the force of his thrust, the wolfskin clad Italian slips on some intestines and falls backward.

Manius rolls over to get his hands under his chest and pushes himself upright. The Bruttian spins around and shoves his spear into Manius' back, slicing through the tribune's red cape. Manius gasps when the spearhead hits him. He falls on his face but he quickly rises up, sword in hand.

The Bruttian stares at his weapon in surprise: the bronze spear point is bent double, deflected by the scale armor shirt that Manius' uncle Fabius had insisted he wear. Cursing his luck, the Bruttian pulls out his sword and springs at his bleeding foe, blade poised to slice into Manius' neck.

A javelin point suddenly blooms from the Bruttian's chest. The barbarian stares at the spearpoint, watching his lifeblood pour out around it.

IV. Coming Home

A stocky centurion puts his foot into the Bruttian's back and yanks out his javelin, holding it ready for another killing thrust. The Bruttian staggers about, vomiting out his lifeblood. He careens toward Manius, convulsively thrusting his sword at him. The young tribune easily deflects the weak blows and watches his enemy fall on his face, kicking out his last seconds on earth. When the body is still, Manius kicks it. "Bastard! I should have killed you myself!" he says, grabbing his bloody thigh.

The centurion rushes over to help his commander stand upright. "Gratitude, Vitus," says Manius, "That savage almost had me."

The leathery old soldier merely grunts. "Ah, you likely would have put a blade through his guts in time. Let us get you to the rear."

"That is not necessary." Manius stoops over and pulls out a linen bandage from his belt purse. He deftly wraps his leg and ties a knot with the ends of the bandage. "I cannot retreat to the rear lines. Not while we have the advantage on them. You, Decimus!" shouts Manius, balancing himself on one leg, "Come over here!"

The standard bearer runs over to Manius, carrying his maniple's horse-head figurine on a tall bronze pole. Manius grabs the standard from him. "Get a shield and follow me!" he orders. He nods toward the standard. "If I fall you retrieve it, and keep it upright!"

Manius hobbles forward, determined to join the front lines and lead his men onward. The veteran triarii see him coming; they raise their spears high and cheer the site of an officer carrying the standard. The word carries up to the legion's front lines that Manius is coming. The hastati and principes fight with renewed vigor, and the Bruttians are beaten back.

Standing in the second line with his staunch principes, Manius leans heavily on the standard as he shouts orders and encouragement. Two of his tribunes ride up and force him onto to a horse as they rebandage his wounds. Manius hands the standard to Decimus. "At them," he screams to the front line hastati. He kicks his horse forward, and joins the front line fighters.

IV. Coming Home

Here on the Neto River plains, the battle rages in full between Manius' legion and four thousand of Hannibal's fiercest Bruttian allies. The two armies fight for control of the port city of Kroton, Hannibal's former base of operations. Manius is determined to drive Hannibal's army farther south, but the Romans find these Italians to be a stalwart foe, determined to avenge Manius' atrocities upon their fellows.

As soon as Hannibal's army marched south, Manius' legions marched from his garrison and retook the town after a brief siege. Once inside, Manius left a brutal lesson for any of Italia tribes who would join Hannibal. The skeletons of thirty Carthaginian sympathizers still hang from their crosses at the front gates of the fortress city. The bones are so bleached and picked that even the carrion crows show no further interest in scavenging them. A wood sign hangs beneath each skeleton's feet, with the word "traitor" burned into it.

The angry Bruttians have stormed up from the south, intent on plundering Kroton and restoring it to Hannibal—and taking their countrymen off the crosses. But Manius' legion has met them on the plains, blocking their attack on his base of operations. The Bruttians have stormed into the Romans but the front line hastati have maintained their shield lines and speared them back. Now the Bruttians retreat from the unyielding Roman front, anxious to regroup.

Manius shouts for fresh troops to go to the front lines, replacing the weary hastati. The principes, the legion's principal fighters, turn their shields sideways and shoulder their way through the front row of the retreating hastati. The principes calmly array themselves three feet apart from each other, their scuta held high in front of their bodies, and prepare for the next onslaught.

Across the open field, the Brutii mass up for another charge, lining up a hundred feet from the Roman front. The southern Italians are rangy mountain tribesmen, their heads and bodies bedecked with the skins of wolves and bears. Some wield scavenged Roman swords and shields, others hold Gallic longswords, still others grasp knobby cudgels. All are bloodied veterans of their own internecine tribal wars. They are not daunted at the prospect of fighting the dreaded Romans.

IV. Coming Home

The Brutii mill about, beating their skin drums and chanting war songs about the glory of death in battle. They stamp their feet in unison with their chants, slowly building up the will to dash across the trampled meadow and beat down the Romans.

The war chants conclude and the drums cease. Silence hangs over the field. A wide-bodied elder chieftain steps into the open space and faces the Roman lines, his iron ringmail vest shining as brightly as his polished winged helmet.

The silver-haired giant carefully lays down his body-length shield and his thick great sword. He turns his back to the Romans as his men watch eagerly. Bending over, he pulls up the back of his worn green tunic and waggles his bare ass at the Romans. His men roar with laughter and cheers, beating their weapons upon their shields to create another ear-splitting clamor. The commander takes off his wide leather belt, lined with the dangling ears of his conquests. "I coming to get more ears!" he roars at the Romans as shakes his belt at them, prompting further uproar from his men.

The older man reties his belt. He picks up his weapons and walks alone to the front of the Romans, standing midfield as his horde watches quietly. He pauses for a minute, head held high. Then he screams out a battle cry and strides quickly at the principes. He waves his flashing sword over his head, motioning for his subjects to join him.

The screaming Bruttians stampede across the ravaged grass and crash into the waiting Romans. Their flailing clubs knock against shields and ring against armor. The Romans batter back at them, and the cacophony of battle rises, so loud that the centurions signal troop movements by whistle and hand, not trusting their voices to carry.

The legionnaires behind the front line fling their heavy javelins into the Bruttian troops, felling scores of unwary warriors who neglect to raise their shields. The stoic principes grimly hold formation as the wild-eyed tribesmen charge in and beat at them from every angle. Dozens of legionnaires fall. The second line soldiers quickly pull their wounded comrades to the rear, then step in to replace them.

IV. Coming Home

The Bruttii are fearless and fierce but they fight without discipline or tactic. Two or three warriors assault a single principe, only to be stabbed down by the legionnaire's mates. Dozens of Bruttians fall with side and back wounds, killed by a foe they never faced. Still the tribesmen come on, shoving at each other in their eagerness to get at the Romans, aching for retribution of their fellows' crucifixions. The Bruttians cut down more of the principes, but for every legionnaire who falls, three or four Bruttian corpses litter the ground about him. The Roman steadfastness takes its toll.

The Bruttians again draw back from the unbending Romans. The elder commander raises his blade bolt upright, signaling a pause in attack. The undaunted legionnaires drop their swords to their sides and lower their shields. They casually drink from their water and wine skins, hurling taunts and jokes across the field. Many sprawl on the ground to rest, glaring at their enemies. The centurions walk across the front line, exhorting the soldiers to stay next to their shield mates, ordering the back lines to be ready to step forward. The Bruttian war songs start again, and the tribesmen hurtle back into the fray.

After a half hour of continued battle, Manius can see that the principes' shields are beginning to droop. He calls for a front line change. The refreshed hastati step to the fore and ram their shields into their tiring foe, knocking scores off balance for a killing thrust. Their comrades' death only serves to anger the other Brutti. They stampede into the hastati with renewed frenzy, many leaping high onto the heads of the surprised Romans, knocking them to the earth so their fellows can swarm over them.

With the Bruttians fully occupied with the Roman front, Manius decides that their rear ranks are vulnerable. *Now, quickly, while they are all pressing to get to the front.* He calls over his equite commander. "Cavalry attack to the rear." he orders. The commander gallops away.

The legion's three hundred riders divide into two groups and circle out toward each side, hurtling toward the Brutti's open flanks. When Manius sees the horsemen nearing the enemy's sides, he calls over his senior tribune. "Tell the velites to throw their spears into the back lines when the horns blow."

IV. Coming Home

The tribune nods. "I will send them to the front. They will be ready."

The light infantry trot out toward the front line of battle, waiting in the gap between the hastati and principes. The cornicenes sound the command, and the velites spring into action. Running forward for momentum, the velites fling their javelins over the battling front lines, arcing them down into the Bruttian rear. As the javelins hail down upon the enemy, the Roman cavalry crash into the tribesmen's flanks. The front and side assault jams the barbarians together. The horsemen jump off their mounts and stab into their disorganized enemy, pushing them further into their fellows.

Manius senses a rout is near, and orders his legion to press the attack. One step at a time, the Romans tromp forward and press into the barbarian mob. The legionnaires push the Bruttians back with their unyielding shield wall, stabbing their swords to into any exposed flesh they can reach, knowing a bleeding cut will eventually weaken their foes and leave them vulnerable for a mortal thrust.

The Brutti fight demonically, battling through their wounds, but they are assailed from the front and sides and have little room to maneuver. The Bruttian back lines walk backward, then trot, and then run, dashing toward the local farms' cornfields. Thousands of Bruttii throw down their weapons and disappear into the tall stalks, furrowing their way toward the sheltering hills. The Bruttians in the front line soon follow suit, running to catch up to their retreating tribesmen.

The Roman infantry and cavalry pursue them relentlessly. They grab spears from the enemy corpses and wounded, hurling them into the backs of their retreating enemy. Scores of once-proud warriors fall with javelins in their backs, slain in cowardly retreat before they reach the beckoning fields.

They're going to hide in those damn crops, curses Manius. *We'll have to surround the fields and hunt them one by one.* Then he grins. *Or just burn them out.*

As the front line Brutii near the edge of the fields they pull up and regroup. The elder captain stands in front of them there. He totters on

IV. Coming Home

his feet, his ringmail stained with blood from cuts to his neck and head. The giant bellows out a command, and the Bruttians turn to face the oncoming Romans. The Italians hold their weapons loosely at their sides, as if unconcerned about the approaching legionnaires.

Manius rides at the head of his men, directing the final charge. His head is woozy from blood loss, but he still has the presence of mind to wonder why the Bruttians are stopping so close to escape. *They are going to make a final stand? Fools.*

As he and his men close in on the solemn lines of Bruttii, Manius notes an anomaly in the cornfields. The gracefully waving strands are rippling toward his men from all sides, as when a strong wind blows across a lake, even though the winds waft the other way.

Manius' eyes widen with dawning alarm. He opens his mouth to shout a halt but the first wave of his men are already crashing into the waiting Bruttii. When they do, the first waves of Carthaginians storm out from the fields...

Six days ago, Hannibal walked by these same farm fields, dressed in simple peasant garb, with a beggar's sack slung over his shoulder. As he plodded along the dirt road he noted the height of the nearby hills, the places with the densest trees and the farms with the tallest corn. Most importantly, he noted the direction of the wind in the afternoon. Having thoroughly studied the terrain he returned south to his camp, where he quickly ordered thousands of his men north under cover of night.

The night before the Brutii were to attack Kroton, Hannibal led his army back to the area he reconnoitered. It was a simple task to capture the local farmers and hide his infantry in their fields before sunrise, swords at the ready. Hannibal sequestered his Numidian cavalry back into the forested hills, far from the eyes of any roaming scouts. He concealed himself and his Sacred Band among the hillside trees, waiting until the Romans pursued the Bruttians into his ambush.

Now thousands of Carthaginians, Gauls, and Libyans pour out from the croplands, lusting to fight with the outnumbered Romans.

IV. Coming Home

Hannibal's stern Libyans thresh into the legion's vulnerable flanks, while the wild-eyed Gauls join the renewed Brutii in a beserking assault upon the Roman center, madly hacking and slashing at any who stand in their way.

Hundreds of Numidians ride down from the hills, swifter than the wind. The African riders cut into Manius' equites. Their nimble ponies whirl about their heavily armored opponents, and their darting spears find fatal gaps in the Romans' armor.

The Numidians gallop out from the remnants of the Roman cavalry they have just destroyed. They circle behind the Libyans and charge into the legion's rear lines. With infantry on three sides and cavalry at their backs, a noose of death tightens about the battling legionnaires.

Manius watches the encirclement unfold. His stomach sinks with dread realization. "Close ranks," he screams. "Man to man, close the shield walls!" He watches his men being slaughtered, and sorrow pierces his heart. *You can die up here or die with them,* he thinks. Manius clambers down from his horse and limps over to join his diminishing front line. He sees seven enormous Gauls surrounding three of his principes, who stand back to back to fend them off.

Manius draws his gladius and rushes forward. He crunches his sword into the spine of a stout chieftain who is busy beating a centurion to his knees. The chieftain screams and falls to the ground, scrabbling at the bloodied earth beneath him. Manius hacks off the barbarian's head and brandishes it at the enemy lines. "Here's your leader, pigs!" he shouts.

He hears a scream of rage and turns face a half-dozen onrushing Gauls, furious at the death of their leader. *It is your time,* he concludes, *do honor to Uncle Fabius.* The young man spits at them and raises his sword high. "For Rome and victory!" he shouts, and rushes at them.

Manius blocks the first sword blow with his shield. Ducking out from behind his scutum, he impales the chest of the Gaul facing him. With sword and shield occupied, he is easy prey for the other two Gauls, and they lance their blades into his legs, bringing him to knees.

IV. Coming Home

Apologies, uncle, is Manius' last thought, before a greatsword cleaves his helmet.

As dusk approaches, the last dozen legionnaires are surrounded, several so wounded they cannot raise their swords in defense. Hannibal shouts for his mercenaries to capture the remaining Romans, but it is too late. The bloodlust is upon the Gauls and Brutti, they swarm over the last legionnaires, stabbing them down and decapitating them.

Disgusted at the slaughter, Hannibal motions for his officers to follow him away from the corpse-strewn field. "We can do no good here," Hannibal tells them. "It is time to march on Kroton." Hannibal and his commanders ride slowly toward the city as their small army regroups and follows along.

Once away from the stink of gore and feces, Hannibal takes a deep breath and lets his eyes roam over the lush countryside, enjoying the farmers' carefully tended groves and fields. He reaches into his belt pouch and extracts a figurine his father, a replica of the original that Hannibal gave to a dying young soldier at Cannae.

Hannibal looks down at the little statue of Hamilcar Barca, the Thunderbolt, the bane of the Romans in the first war. He thinks of his vow to his father, to be ever an enemy to Rome. *But I did not vow to be an enemy to all of Italia*, he decides. *These people can be my friends. And allies*

Hannibal halts his horse and turns to his Sacred Band leader. "Make sure the farmers are released unharmed. Tell the men that any who violate the peasants' families or property will be slowly disemboweled while they hang on a cross. Understand?" His Sacred Band captain nods, and Hannibal continues on. *By Baal's balls, we don't have to kill everyone in this country, do we?*

The Carthaginian army camps few miles outside Kroton's walls, near the beautifully colonnaded Temple of Hera.[xxxviii] Three Carthaginian envoys approach the garrison commander with Hannibal's terms: the soldiers inside must surrender immediately or face a brutal takeover. If they resist, thirty new crosses will be staked outside the walls, each

IV. Coming Home

with a Roman officer stretched across it.

The next day Kroton's gates fly open and the Roman defenders march out with full armament, defeated but proud. After they are disarmed, Hannibal oversees a swearing in ceremony with his captives, in which they promise to march back to Rome and report their merciful treatment to the Senate. The lead tribune swears to give the Senate Hannibal's final proposition: make peace with him now, or he marches on Rome.

The next day Hannibal gathers his men into formation on the fields by the front gates of Kroton. They watch the Bruttians taking down the crosses of their crucified countrymen, arranging each skeleton on a massive pyre.

The Gauls, Libyans, and Numidians watch the cremation of the remains in silence. After the final timbers crumble to ash, Hannibal releases his army to a victory celebration in town. Hours later, as the music and laughter fill the starlight night, Hannibal watches the proceedings from atop a guard tower. *A fight, funeral, and feast all taken together*, he muses. *This should unite them as warriors.* He grins ruefully. *That is, if they don't kill each other in a drunken brawl tonight.*

Hannibal bends backward, massaging his back. *Enough thinking, old man, you have earned a good night's sleep.* With a heavy sigh, fearsome Hannibal steps his way down the curved stone steps from the tower, seeking only a hot meal and a warm bed.

* * * * *

SERVIAN WALL, ROME. "Salve, Romans. Salve!"

Returning from his meeting at the Temple of Bellona, Scipio shouts his salutations at the knot of citizens who are ecstatically calling his name. He rubs his tiring forearm and smiles, flicking the reins on his black stallion. *By Mercury's winged helmet, I'm tired of waving at people! I should have entered Rome with that ragged cloak and old mare.*

IV. Coming Home

As he trots past a corn field, a quartet of freedmen lean on their hoes and wave at him. "Scipio! Scipio Imperator! Salve, Scipio!" they shout.

Scipio grins and waves. *Well, at least some of the country folk remember me, triumph or not. That bodes well for my election.*

The mighty stallion clops along at a leisurely pace. Scipio feels the weight of command fall off his shoulders. He studies the groves and fields that flourish along the main road to Rome, recalling the times he and Laelius raced their horses down to Ostia, when their only worries were preparing their homework for their Greek tutor Asclepius. Off to the side of the road he sees the weather-beaten statue of Roma, goddess of the city, its arms outstretched in welcome. *Thank you, Goddess. It is good to be back.*

Then it finally occurs to him: he has finally come home, home to Rome. For the first time since he has landed, Scipio feels the heart flutter of homesickness cured. His eyes film with tears and he quickly wipes at them, concerned that his surrounding guards will think him weak.

Scipio draws nigh to Rome's daunting Servian Wall, rising thirty feet above the twelve-foot battle trenches dug at its feet. He pauses beneath the arched main gates of the Porta Carmentalis and scratches his head, puzzled. The gates are closed in the middle of this quiet day, with no threats about. There are no guards in front of the portal, only a few men languidly watching from the top of the wall.

Citizen Scipio dismounts and walks toward the gates, knowing a general who has just resigned his command must enter Rome on foot.[xxxix] He walks up the gates and pounds on them, still puzzled at the lack of sentries. *Discipline has grown lax, I must talk to the consul about this.*

The massive gates open a crack, groaning loudly on their thick iron hinges. Two stern-faced legionnaires slide out to confront him. "And you are who?" one of them asks brusquely. Scipio blinks in surprise.

"I am Publius Cornelius Scipio, governor ... former governor and

IV. Coming Home

proconsul of Iberia."

The legionnaire looks at his compatriot, who nods curtly. "Best give him admission, whoever he is" the other says. A humbled Scipio starts to ease past them when he notices that they both suppress smiles. *What is going on with these fools?*

Four other soldiers join the guards. They quickly shove the groaning gates wide open. There, standing at the entrance, Scipio faces a sheer cacophony of screams and cheers. The people of Rome have filled every inch of ground in the streets and steps about them. They hang from the buildings and statues, cheering his name and throwing flower petals, wildly blowing horns and trumpets. Rome's citizens have decided that Scipio will receive his triumph, their way.

One of the gate guards bends to his ear, shouting so he can be heard. "Apologies for my rudeness, General, but I had to play my part!" He motions for Scipio to follow him and he marches ahead, joined by a century of soldiers who form an honor guard about Scipio, leading him toward the Forum.

Scipio's army guards soon join them, leading a chain of oxcarts that carry the plunder of Iberia: seven tons of silver, and massive sacks of plundered coins.[xl]

Scipio dismounts and flips the reins of his horse to a nearby centurion. He strolls along with his personal guard, his eyes roaming over the sea of people waving at him. *Is this all for me?* He waves at the cheering throngs and smiles awkwardly when several red-faced young women rush out to kiss him. Scipio runs his hand across his brow as if he mopping sweat from it, artfully wiping away his tears. *Gratitude, Fortuna. I am truly home.*

The procession enters the vast Forum Square. It wends its way through the thousands gathered there and halts in front of the Curia Hostilia. Scipio sees Amelia and Pomponia standing on a cleared space atop the stairs of the senate house, and his smile widens to split his face.

IV. Coming Home

Pomponia shines in a snow-white gown belted with golden chains, her face streaked with tears. Amelia is a pace behind her, garbed in a flowing maroon gown, a gold pendant of Nike hanging from her neck. Her eyes meet Scipio's, and close slowly in acknowledgement and respect of her beloved. Scipio waves at her like a schoolboy, ecstatic.

Several dozen senators also stand along the top steps of the Curia. Most of them wave and salute, but others glumly watch the plebs' celebration, angry it was done without Senate approval. Cato, Flaccus, and Fabius stand to the side of the group, their arms crossed over their chests, looking as if Rome had just lost the war.

Scipio walks up the steps and stands at the tall rostra placed there for him. He delivers an impromptu speech about his Iberian campaign, one that echoes the achievements he just described to the Senators at the Temple of Bellona. With a flourish of his hand, he indicates the oxcarts of plunder that are trundling into the Forum. He details the wealth he has brought to Rome and the civic improvements the money can bring, eliciting more cheers. As the crowd chants his name, he raises his hands over his head. *And now begins my consular campaign.*

Several hours later Scipio is at home with his family. He walks about the city manse, stopping to converse with the slaves and freedmen, feeding tidbits to the family greyhounds. His brother Lucius soon gallops in from Ostia and joins the family. As Lucius dusts off his riding clothes he informs Scipio that Marcus Silenus and Laelius have just arrived in Rome, and will confer with him on the morrow. *We all are back here safely,* Scipio muses. *It is beyond belief.*

With the greeting formalities behind him, Scipio, Pomponia, and Amelia repair to the dining room and recline on the dining couches, eager to celebrate the family's reunion. Lucius soon joins them. He eases himself onto a couch, a distracted look on his face, as if his mind is elsewhere. Amelia reclines on a couch perpendicular to Scipio's, that she may hold his hand while they dine and converse.

The house slaves bring food and wine throughout the family's three-hour meal. It is a sumptuous feast, Pomponia has spared no expense for her returning sons. They dine on boar, goat, peacock, and ostrich, with

IV. Coming Home

a huge tray of Scipio's favorite, roasted mice rolled in honey and poppy seed.

The wine and talk flows freely, and the hours flow past, unheeded. At Scipio's request there is no talk of the war, and so the conversation turns to the politics of past years. Pomponia recounts her efforts at promoting land reforms for the plebs and reducing the slave population so that freedmen can find more work. Amelia explains her propagandistic efforts to promote the campaigns of the ill-fated Marcellus, the Sword of Rome, and of Nero, so recently fallen from grace. Scipio listens avidly to all his family's tales of success and disappointment, happy to hear anything that does not involve death and destruction.

The conversation soon turns to the consular elections, and Scipio at last adds to the talk. "I am thinking about running for consul. That is the only way I can get the authority and resources to eliminate Hannibal."

Pomponia claps her hands. "It is a brilliant idea. Amelia and I had thought you might. We have planned how we can help you."

"Gratitude for that," says Scipio, "but I do wonder if I should run. After all, the Latin Party will vehemently oppose my nomination."

Pomponia spits out an olive pit into a bowl held by a waiting slave. "So what? They cannot stop you. Did you hear those people out there? The citizens love you! You brought victory to Rome after years of defeat."

Scipio pulls out his battered figurine of Nike, smiling at Amelia. "Yes, I had Victory with me in every battle, and have brought it back from Iberia." Amelia reaches out and squeezes his hand. "The gods have blessed you. And me."

"There are other concerns," continues Scipio. "Suppose I manage to get elected. The Senate would have to decide if I am to go to South Italia or to Sicily. Flaccus and Fabius may use their influence to send me to Bruttium in the south. I need to be in Sicily, not Bruttium! From

IV. Coming Home

there I can launch an assault in Africa, and draw Hannibal from our shores."

"The Latins cannot prevent you from being elected; you are too popular, my love," says Amelia. "But I see your point, they can keep you from going to Africa by designating Bruttium as your province of assignment."

"Hmm, that is a point for us to consider," Pomponia says, biting her lip. She dips her hands into a fingerbowl and a slave rushes to bring her a thick nubby towel. She dries her fingers and holds up the towel. "Have you noticed how soft these towels are? They are made from some Egyptian fabric they call 'cotton.' It is wonderful! I am having a dress made of it for the games."

"Best the Latins don't find out about your cotton," Lucius chuckles quietly. "They would curse you for not using good Roman cloth."

Pomponia smiles ingratiatingly at her eldest son, her eyes sad. She has noticed her once-carefree boy has had a haunted look about him since his return from Iberia. *He so quiet and reserved now,* she thinks. *As if he is hiding inside himself. Something happened to him over there.* She shrugs off her worry and looks back at Scipio.

"The Senate may not support you going to Africa, not with Fabius and Flaccus in power. They will push to campaign against Hannibal in Bruttium."

"Then I would be forced to defeat Hannibal in Italia," says Scipio dejectedly. "And once he is defeated, the Latins will push to declare the war is over, so that Rome may return to colonizing Italia's agricultural lands. And Carthage will be free to gather power and mount another attack." He shakes his head. "They still think like farmers. Like Rome is just a big farm town, not a budding empire."

Pomponia sighs. "That is how they would see it. *Absens haeres non erit* (out of sight, out of mind*).* If Hannibal is gone from our shores, the war is over to them."

"Perhaps there is a way out of this mess," Amelia interjects. "What if

IV. Coming Home

the other new consul could not leave Italia? Then you would have to go to Sicily for your consulship. And you could go to Africa from there."

"Yes, but why couldn't a consul leave Italia?" Scipio asks. Because he's too old to travel to Sicily?"

Pomponia smiles at Amelia. "Ah, I see it. A priest could not leave Italia because the law would not allow it." Amelia nods. "Just so. Religious law."

"Well, then, now our chickens are cackling!" says Pomponia, downing her half-full cup with a flourish. "We had best get to work, Amelia. The elections are coming in two weeks, and we have developed what you call 'propaganda'. There are slogans and banners to be made." She looks mischievously at Scipio. "But the propaganda is not for you."

"I am still confused," Scipio says. "Who cannot leave Italia? Who else would you support? You have another Hellenic in mind?"

Amelia smiles. "Not a Hellenic. Or a Latin. A priest. You need a certain priest to be elected as coconsul with you. A most important one."

"I swear to Olympus, Jupiter is clearer to me than the mind of a woman!" Scipio drains his cup with a flourish.

"We are speaking of Publius Licinius Crassus, The Pontifex Maximus of Rome. The head priest of all the pontiffs. By law, he is not allowed to leave Italia, in case he is urgently needed. "

Scipio blinks at her. "You think a priest can get elected consul?"

Pomponia nods her head vigorously. "I am certain of it! Crassus' family are plebians, not patricians.[xli] He will have the people and the Tribunes of the Plebs behind him."

"And the Senate would have to elect him if the people support him," interjects Amelia. Her eyes sparkle with excitement. "Several weeks ago they almost rioted over the imported slaves taking their jobs. The

IV. Coming Home

Senate is afraid to displease them."

"Do not be so sure he'll get elected," mutters Scipio. "There are many worthy candidates, I would think."

"But none that will be seen with you at the gladiatorial games three days from now," Pomponia remarks. "We've asked Licinius to sit next to you." She looks innocently at her son. "Oh, did I forget to mention it? The curule aedile is sponsoring a gladiatorial combat in your honor."

She smiles. "As the city magistrate, the aedile was happy to gather public recognition for his personal generosity, once we provided him with a large purse of the 'support' you sent from Iberia."

"You will have the place of honor, of course," Amelia says. "And after Licinius offers a ritual sacrifice to open the games, he will be sitting next to you!" She claps her hands like a child. "You see? It's all so simple!"

"Very well, make it so. Gods take me to Hades, I am grateful I'm not scheming against you two." He laughs. "I am happy to settle for Hannibal!"

* * * * *

FORUM ROMANUM, ROME. Clad in a toga candida, the chalk-white toga of a consular candidate, Scipio snaps his fingers enthusiastically, joining with the plebs and patricians as they applaud the exiting jugglers. The three ropy men bounce two stuffed leather balls on their knees as they prance off from the ring, their leather spheres never hitting the ground. Behind them a woman stands atop a cantering roan mare, juggling five peaches as she follows her fellow slaves toward the Temple of Saturn at the end of the Forum.

The crowd cheers as the performers depart, and guest of honor Scipio feels obliged to pay them the ultimate recognition—he waves the flaps of his toga at them. The crowd roars with approval, indicating their support for the man they believe will finally end the war.

IV. Coming Home

Publius Crassus reclines in his throne-like seat next to Scipio. The two men are perched at the top of the Senate chamber steps where they are accompanied by a host of nobles and war heroes. Crassus, The Pontifex Maximus, is a taciturn and doughy older man, inclined to smile only when being cheered by the crowd—and then only if it is very loud. But he is with Scipio today, and so Crassus has been smiling frequently.

Pomponia and Amelia occupy seats to Scipio's right. Pomponia is draped in an elegant cotton dress that matches her flame red hair, which has been coifed high atop her head. Amelia's auburn curls cascade down to the shoulders of her green silk gown, her hair held in place by a thin golden circlet. Admiral Laelius and Legate Marcus Silenus stand behind Scipio, receiving their own applause as Scipio's two Iberian commanders.

In the few days since he has returned to Rome, Laelius has already managed to find the most ornate and dazzling Greek toga in the city. He wears the black and gold robe proudly, savoring the disapproving looks of Cato, Flaccus, and the rest of the Latins.

Laelius leans to Scipio's ear. "My gods, Amelia and your mother are beautiful," Laelius exclaims. "I had to dress up just so they would not shame me. Marcus, apparently, is impervious to such feelings." He glances over at stolid Marcus Silenus, who is simply attired in armor and sword.

"Leave him be," chirps Scipio. "I had to bribe him just so he would wear the sword of honor I gave him."

Laelius glances over at the gold-pommeled sword that rests in Marcus' dented and bloodstained scabbard. "You know, that is the only thing he has that I would want—other than his courage, strength, ferocity—the little things."

With the jugglers gone, the crowd quiets, waiting Scipio's signal to begin the main event. But Scipio is enjoying the attention, and he tarries to give it. With timing born from his natural instinct for drama, Scipio raises his right hand just as the crowd begins to mutter restlessly. "Let the contest begin!" he shouts.

IV. Coming Home

A quartet of trumpets blares the signal. Six leanly muscular men march out, handsome young men without a blemish upon their smooth-muscled bodies. The young men move with the fluid grace of marathon runners, their slim legs rippling with muscle. They stride toward the middle of the ring and bow toward Scipio.

Two middle-aged referees follow behind the youths, retired centurions who will oversee the individual battles and judge the victors. Scipio has publicly insisted there be no deliberate fights to the death—he is weary of people dying on his account. His edict has prompted the six young nobles to volunteer for the engagement, hopeful it will further their own political careers. They are all patricians from Rome's most powerful families, trained since birth to fight and command.

The six patrician nobles carry shields filigreed in gold, bearing the double-eagle standard of the Roman army. They all hold a standard issue gladius in their hand, the traditional short thrusting sword that Scipio has abandoned in favor of his falcata-based gladius hispaniesis.

"Isn't that Valerius Maximus' son?" Laelius asks.

"Yes. He volunteered for the fest, in honor of Scipio."

"I know him," Marcus states. "A soft-bellied pumpkin."

"Compared to you," Laelius sniffs, "we are all soft-bellied pumpkins."

The trumpets sound again. Six thick-chested men tramp out into the ring; iron-thewed men with stout bellies to protect their organs from killing slashes.

"Ah, the gladiators," Marcus says admiringly.

The patricians' opponents are six of Rome's finest fighters, stern men who have withstood numerous tests of death in the ring. Four of them are captive Samnites, wearing only a loincloth and shin greaves. They each carry a curved square shield across their arm and grasp a short sword, weapons that are the armament of their ancient nation.[xlii]

The other two fighters are captive Greeks, they wear the hoplomachus

IV. Coming Home

armor of their country. The Greeks stand bare-chested in the middle of the ring, their legs protectively wrapped in leather, sporting a plate-sized shield in their left hand and lance in their right.

"My god, those patrician boys will be killed," exclaims Amelia.

"I think not," replies Scipio. "The gladiators will be crucified if they kill one of their opponents, unless they do it under threat of death." He spreads his hands. "The gladiators must fight to win but not die by the winning. It is a delicate balance!"

"A balance weighted toward the pretty rich boys," mutters Marcus.

The six patricians and the six gladiators line up and face one another. The young men stir their toes into the sand and tramp their feet. They are at once both nervous and eager. The gladiators stand immobile, waiting. There is a shuffling sound from another entry way, and two more men come out into the ring.

A wiry older man walks out into the ring lugging a worn gray goatskin satchel. The old man plunks himself down at the bottom of the steps and eyes the combatants, studying them as if they were livestock he might buy.

"Isn't that your medicus?" Laelius asks.

"I asked him to attend, that he might help the wounded," replies Scipio. "If the medicus says someone is beyond help, that other fellow will do his part."

A short and stocky older man follows the medicus to the steps. He wears only a tattered brown loincloth about his hairy body. His face is covered by a silver mask that shines like the sun itself. He wears a rounded bronze cap with large flying wings on it, symbolizing that he is Hermes, the messenger god who conducts souls to the underworld. The burly man drags along a stout oak cudgel, its knotted top mottled with dark brown stains.

The combatants turn and face Scipio. After a significant pause, Scipio rises slowly from his seat and beckons for Crassus to stand with him,

IV. Coming Home

playing the moment for maximum publicity. The crowds' impatient murmuring rises slowly. As it reaches the critical tipping point into unrest, Scipio raises his extended right arm and swings it down with a flourish. "Commence!" he orders.

The twelve men leap into combat, each engaging the man closest to him. The patricians fight methodically, in the manner they were trained. They keep their thick bossed scuta in front of them, using their gilded shields to shove back their opponents. Stepping lightly and gracefully, they aim their short thrusts at the gladiators' unprotected chests and arms.

The young men try to fight shield-to-shield as legionnaires would, but the gladiators wisely move to the men's flanks and backs, separating the combatants so the noblemen must fight them singly. The two referees scamper from match to match, looking for a disabling wound that would end a contest. The man with the Hermes mask stands immobile, clutching his cudgel and carefully observing each engagement.

The crowd screams and curses, delirious with blood lust and delight. Men fistfight each other in the stands, arguing lividly over who will win the duels. Dozens of women bare their breasts at the gladiators as a symbol of their love for them. Old patricians mutter quietly to each other, reminiscing about great warriors past, dropping denarii into the bettors' palms as they make their wagers.

The Forum square has become a melee of six pairs of men scrambling about, darting and thrusting at each other. The din of their blows is drowned in the sea of excitement above them, only their screams of pain can penetrate the tumult.

A hoplomachus gladiator pushes aside the shield of his youthful opponent and jabs his lance deep into the man's thigh. The patrician shrieks, drops his shield and falls to the ground. He curls into a ball and raises his right arm in supplication, his eyes bulging with fear. The gladiator raises his spear high in the pose of a killing blow, and looks at the referee.

IV. Coming Home

The crowd chants "Habe, hoc habet (He's had it!)" The referee nods and shoves his staff between the gladiator and the fallen patrician, ensuring that the victor cannot deliver the death blow. The referee grabs the gladiator's arm and thrusts his hand up, signaling his victory. The crowd cheers heartily as the panting gladiator steps to a corner of the ring, his combat done. Within minutes he is joined by a patrician who gashed open the sword arm of his Samnite opponent, ending their duel. As the two men stand silent next to each other, a pair of slaves runs out and drags the wounded patrician to the waiting medicus, amidst a chorus of boos and taunts.

Marcus Silenus leans over to Laelius. "That Samnite could have used those wounds to lure his opponent closer, and cut out his guts," He sniffs. "He is weak or stupid, especially for a gladiator!"

Laelius shakes his head and rolls his eyes heavenward. "You sound like you are still playing the role of trainer," Laelius says. "Or is it that you want to cut out a patrician's guts yourself?"

Marcus does not reply, but a smile twitches at the corners of his mouth.

Soon another gladiator joins the two victors, bleeding profusely from a stab in his shoulder. The medicus washes his wound with vinegar and stitches it up with a thin flax thread, covering it with a linen bandage. No stranger to Greek doctoring, the gladiator grunts his thanks and sits down to watch the rest of the matches. A lump of bread lands at his feet, thrown from the appreciative crowd. He dusts the sand off it and chews moodily, his eyes fixed on his fellow warriors.

Two comely young patrician women come over to stand behind the fighter, cooing invitations to meet with them that night. The gladiator grins and looks at the medicus. "It looks like you will be fine," the doctor comments, and returns to his post, standing next to the man with the Hermes mask. The gladiator nods at the women. One drops a parchment scrap into his palm. He sees an address is written upon it, and a time. He grins.

The final three pairs of combatants are evenly matched, and the bout

IV. Coming Home

lingers on. The youthful patricians move quickly and energetically, while the wily gladiators slowly stalk them, trying to wound or trip their opponent.

One patrician charges his hoplomachus opponent. He suddenly thrusts out his shield, hoping to surprise the gladiator. The Greek rams his small shield into the Roman's scutum and steps sideways, deflecting the patrician's charge. As the young man rushes past, the gladiator lashes out his foot and trips his opponent. The youth crashes to the earth, his armor clanging about him, momentarily stunned. The crowd roars with laughter, and the young nobleman's face reddens.

The Greek steps over his opponent and raises his lance, looking at the referee. The patrician drops his shield as raises his hand with his index finger extended, as if to signal surrender.

The crowd again chants "He has had it." When the referee raises the gladiator's hand, the stout old warrior lowers his lance, grateful to be done with chasing the energetic youth.

The defeated patrician suddenly vaults up from the ground and shoves his short sword deep into the man's lower stomach, carving the blade sideways to cleave his bowels asunder. The gladiator moans with pain and falls to the earth, curling into a fetal ball.

Fruit and stones rain down upon the patrician, hurled from the jeering crowd. The man with the Hermes mask leaps to his feet and lumbers over to the fallen warrior. He pulls off the gladiator's helmet, grabs his cudgel with both hands and swirls down it in a vicious arc, bashing in the man's forehead with a loudly audible crunch. The gladiator's eyes start from his head, and he slumps silently to the earth.

The executioner bends over to gently close the warrior's sightless eyes and crosses his hands over his chest. "May Charon take you safely to the underworld, warrior," he says. With a disdaining look at the treacherous patrician, the man walks back to the medicus and plops down upon the lowest step, wiping his cudgel across the sand.

The remaining Greek gladiator has been carefully fighting his

IV. Coming Home

opponent, hoping to wear him down so he can disable or disarm him. He hears the crowd chant "He's had it!" Driving his opponent into retreat, the gladiator glances over to see his comrade standing over his fallen opponent, who has his finger raised in supplication. He turns back to engage his trembling opponent, when he hears a roar from the crowd. The gladiator looks over and sees the treacherous patrician cut into his fellow gladiator's stomach. He hears the crowd jeer their disapproval.

"You cowardly shit!" the gladiator screams.

The Greek whirls into his opponent. Heedless of his own safety, he feints forward, luring the Roman's blade toward him. He swipes his small shield into the patrician's sword arm and knocks the blade flying.

In a single motion the gladiator throws down his lance and grabs his sica from his belt. He stabs the short sword into the youth's left underarm and slices the blade down to his ribs, inflicting a long but shallow cut. The patrician shrieks in pain and runs to the exit, clutching his side. Without a backward glance the Greek strides over to the patrician, catching up to him as he walks over to join the other victors.

Hearing the crowd roar, the young man turns to see the hoplomachus bearing down on him. He spits at the gladiator and crouches into a battle stance. Bearing only his dagger, the Greek gladiator rains blows upon the noble's shield and helmet, turning sideways to dodge his opponent's longer blade. The gladiator's furious assault drives the Roman backwards, and he begins to stumble.

A referee walks toward the combatants. "Here now! Break it up! The boy's had it!" The referee bawls at the hoplomachus.

The Greek realizes he only has a few seconds left for his vengeance. He raises his sword hand as if to jab at his opponent's helmet. When the patrician steps back to evade the dagger, the Greek pivots on one foot and thrusts out his other one, kicking the patrician squarely in the chest.

The young man plummets backwards and the Greek is instantly on

IV. Coming Home

him. He slashes the hamstrings of the Roman's right leg, crippling him for life. With a final, disdainful kick to the Roman's buttocks, the gladiator turns from the wailing youth and stalks to the victors.

As two slaves carry the hamstrung warrior between their shoulders the crowd's chants grow louder. Some scream "Kill him, kill him!" lusting for the gladiator's death. Many others shout out "Victory, victory!" They are delighted that a commoner has brought down a patrician.

When the gladiator reaches the side of the ring he pulls off his helmet, revealing a brown bearded young man with a hawk like nose and pointed chin. He ignores the shouts directed his way as he watches the final gladiator pummel his opponent's helmet with the butt of his sword, bringing him to his knees. A peach bounces off the Greek's head but he ignores it, watching his brother in arms.

Marcus Silenus steps down to stand next to Scipio, and leans into his ear. "That man has skills our soldiers could use." he says, and steps back to his place.

Scipio glances briefly at Marcus and chews on his lip, thinking. He knows the Greek will likely be dead before sunset, slain by one of his own that the victim's family has bribed to kill him. Or worse, the family will purchase him for extended torture. *Marcus is right. The man knows how to use elusiveness and surprise. The same tools Hannibal uses. And myself.*

When the horns signal the end of the match Scipio rises and extends his hands toward the crowd, waiting patiently for them to fall silent.

"Citizens of Rome," he bellows, dissolving the last of the crowd's murmurs. "You have brought me great honor with your presence today. I thank you." The crowd claps and cheers, grateful that a nobleman recognizes their presence. *They like humility. I must remember that.*

"We have seen many talented performers today," Scipio continues, "But none so valiant as those who fought today, all warriors that are worthy of Rome."

At those words, Laelius rolls his eyes and leans toward Marcus.

IV. Coming Home

"Except for the patricians, I would say!" Marcus gives the barest of nods as he continues to watch his commander, knowing some plan is unfolding with Scipio's words.

"In commemoration of this glorious event, I hereby declare that all of today's victors, both gladiators and noblemen, will become members of my Honor Guard. They will join me in defeating dread Hannibal and in overthrowing Carthage! Victors step forward!"

Amid the crowd's cheers, the four gladiators and two patricians walk over to face Scipio. He stands with arms upraised as if he is a god blessing mortals. "If I am elected consul...*when* I am elected consul, will you men join me in final battle against Carthage?" Hearing the crowd's roars of approbation, the fighters know they have little choice. One by one, they raise their swords to Scipio, and the volume crescendos.

"Be it so!" Scipio yells triumphantly, prompting more roars from the crowd. Scipio extends his hand to Crassus, the Pontifex. Together they exit the Forum, accompanied by Pomponia and Amelia. The crowd chants "Scipio, Scipio!" until he it out of their sight.

Cato looks inquiringly at Flaccus, who has been watching the events unfold. Flaccus closes his eyes and purses his long, thin lips as if he has bitten into a raw olive. He shakes his head forlornly. "He has the people in his purse now. He will be elected."

Cato's frowns deeply and looks away. "May Pluto take him!" he says. "He'll drag us all to Africa!"

"We are not yet done, young man," replies Flaccus. "Consul or no, we have the Senate power to usurp his Africa plans, should he want to venture into that insanity." He points over at General Fabius, who is conversing intently with the Senate leader.

"To fight a dog you bring a bigger dog," Flaccus says. "To fight a general you bring another." He waves his hand at Fabius. "General Fabius, may we talk for a bit?"

* * * * *

IV. Coming Home

HIPPO REGIUS, NORTHERN AFRICA. Masinissa's bireme coasts into the tiny bay below the shoreline's rocky promontory, followed by his house-sized transport. The two ships have just completed their journey from Iberia, and are home at last. The Numidians beach the two ships in a tree-shrouded cove and throw branches over them for camouflage.

Masinissa has landed ten miles from the prying eyes of mighty Hippo Regius, the city his deceased father, Gala, had built when he and his Massylii ruled western Numidia. Masinissa has heard that Syphax and his Masaesyli army has ventured here and are ravaging the borders of his tribal lands. He is not sure whether Masaesyli or Massylii rules his former stronghold, so he and his eight guards will have to steal into the city, returning to his homeland as spies.

Masinissa does not feel fear or regret at his return to a hostile homeland. For him, his arrival is the first step in fulfilling his dream: to reclaim all of western Numidia for his tribe, uniting east and west nations into one mighty country that will rival Carthage itself. To do this, he has covertly abandoned his alliance with Carthage and sold his future to the Romans, and to Scipio in particular.

The Numidians pull their horses to shore and prepare to reconnoiter. Masinissa leaves four guards with the ships and ventures out with the other four. Soon they are darting among the bushy trees scattered among the fertile plains outside of Hippo Regius, zig-zagging up a dirt trail toward the hilltop city center. Finding a grove of trees near the city walls, they tie their horses to them and proceed on foot, cloaked in worn gray robes.

It is a simple matter for Masinissa to elude the guards stationed about the borders of this low walled city. As a child he made a game of sneaking past them, finding the gullies and scrub that hid him from their sight, mastering the skills of elusiveness that have made his Numidians the infamous "ghost warriors" of the war, men who appear from nowhere to destroy their foe.

As night settles into the bayside city, Masinissa and his men glide quietly through its streets, lugging along the large wicker baskets of a

IV. Coming Home

street merchant. He notices a number of guards bear the tribal markings of his uncle's Massylii tribe, not his father's, and he realizes his own people no longer control his father's home. *Are these men enemies or allies?* Masinissa wonders. *I have to find out who controls this town.*

Masinissa sends two of his guards back to the ships with word that he will be detained a day or two. He and his guards spend the night at a rooming house on the edge of the small city, a place where no questions are asked of men with money.

The next day he and his men are sitting in the town square, huddled against the stone walls of the government building. They hunch over their begging bowls with their hands clasped in supplication, looking at nothing but seeing everything. Morning creeps on to early afternoon, and the three beggars' bowls fill with small coins—war has not affected his people's legendary generosity.

Finally, Masinissa sees what he has come for. Two tribal leaders enter the stone block meeting hall next to him, men from his uncle's tribe. He watches anxiously, but no chieftains appear from his own tribal group.

Four armed warriors walk into the square, and Masinissa's body tenses. Two of them are officers of Syphax's tribe, his sworn enemies, and the other two are Carthaginians. He forces his head down to avoid staring at the unwelcome alliance, breathing heavily with anger—and confusion. *Why would Syphax ally himself with Carthage, when he has signed a treaty with the Romans? The bastard does not need Gisgo and his minions to fight me, he has a hundred thousand warriors.*

Masinissa frowns. *Hmph. Gisgo must have offered him something really precious for him to betray his alliance with Scipio.* And then, with a sickening lurch to his stomach, it occurs to him. *Sophonisba.*

Masinissa rises abruptly. He hurries out of the square, and his men rush to catch up to him. The young prince weaves through the back streets until he is into the tent slums of the city, a place where the city militia rarely venture.

Motioning for his men to follow, Masinissa slides two stones blocks

IV. Coming Home

from the base of the wall and plunges into the outlying scrub. He scrambles frantically through the roughlands and bushes, heedless that he can be seen from the walls. His companions follow as best they can, looking back anxiously to see if any sentries have spied them, wondering if their leader has lost his mind.

The three men are soon at the grove, gasping for breath. Masinissa vaults onto his horse and gallops back toward his ships. His guards jump onto their mounts, looking at one another with fearful exasperation. The trio dashes across the plain riding at full gallop until they are back at the landing cove. Masinissa leaps from his still moving horse and trots toward the grounded ships.

"Pack up for a long journey," he bawls to his men. "I am going to find Gisgo."

At dusk Masinissa rides out from the ships with four of his men, galloping hard toward Carthage, two hundred miles away. For five days the men ride through the desert plains and mountains of Syphax's realm, heading east toward Gisgo's domain. Each day Masinissa's men have to cajole him into stopping before he kills them or the horses. The regal young prince takes little food or water, consumed with dread about his beloved's fate.

On the fifth day Masnissa's entourage arrives at a hilltop overlooking Carthage. The vast metropolis sprawls below them, its wide streets lined with elegantly carved statues and stately trees. Hundreds of spear-carrying guards patrol the twenty-mile circumference of its thick stone walls, their white linen armor shining like polished eggs, their domed brass helmets blazing in the desert sun.

But the city's splendor is lost on the young prince; his heart is filled with dread. Before his men can stop him, Masinissa gallops down the hill toward the city gates. Masinissa pulls up beneath the forty-foot walls that surround the gigantic main gates, a portal so large a hundred men could march abreast through it.

Several sentries peer out from the twin towers flanking the gates. "What is your business here?" barks a leathery old guard.

IV. Coming Home

"I am Masinissa, rightful king of all Numidia. I have come from far Iberia to meet with General Gisgo."

A bushy-bearded man of slight frame limps to the fore of the sentries. The indigo-plumed crest on his helmet identifies him as the captain of the guards. He sneers down at the regal young Numidian.

"General Gisgo has been expecting you for some time," he says curtly. "Wait here." Masinissa stirs restlessly on his horse, and finally dismounts to stand next to it. *Does Gisgo know I met with Scipio?* Masinissa wonders. *Is that why I'm denied entry? How could he? Am I walking to my death?*

The captain reappears on the parapet. "General Gisgo is engaged for the rest of the day. He will see you tomorrow morning, when the phoenix flies from this tower."

Masinissa blinks incredulously. "You did tell him that Prince Masinissa calls on him? Recently arrived from Iberia?"

The captain barely masks his sneer. "I did tell him, *Prince* Masinissa. He said for you to return tomorrow."

Masinissa swallows his rage and looks at the captain. "And what of his daughter Sophonisba. Is she well?"

The captain merely blinks at him, and turns to leave. "Tomorrow. When the flag flies."

The captain shouts an order to his men, and they resume their patrol about the parapets. Masinissa mounts his horse and stands in front of the gates for half an hour, looking expectantly at the walkway. Finally, he turns and leads his men into the hills, glancing back at the merchants and peasants that the sentries wave in through the gates. *I should have posed as a peddler or beggar*, he thinks ruefully. *But how could I know he would treat me like this?*

The next morning Masinissa and his men approach the open main gates where the phoenix flag proudly flies. As he draws near, the gates close in front of him. He is left waiting with several farmers towing

IV. Coming Home

oxcarts of vegetables into the city. An hour later Gisgo appears on the parapet, flanked by his Sacred Band. He stares down at his former ally.

"Why won't you admit me?" demands Masinissa.

Gisgo shakes his head. "You are not welcome here, Prince, it is best you depart." Gisgo smiles haughtily, "I only grant you audience out of respect for your past services." He grins at his Sacred Band guards. "And to get rid of you!" The guards laugh uproariously. Masinissa's hand creeps toward his throwing dagger.

He does not know about my pact with Scipio, Masinissa realizes, and stays his hand. "Why should I have to depart?" Masinissa asks. "We are allies."

Gisgo stares out into space, as if studying the hills behind the Numidian. "I have a new ally now," he says flatly. "Syphax and I have struck a bond. He has deserted Scipio. He fights for me."

And you for him, bastard. Masinissa swallows hard, forcing himself to pose the question he dreads to hear answered. "But I am betrothed to your daughter, am I not? Sophonisba and I are to be wed," he says, his voice trembling in spite of himself. "I would do nothing to break our agreement," Masinissa adds, hating himself for his toadying.

Gisgo snorts. "Betrothed? You have tarried too long, rebel. Sophonisba has wed Syphax."

The words ring in Masinissa's head. His heart pounds in his ears. There is a flash of light. A guard screams as the throwing knife pierces his eye, missing Gisgo by a hair's breadth. Gisgo dives under the protective parapet as his Sacred Band form a shield wall in front of him. The tower guards rear back to throw their spears, but the prince has already vanished into the plains.

"Bring him to me!" bawls Gisgo. "Bring me his head!" By the time the Carthaginian cavalry storm out from the gates, little can be seen but a distant cloud of dust.

The erstwhile prince of Numidia gallops for hours. He and his men

IV. Coming Home

pound across the coastal ridges and forests until he is far from the humiliation of Carthage. As their horses begin to flag Masinissa pulls up in a meadow veined with small streams from the hills. He jumps off his horse and rushes to a nearby stream. Kneeling next to it, he laves his face again and again as his men watch, puzzled.

Masinissa rises and faces them. His face streams with water, and perhaps more. "You will return to the ships and wait for me," he says huskily, and swallows before he continues. "Seven days. If I am not back, return to Iberia and bring all our men back to our tribal homeland."

The men stand silent, looking sullenly at one another. "Where will you go?" one finally ventures.

"I am going to pay a visit to Syphax in the city of Siga," Masinissa replies. "That is another thing that once was ours, that the bastard has taken from me." He clenches the pommel his sword. "I go to reclaim them both..."

V. DEPARTURE

CURIA HOSTILIA, ROMAN FORUM, 205 BCE. The last of the twenty senators files in from the rear chambers, taking their seats in the back rows of the Senate. They are all Latin Party members, entering late to signify their disapproval of the man who will be addressing them this morning. The senators join the rest of their party on the right side of the curved rows of seats. The Latins congregate so that their protests might have a conjoined force, for they fully expect to jeer the Hellenic sympathizer who ordered this convocation.

Consul Publius Cornelius Scipio faces his Senate, a slight smile on his face. Scipio wears that most glorious of togas, the consular toga picta, a solid purple toga resplendent with a gold embroidery of eagles and warriors along its borders. He wears the regal toga as a sign that he is no longer the boy the senators scoffed at when he volunteered to face the Three Generals in Iberia. He is a consul, and he will not be disrespected.

Now, even the crustiest Latin cannot help but notice the utter confidence of his bearing. Scipio's head is held high as he coolly watches the last of the Latins take his seat. When all have finally seated themselves, he walks out from behind the rostrum and stands in the middle of the semicircular stone floor.

"I am honored to be addressing you today, fellow senators," Scipio begins, pacing slowly in front of them. "When last I came here I volunteered to go to Iberia and take on the task of conquering my father and uncle's killers, the indomitable Three Generals." A slight smile crosses his face. "At that time no general would take this task upon themselves, thinking it impossible. No one..." Scipio pauses, letting the weight of his words sink in. "And now my deeds are done, my commission in Iberia has expired, and my campaign's achievements are a matter of record. And the future lies ahead."

V. Departure

Scipio glances toward open doors of the Senate entrance, where a group of men can be seen gathering in the hallway. Scipio gestures toward them. "Before I speak to you of my intentions as consul, perhaps you should know how our Iberian campaign fared, from the mouths of those who live there. They have more to say than my scroll of accomplishments could ever hope to tell you."

Scipio motions for the group to come forward. Ten middle-aged men stride into the room. They are clad in rich, multicolored robes of silk and linen, bedecked with jeweled rings and silver wrist clasps—obviously men of wealth and import. They approach Scipio, bow their heads to him and turn to face the Senate, their faces dignified and stolid.

Scipio nods toward the group and looks at the Senate. "This is a delegation that arrived yesterday from Iberia," he says, smiling back at them. "They tell me they were sent by their people and their senate, to speak to you about the war in Iberia. They are all from Saguntum, because it is our largest and richest allied city."

Scipio smirks, eyeing Flaccus. "I thought you should hear testimony, because some have accused me exaggerating the breadth of our achievements there, though I cannot guess who would perpetrate such lies!"

Scipio bows toward the group and gestures for them to approach the speaking rostra. A stout man in an orange silk robe steps up to the speaker's platform. His hands nervously clench its polished teak border. He pulls at his bushy gray beard. "Guh, greetings, Senators," he stammers. "It is an honor to be here."

"We are emissaries from Saguntum. We have been sent by our senate and citizenry." The man blares so loudly that several senators clap their hands over their ears. The delegate blushes, and softens his tone. "I am Senator Baldomero." He looks about anxiously, unsure of what to do.

"Continue, Senator," urges Glabius the Senate leader, a wizened old praetor who sits to the side of Scipio. Baldomero nervously clears his throat to speak.

V. Departure

"As you all would know, we have been ever loyal to Rome, but the Carthaginians came and overwhelmed us. When they killed Publius and Gnaeus Scipio, we lost our last hope and succumbed to the Three Generals." He bows his head, ashamed. "We thought we would be slaves to Carthage forever."

He turns to his compatriots and smiles at them before returning his attention to the Senate, his seamed eyes shining. He waves his right hand toward Scipio. "Then, to our surprise, you sent us General Scipio here, seeing him now makes us think we are the most fortunate people in all Saguntum! For we have seen him declared consul—the man who was our hope, our succor, our salvation—and we shall be reporting the sight to our fellow citizens!" [xliii]

Scipio looks challengingly at the senators, enjoying the Latins' discomfiture. "Many thanks, honored Baldomero. I hope to see you addressing our people in the Forum tomorrow."

With those words the Iberian Senator bows deeply, as do his compatriots. They file from the Senate chambers. The senators applaud loudly—Saguntum has long been one of Rome's most valuable allies. The applause continues until the retinue disappears.

Flaccus looks at Fabius, his lean face ugly with disappointment and anger. Fabius waggles his right index finger at him. *Just wait and see*, he signals. Flaccus nods, knowing Fabius will attack Scipio's plan.

Glabius raises himself up on his stout wooden staff and bangs it on the floor, calling the Senate to order. He turns to Scipio. "Ah, yesss... gratitude for introducing this delegation to us, humm ... we are delighted that our allies so value you. Yes, hum..."

The leader blinks several times, trying to recall what he is to do next. "Oh yes! Now, if you will, Consul Scipio, we need to hear your plans! You will go to Sicily, of course, since Consul Crassus cannot leave Italia, that is."

General Fabius levers himself upright and stares haughtily at the young consul. "Tell us now, young Consul. How do you plan to

V. Departure

conduct the war?"

Scipio gives the barest of smiles. His eyes twinkle. "I am not here to conduct the war, but to finish it," he declares. [xliv]

Fabius bobs his head, as if he is hearing something he expected. "I think you seek glory over victory, now that you have had a taste of both."

The old general spreads his sinewy arms out toward his fellows, turning about as he speaks. He ignores Scipio. "If your goal is the supreme glory of finishing off the Punic War, why not go straight from here and focus hostilities where Hannibal is located? Why not do that rather than take the circuitous route you propose of crossing to Africa and hoping that Hannibal will follow you there? You could go to Carthage later, after you have vanquished Hannibal here!" [xlv]

Scipio takes deep breath, preparing his rejoinder. He knows that Fabius' argument has some strategic plausibility, but he knows it is mainly motivated by the Latins' desire to take over the farmlands in Northern Italia once Hannibal is gone or defeated—and Carthage itself will be forgotten. *They still think like farmers*, he muses. *Carthage rises as an empire, and they want Rome to stay a village. Enough of this shit.*

"Quintus Fabius, I shall have the adversary you tender—Hannibal, that is—but let me draw him after me rather than have *him* hold me here." His voice rises, his head pointed to the heavens. "Let me force him to fight in his own country and in Carthage. Rather than some crumbling forts in Bruttium. Carthage will be the prize!" [xlvi]

Scores of Hellenic and undeclared senators rise to their feet and cheer, while the Latins jump up and boo, pointing their thumbs down. Cries of "Victory!" "Nay!" "On to Africa!" and "Embezzler!" ring off the stone walls, as the staid Senate erupts into a verbal free-for-all.

Glabius booms his staff onto the floor, his flaccid arms wobbling with the effort. He glowers at the squabbling senators and raises his staff high, signaling them to quiet. "Fabius has the floor," he shouts.

Fabius walks from his seat and stands next to Scipio, facing the

V. Departure

Senate. "When you consider this matter, fellow senators, do not forget that General Mago is rumored to be making his way to Rome from North Italia. A campaign to Africa would take away our best legions and ship them to Africa, while the Barca brothers move to join forces. Hannibal himself could not have planned a better way to weaken us!"

Another round of protests and cheers erupts. Scipio can hear the affirmations are outnumbering the dissents, and he knows his proposal is in danger. His anxiety rises, and his right hand begins to shake. He clenches his fist to disguise it, biting his lower lip with fearful realization. He must risk all or lose all.

"Hear me" he bellows commandingly, "Hear me now! Beyond the two consular legions that are my right, I will not levy any of our troops for the campaign. None!" These words quiet the tumult to a murmuring skepticism, and Scipio knows it is time to propose the undesirable. "I will make my own army from volunteers, if you will grant me the authority!" [xlvii]

Scipio sees many nod their silent approval. *Time to make my final offer, gods help me if they accept it!* "Senators, I expect the usual consular allotments for my legions, and ships appropriate for a campaign. But I will raise all my campaign's money and resources from contributions. Do you hear me? Rome will not pay for Africa, though it gain unimaginable fortune from the venture!"

The senators erupt into more internecine arguments, but Scipio can tell that the tide of agreement has swung his way. Following the Senate custom, each senator stands and declares his approval or disapproval of Scipio's proposals.

Flaccus grins at Scipio's words. *He has fallen into the trap.* He looks at Fabius until he catches the old general's eye, and winks. Fabius nods imperceptibly, and resumes his seat.

When the last senator has spoken, Glabius shakes himself from his drowse and rises from his chair. "If there are no further replies to Scipio, I call the vote!" the old man bellows sternly. Several Latins and Hellenics stand up and raise their hands to speak.

V. Departure

Before Glabius can call on any of them, one of the senior senators stands up to speak. He is well into his seventies, pale and thin with age. But his back is ramrod straight and his grey eyes are steady and clear. A former general, he is one of the most respected men in Rome, an independent thinker unaffiliated with either party. He looks inquisitively at Scipio, his expression free of acquiescence or challenge.

"Consul Scipio, I have heard that if we do not grant you leave to venture from Sicily to Africa, you will take your proposals to the people themselves.[xlviii] Is that correct?"

Scipio looks challengingly at the Senate, then slowly grins. "You have the truth of it. And when I do, our esteemed Saguntine emissaries will address them, too. They will tell the citizens what they have told you."

Many of the senators frown at these words. If they vote against Scipio they will risk their own bills to vengeful vetoes from the Tribunes of the Plebs. Several of the most vociferous Latins sigh heavily, and sit down. Seeing their opponents refrain from attack, the Hellenics quietly sit down, wanting to let well enough alone.

Glabius peers into the senators' faces for five heartbeats, waiting for another speaker. When none speak out, he calls for a vote. Those in favor of Scipio's proposal are to stand on the left side of the room, those opposed will gather on the right.

The Hellenics quickly group to the left, with several abashed Latins joining them. The undecided senators see that the two Tribunes of the Plebs are standing in the rear of the chambers, the men who are eyes and ears of the citizens. They know the commoners will learn how they voted, and they move to the left.

An overwhelming majority approves Scipio's proposal. Scipio bows his acknowledgement of the vote. *Fortuna bless me, they accepted my proposals. Now what do I do about it?*

The Senate leader calls for the vote to be recorded and immediately raises the next issue of discussion, troops and resource allotments for each of the consuls. Knowing this is a privileged discussion, Scipio

V. Departure

turns about and walks toward the open doors.

Before Scipio can exit, Fabius rises and shouts at him, his voice quaking with anger. "When you catch sight of Africa from the sea, Publius Cornelius, you will certainly think your assignments in Spain to have been child's play!" [xlix]

Scipio stops. He turns around slowly and looks Fabius in the eye. Then he smirks. "Good, I am ready for some adult entertainment, after dealing with fussy children!"

He raises his hands to silence the laughter. "Italy has been tormented for too long. Let her finally have some rest, and let Africa have her turn of burning and devastation." [l]

The young consul spins on his heel and marches out, leaving a red-faced Fabius behind him.

* * * * *

ESTATE OF LUCIUS VALERIUS FLACCUS, SABINA VALLEY. Flaccus, Cato, and Fabius recline on couches placed in the garden patio of Flaccus' sprawling estate, perched atop one of the valley's highest hills. They are taking an evening meal there, all but unaware of the setting sun casting its fading rays across the lush rolling hills of Rome's outskirts, turning the windswept wheat fields into waves of rolling gold.

"Think what would happen if the young fool should somehow win a battle in Africa, or broker some type of peace there. The Scipios would control the city for years. And Amelia's clan, the Amelii, they would be right next to them!" Flaccus' jumps from his couch and stalks about the paved patio, his face flushed with anger. The three men have come here to conspire before the Senate votes on Scipio's troop allotments tomorrow. Their mood is grim, now that Scipio has been granted the commission to Sicily.

Cato turns to Fabius. "General, you have been give a triumph for your battles against Hannibal. Can you convince them that we need all our legions here to fight him?"

V. Departure

Fabius stands up. "Well, we do need all our legions here, some are still too raw to send against Hannibal or Mago." He sputters a laugh. "The other generals, I think they would be sympathetic to that idea."

"We cannot forbid Scipio to go to Africa. As governor of Sicily that is part of his responsibility. The people would riot if they found we put a halter on him. He has promised to go there and end the war."

"That leaves us little choice, then." muses Fabius.

"Perhaps it leaves us the best choice of all," adds Cato. "Remember when Scipio volunteered to go to Iberia? We gave him two legions and 'permission' to recruit the rest as best he could." He stands up, excited. "Deny him the two consular legions that he requested, but grant him permission to raise whatever he men he can muster here in Rome."

Cato's eyes gleam triumphantly. "We are down to recruiting slaves for our legions. Let him see how much luck he has trying to find his own recruits here!"

"He is a consul, Cato," grumps Flaccus. "He has to have two consular legions. We cannot be so transparent as to deny him his rights."

Fabius spreads his hands and cackles. "Oh no, we do not deny him, we leave open the opportunity for him to recruit two veteran legions if matters dictate he do so. The ones in Sicily! They will be his consular legions."

Flaccus smiles. "You mean the Cannenses, the two disgraced legions who lost to Hannibal at Cannae?"

Fabius nods. "Just so, the fifth and the sixth.[li] And whatever is left of Marcellus' old legions that failed at Herdonia. Those men have done nothing in Sicily since the Senate exiled them there. All they do is eat and lay about, getting old and drawing pay. Let him go to war with two legions of old men and failures!"

Cato rubs his chin, thinking. "In truth, we do not have the ships he would need anyway. You could allot him a few quadriremes and transports, enough for Sicily but not enough to for him sail to Africa

V. Departure

and keep supplies coming to him from Sicily."

Flaccus grins. "Ha! Let that son of a bitch fight Carthage with recruits and cowards—if he can even get them there!" He shrugs. "And if they are wiped out, the loss in minimal."

Flaccus sees Cato and Fabius staring at him, disgusted. "Why not? He *is* a true son of a bitch, the son of that meddling bitch Pomponia." He shifts uneasily in his seat. "I have not finished with her!"

"Then we have a proposal to take into the Senate," says Fabius. "We keep our best legions and let Scipio have whatever he may scrounge!" The old man sweeps his arm out to emphasize his point, and it smashes into an aged slave bringing them a tray of wine. The gaunt little man falls to one knee to grab the bronze goblets clattering across the stone steps.

"Apologies, Dominus, Apologies! I will bring more wine."

An embarrassed Flaccus pushes him away from the mess. "Off with you! I will have it cleaned up. Go!" The slave scrabbles together the goblets and trays and scuttles from his angry master.

"Why don't you sell that old goat?" snarls Cato, wiping at a wine stain on his old worn tunic. "He has certainly outlived his usefulness."

"He has been in my family for decades," replies Flaccus, avoiding Cato's accusing eyes.

Cato sniffs. "Slaves are livestock. You sell them when they are no longer of profit to you." [lii]

Flaccus blinks at him, and grins self-consciously. "Well, perhaps I am too soft, then," he chuckles. "But my mind would bother me if I did sell him. I could not engage in such miserly behavior."

Cato shakes his head in disgust. "It is a matter of standing by our honored agricultural principles of utility, valuing only that which is useful. You should know that."

V. Departure

Flaccus nods. *And you are outliving your utility to me*, he thinks. *Gods save us if we have a nation of Catos.*

"That does remind me," continues Flaccus, looking at Fabius "When we present the Senate proposal we should push to have friend Cato elected quaestor to Scipio. That will give us a pair of eyes to follow him. We will see if those rumors about him smuggling plunder are true." *And it will get Cato away from me for a while.* Flaccus rubs his hands eagerly. "Who knows? We may yet try the people's 'hero' in court for theft!"

"I am grateful for such an office, should the Senate think I deserve it," intones Cato. "But I have told you before: I lie for no man, and I lie about no man."

Flaccus grins fatuously, his sly eyes belying his smile. "Oh no, we would not expect such, most honorable Cato. You have only to be yourself. That will more than suffice!"

The next day, Scipio and Coconsul Publius Crassus are called in separately to receive their army designations from the Senate. Crassus is assigned to Bruttium, there to prevent Hannibal from gathering strength and heading toward Rome. As is customary, Crassus is assigned two consular legions, two of the four that are presently surrounding Hannibal. He is also assigned the standard budget of grain and payroll to sustain his army for a year. The Pontifex windily accepts the terms and leaves to prepare for his departure.

Scipio enters the chamber. His heart beats anxiously but he holds his head high. Glabius wastes no time in preliminaries, having heard enough speeches in Scipio's last visit. Scipio is bluntly informed that he is assigned to the region of Sicily, the enormous island that is the geographic bridge between Rome and Carthage. Glabius unrolls a papyrus scroll and proceeds to read it out loud before the Senate.

"Publius Cornelius Scipio. You are hereby granted leave to cross to Africa, if you think it is in the interests of the state," [liii]

Scipio scowls "The interests of the state? Do you think I would do it

V. Departure

for personal enjoyment?"

The Senate leader coughs, and continues. "In Sicily, you will have the thirty ships that retiring consul Gaius Servilius had commanded.[liv] You may take whatever ships you can acquire on your own, in keeping with your promise to find your own resources. You are granted leave to appoint your own commanders for your army and navy."

Scipio blinks incredulously "Only thirty warships? To protect Sicily and the coastal waters? And for a war in Africa?"

Glabius drones on, heedless of Scipio's sarcasm. "In keeping with your promise not to levy troops, your army will be composed of whatever volunteers you may recruit in Rome and Italia, and whatever supplies you may gather from the allies before you leave.[lv] You may acquire your consular legions from the troops in Sicily, there are more than enough soldiers there." Glabius rolls up the scroll and gives it to Scipio. "That is all."

"You have chained me!" Scipio blurts, his face reddening. "What profit is it for me to be granted leave to attack Africa, if you do not even provide me some proper legions? And throw me a few tired old ships that must stay in Sicily? Would you send a legionnaire to war without sword or shield? By Mars' spear, this is an insult!"

Flaccus stands up and waggles his finger at Scipio. "In spite of the plunder you brought from Iberia, our war budget is facing a financial deficit.[lvi] We have had to sell valuable farmland in Capua to meet our military expenses. Be not so childish as to think you are the only general with needs!"

A young senator stands up, eager to console Scipio. "You might get more men, General. You have leave to gather what troops you may find in Sicily. There are good men there. Please be patient."

Scipio snorts his derision, and the red-faced young senator quietly resumes his seat.

The conqueror of Iberia looks across the faces in the Senate. Some Senators look disappointed, and others delighted, still others merely

V. Departure

bored. Scipio measures his words carefully before he speaks. "This has all the markings of a Senate compromise, an ill-made mess of contradictions. I could not go to Africa without more legions."

Fabius stands, evidently pleased at the turn of affairs. "Africa? You can best end this war by keeping Sicily from the enemy, while Crassus and the praetors wear down Hannibal until he goes home."

Scipio looks wonderingly at the august body. "And what would Hannibal do when he went home? He would recruit more warriors! You just do not grasp it. The tides of history have changed. The sea is no longer our protector from invasion, it is the means for enemy incursion. [lvii] To end the war we must strike our enemies' heart, not run them from our shores."

Scipio throws up his hands. "I promised my father I would protect Rome and I will do it the only way I know. I swear upon my unborn children, I will not be stopped by your tepid rules and compromises. Africa will fall to my sword!"

He points his finger toward the open doors of the Curia Hostilia. "Two days hence, I address the people about my needs. We will see where their sympathies lie!"

Scipio stalks from the Senate chambers, heedless of the applause and jeers.

SCIPIO DOMUS. Consul Scipio pads through the atrium carrying a small silver plate of food. He pauses before a large alcove near the front door, a recess that contains the family lararium. Scipio places a plate of olives and cheese on a narrow shelf that holds statues of Janus, god and protector of doorways, and Vesta, goddess of hearth and nourishment.

"Please protect our family, and bring them health," he prays to the clay figures. "I fear we are in great danger from our enemies."

Scipio steps back from the alcove and turns to the wall next to it. He raises his right arm. "Greetings, Scipios," he says reverently. "I hope you look upon me with favor."

V. Departure

There, arranged in a pyramid, are six wax death masks of his ancestors, legionary generals all. His father's mask is at the top, its eyes closed in a peaceful repose that belies his agonizing death. Scipio swallows hard and looks up at the likeness of stern but loving Publius Cornelius Scipio, feeling like a boy again. He bends to one knee and bows his head.

"Father, I work to fulfill my promise to you. I will defend Rome from its enemies, no matter the cost. And if Fortuna smiles on me, I will defeat Hannibal and end these fourteen years of strife."

Scipio rises and stares at the mask, feeling his right hand twitch. "Father, I do not have enough ships or men to conquer Africa, should Hannibal come there to meet me." He smiles boyishly. "If you should see Fortuna where you are, please ask her to favor me with a few more legions. And a dozen more quinqueremes!"

"You have always made your own fortune, son. That was how you became General Scipio."

Scipio turns to see his mother watching him. Her hands are clasped to her breast, eyes shining with pride. "And now you are a consul! Your father would be so proud of you!"

"You and Amelia are the reason I am a consul, mother. I know naught of politics, but you rallied the people to me."

"We rallied them because you gave them hope, because you have defeated all you opposed. And they know you will do the same against dread Hannibal."

She looks up at her husband's mask, her eyes distant. "Would your father were here to help you save Rome. Since Marcellus fell to Hannibal, all others fear to fight the Carthaginian. But the Sword of Rome would fight him without hesitation." She smiles at her son. "As would you, if given the chance."

Pomponia walks around Scipio to stand in front of him, dignified as a queen. She places her hand firmly on Scipio's shoulder, and looks commandingly into his eyes. "Dear heart, you must rally the people to

V. Departure

help you build an army, while you still have their ears. As the poet says, 'act now, the time for profit is short.' I fear the whisper campaigns of the Latins will soon be starting again."

"But I have no soldiers or funds. And only a few ships to take with me. What can I tell them that is promising?"

Pomponia shakes his shoulder, as if he were a naughty boy. "What you have always told them: the truth in your heart, no more or less." She smiles conspiratorially. "Tell them of your dreams. Your speech about Poseidon helping you take Carthago Nova is a legend."

Scipio nods. "I hear you, Mother. I will speak to them in their words, about the truth."

"Ah, we knew you would!" says Pomponia. "Amelia has already started the propaganda for your cause. By tomorrow banners will be flying in Rome and the allied towns. Slogans will be painted on the walls. They will call upon all Romans to join your army." She glares at her son. "But you must act now upon our initiative!"

Scipio kisses his mother's cheek and wanders off toward his room, lost in thought about stratagems for waging his political war in Rome.

Four days later, Scipio stands on the top steps of the Senate building, facing the thousands of freedmen and nobles who have gathered in the square to hear his first consular speech to the public. People are draped over all the statues and columns surrounding the Senate, but the chamber's wide steps are kept clear by Scipio's consular guards, to protect Scipio from his admirers. A man-sized plaster statue of the multi-headed Greek monster Hydra stands next to Scipio. A score of senators surround the statue, looking curiously at it.

Scipio has donned the same ceremonial armor he wore six years ago, when he volunteered to take the war to Iberia—when he was an untested boy trying to sway the crowd. But this time his iridescent bronze is backdropped with the dark purple of a consul's tunic, and a blood red cape flows down from his shoulders. This time, his once-smooth face is lined with the tolls of sickness and leadership. Even so,

V. Departure

his eyes shine with confidence and his chin is held high. He is ready to fight for his campaign, on the battlefield of Rome's Forum.

Scipio faces the cheering crowd. He raises his arms high as they chant his name, but he quickly lowers them when he sees his hands are shaking. *Steady. Show confidence or you will lose them.*

Scipio's coconsul, the Pontifex Maximus, opens the ceremony with the customary sacrifices and prayers to the gods. At Scipio's behest no animals are killed today—only wine, cheese and fruit are burnt in a sacred votive, food sacrificed as symbols of life.

Two Hellenic senators provide some extended laudations about Scipio's achievements. Scipio stands immobile during these long speeches, his face a stone. The crowd stirs restlessly, waiting for their hero to speak. When the second senator has finished, a juggler dances to the front, bouncing four balls of his knees. He juggles the balls with his hands and his mouth pipes play a lively tune while he performs a prancing dance. The crowd laughs and applauds, flinging small coins and the cavorting performer.

Scipio smiles with satisfaction. *Now they will not be so bored.* Scipio hired the juggler after watching him delight the crowd at Scipio's gladiatorial games. He knows the crowd needs a diversion from any more speeches, if they are to attend to his own. They also need a reminder of the games that celebrated his Iberian conquest.

When the juggler has pranced away, Scipio walks to the edge of the top step and stands silently, his cape flapping in the breeze. His penetrating eyes roam across every corner of the multitude, staring into individual faces, giving his people the impression he is looking at each one of them.

"Salve, citizens of Rome!" Scipio shouts, spreading wide his arms. "Gratitude for electing me as your consul." Scipio descends four of the steps, drawing closer to the crowd. "Now I ask you to have faith in me once again, and join me on a mighty adventure to Africa, where I may accomplish what you elected me to do—end this war!"

V. Departure

Cheers rise from the crowd, and the shouts crescendo as he steps closer to the citizenry, pausing to spread his hands across the multitude. Scipio descends several more steps until his feet are near the citizens who crowd the base of the steps.

"As you all know, Hannibal's army is camped on the shores of Bruttium, by Kroton. Our generals fear to engage him there; instead they stand passive, watching him gathering his strength. Soon the Carthaginian will again venture forth to capture our provinces, ransack our towns, and assault our cities. Another Cannae could happen if we ignore him. But I say that shall not be!"

The crowd roars its agreement. Scipio marches back up the steps to stand next to the Hydra statue. Once again, he raises his arms high and quiets the crowd. "You all know the legend of the Hydra, the many-headed beast that sprung a new head for every one that was cut off, killing all until Hercules slew it. Citizens, I tell you now that Carthage is our Hydra. Its heads are their generals, stern commanders such as Mago, Hasdrubal, and Gisgo. I have defeated all of them, and cut those heads from the Hydra. But two more have sprung up to attack us—dread Hannibal moves north to join his brother Mago, and together they will march on Rome!

A muttering cry of dismay wells in the crowd. "Yea, but even Hannibal is but another head of the Carthaginian Hydra. If we cut his head off here in Italy, more generals will spring forth from its African body. We must kill the beast itself, and its heart beats in Carthage!"

Scipio raises a clenched fist, slowly turning to every part of the roaring multitude. His face is determined but his eyes exult, as if witnessing Carthage's defeat already.

Standing in the back row behind Scipio, Cato watches with resentful respect. *The patrician whelp can speak, I give him that.*

Flaccus slouches in the front row, his disgust plain on his face—he knows Scipio is winning over the people and the Tribunes of the Plebs. Flaccus begins his plans to hobble him.

V. Departure

Fabius merely watches from his seat to the side, waiting patiently for the fuss to be over, unalarmed at Scipio's triumph. He believes Scipio has been given an insurmountable task, and all his talk is nothing but crow-pleasing rhetoric. His Fabian strategy of conquest by attrition will be the solution to Hannibal, he is sure. Scipio will probably kill himself with his rash assault on Africa, and Fabius will not have to worry about him.

Scipio flashes out his falcata and holds it high, making sure its brightly polished blade is angled to catch the sun's rays. The weapon gleams like a thunderbolt from the heavens. The crowd stills. "To slay a Hydra is a formidable task, even Hercules required the help of the gods. And so I need your help, citizens of Rome, that we might slay our beast." Scipio turns and walks back up the steps.

"How can we help?" cries a voice from the crowd. "Go destroy Carthage!" rings out another.

Scipio walks over to the Hydra statue and puts a hand on its neck. He raises his sword high above the statue, gazing at the rapt crowd. The square is silent save for the crying of babies and the barking of dogs.

"Centuries ago, we Romans left our fields to repel the Sabines and Samnites, way back when the godlike Dentatus led us to victory. I ask you now, join me to repel the Carthaginian menace. We will not wait for the enemy to come to our walls, we will carry the war to this aggressor in his own land! We will break down Carthage's gates before they break down ours. Then the Hydra's heads will threaten us no more, because we will have killed its body!"

Scipio arcs his blade into the trunk of the plaster statue, his face grimacing with effort. The cleaver-like falcata explodes the plaster Hydra, sending its pieces flying into the crowd. The heads break apart and roll down the steps to the outspread arms of the crowd. Scores of Romans scramble about the steps, grabbing at shards of the crumbling heads, triumphantly holding them aloft. Deafening chants of "Scipio, Scipio!" ring throughout the square.

Scipio feels his right hand tremble. He is at the moment when his

V. Departure

campaign will be won or lost.

"I have no legions to go with me, my people. I have only you. You must be my army!"

Scipio spreads wide his hands. "All who will join me, step forward." He looks at the people in front of him and pushes his arms out, as if shooing them away. "Make way for Scipio's citizen army, my friends. Those who will fight for me, step out now!"

A score of young men jostle their way to the front. Then two score, then a hundred. Then several hundred. Then thousands. Scipio watches in awed amazement. He swallows hard, willing his eyes not to tear, struggling to maintain his gravitas.

The men continue to step forward, men of all ages and social strata, their faces firm with noble purpose. Scipio sees an entire legion of volunteers forming before him. *I am blessed,* is all he can say to himself, over and over.

The additions finally start to dwindle, but by now the volunteers fill half of the Forum Square. Scipio points to five tables placed on the adjoining temples' steps, each attended by two of his centurions "My men are there at those tables in front of the temples," he shouts, his message echoed by his guards standing below him. "See where the cohort standards are displayed? Give my men your name and origin and they will place them in the books. If you meet our age and health requirements you will become a soldier in our new army. You will become part of the legions that will be known forever as the saviors of Rome!"

Scipio looks past the volunteers to the people gathered along the sides and back, at the women, elders, children, and handicapped. "Those of you who must remain here, you can also serve. We have need of grain, weapons, tools, and shipbuilding materials. Can you help us? We have sent requests for help throughout the Italia provinces, but your gifts are needed, too. Bring what you can spare to the Campus Martius. Spread the word to your countrymen."

V. Departure

As the volunteers press to be signed in, Scipio gives them a final message. "In a fortnight I will meet you here, bring what food you can spare from your family. Bring any who would join us, be they slave, patrician, or plebian, I care not. The sword knows not the hand that wields it, it cuts for all the same!"

The crowd erupts with cries of "Scipio!" "Imperator," and, for the first time in history, "Scipio Africanus!" Scipio strides away from the front steps, brushing at his eyes. *Thank the gods, I will yet have my army.*

The days that follow are an overwhelming endorsement of Scipio's cause, and of the man himself. Recruits walk in from all parts of Italia: Etruria, Latium, Samnium, and Campania—even from as far south as Apulia and Bruttium. Most are humble working men determined to be part of something greater than themselves. But hundreds more are young patricians, enraptured at the thought of fighting war in far-off Africa, of gaining glory and political advancement.

Within two weeks of his speech, Scipio's volunteer army swells to five thousand able-bodied fighters. Among them are over a thousand ex-legionnaires, as well as hundreds of freed slaves, all afire with the urge to fight for the man who conquered the Three Generals. Another week, and Scipio's volunteer army passes seven thousand. [lviii]

Over the next week, Scipio watches his new men file into the expansive Campus Martius, there to begin their training. The outlying Field of Mars becomes a city of lean-tos and roughspun tents. Amelia's gaily decorated banners serve as standards to mark the training areas, each banner displays a training symbol of sword, pilum, shield, or horse.

Many plebian men and women come to visit, eager to give to the cause. They come bringing food, livestock, tents, cloth, family treasures, and coins—bringing anything that will make them become a part of the grand undertaking.

As the city energizes to the purpose of war, the Latin Party wisely retreats into the background. No one speaks against Scipio's plans. Even the dauntless Cato has quieted his tongue, content to concentrate

V. Departure

on his farm and on his new duties as Scipio's quaestor.

The furor raised by the tide of volunteers has barely subsided when more donations arrive—Rome's allies have answered his call for supplies. The township of Caere carts in tons of grain. The miners of Populonum trundle in groaning oxcarts of iron for weapons. The Camerinum volunteers march in as a cohort of six hundred trained men, each armored and ready for battle. The smiths of Arretium send three thousand pairs of shields and helmets, along with thousands of new javelins.

And there is more from other townships and states: keels, pots, shovels, and money.[lix] Rome becomes a madhouse of transport, as the city's aediles scramble to find storage for all the gifts. The road to the Servian wall becomes lined with ship-sized wagons bearing load upon load of trees from the hardy northern forests. Enough timber to build a fleet of warships.

Time and again, Scipio visits the Temple of Mars to offer sacrifices and prayer, impelled by the urge to thank some higher power for the gifts bestowed upon him. *God of War, help me live up to these people's sacrifices,* he prays, prostrating himself before the statue of Mars. *Now I must defeat Carthage for all of Italia, not just Rome.*

His heart is satisfied with his prayers to the gods, but his head knows that he must attend to the minutiae of army supply and training if he is to win an extended foreign campaign. Logistical planning then dominates his time.

Exerting his consular powers, Scipio locates every shipwright in Rome and Ostia and sets them to work on building his new fleet. His dictate is simple and nonnegotiable; they have forty-five days to construct ten quadriremes and twenty quinqeremes.[lx] He intends to build a convoy of warships that can challenge any Carthaginian fleet between Sicily and Africa.

Scipio then turns his attention to his new army's weaponry. Following the advice of his Iberian armorers, Scipio arranges for the donated iron to be watered regularly and exposed to the hot sun, so that it may rust

V. Departure

as quickly as possible. Once the rusted impurities are removed there will be a steely metal for his new army sword, the falcata-based gladius. A metal that will make this gladius hispaniesis stronger and more flexible than any Roman blade before it.

Scipio personally inspects all the donated wheat and barley, allotting inferior grains for animal feed, intimidating the local grain merchants into bringing more to add to his stores. Even the soldiers' clothing becomes an object of his attention. Shoemakers are hired to make thousands of the hobnailed caligae he used for the Iberian campaign, Scipio insisting they be designed for the North African desert climes. The traditional Roman sarcina pack is lightened in weight, as Scipio anticipates rapid marches across the vast African plains.

Scipio is everywhere. He inspects everything, demands everything, compromises on nothing. He is a man on fire with purpose.

With Marcus and Laelius' help, Scipio organizes a rigorous training program for his recruits. A third of the Field of Mars is cordoned off for battle practice. Hundreds of heavy wooden practice swords are purchased, along with wickerwork practice shields. Marcus Silenus is again recruited to become the lead trainer, a task he readily embraces. Almost everything is in place. There is but one final detail to conclude.

Scipio meets with the four gladiators who are part of his Honor Guard, to plan how his legionnaires can learn to fight like the criminals and slaves of the ring. Like their general, Scipio's soldiers will be men of surprise.

* * * * *

SIGA, NORTH AFRICA COAST, 205 BCE. With a final shudder, Syphax expends the last of his seed into his immobile bride.

Sophonisba lies beneath her new husband, eyes staring at the deer running free on the Greek tapestry she had mounted on the ceiling. Her hands rest lightly on Syphax's sweaty back, just enough to maintain contact, and then fall to her sides. She forces a smile as her hawk-faced husband pushes up from her. "Was it enjoyable for you?" she asks

V. Departure

dutifully.

The King of Western Numidia rolls over and slides his hand over her naked body, lingering possessively on her breasts and mound. "Fucking you is like making love to a goddess." He says. "You were worth my deserting the Romans, though Scipio may burn my realm."

Sophonisba raises herself on one elbow, her full breasts swaying. Her palm wipes his sweat from her body, flinging it from her as if it were poison. She pushes her long raven hair back from her oval face and smiles mechanically at Syphax, her eyes downcast. "I am pleased you so value me. My father will be pleased, too."

Syphax snorts. "Ah, Gisgo! He had best follow through with his promise, and squeeze more mercenaries from that Council of Elders! We will need them—Scipio will be quite angry that I broke our agreement." He looks about Sophonisba's lush palace chamber. "And that 'friend' of yours, the rebel Masinissa, he is rumored to be about here, isn't he?" He carefully studies her face. "Does that excite you?"

She looks away toward the door. "He was but a flirtation, my king. The boy has certainly found another lover—or three. I care not."

Syphax sneers. "That 'boy' is a usurper and a murderer." He looks around again, suddenly anxious. "I will double your guard tonight, in case the scum should try to sneak in on you." Sophonisba shrugs, willing herself to sound bored. "No matter. If it is your will, be it so."

Syphax dons his silk night robe and shuffles toward the door. "I leave for Carthage tonight. I will return five nights hence." He leers at her. "We will be together then, my treasure. And I will make up for our lost time."

Staring at his back, Sophonisba grimaces. "Rest assured, I will count the days until you return," she replies.

As soon as Syphax departs her chamber, Sophonisba calls in her attendant. "A hot bath. Immediately!" Her middle-aged attendant is moving to the task before Sophonisba finishes her command, wise in the ways of her mistress' needs. Sophonisba rushes to a bowl filled

V. Departure

with rose petal water. Grabbing a linen cloth she laves her insides, time and again, stifling sobs as she reaches for another cloth. The attendant declares her bath is ready and Sophonisba patters barefoot to the adjoining bath room. With a relieved sigh she immerses herself in the bronze tub's steaming, fragrant, waters.

Minutes later, Sophonisba orders the water changed and immerses herself again, scrubbing vigorously with a sponge. Finally she dries herself and slips into a thick thigh-length red tunic. She sits at her stone dressing table, distractedly brushing her hair while she contemplates her predicament.

"Is there anything more I can do for you?" queries her attendant. "I wish you could," Sophonisba wistfully replies. Waving her hand toward the rear door, she dismisses her staff for the night.

After all her attendants are gone, Sophonisba rises from her chair. She walks over to the statue of the goddess Tanit which she brought with her from Carthage. She looks about to affirm no one is there, picks up the statue and pushes her finger into a hole in its bottom. Easing her finger out, she extracts a small glass bottle capped with wax, its outside sticky with a glue sealant to keep its contents fresh. She peers inside, assessing the freshness of the blue berries and ground leaves contained therein, the fruits of the deadly North African belladonna plant.

Sophonisba stares at the bottle, as if looking for a sign from it. "Sweet surcease," she says to herself. "Is tonight the night?" For the twentieth time, she rehearses what she will do. *Just a warm cup of wine with my little bottle stirred into it, and all is gone. First a letter to my father, that he will know what he has done to me. Then my path is free.* She stares at the bottle. *Tonight?*

Her reverie is interrupted by a thump outside her chamber. There is the edgy rasp of a sword being hastily drawn, followed by a heavier thump against her door, as if a body collided with it.

"Sophonisba?" comes a muffled voice from the other side.

She hurriedly stuffs her bottle back into the statue. "I am to be left

V. Departure

alone," she barks peremptorily. Yet her heart flutters at the memories the voice calls up. *Could it be?*

The chamber door is shoved halfway open and Masinissa shuffles in, his back bent to her as he drags in an unconscious guard. He hears her gasp of surprise and raises a warning finger to his lips, grinning deliriously nonetheless. Within moments she feels his strong arms about her. Sophonisba gently strokes his face, drinking in his scents and sounds, kissing him again and again. A blessed eternity passes.

Finally, Sophonisba stands back to look at him, his tall sinewy body clad in the worn gray tunic of a slave. "How did you..?" she starts to ask, but Masinissa silences her with a kiss. She pushes him away, her face concerned.

"Syphax, he ... he said he is sending more guards to me, they may be here soon," she blurts. "Oh gods, please, do not let me lose you now that I have found you again!"

Masinissa slants his eyes toward the door, listening. He smiles tenderly, his eyes sad. He lightly strokes his finger across her full lips, as if tracing their memory. "I will go, so I do not put you at risk. But I will be back." He stares hard into her eyes, as if reading her deepest thoughts. "And you will wait for me, will you not?"

Sophonisba swallows her tears and nods mutely, her eyes staring beseechingly at him. "I will. But come soon, my heart. Else only my body remain."

The prince's eyes widen fearfully. "Do not say that! Keep your mind to a good turn, promise me you will. And I promise you, we will be together soon."

Masinissa clasps her to him one final time, savoring the feel and scent of her. With a final kiss, he turns and pads toward the door, pausing to look down at the guard. "And what of...?"

Sophonisba waves her hand dismissively. "When you are safely out of reach, I will shout the alarm, and tell them you ran from my chambers." She smirks. "Do not fear for me. Syphax would not harm a hair of his

V. Departure

most precious possession."

Masinissa gnashes his teeth, looking at her and at the door, knowing it would be impossible to escape with her. "On my life, I swear. I will return to you as a king." He slips out the door and quietly closes it.

Sophonisba throws herself onto the bed's rumpled covers, and sobs into her pillow. *Oh love, please hurry. Lest my little bottle rescue me first.*

* * * *

CITY OF CARTHAGE, NORTHERN AFRICA, 205 BCE. "Would you favor a savory slice of she-camel, honored sir? What about a bowl of hedgehog in garum sauce? The hedgehogs are very good this time of the year. Or some fresh peacock, a bird fit for royalty such as you!"

Sensing a sale, the anxious little food merchant has left his back street stall to scamper after the two Carthaginian senators. The politicians converse intently with each other, heedless of his wheedling as they stroll to the Senate house. The merchant scurries back to his stall. He dashes back and stands in front of them, holding out two small red clay bowls.

"A sample?" he croons. "Just a little gift from a man who so admires our hard-working politicians." He wafts a bowl under his own beaked nose, sniffing theatrically. "Mmmm, fresh snails in cumin sauce. The gods pray for such savories!"

The two senators pause before the plucky little businessman, amused at his timid persistence. The tallest senator is a caramel-skinned man with gray hair cascading in ringlets to his wide shoulders. He grins at his younger companion, a slim and well-formed young man who crinkles his grey-green eyes with mirth.

"I admire his persistence, Mintho, should we try it?" says the elder senator.

The younger man is a new senator, but he is wise enough to know he should follow his elder's lead, particularly when that elder is the

V. Departure

Council Leader. "It smells quite good, Salicar. I have had naught but honeycombs and bread to break my fast."

The tall older man laughs. "You say you had nothing but combs and bread? That would last me an entire day! Ah, the energies of youth!"

Salicar gestures for the bowls. The merchant hands one to each, his head deeply bowed.

Salicar takes his bowl and grabs the merchant's thin wrist in a viselike grip, prompting the little man to gape in terror.

"A coin, Mintho," says the elder. "A good one."

Mintho fumbles for his purse inside his toga. He places a silver coin in the shaking palm that Salicar holds open. The coin bears the stamped image of Hannibal's father—Hamilcar Barca, the Thunderbolt—clearly a coin of high value. Salicar releases the merchant's wrist. The little man clutches the coin tightly, amazed at his good fortune. With a nod to one another, the senators raise their bowls and slurp down the fragrant snails.

Salicar smiles, smacks his lips, and nods to the merchant. "Fit for a god," he says, "But a minor one. Next time, add some anise." The two return the bowls and walk past the vendor as he bleats out his promises to do better.

The senators turn off the Avenue of Merchants and enter the vast square that surrounds the palatial Senate house. Salicar pauses here, as he often does. His eyes take in the perimeter of palaces and mansions around the massive square, each building fronted with elegantly carved Phoenician and Greek statuary. Looking up the side streets, he sees rows and rows of immaculate stone houses, all owned by the residents of Carthage's working class. Without exception, they are well-maintained structures, rows of two-story dwellings that extend down toward Carthage's enormous circular port.

Salicar smiles to himself, as he always does when he comes here. *This is the most magnificent city in the world*, he muses. *We cannot let it fall to Roman ruin.* He faces Mintho. "We have to win this war," he

V. Departure

declares. "No treaties. Rome must be destroyed before they destroy us!"

Mintho shrugs. "That has proven to be a difficult course to pursue. And our 'birds of peace' senators will be chirping again today."

Salicar takes a deep breath and exhales. "I may have an untoward resolution to that problem," he replies, "Though it grieves me to use it."

The two senators ascend the sweeping marble steps up to the Senate house. They seat themselves in the open-air semicircle where the Senate has decided to meet today, that they might enjoy the warm and sunny weather. The senators converse about the rumor that Consul Publius Scipio is planning to attack Africa from Sicily,

Carthage's two ruling suffetes arrive to open the meeting. They are aged men in floor-length purple-bordered togas. The sufetes shuffle slowly up to the governmental altars. Once there, they sacrifice a goat to Baal for enlightenment and conduct an augury of its remains. The suffetes declare the signs to be too vague to draw a conclusion, prompting a muffled chuckle from Salicar. *As if they ever do anything but conclude there is no conclusion.*

Their religious duty completed, the suffetes turn the chamber over to Salicar. As the Senior Elder of the Senate, known in Carthage as The Council of Elders, he is charged with managing today's debate. Today's meeting is about the conduct of the war against Rome. The senators are anxious to argue about Carthage's next course of action, spurred on by the rumor that Consul Scipio will invade Africa.

Salicar opens the floor for discussion, and a heated debate ensues between the peace and war factions. The bejeweled merchants and businessmen of the Senate argue vehemently for another treaty with Rome. They want Carthage to return to the trade and commerce that have made it the wealthiest city in civilization—and made them some of the richest men on earth.

The merchants are opposed by a score of senators from the powerful Barcid family, the clan from which Hamilcar and Hannibal are

V. Departure

descended. The Barcids sit together with arms crossed, severe men without adornment or humor. Each stands and speaks in turn, though they all say the same thing. They all demand a stronger commitment of troops and resources to Mago and Hannibal Barca, so the two can defeat the Italia legions and march on Rome, to force its surrender or burn it to the ground.

Salicar deftly manages the heated arguments. He calmly quashes those who speak out of order by threatening to have them arrested, and raises his staff of office when a senator speaks too long. Though he appears calm on the outside, his heart races with anxiety that this meet will end in another stalemate. Time grows short to stop Scipio, and to resupply Hannibal's army.

In the fourth hour of debate, with the tide seemingly turned toward treaty, Salicar calls himself as the next speaker. He walks up the steps to the speaking platform in the center of the semicircle, a limestone slab embraced by a floor carving of the outstretched arms of Tanit, goddess of war and fertility. When the chamber has stilled, Salicar holds up a sealed goatskin scroll, that all may see it.

"I have a written statement from the Tribunal of the Hundred and Four," he says. The senators murmur with dismay, fearing the Tribunal will dictate some course of action to them.

The Tribunal is composed of the most powerful and elite families of Carthage, men nominated for life by the Senate. Created to audit the conduct of generals and officials, the Tribunal is a terror to those that oppose its will—and the whims of its individual members. Lately the Tribunal's crucifixions of generals and officials has increased, with even a lowly magistrate being nailed to a cross last week. To oppose the Tribunal is to flirt with death, as every Senator knows too well.

Salicar brandishes the scroll. "The Tribunal has observed our extended disputes on this issue, and has seen fit to issue an opinion. I have not yet read it." *But I have been told its contents. Be prepared, Senators.*

Salicar breaks the seal and scans the message. He looks at the

V. Departure

hundreds of senators. "It is brief, as are all of their missives. I will ask our Speaker to read it."

Salicar hands the scroll to a nearby senator, known for his oratorical skills. The portly youth clears his throat. "In the matter of the resolution of the second war with Rome, we recommend continuing our present course of action. That is, we should continue to support our generals in the field with increased manpower and supplies, whatever the cost. We believe it best to double the proposed allotments of both." Amid cheers and boos, the Speaker returns the scroll to Salicar.

By the time Salicar has rolled up the little scroll he knows the issue has been decided to his liking. He has only to look at the faces of his alarmed opponents.

One of the peace party senators ascends the platform. He is a wealthy spice merchant who has had frequent dealings with Rome. He gives an impassioned speech for an immediate treaty. When he concludes, he receives very few cheers of support: the Tribunal has already spoken against him.

"Sit down, coward," shouts Boumca, a young Barcid captain.

The old spice merchant shakes his head. "You do not know these people, Boumca. They will not give up, no matter their losses. We cannot win a war with them."

This is going nowhere, Salicar decides. He abruptly calls a voice vote, eager to use the missive's momentum for his cause. The proposal to increase the war effort wins with overwhelming support.

"Now, we must designate the proper resources for Mago and Hannibal," Salicar announces. The Senate then turns to the matter of money, troops, and supplies for the two generals. Four older merchants address the Senate as a group, with a list of moderate allotments that will not overspend the annual budget. The Barca senators demand that Mago and Hannibal receive immediate support, else Scipio may soon be at Carthage's gates.

The specter of Roman legions on African soil is enough to sway many

V. Departure

senators to the Barca stance. As Boumca speaks, scores stand up silently, indicating their support of him. Salicar shakes his head, amused. *This Scipio has done more to support our war effort than I have. They fear him more than the god of the Underworld.*

The war supporters win sizable money and troop allotments for both Hannibal and Mago, to be delivered to them as soon as possible. As the final vote is reported, Salicar and his Barcid allies smile.

The senior senator pushes through the crowd of politicians. He finds young Minthro and slaps him on the back. "Rejoice, young man! We are mustering an indomitable force against Rome!"

Mintho grins. "What a turn of events! We may yet make Rome a smoking ruin. And see Scipio on a cross!"

* * * * *

FIELD OF MARS, OUTSKIRTS OF ROME. "Again, lift!" shouts Marcus Silenus, glowering at his new recruits. "Use your legs, curse you, not your back!" Clad in full battle armor, the redoubtable commander stalks among his anxious trainees, searching for the slightest imperfections in behavior or attitude.

Ever eager to teach, Marcus has gladly reassumed his role as trainer of legionary recruits. But the crusty ex-centurion does not suffer fools lightly, and his patience with this motley crew of farmers and fishermen is growing short.

They think they are soldiers because they have weapons, he fumes. *As if wearing a crown makes you a king.* Marcus is angry at their lack of gravitas and conditioning. He knows they are not prepared to fight for hours in the hot African sun, much less to methodically fend off a rampaging barbarian horde. *The first Gaul that comes at them, they'll shit their subligalculum and run.*

The short, blocky officer has ignored his recruits' entreaties to learn more sword fighting, telling them they must first strengthen their legs and torso. Today they will indulge in Marcus' favorite training exercise, lifting and hurling boulders—at each other.

V. Departure

Hundreds of recruits stand in pairs across the Circus Flaminius, the racing track that abuts the Campus Martius. Dressed in padded fighting vests, the men use both hands to heave their cabbage-sized boulders underhanded to one another. They catch the rocks and quickly pitch them back, time after time. Their breaths come shorter with each throw.

Many bend over and place their hands on their knees, prompting Marcus to kick their backsides. "No matter how tired you are in a battle, you keep your head upright, and your shield high!" he bellows, as he boots another stooped recruit.

Marcus stalks through the ranks, correcting their stances and throws. "All at once! Lift with arms and legs all at once," he orders, striking errant practitioners with his vitis, a yard-long trainer's cudgel. "Any who cannot get it to their chest get a week's ration of barley instead of wheat."

The legate walks between the lines, glaring balefully at any who smile or laugh, pausing periodically to correct an errant posture or motion. "Swordplay begins in the legs. Men are killed because their legs tire, not their arms!"

Marcus hears rough laughter. He looks over to the edge of the training circle. A barrel-bodied Gaul is flinging his practice boulder at his Roman companion, a slim young fellow who is a head shorter. The Gaul picks the boulder up in one plate-sized hand and flings it underhanded at the Roman youth, who gamely catches it but is knocked sprawling.

The youth rises silently, his face stoic. He picks up the boulder and hoists it back at the Gaul. The barbarian fields it easily and viciously returns it, again knocking the boy to the ground. Marcus watches the scenario unfold several times. *The boy has sand in him*, he thinks. *But that bully needs a lesson.*

Marcus he steps over to the dueling pair, his hands clenched behind his back. The pair halts their routine, watching Marcus nervously. He turns and faces his recruits.

V. Departure

"You may wonder what those larger boulders are for," says Marcus, pointing at four piles of head-sized river rocks. Those are your next lesson. When you can return those a score of times in succession, you are absolved of any further practice on them. Until you do you will not quit, though you have to tote your rock onto Scipio's ships for Sicily!"

He holds two fingers in a V-shape and points them at all the watching faces. "Today you succeed or fail as a pair, as you do when you fight. The man next to you is as responsible for your life as you are for his." He glances over his shoulder at the Gaul. "You always support your brothers in arms, so they will support you."

Marcus casually walks over to the Gaul, who watches the diminutive commander with a slight smile. "Some may think it easy to lift such a rock as you have in your hands, but it is the repetition that drains you, just as the length of battle can weaken the strongest of men who do not have stamina. Let me demonstrate."

Marcus walks to a boulder lying between the piles, the largest stone on the field. He pulls off his helmet, belt, and cuirass, leaving him only a simple gray tunic and sandals. In one smooth motion, the commander bends and effortlessly sweeps the boulder up into his arms. He trudges over to the Gaul, his face expressionless. The men goggle at their leader's bare arms. Every muscle and vein is swelled and visible, as if his limbs were carved from the rock itself.

Marcus steps in front of the large Gaul, bouncing the boulder in his hands. Without a word Marcus pitches it at him. The Gaul catches it and pitches it back, not daring to throw it violently. Marcus catches it, bending his knees to absorb the force, and easily returns it. And the duel is on. The two pitch it back and forth for a score of times, then another ten. And then another ten. The Gaul is now bathed in sweat, his body stooped, his throws coming from his shoulders and arms instead of his lower body. Marcus' form has not altered, he throws with his legs and torso as the impetus. Sweat runs down Marcus' entire body, but his face is impassive, save for his feral peridot eyes, which always stare into the Gaul's face.

Finally, the Gaul's throw falls short. Marcus steps forward two paces

V. Departure

to reduce the throwing distance. He picks up the boulder and resumes the drill. Then the Gaul's return falls even shorter, and Marcus steps forward again. Finally, he is face to face with the exhausted giant, who cannot pick the stone off the ground. When the Gaul drops the stone between his feet and slumps, Marcus puts his hands between the man's arms and lifts him upright. He leans toward his ear. "Do not ever humiliate your sword mate again," he whispers harshly, "or I will choke the fucking life from you."

Marcus stands back. The barbarian blinks in fear and returns to stand next to the Roman youth. Marcus drops the boulder and walks to the edge of the training circle, that all may see him. He stands silently, daring anyone to make a noise. The field is so silent the men can hear the Tiber River sloshing along behind them, punctuated by the screams of its gulls.

"Do you think I became legate by some patrician's favor?" Marcus snorts. "By a purse dropped in a senator's waiting palm? I fought my way up from the sewers, with all to gain and nothing to lose. I say to you now, your will is your only limitation. What you do not will for yourself, you will not have. What you do, you will."

With those words Marcus walks back to his boulder, picks it up, and hurls it toward the far pile. It sails past the stunned recruits and cracks into the stones. "Your will is your greatest ally. Never forget that."

Soon, Marcus Silenus dismisses the weary men for a midday meal. They are given fruit, cheese, and buccelatum, the same hard-baked biscuits that were the staple of Scipio's fast-marching Iberian legions.

While the men stretch out in the sun, Marcus directs the camp slaves to bring out the wooden swords and practice shields. The recruits' "reward" for their completing their conditioning work is to practice one-on-one sword fighting under Marcus' careful eye...

When the recruits return to their training space after the meal, they see a new man standing next to Marcus Silenus. The man is fleshy across the stomach and chest, but he has the rocklike shoulders and forearms of a heavyweight wrestler. Marcus holds up the man's right hand.

V. Departure

"This is Praxis, late of the gladiatorial games you witnessed here." Marcus turns the Greek's arm to show the letters and numbers tattooed on the inside of his forearm, the brand of a slave gladiator. "General Scipio has made this man part of his Honor Guard, his protector for life. That is all you need to know about his value. Praxis is here to teach you the Way of the Gladiator, that you may confound your enemies with the unexpected."

Marcus peers over his group of trainees. "Lupus, come forward!" Marcus shouts. "Bring your weapons."

A middle-aged Thracian steps forward, lugging a shield and a wooden gladius. He is an angular man who seems to be all joints, bones, and ropy muscles, more skeleton than man. Lupus is Marcus' prized trainee, a former legionnaire who fought with Fabius in his early campaigns against Hannibal. Marcus has seen the old soldier best a score of his fellow recruits, scoring kills with only a feint and a thrust. Soon Marcus will make him a tribune in his First Cohort, but for the time being he must serve as an example.

"Lupus, I would have you fight Praxis, that our men may learn how to fight against an experienced opponent." Marcus says.

The legionnaire touches his blade to his forehead, signaling his acknowledgement. Marcus nods toward Praxis. The two men step in and begin circling each other.

Without warning, Lupus barges his shield into Praxis' own buckler, attempting a quick knockdown. Instead of engaging Lupus with his sword, the gladiator spins sideways, reducing his target area. He steps in and slides past Lupus, fetching him a clanging blow on the helmet as he passes. Lupus ignores the blow and whirls to face Praxis, just in time to ward off a cleaving stroke at his sword arm. The legionnaire follows with a low thrust that Lupus turns aside with his shield.

The two combatants parry and thrust, using their shields and legs as much as their swords. The hefty Praxis ably dances away from Lupus' determined charges, seemingly playing with him. Lupus stalks after Praxis, watching his stomach.

V. Departure

"Do you see how he watches the man's gut?" says Marcus. "A man can feint with his head or shoulder, but the gut, it stays where it's at."

Swift as a striking snake, Praxis darts down and whacks Lupus across his bare shin. Lupus howls and jumps away on one foot. Marcus grabs a wooden sword and pitches it to Praxis. "Dimachaeri style!" Marcus orders.

Praxis drops his little shield and catches the sword. He whirls the two blades in his hands, grinning in anticipation, and stalks toward Lupus. With a roar, the old legionnaire lowers his head and charges. Praxis rains blows on Lupus' helmet and shield, and he stumbles backwards.

"You see what two swords can do?" asks Marcus. "When you have lost your shield in a melee', use another sword as your shield, and attack your opponent. Your best defense will be your offense."

Lupus retreats, but he is not cowed. He crouches under the blows but watches Praxis' torso. Praxis raises his right sword high, intending a mighty blow. When Praxis' sword is over his head, Lupus springs forward. He crunches his shield into Praxis' body, a classic legionnaire move, and a dazed Praxis tumbles to the earth, his wooden blades tumbling from his hands.

As Praxis lies supine, Lupus scrambles in for the victory stroke. He steps next to Praxis and pulls his arm back to thrust his wood blade toward the gladiator's neck. As soon as Lupus cocks his elbow, the big man rolls onto his left side and sweeps his right leg under Lupus' feet, hooking his left ankle and pulling it out from under him.

The gangly warrior crashes to the ground. He quickly scrambles up to regain his feet, but it is too late. Praxis has jumped onto Lupus' back and plowed his face into the earth, pulling one arm behind Lupus' back as he throttles him with his thickly muscled forearm.

"A kill," says Marcus flatly. The gladiator immediately releases Lupus. He extends his hand and yanks him to his feet.

The recruits snap their fingers in applause, and Lupus bows his head before the panting older man. "You are the best I have ever seen,"

V. Departure

Lupus gasps, dabbing his bleeding elbow into his padded tunic.

Praxis laughs heartily. "Me? I tell you now, even two of me would fail with such as he," he says, as he inclines his head toward Marcus Silenus. The gladiator faces the recruits and laughs pityingly. "You know not who you have training you, striplings."

Marcus gives the briefest of nods. "Gratitude." He turns to his trainees. "As General Scipio has taught all of us, doing the unexpected gives you and advantage. Anticipating it gives you another. Now hear me. You will fight as a legionnaire when you are in formation. But you will learn to fight as gladiator when you are in a melee'."

Marcus picks up a sword and stands in front of Praxis, looking at his pairs of men. "Time for another lesson. Get into your pairs. One of you will become me, the other becomes Praxis. Choose!" The pairs mutter and point their training swords at one another, assigning roles.

Marcus grabs a shield and wooden sword. "Watch us, and follow our moves. First, the kick..." Praxis and Marcus engage one another, choreographing an attack in slow motion, with Praxis kicking Marcus back and thrusting his sword into him. Slowly, awkwardly, the men mimic the master fighters' coordinated moves, learning the ways of the dance of death.

ROME. With a forlorn bleat, the sheep falls flat and bleeds the last of its life into the waiting blood cup. Even as the unfortunate animal breathes its last, the downy-cheeked haruspex deftly opens the beast's stomach with his long, keen, knife. Severing the veins and tissue about the liver, he cups his hands around the saddle-shaped organ and eases it from the sheep's still-throbbing body. He places the liver into a wide and shallow bronze bowl as his acolytes chant the ritual prayers for a divination.

Scipio, Pomponia, and Amelia stand to the rear of the haruspex. They await the priest's prediction of the success of a war in Africa. Scipio has a look of resigned disgust, like a boy who has had to dress up for a dinner party. "How long does this take, Mother?" he whines.

V. Departure

She frowns at him. "Shhh. Not long. You know you have to get the divinations for your campaign before you leave. The people would be aghast if you did not tell them the signs were favorable."

Scipio purses his lips. "We should have gone to an augur, they would give us a prediction."

"You want a prediction from someone who watches the flight of birds? How silly that would be! Besides, this young man is a prodigy," says Pomponia. "People say he has the gift of foresight. He is almost an oracle!"

"Hmph," snorts Scipio. "I prefer to be my own oracle! How can you tell the future from looking at a sheep's' guts? Aristotle would blush at such practices. He was a rational man, and I am too."

Amelia places a hand on his shoulder and playfully shoves him. "Peh! This coming from a man who follows his dreams?"

"My dreams have proved to be true," he growls. "Well, most of the time, anyway."

Scipio peers over the soothsayer's shoulder and steps back to rejoin his family. "Did you see the sheep he is using?" he whispers. "It's sickly! I wouldn't feed its meat to a dog, and he is using it to predict the future!"

"Shush," Pomponia hisses, her finger between her lips. "You have too much faith in your 'rational' Greek brain. The gods will send us a message through the sheep, whatever its condition."

Hearing them muttering behind him, the haruspex looks over his shoulder and glares reprovingly at them until they are quiet.

Scipio shifts about impatiently. He reaches into the belt purse hiding underneath his purple bordered toga and extracts his figurine of Nike. He holds it up to Amelia. "See, I still carry your gift everywhere," he says.

She smiles and bends to kiss his cheek, giggling like a naughty child.

V. Departure

Scipio smiles back at her. "I believe in this more than any priest. It reminds me that fortune lies within my own efforts—not some sheep's ass."

Scipio recalls a speech Cato made in the public square against the "effeminate" practices of divination, with Cato saying that he wondered that one haruspex did not laugh when he saw another.[lxi] *And here I am with one of them*, he thinks, embarrassed. He taps his right foot, more impatient than ever.

Finishing his entreaties to the gods, the haruspex pulls the blood-drained liver out of the bowl and places it on a marble slab. He grabs his razor sharp knife and smoothly slices the sheep's liver lengthwise. The haruspex pokes the two pieces apart with the tip of his blade, and peers into the globes of the liver, searching for signs. "Hmm, there are portents here, of certitude."

After several long, silent moments, the haruspex looks up from the liver. He flicks his knife toward the family, beckoning them to approach. The priest points at the right lobe of the liver. "See this? This is the hostilis part,[lxii] where the gods tell us about the fate of your enemies. See how darkly streaked it is? This means that your enemies will suffer great misfortune against you, Consul Scipio."

Amelia and Pomponia nod smugly, looking at Scipio as if the soothsayer's words justified their coming here. Scipio merely looks into the bloody organ and points to the left portion. "And what about these two spots? Are they about my finances, my sexual life—do they say I will be coming into riches?"

The divinator sighs. "That is the familiaris portion, it foretells the fate of your family network, and of those you love." He pokes at the two dark spots and stares at their position within the globe of the liver. He shakes his head. "Apologies for what I tell you. If you continue your present course, your enemies will suffer grievously. But two that you love will suffer a grievous fate, though I do not know what it will be."

Scipio's face darkens. "What? You dare tell me that two people in my family will die, because I go to conquer Carthage?"

V. Departure

The haruspex slowly shakes his head. "Not your blood family only, but the 'family' of those you most care for, the family of those you love. Perhaps they die, perhaps . . . who knows? But misfortune will happen."

Scipio's face flushes with anger—and fear. "Liar! Who put you up to this, the Latins?"

The young man blushes but he stares coolly into the consul's burning eyes. "I simply report what the gods tell me here," he says, poking the animal's liver. He gives his bloody knife to an acolyte and looks at Scipio. "You may not like me but I will tell you this: our lives will be intertwined, that is why the gods sent me this message to you. May Fortuna smile upon you, Consul Scipio."

Scipio stalks toward the temple door. Pomponia and Amelia hurry to catch up to him.

"You are being a rash boy," scolds Pomponia her sandals clapping as she paces after her son. "He is a brilliant young man, and we can use him in the Party."

"Who is he?" Scipio snorts.

"Tiberius Sempronius Gracchus," Pomponia replies. "He is the son of that consul who was killed several years ago, a man who was very popular with the people."

Scipio shrugs. "His father was a good man, a good soldier. But this, this poking about at livers, this is lunacy. And he says he will be connected with me in the future. Well, not if I can help it."

Pomponia rubs her chin, and looks sideways at her son. "If we get him to join the Hellenics, you will see him again."

Amelia nods. "He could be very useful as Rome's chief augur."

"Pish! He is naught but a doomsayer!" barks Scipio. He stalks furiously through the bustling streets of Rome, his guards forming a wedge in front of him.

V. Departure

The family returns to the Scipio domus. Scipio goes to the atrium and pours himself a glass of wine, not bothering to water it, and plops onto a low-slung couch. And there he sits, sulkily, alone.

After a second glass of wine, Scipio jumps up and hurries to his scroll basket. He yanks out an armful of his most-studied scrolls: the historic accounts of Xenophon's campaign, Alexander the Great's victories in Egypt, and Rome's first war against Carthage. For hours he pours over the familiar manuscripts, inking notes on a blank roll of papyrus, muttering to himself, rubbing his weary eyes.

Amelia and Pomponia peer in and see him pouring over the scrolls, furiously scribbling down notes. "Let us leave him alone," Pomponia says. "What you see, that is his way of protecting us from the haruspex's prediction. He is trying to eliminate any possibility he could fail."

The hours bring dusk, and Scipio finally rolls up the scrolls and eases them into the basket. Rubbing his weary eyes, he sprawls out on one of the dining couches, and pops a grape into his mouth. Scipio is satisfied for now, having reevaluated his strategy, tactics, weaponry, and logistics. *I can take all the lands about Carthage, if I first take the fortress at Utica. Then he will have to come after me.*

Scipio's eyes wander about the room in which he studied as a child. he laughs darkly to himself. *Oh, to be back when my words did not prompt action, when my decisions did not have consequence.* "Whom the gods would curse, they first make powerful," he says to the deities depicted on the wall frescoes.

Scipio retires to his room for a nap. Hours later, he emerges for the evening dinner with his family and Laelius. They lay about on the couches, joking about the antics of irascible Cassius, the one legged veteran that Marcus Silenus sent to 'help' Pomponia.

The family trades opinions about the management of the family farms in the Sabina Hills. "The ranks of Rome's unemployed swell to the size of an army," Pomponia declares. "From now on we will employ freedmen instead of slaves. We can afford it."

V. Departure

Scipio sits quietly, lost in thought.

"Someone is brooding too much," says Amelia. She walks to his couch and plunks herself on top of him, knocking him onto his back. They wrestle about, laughing like children. He pins her arms and kisses her. She wriggles free and pushes him back, smiling into his eyes. "I'm sure that priest likes to be dramatic," she tells Scipio. "And predictions of misfortune are talked about more than ones of the good. Do not worry over his words!"

Lucius laughs, an all too rare occurrence lately, and the family stares at him. "I'd rather augur bird shit myself than trust a priest!" he declaims.

Scipio nods gratefully at their solace. "In truth, I do put more trust in my dreams than the interpretations of a boy," he responds. "But he was so sure of what he said!"

"As most men are," quips Pomponia. She picks a slice of peach off a platter. "Even when they are obviously wrong."

Laelius toys with his wine cup, peering inside and rolling it about to look at its gleanings, as though it were an augury itself. "You know, Scippy, you have taken back Iberia, and enriched Rome with all its silver mines. As for that bad old Hannibal, he is contained in Southern Italia and Rome could soon send a dozen legions there to throttle him." He studies the frescoes on the wall, dwelling on the one of frolicking centaurs. "You have done your part. You don't have to do any more."

"The war is not over while Carthage stands unchallenged," Scipio says. "I am not yet finished."

Pomponia looks endearingly, pityingly, at her beloved boy. "Son, I know you promised your father that you would protect Rome, but you have fulfilled that promise. Do not let that worry you. Take over Sicily, control the sea lanes. Let others go to Africa, if needs be."

Scipio casually reaches over to take an olive from a slave's tray and pops it into his mouth. When he turns back to look at them, his eyes shine with a determined ferocity.

V. Departure

Amelia bites her lip, she has seen that look before. "What is it, my love?"

"*I* will win this war, not someone else," he blurts, his fists clenched. "I have come too far to let someone else have the glory. You would have me squat in Sicily like an old woman on a toilet? I will end it myself, with Carthage begging for peace at my feet!"

Laelius looks at Pomponia and Amelia, and sees the shared concern on their faces. *The ram has touched the wall. We can but help him do it.* A resigned smile comes across Laelius' face. "Well, General or Consul Scipio, or whoever you are now. I guess I had best get ready to help you."

"And I," says Lucius, to the surprise of everyone.

Scipio's face softens. "Forgive me, beloved family. I have come so far, seen so many of my men die for our cause. To leave it unfinished would be intolerable." He laughs ruefully. "I can only hope the Senate sees fit to grant me more manpower and resources when I get to Sicily."

Laelius opens his arms expansively. "How could they not, Imperator? You are the people's chosen one. I heard the plebs, they are already giving you a new surname of virtue. They call you Scipio Africanus, the conqueror of Africa."

* * * * *

SABINA VALLEY, 205 BCE. The oaks are filled with chirping blackbirds singing praises to the morning, but Cato cannot hear their joyful songs. He is absorbed in worship of his childhood hero. Cato stands at the crumbling wood hut of Manius Curius Dentatus, the simple farmer who put down his plow to lead Rome's soldiers to victory over the Samnite army, ending the war. As he does in times of dilemma, Cato asks himself, *what would noble Dentatus do in such a situation?*

Cato is perplexed. Flaccus is his friend and sponsor, a man who fights for the noble Latin cause of preserving Rome's traditional agrarian

V. Departure

values of material austerity and moral discipline. Yet he is an arrogant patrician that uses blackmail, slander, and bribery to promote these noble aims. His admired mentor, the renowned General Fabius, argues against Scipio going to Africa to conquer the city of Carthage. But Cato himself has ended many of his speeches with the enjoinder "Carthage must be destroyed." He agrees with the ends of both, but not their means.

And then there are the Hellenics. They work to pass bills that would help farmers and common workingmen, the people of Cato's humble origins. They would save the small farms of Cato's youth, the ones that are being gobbled up by accursed latifundia, the large estates such as Flaccus owns. Yet the Hellenics espouse the cultivation of fripperies such as mass culture and education, policies he knows would weaken the stoic agrarian traditions that made Rome great. *Who to serve? For one I embrace the cause but am repelled by the people, while the reverse is true for the other.*

As he stares at the humble hut, the place where Rome's most honored hero elected to live out his days, he finally decides. *The cause comes first, whatever means are used to attain it. The Latin way will preserve Rome, while the Hellenics' would destroy it. But I must avoid the taint of Flaccus' practices.* Cato shrugs. *At least I can serve Rome by keeping an eye on Scipio's wastefulness, now that I am his quaestor.*

Cato steps inside Dentatus' home. He looks at the fireplace where the hero was roasting turnips when the vanquished Samnites appeared, offering Dentatus carloads of treasure if he would lobby for their interests. Dentatus rejected them, that he might preserve the purity of his simple farming life—and of himself.

I must do the same, spend my censorship pay on the simple purities of acreage, seeds, and tools. He breathes deeply, savoring the faint acrid traces of the fireplace's long-extinguished fire. *Best get back to work. The fields must be tended before I leave for Sicily.*

Cato trudges back up the hill and down into the adjoining valley, back to his small plots of wheat fields and olive groves. He can see his ox and plow waiting for him, just where he left them to visit the shrine.

V. Departure

His stern face cracks with a tight smile. *Gods burn cursed Carthage! I want to be done with war and live in my fields.* He picks up his plow, snaps the reins, and calls for his slaves to follow him, pulling out the rocks he unearths.

A mile from Cato, Laelius slowly rides along the main Sabina farm road, surveying the valley's lush wheat fields and thick olive groves. He is out shopping for a place in the country, a place far from the stinking dock streets in which lived as an orphan, as far as possible from its memories of rapine and murder. *I could have a nice small farm here. Raise grapes and drink my own wine!*

He notices that there are several modest stone block farm houses scattered throughout the valley floor, likely for farms of twenty or thirty acres. Laelius glances at the large villas perched on the low-lying hills above the valley. He wrinkles his nose. *Who do I want as my neighbors? Cultured and snobby patricians, or honest and simple farmers?* Then he laughs. *I would rather be the best dressed and most despised commoner*, he decides.

Then he thinks of the wealthy Scipios, and how they took him in from the alleyways of Rome. *I can't be such a snob. Some of the rich have morals—just not that many.* He looks up at the well-tended gardens that surround Flaccus' courtyards high above him. *Besides, I would need a place to entertain the Scipio family. A place where Amelia and Scippy's children could play.* He grows wistful, and sighs. *Ah, children ... There are advantages being attracted to women.*

As he rounds a turn in the road, he sees a line of slaves sprawled out next to a freshly plowed field. The lean men are all clad in worn gray tunics of roughspun, the tatty wool dark with work sweat and grime. The sweaty workers pass around a pottery flagon of watered vinegar, each taking a deep draft. Laelius notices the fields about them are immaculately kept, each row of wheat straight as a spear, the ground beneath the squat, thick, olive trees is barren of leaves or fallen limbs. *Whoever owns these fields is a careful farmer. I'll ask him what's good to buy around here.*

Laelius turns to the nearest slave, a leathery old Thracian. "Who owns

V. Departure

these fields? I need to talk to him." The slave looks down the row of his coworkers, and points to the dirtiest of the lot, a man in a tattered gray tunic. "Ask him," the slave says in broken Latin.

Laelius eases off his horse and picks his way through the serried rows, carefully stepping over the clods of manure that line the spaces between them. "Greetings, slave," says Laelius. He picks his way toward the worker, who is tipping out a wheelbarrow of ox droppings.

"Can you tell me where the owner is?" Laelius inquires. The burly man pivots the barrow sideways, shaking out the last of the manure. He turns and fixes Laelius with his icy gray eyes. "That would be me, Hellenic," he replies, wiping his hands on his tunic.

Laelius stares harder at him, and grins. "By Jupiter's cock, it is Cato himself! I should have known it was you, no slave would dirty their hands as much as you do!"

Cato eyes Laelius speculatively. "You dress finer than my wife," he notes. "And you probably have on more perfume. Is that what your General Scipio taught you? To dress like a woman?"

Laelius' face reddens. "Aye, and to fight like a warrior born! You think him soft-handed, because he is a Hellenic? I tell you now, more than once we have had to pull him from the front lines, lest he lose our war with the folly of his bravery."

"All I see is a waste of good money," Cato replies, closing one nostril to snort out the other. "But then, you are a ward of the Scipios, you are accustomed to such extravagance." He looks challengingly at Laelius. "I hear he has wasted much coin on lavish parties for his men. And has likely stolen more."

Patience, Laelius tells himself. *He wants you to say something he can use.* "You are a pumpkin. All he has done, he has only done for Rome. Now Rome is afloat in the silver and treasure he has brought home, no matter what the greedy Senate says about their barren coffers. The mines of Iberia work for us now. What care you if a few sesterces happen to be left unaccounted?"

V. Departure

"The amount is not the judge of a crime. A thief is a thief," Cato retorts. He waves over at his resting workers. Cato's slaves vault to their feet, knowing the consequences of ignoring his orders.

Laelius' eyes darken. "Have a care, little man. You speak of the best person I have ever known. Would you were so blessed in your character, you would not treat those under you so cruelly."

"I treat them no worse than I treat myself," growls Cato. "I eat what they do, drink the same wine, wear the same clothes."

Laelius sighs, and turns his horse to go. "Ah, and there's the tragedy, you do it to yourself. And more so that you urge others to mimic you!" He laughs bitterly. "A nation of Catos! What a sight that would be, stern little men in mud huts eating turnips. Amelia was right. You want to make a nation that is powerful, but not one that would ever be great."

The field workers march up to Cato, and he motions for them to spread out the manure. He smiles spitefully at Laelius. "I will be your quaestor in Sicily, Admiral. The overseer of your finances and morality. Do not forget that. I shall have my eye on Consul Scipio. And on you." He grabs a hoe and begins chopping the manure clods apart.

"Have a care yourself," says Laelius coolly. "Scipio is not the boy he was when he left for Iberia. I fear he has grown more like you, which should worry you deeply."

"Pfeh! Large talk! What have I to fear from you, a man who takes it in the ass?" snorts Cato.

"And who gives back as well as he takes!" chortles Laelius. He steps next to Cato, his grin frozen on his face. "Perhaps you would like to try my mettle, my hard-handed little friend. Just me and you."

The slaves halt their work and stare at the two men. Cato drops his hoe and peers into Laelius' frigid blue eyes, his hands balled into fists. Laelius' eyes never leave Cato's, and his smirk never leaves his face. But Laelius' fluid muscular body tenses into a crouch, ready to spring.

The slaves stir uneasily in the unbearable silence. "Master? Are we

V. Departure

ready?" says the eldest.

Cato turns his head, holding Laelius' gaze as long as he can before he looks at his slave. "Get back to work," Cato picks up his hoe/ He steps into the adjoining row. and turns his back to Laelius, chopping furiously at the fist-sized dirt clods.

With a derisive snort, Laelius stalks back down the row and springs onto his horse. "The offer still stands, plow horse," he shouts to Cato. "Any time you want."

Laelius wanders down a narrow road that borders Cato's field. He looks back at Cato and bellows out a lewd song about a cruel farmer who leaves his wife for a sheep—with the sheep leaving the farmer for a kinder man.

Cato glances up and sees Laelius is watching him. He spits, once, and returns to his hoeing. *Effete fool,* he fumes. *He's lucky Marcus Silenus hasn't strangled him.*

AVENTINE HILL, ROME. He has come back. Drawn again to the place of his birth, to the stinking hovels in which he once played, then fought—then killed.

Marcus Silenus tramps down the narrow cobbled street that cuts between the rickety towers of insulae. His hobnailed caligae beat a strident tattoo on the worn river stones beneath him, making Marcus frown. *I should have worn my old sandals. I sound like one of those cursed tympanum players, beating their hand drums down the street.*

Rome's greatest warrior is hooded with the same dingy gray cloak he wore on his last visit to these apartment buildings. He forces himself to slump and walk slowly, lest he betray himself with his military bearing and stride. Walking slowly does not come easy to him this afternoon; impatience eats at him. *I wonder if she is still there? The child must have grown big in these last three years.*

Two burly men walk toward him, veering over to block his path. Marcus raises his head and stares into their faces. The men hurry past. *I should have taken them down, now they'll rob someone else.* He sees an

V. Departure

elderly man lying drunk in an alleyway. *At least I got old Cassius out of here*, he consoles himself.

A small child wanders toward Marcus, drawn to the sound of his tattooed footsteps. The boy pulls up a corner of the knee-length grain sack he wears and stuffs it into his mouth, his eyes large with wonder.

Marcus stops. "Here now, take that out of your mouth," he grates. The child's lips tremble, and his eyes moisten.

"No, no, you're a good boy," Marcus says softly. *Idiot! He's just a child.* He reaches over and gently, irresistibly, tugs the fabric from the child's mouth. "This will taste better," says Marcus.

He fumbles inside his cloak, reaching across his throwing knives and dagger to his left belt pouch. Marcus pulls out a small triangle of finest linen and unwraps it, exposing the five honey-covered nuts inside it. *Have to save some for her boy*, he tells himself.

Marcus plucks out a candy out and gives it to the child. The boy immediately stuffs it into his mouth. He smiles a gap toothed grin, patting his hands together.

Marcus watches him chew the candy. "Take it easy, make it last," he enjoins. He gives the boy another one, and watches as he devours it. When the child is finished, Marcus strokes his bushy black head. "Go with the gods, son." He tucks the linen into his pouch and resumes his way.

Soon Marcus walks into an ancient courtyard ringed with five mud and brick insulae. He heads for the center one that holds his childhood home.

"Do you require a burial, honored Legate? Perhaps a funeral procession? We make excellent masks!"

I am recognized, curse it. Marcus faces the indigo robed undertakers. They stand inside their oak plank stall, grinning at Marcus as though he were an old friend. The gaunt old men proudly hold out several of the wax death masks that dangle across the stall's overhead slats.

V. Departure

"Look how realistic," says one undertaker, "and he has been dead for over two years. He never looked this good in real life."

"I do not require anything," says Marcus. "But I may soon make some business for you." He grins wolfishly. "Do you have a stall in Africa?"

As the undertakers stare in bewilderment, Marcus marches up the entry stairs, scattering the chickens perched on its warped wooden steps. He trudges up the rickety staircase to the insula's fifth floor, edging around the mothers and children that line the staircase.

Marcus walks down the hallway to his birthplace apartment, a place that he visited three years ago, where he first met the young woman and her child.

This is the same old horse blanket, he thinks, fingering the worn wool sheet that dangles in front of the door. *I thought she might buy a new one with the money I gave her. Probably spent it on the boy.*

A dark-skinned arm pushes the blanket aside, and a pop-eyed little man stares belligerently out at Marcus. "What you want?" he demands, "I busy."

Marcus pulls back his hood and stares into the man's eyes. The man studies his hands, suddenly interested in his fingernails.

"I am looking for the woman that used to live here." Marcus says. "Are you her husband?"

He laughs. "Husband? Me? Thesus no marry, whores cheaper! Her husband die in war, fight for General Scipio. She no have money." He points to the tiny apartment's roof. "I take her place, leave mine. Less pigeon shit. Glad she gone."

Marcus feels his pulse pound. He quells an urge to squeeze the man's throat until his eyes pop out of his head. He takes a step closer and leans into his face. "Where is she?"

Thesus shrugs. "Who care? She no pay debts, out she goes!"

V. Departure

Marcus reaches out with his left hand, grasps the man by the neck, and lifts him off his feet. His right pulls out a handful glittering silver denarii. He holds the coins in front of the choking man's nose. "I will ask you again. Where is she?"

Claudius gulps for air. "Quentius Cento took her. Big house on Caelian Hill. She a nexus for him."

Marcus relaxes his grasp, and the man collapses to the floor. The legate extends his left hand and sprinkles his coins over Thesus.

"A nexus?" Marcus asks. "She is a bond slave?"

Thesus crawls across the floor, picking up the coins. "Cento pay her debts, he own her. Warm his bed, I bet."

Marcus shakes his head. "You are lying. Bond slaves were outlawed ten years ago." [lxiii]

The man cackles. "You think so? You think slavery stop because rich men pass paper law? I have two nieces, they nexi in whorehouse. You go tell them, maybe they go free!"

The legate marches swiftly out the door, his hands balled into fists. He hurries down the steps and rushes out into the street, heading for the west end of the city. Within the hour Marcus is stalking up the side of the tree-covered Caelian hill. He splashes across the aqueduct, and marches into the lushly landscaped gardens of a hilltop villa, heading for its brass-studded entry doors.

Two muscular young men appear at the top of the walkway, their squat knobby cudgels dangling at their sides. They glare imperiously at the short stocky man trudging up the marble steps toward them.

"You are trespassing on the property of Quentius Cento, little man," shouts the tallest one, slapping his club into his palm. "Leave now, or you will become an object of our amusement." The other man grins at these words.

As Marcus nears the top he reaches into his cloak. His hand slides

V. Departure

across his belt and pulls out one of his throwing knives, his eye on the largest man's chest. He pulls one from his belt sheath, then puts it back. *They are only doing their jobs*, he reminds himself. He steps onto the villa threshold and stops in front of the smirking guards.

"I am Marcus Silenus, Legate to Rome. I demand an audience with your master."

The two men study his tattered cloak and splotched tunic. The tallest one grins, and takes a step closer to Marcus. "A legate's pay must be poor these days, if you have to dress like that!"

"Another good reason not to join the army," quips the other. "Now begone, old man, before we beat your head into mush!"

"If you were in my army, you would learn how to use those things," Marcus says, pointing at the nearest man's club. He crouches down. "Apologies, but I am in a hurry."

Marcus' left leg flashes out and scoops the man's feet out from under him. The guard crashes onto his back, stunned. In one swift movement, Marcus straddles the guard, knocks him flat, and yanks his cudgel from his slackened grip.

The second man rushes at Marcus, swooping his club at Marcus' skull. Marcus springs away from his victim. The cudgel whooshes past his ear and thunks into the ground. Marcus swings his club sideways, crunching it into the man's ribs. The guard doubles over, howling with pain. Marcus grabs the man's weapon and flings it down the hill.

"Be lucky I did not want your heads, boys," he says. "Stay here, and you will live to see the morning." He stalks through the entryway and into the vestibule, swinging the cudgel at his side.

The household attendants scatter before this grim shabby man who brandishes a club. They yell for their master.

Marcus stalks quickly through the atrium and into the hallway, sticking his head into every side room. *Jupiter's cock, I wish I knew her name so I could call her!*

V. Departure

Stepping out into the peristylium, he finds her in the open air gardens in the center of the manse. She is there, standing next to a squat marble statue of Diana, scrubbing the goddess' bird-stained bow and arrow. The slim young woman bends over and dips her rag into the small water jar that her toddler son solemnly holds for her. Her globe-shaped buttocks swell against her flimsy tunic, and Marcus feels himself swell.

"Come, we are going!" says Marcus to her back. The woman turns to face him, and her jaw drops open. "You!" she says. "The legionnaire!"

"My name is Marcus Silenus, and we are leaving. Now!" He takes the pottery jar from her son. He cries out, and Marcus empties the water and gives it back to him. "As you wish," he tells the child.

Marcus squeezes her hand and points toward the garden exit. "You are slaves no more. Follow me."

The woman picks up her son and scurries after Marcus. The trio hurries through the empty atrium toward the front door. They enter the vestibule and find the exit blocked by Quentius Cento, a fleshy, frog-faced man of middle years. The toga-clad Quentius stands in front of his two sword-bearing guards.

"You presume to take my property, beggar?" He looks at his guards. "Kill him."

The two young Thracians step around their master, swords at the ready.

Marcus' hand flashes sideways. The nearest guard drops his blade and grabs his sword shoulder, pulling at the throwing knife embedded to the hilt. The second man halts, wary of this raggedy man who crouches before him with another knife in his palm, looking at him as if he were prey.

"Quentius Cento, I am Marcus Silenus, Legate to Consul Publius Cornelius Scipio," Marcus booms. "Call your man off or I will kill him."

Cento peers into Marcus' yellow-green eyes. "You come here? For

V. Departure

this woman?"

"She is a friend of mine. You hold her illegally as a bonded slave. She goes with me or I will report you to the Senate."

"I paid good money for her. Paid all her debts!" Cento protests.

No sooner have the words left his mouth than a heavy leather purse flies into his face, knocking him onto his back. Silver and gold coins spill onto the floor. "That should pay you in full. And if it does not, come and see me for the rest. I will give you what you deserve."

Marcus strides past the fallen patrician. Cento's two guards flatten against the wall. They know well the name of Marcus Silenus.

Prisca and Marcus weave down a side path to the bottom of the hill and enter the main street leading to the Forum. The woman tugs at Marcus' tunic sleeve. "Wait, not another step!" she says, stepping in front of him.

"Are you who you say you are? A legate?"

He manages a tight smile. "Apologies. I am too focused on task to remember the proprieties. Yes, I am Legate Marcus Silenus of the Roman army." He looks expectantly at her.

"Prisca Valeria," the woman says, bowing her head slightly. She pulls her son in front of her and puts her hand on his shoulder. "This is Florus. My husband and I called him that because his cheeks bloom with color." She suddenly begins to sob, pulling her son to her. "Ah gods, are we truly free from that monster?"

"All will be well, as soon as we leave this city," Marcus replies.

He bends over and picks up Florus. "Will you come with me, little man?" he asks the child. "I will take you for a horseback ride!" Florus' eyes widen. His smile splits his face.

Marcus puts the four year old onto his shoulders and trots toward the city center, with a bewildered Prisca following along.

V. Departure

Within the hour they are at Rome's main stables, a checkerboard of small holding pens. A wizened stable hand rushes out to Marcus, grasping his hand in both of his. "Ah, Marcus Silenus, it is an honor! My boy talks of you all the time! He is a ballista operator in the third legion, you know."

Marcus smiles. "I would be pleased to meet him someday, Philo. Can you fetch us a wagon?"

"Let Mercury lend wings to my feet!" Philo exclaims, scurrying for the corrals. He soon rides back upon a two wheeled carriage pulled by a pair of chestnut mares. "This is my best cisium. It has a new wicker body and a freshly waxed leather seat!" He glances at Prisca. "Perfect for such a beautiful lady!"

"I will have to pay you tomorrow," Marcus replies. "I just threw my money away."

The old stable master grins. "Ah, I do the same. With my gambling and women, the coins fly out the door!"

Marcus takes the reins of the small carriage. "Prisca, would you accompany me to my home? You will be safe there." His face reddens. "There are others living there. We would not be alone."

Prisca nods, and laughs. "Of course. It is not as if I had anywhere else to go." She lifts her boy onto the seat and plops down next to him. Marcus vaults in alongside her, and snaps the reins. The cisium rumbles down the cobblestoned street toward the Porta Collina, Rome's northernmost gate.

Three hours later, Marcus and Prisca are deep into the fertile groves and fields of the lower Sabina Hills, watching the blue green Tiber flow past on their right. Marcus turns onto a narrow side road and wends his way between two prominent hills, waving at the freedmen harvesting the olive groves. He pulls up before a sprawling one-story farmhouse of white stone walls and red tiled roofs. A young boy rushes out and grasps the carriage reins.

"Salve, master," the boy chirps. "All is fine. The harvest is coming in

V. Departure

heavy. We will have lots of oil!"

Marcus helps Prisca down. She grasps Florus' hand and looks about the immaculately tended estate. "This is yours?" she asks.

He nods. "I needed a place away from the city. Too many people, not enough air." He turns to her. "This could be your home, too."

"You want me to stay here?" she asks, incredulous. Her eyes narrow. "What would be my duties?"

Marcus blinks at her. "Why, to be my wife. To manage it when I am away." He looks at the ground. "To take care of our children."

Prisca shakes her head. "We have only met twice, friend Marcus."

Marcus takes her hand, and holds it lightly in his calloused palm. "I have no family. I have no heir. War is coming to me, and I do not know what it will bring." He smiles at Florus. "And your son is strong and brave, as is his mother." His eyes light up. "I will finally have a family, and be a paterfamilias!"

"You are the finest man I have ever met. But you do not know me, Marcus Silenus. I am a woman of many moods," says Prisca, squeezing his hand.

"I do know you, Prisca," he continues. "You are one of us, a poor person—people who have a street spirit no matter how rich they become. When I found you living in the same apartment where I was born, I knew it was a sign from the gods. We were fated to be." He smiles shyly. "If you would have me."

Prisca takes his iron-cabled forearm in both her hands. She raises it to her face and kisses his wrist. "I only wonder how I can ever repay the gods for bringing you to me. I am yours, Marcus Silenus, in body and spirit..."

A week later the rustica villa is alive with pipers, tympanum players, and jugglers. Marcus stands out on his stone block patio, looking decidedly uncomfortable in his snow white toga. Prisca stands next to

V. Departure

General Scipio, robed in white with a flame-colored veil over her face.

Scipio takes her hand and places it in Marcus' leathered palm, giving her away to her husband. The priest blesses their exchange of vows, and crumples a sacrifice of wedding cake onto a small altar of Jupiter. Marcus and Prisca feed each other a piece of cake, sealing their vows. The bride and groom lead a procession around the perimeter of the farmhouse and into the front door, as the wedding invitees fling walnuts about their heads.

The wedding feast begins. Pomponia, Amelia, Lucius, and Scipio recline on couches about the happy couple, as the attendants rush about with plates of wedding food.

A beaming Laelius weaves over toward the wedding couple, already deep into on his third cup of wine. He walks behind the reclining Marcus and leans near his ear, that he might be heard over the pipers and drummers.

"I truly cannot believe it!" he blurts. "How did you find such a beauty and talk her into marrying you? Did you bribe her? Threaten her life?"

Marcus wipes his ear and turns his head sideways. "Fortuna drew me back to the place of my birth. Everything happened from there."

"The goddess certainly smiled upon you. But I must confess, I never saw you with a woman—or a man. I did not think marriage was in your destiny. And now you have a wife and child!" He shakes his head.

"I have never been concerned about returning from a war before," Marcus says softly. "But this Africa campaign, where Hannibal himself may engage us ... I thought it was time to make preparations."

"Psh!" exclaims Laelius. "You are indestructible."

Marcus lifts his cup toward Scipio, reclining on a couch opposite him. "I have an uneasy feeling about Africa, though I trust that our leader and friend will have made every possible preparation for victory. Pray to the gods that I am wrong."

V. Departure

* * * * *

CAMPUS MARTIUS, OUTSKIRTS OF ROME. "We will start as work soon as we come to Rome, King Scipio," says the muscular old Iberian. He points to a house-sized pile of rusting iron blocks. "We keep the iron watered and in the hot sun every day. Look at all that beautiful rust!" He takes his smith's hammer and clangs it off the side of a thick ingot. A patch of rust falls off. "Look at that lovely pure iron, rust takes them bad things away! We make good steel, King, you get good swords soon."

Laelius smiles. "You are 'King' Scipio now? The Senate had best not find out!"

Scipio shoves him away. "Be tolerant of his language, the man's Latin is better than my Iberian! And there is no Iberian word for 'consul,' anyway." Scipio picks at his purple bordered tunic, a slight smile on his face. "Besides, 'King Scipio' has an attractive sound to it."

Laelius throws up his hands in mock alarm. "Now you want to be King? I'm not sure I can endure an entire morning of weapons inspection with you today, if you are going to take that attitude!"

Scipio rolls his eyes. He turns back to his arms craftsman. "Excellent work, Lagunas. I want those blades so flexible they can be bent double. And I will test them myself!"

Scipio walks past several armorers' stalls until he comes to one that houses a famed javelin and spear maker. The lean Roman is busy directing his slaves to hammer out the ends of Scipio's new double-pointed spears.

"How goes it Didorus?" Scipio asks the freedman.

The armorer grins, his teeth shining in his soot-blackened face. He holds out a six-foot javelin. "See for yourself. I've added that second spearpoint on the bottom. And improved the balance."

Scipio hefts the spear in his hand. "Let's try it," he says, looking at Laelius. He whirls and jabs the spear toward Laelius. Laelius pirouettes

V. Departure

sideways and the spear passes by him, clanging against an iron-covered stall post. The spearhead bends back upon itself, useless. Scipio pulls the javelin back and spins it around so the other point faces out. He hurls it at a nearby fence, where it thunks deeply into a wooden railing. Scipio nods his satisfaction.

"Very good. Even with the point broken, the spear has enough balance for another good throw. Now our soldiers can fight on if the first spear point breaks." He hands the weapon back to Didorus. "Give me twelve thousand, just like this."

"Twelve thousand? That's a lot of spears," observes Laelius.

"Enough for two legions," Scipio replies. "When we get to Sicily, I'm going to build two of the largest legions in history, about six thousand men in each, instead of four thousand." [lxiv]

Laelius wrinkles up his face and squints at Scipio. "What? I thought you wanted more maneuverability."

Scipio shakes his head. "I want more maneuverability within the legions. Its ten cohorts will move independently of each other, each unit of six hundred men moving as one legionnaire. We need the larger legions to withstand the shock of attack." He smiles. "Two more changes to irk my traditionalist friends!"

"So you plan to change our swords, spears, legions, cohorts—all to suit your whims?" Laelius exclaims.

"All to suit our needs," answers Scipio. "Our Africa army will be small, and filled with inexperienced soldiers. If we face Hannibal there, we have to employ new tactics and weaponry if we are to have a chance."

"Well, he has certainly won enough battles against the old ways of fighting. Perhaps you can trick the trickster, and for once give us the element of surprise."

Scipio laughs, and shakes his head. "Perhaps. But gods help us all if Mago should join him."

V. Departure

*   *   *   *   *

LIGURIAN ALPS, NORTHWEST ITALIA, 205 BCE. Mago can see them, even though the mist is heavy in the valley. The drifting sea of shadows tell him there are thousands of men milling about down there, men who may be waiting to destroy his army. He paces out front of his command tent, wringing his hands to fend off the morning cold. *Maybe it's not the Montani. Best check before we attack.*

The wiry general turns to the one-handed giant who serves as chieftain of the Inguani. "Are those your enemies down there, Asrix? The ones we are supposed to attack?"

The barrel-chested chieftain thumps his spear upon the ground. "Montani pukes down there! Horse-fuckers, baby-eaters! They steal our women! Now we kill all!"

Mago blinks up at the auburn-bearded barbarian. "Well, I shall interpret that as a 'yes'," he says calmly.

Asrix snuffs loudly, baring his snaggled yellow teeth. "We kill now! All dead!"

Mago frowns at these words. He waggles his finger under the nose of the towering chieftain, as if chiding an errant child. "Remember our agreement. If they surrender we take prisoners, not heads! Understand?"

The chieftain chews moodily on his drooping mustache. He shakes his head. "No prisoners. Kill all. No more trouble!"

Mago throws up his hands. "Aaagh! I hate these stone-headed savages!" He turns to Baelon, the stout old chieftain of the neighboring Ligurians. "This is what I feared would happen," Mago says. "He wants to wipe them out. I need prisoners for Carthage!"

Baelon sniffs. "He is scared, that is all. The Montani tribe greatly outnumbers the Inguani. He fears revenge."

Mago paces about, rubbing his chin. He turns to Baelon. "Tell Asrix I

V. Departure

promise that none of them down there will threaten him again. He can take my head if I lie."

Baelon steps past Mago and speaks to Asrix in his native tongue. Asrix shakes his head. Baelon replies stridently, shoving the chieftain. Asrix nods reluctantly, and Baelon walks back to Mago. "His men will cease fighting when you sound the call."

Mago looks over the glowering Asrix. "He doesn't look like he's happy with that."

Baelon shrugs. "Who cares? He will do it. He swears on his children's eyes. What more could you ask?"

Asrix stalks away toward his men, clearly angry.

"What did you tell him to get him to agree?" Mago asks.

"That you would give him the Montani's lands," Baelon replies casually. "And that you will marry one of his daughters."

Mago's eyes start from his head. "Married! I'm already married, and I don't need an Inguani wife following me around! I march on Rome, and it is two full moons away from here!"

Baelon waves away Mago's protests. "You have much wealth and power, you can afford many wives. Why not take one more? You marry, fuck her for a while, then leave for war. And you don't come back. It is no problem!" He frowns reprovingly. "You are a strange man."

"I hope to stay strange, then," snipes Mago, already walking back toward his Libyan phalanxes. "Now get your men into the center lines." Baelon thumps his chest with his fist, signaling his affirmation. "You will have a long fight today, Carthaginian," he adds. "Montani are strong warriors."

V. Departure

LIGURIAN ALPS

MONTANI

LIBYANS   LIGURIANS   INGUANI   BALEARICS

NUMIDIAN CAVALRY

ELEPHANTS

MAGO'S CAMP

205 BCE
MAGO BARCA
VERSUS THE MONTANI

"Well, I have a surprise or two for them," the general replies. "We'll see how strong they are then."

As he takes the reins of his horse, Mago grins with anticipation. *Let's see if Scipio's little trick will help me beat these savages. It worked well enough against me at Ilipa.*

V. Departure

Mago rides down the hill toward the wide plateau where his army is arrayed. He moves past the Numidian cavalry waiting in the rear, then pauses atop a small rise at the plateau's edge. He can see the Montani horde massed a half mile east of his men, their tall spears glistening in the rising morning sun. Their rude lines stretch back to the cloud-clawing Alps that sprawl behind them.

A falcon swoops across the brightening sky, screeching its presence to the world. *A bird of prey visits us. That is a good omen. The gods are telling me to swoop down on my prey.* He grins. *Yes, beasts may decide this battle today.*

Mago leads his men down from the plateau to the waiting Montani. The Montani's battle horns echo across the valley. Now he can clearly see his enemy; a mile-wide line of men four deep, standing in uneven lines interrupted by the scattered cavalry. *Hmm, there may be eight or ten thousand of them down there. All of them are probably experienced fighters. But their lines are disorganized. Typical barbarians. Big and crazy.*

The Montani are as tall as the neighboring Gauls, with whom they have intermixed. Many of them top six feet. They carry the same oblong shields and long heavy swords as Mago's Inguani and Ligurians. *Large men with larger weapons*, thinks Mago. *What do these people eat to get so big? Each other?*

As Mago's army descends onto the level ground, he shouts for his divisions to assume formation. The horns sound. The Libyan commanders lead their infantry past Mago's left side, securing his left flank. The gargantuan Korbis leads three thousand Balearic infantry into the right flank, lightly armored men who count on mobility as their defense.

Baelon and Asrix's men occupy the center sections, marching along in loosely organized rows that Mago knows will dissolve in the heat of battle. Mago tries to ignore the two tribes as they curse and insult one other, each betting they will take more heads and plunder, each joking about the other's sexual failings. *Gods below, they are worse than children*, he thinks. The mountain tribesmen are brash, but they are

V. Departure

apprehensive. They know the mettle of these Montani.

When the two armies draw within three spear casts of each other, the Montani set up a deafening clamor. Thousands of thick-armed warriors beat their short handled battle axes on their shields. The sea of noise drowns out Mago's commands, forcing him to gesture his orders to his commanders. In the midst of the deafening din, Mago smiles. *I see Asrix's point. I wouldn't want to leave any of them around to come after me either.* And then, sadly, *What might Hannibal have done if he had those brutes fighting with him years ago? We might be dining in Rome by now.*

Mago heaves a heavy sigh. *Best to get on with it.* He signals for the call to attack. The Carthaginian horns blare out their signals. The Montani erupt in a mighty shout and tramp toward the Ligurians and Inguani.

Mago's center lines halt momentarily. The Inguani and Ligurians stand immobile, dangling their swords at their sides, cursing with impatience. There is a flurry of movement behind them. Hundreds of Balearic slingers slip out between the forest of barbarians, slim youths wearing only a light brown tunic and sandals. The skirmishers rush into the clearing between their men and the advancing Montani.

The Balearics plant their feet into the frozen turf, facing their enemy sideways. They unfurl the shortest of the three slings wrapped about their heads, the one designed for short range throwing. Each slinger stuffs an egg-shaped river rock into their sling's leather pouch, hefting the stone to measure its throw.

The Montani draw within two spear throws. They laugh at the diminutive foes facing them. Several barbarians fling their spears at the slingers, but the wiry youths readily dodge them. Mago waves his right hand, and the horns sound again. As one, the Balearics whirl their slings over their heads and whip them forward, the stones arcing down into the Montani's rear lines. The missiles ring off helmets, thud off shields, and crunch into bodies. There are scattered screams and grunts as scores of Montani are cudgeled down. There is no more laughter.

V. Departure

The mountain tribesmen raise their shields high and march forward slowly, as the slingers rocket their stones into the faces of the front line Montani. A bare-headed chieftain rides out in front of his tribesmen, his face red with anger. Ignoring the stones that whiz past him, he curses his tribesmen for being cowards. The chieftain gallops forward, rocks ringing off his shield, and stampedes into the Balearics, scattering them like sheep.

The abashed Montani regain their nerve and charge toward the Balearics. They volley their spears into the slingers, too many for them to dodge. Dozens of youths fall to the earth, pulling at the spears that have pierced their vitals. The remaining islanders sling a few more volleys, slowing the Montani attack, then dash back to the rear lines.

Mago gallops out in front of the center-line Ligurians and Inguani, arrayed in a silver helmet and a rock-hard cuirass of glued white linen, his purple cape flowing behind his broad shoulders. He faces Asrix's and Baelon's men. "Follow me!" he shouts.

Mago trots forward and flings his spear into the onrushing horde, then pulls out his gleaming curved sword. Seeing their general riding ahead of them, his armor glinting like a beacon, Asrix and Baelon run to follow him, screaming their tribal war chants. Their men quickly follow, swords drawn and ready.

Mago's allies run at the Montani, and the left-flank Libyans march steadily forward. As Mago ordered, the Libyans lag slightly behind the onrushing Ligurians and Inguani, waiting for their advantage.

Korbis leads the Balearic light infantry forward on the right flank. His eyes gleam with battle lust. "Today we kill them all!" he shouts to his men. "Every man takes a head, or he does not come back!"

With a mighty shout, the Ligurians and Inguani collide with the onrushing Montani. The armies' battle horns are drowned beneath the din of iron clashing upon iron, the crunch of blade into wood.

The Montani rush to battle in tightly knit clans, leaving gaps that are loosely defended by the men behind them. They swarm across Mago's

V. Departure

front lines, heedless of the spears that strike down their fellows.

The Montani hack at any man within their reach, their thick hand axes splitting shield, helmet, and skull. In their haste to kill and plunder, the Montani in the rear shove their kin forward into Mago's men. The Montani attack line becomes a thick mass of fighters.

The fierce Ligurians and Inguani stand their ground. They scream with the terrified joy of battle as they hew their thick blades into the heads and shields of the Montani, shoving their long swords into the bodies of those who lower their guard.

Asrix leads his Inguani into a charge at the heart of the thickly pressed Montani. He drops his shield and grabs his long sword with both hands, battering down any that confront him, as his men follow him deeper into the Montani line.

The center of battle becomes a great crashing melee of battling barbarians. Heedless of discipline or formation, the two sides rush into any opening they can find in the other's lines. The battle devolves into a milling, deadly brawl.

Baelon falls, pierced by a Montani chief's sword thrust into his liver. He pushes himself to one knee, only to have his gigantic foe yank Baelon's helmet back and strike his head from his shoulders.

The victorious Montani holds his grisly trophy aloft, prompting cheers from his tribesmen. Baelon's kin scream with rage and swarm over the Montani before he can escape to the protection of his men. They cut his limbs from his body, flinging the arms and legs at his kinsmen.

The Montani on the left flank charge toward the oncoming Libyan phalanxes. The front line Libyans kneel down and plant their long spears into the ground, creating a bristling spear wall. The front line Montani are pushed into the wall by the men behind them —scores of them scream in agony as they are impaled upon the unmoving lances. The Libyans kick the bodies off their weapons and stand up, ready to thrust their spears into the next wave.

The Montani continue to batter against the phalanx' shield wall.

V. Departure

Dozens of tribesmen dive to the ground and pull a warrior's feet out from under him, heedless of the Libyans' thrusts into their shoulders and backs. Pairs of them gang up on a single soldier; one occupies the soldier's shield and sword as the other chops their ax into the greaves around the Libyans' lower legs, breaking a leg or hewing through a shin. Clusters of Libyans fall, and the Montani rush into the breaks.

The tribesmen suffer heavy losses, but they penetrate into the Libyans' second line, killing scores of the Africans. But the staunch Libyans have fought many battles, and they refuse to panic.

Hundreds of fresh soldiers rush into the gaps in the front two lines of the phalanxes. The replacements lance into the Montani, cutting into their backs and chests. The grim Libyan officers shove the replacements into any place a Libyan falls, and the phalanxes slowly beat back the Montani.

On the other flank the Balearics have engaged in a deadly dance with the warring barbarians. The quick-footed light infantry spread out for mobility, creating wide gaps where they can move. When a Montani charges an islander, he ducks and sidesteps the barbarian's deadly ax swings, countering with a wounding stab to the arm or shoulder.

The Balearics' elusive tactics begin to tire out their heavy opponents. The Montani begin to hold their shields low, and their ax swings slow. The Balearics become more aggressive, darting in for stabs to the giant barbarians' chests and stomachs.

Scores of Montani stagger from the fight, bleeding from multiple cuts. More fall where they stand, too weak to fend off the final blow to their throat or torso. But the fight is not a rout: many an unwary or slow-footed islander is knocked down by a blow from an ax or sword, to be chopped to pieces before he can rise.

Korbis does not duck or dodge. He delights in trading blows against opponents his own size, savoring the force of his enemy's ax blows as they thud into his shield, tingling his brawny forearm.

"Come on!" he screams at them, grinning like a madman. "Come kill

V. Departure

me if you can!"

Korbis uses his heavy falcata to chop apart the unrimmed wooden shields of his opponents, hewing off chunks until nothing remains to stay his thrusts to face or heart. Soon he fights in the midst of an island of dead barbarians.

The Montani chieftain sees the futility of battling the elusive islanders, and he waves for his men to follow him. The chieftain wisely runs around Korbis and his guard, ignoring the Balearic chieftain's challenges to fight him. Instead, the Montani leader rushes his men through a field of Korbis' dispersed light infantry and heads in to attack the right flank of the Inguani. With a roar of dismay Korbis wheels about and runs after the barbarians, motioning for his men to follow him to the rear.

The center line fight rages on, with little ground given on either side. After bloodying his sword on a few stout warriors, Mago has retreated to a rise behind the front lines, an elevation where he can best direct the battle. He sees the Montani pouring in from his right flank, pursued by the Balearics, and his eyes widen with alarm.

Mago turns to his Sacred Band captain. "I need you to attack the right side," he bellows, pointing his sword at the incoming Montani. "Every man picks a Montani. No one returns without a kill!" Two hundred of Carthage's finest swordsmen trot down the rise and join the Balearics.

The Montani rush at their new foe, expecting them to dodge away like the Balearics. But Carthage's Sacred Band warriors do not run from anyone. The Carthaginians expertly deflect the ax blows and shield thrusts, countering with lighting quick cuts to the barbarians' ribs and neck. Soon hundreds of Montani are dead or writhing on the ground, and their flanking penetration is halted.

The battle rages for another hour. Mago watches it with rapt attention, and his disappointment grows. *The Inguani and Ligurians are starting to walk away from the fight. Time to bring on the beasts.*

"Zinnridi!" he shouts to his officers. "Get me Zinnridi!" When his

V. Departure

second in command appears, Mago points at the back of his army, toward his camp. "Bring them up," Mago orders. His commander gallops back behind the rear lines.

Minutes later, the earth rumbles behind Mago. The ground begins to shake. Then they appear.

A score of rampaging elephants barges past each side of Mago, nightmare beasts draped in Tyrian purple chain mail, with spear-toting mahouts riding high upon their backs. A dozen Libyans trot alongside each elephant to protect the beast from sword attacks, a protective trick Mago has learned after Marcus Silenus stampeded Carthage's elephants at the Battle of Ilipa.

Looking like monsters from the underworld, the trumpeting beasts stampede down the rise and rush into the gaps between the center infantry and the flanks. The elephants trample into the astounded Montani. They crush scores of fear-paralyzed warriors, as their mahouts strike down dozens with their twelve-foot spears.

Many of the Montani drop their weapons and run for their lives, calling for their gods to save them. In their frenzy to escape, hundreds of the barbarians careen into their own men. They knock their fellows into disarray, leaving them vulnerable to killing attacks from Mago's Inguani and Ligurians, men who have no fear of the beasts they have camped with.

Seeing the Montani crumble, the Libyans press their advantage and push into the left flank. Mago knows the momentum is his, and he has to seize the opportunity. And so he plays his final gambit.

The battle horns sound a charge, and the entire rear of Mago's army springs into action. Thousands of Libyans trot out from the rear, fresh phalanxes that sweep around the Montani's left flank, heading for the rear lines. To the right, Mago's peerless Numidian cavalry whirl out from behind the scattered Balearics. They storm around the edge of the engaged Montani and loop into the back, dashing about to spear down the rear lines of Montani.

V. Departure

Now chaos reigns among the enemy barbarians. Mago's men begin to close their circle of death about their desperate opponents, ignoring the hundreds of them who dash for the hills. The Libyans methodically spear down their outnumbered enemies, closing in toward Mago and his center line.

Soon the battle has become a methodical execution. The Ligurians and Inguani watch each other overwhelm knots of unyielding Montani. They argue over who has taken the most heads, as they toss them into a pile and stalk back to slay the last of their surrounded opponents.

The fall sun casts its long shadows over the stinking charnel field as the deafening crash of battle mutes to the scattered clashes and screams of final combat. Mago calls a halt to the slaughter. He makes it a point to issue the command while he and his Sacred Band stand next to Asrix, to ensure his compliance.

The hundreds of remaining Montani are carefully tied up and led off. The Inguani and Ligurians wade through the rows of the fallen, cheerfully stabbing out the life of any enemy who cannot rise.

Mago calls over Asrix and points at the prisoners. "I am sending them to the slave markets of Carthage. They will never come back. I have kept my promise to you." Mago smiles. *This will show the Senate we can win in Italia. Then I will get more troops from them. Maybe Hannibal will get some, too.*

The Carthaginian's green eyes gleam with triumph and anticipation. He can see himself leading a vast army to the gates of Rome, where he will be reunited with his brother Hannibal. There, they will watch the city burn, his Libyans killing every pestilent Roman who runs from its flames. He scratches his shoulder and smiles. *It is good to have a purpose in life.*

Asrix shakes his sword at Mago, and grins. "Good. You take all away, keep promise." His grin widens. "Now you keep other promise. You marry my daughters."

Mago frowns, then his eyes widen with alarm. *Baal's breath save me,*

V. Departure

did he say 'daughters'?

* * * * *

ROME. "Are they coming?" Scipio asks for the tenth time. Rufus stares down the street, rubbing his rheumy eyes. "I do think I hear the flutes, he says with a smile. "But it could be the wind..."

"Bother you, Rufus!" Scipio says peevishly. "Amelia and I just took our vows with the priest over at her house down the street. The wedding party should be right behind me. Tell me you cannot see a crowd coming down here!"

Rufus pretends to stare harder, as Scipio notes the faint sounds of music. "Ah, they approach!" adds Rufus needlessly.

Scipio peers down the street. Minutes later, he watches the dancing, laughing, crowd materialize before him. His beloved bride walks along in the center. Scipio runs to the doors and flings them open, his heart hammering with excitement. *At last!*

Amelia passes through the doorway of the Scipio manse and into the entrance hall, carried in by her younger brother and two laughing cousins. The rest of the Aemilii Paulli network flows in, eager for the ceremony—and the feast. They are roughly pushed aside by the massive Ursus. The garlanded dog presses his way through the throng, searching for his mistress and barking happily.

For now, Pomponia's domus will serve at the couple's new house, because Scipio will be leaving soon for Sicily. But the ceremony is no less joyous for that—it is evident the couple only have eyes for one another, not their surroundings.

Amelia's cousins set her down on the other side of the threshold. She smoothes her ritualistic white flannel tunic and flame-colored veil and stands waiting for her betrothed. Amelia bows her head demurely; a slight smile is upon her face.

Laelius steps in behind Amelia. He carries a torch for her, as is the wedding custom. Acting in the stead of Amelia's deceased father,

V. Departure

Laelius gives Amelia a burning brand from the hearth of her childhood home. He kisses her deeply on the mouth, his eyes moist. "My most beloved friends, finally married. Oh Gods, you two bless me so!" Laelius wears a simple toga. He knows it is the bride's time to shine.

Marcus Silenus stands next to Laelius, looking decidedly uncomfortable in his snowy white toga. His gnarled hands clench and unclench at he waits for the ceremony to start—and end. He glances over at his wife Prisca and her son Florus Silenus. *At last I have a family*, he rejoices.

Pomponia stands behind her treasured friend Marcus, glorious in a flowing turquoise gown, her red hair laced with threads of gold. She leans down to Marcus' ear. "Take heart, my dear, it will soon be over." Marcus merely grunts, but it is a satisfied grunt.

Amelia steps toward Scipio and gives him the torch of her hearth, signifying her move from her parent's house to his own. Scipio gives her the torch from his own fireplace, indicating his acceptance of their sharing a home. Next to them is a small brazier of burning wood and a shallow bowl of water. Amelia touches both of these essential elements of life, sealing her bond with Scipio.

The pronuba joins their hands, and the matron of honor steps away as the priest comes to the fore, gesturing for them to repeat their earlier vows.

Scipio stares deeply into Amelia's teary green eyes. Her voice trembles as she chants to him "Ubi tu Gaius, ego Gaia (where you are Gaius, I am Gaia)," and squeezes his hand.

"Ubi tu Gaia, ego Gaius," he replies. Scipio reaches to Amelia's waist and unties the knotted rope he placed there for their engagement. With that, the formal marriage ceremony is finished

Laughing with delight, the women pelt the couple with walnuts to make their marriage a fertile one. The men from both families join in a bawdy song about the marriage god Hymen visiting the ceremony and fleeing when the bride is penetrated. Several of the drunkest ones act

V. Departure

out the words as they sing, and are pelted with nuts by their disapproving wives.

As the men sing, the pronuba leads Amelia into the couple's new bedroom and gently undresses her, easing her naked body under the snow white marriage linens. Soon Scipio joins her, pushing his way through the dense collection of wreaths and flowers that veils the doorway and surrounds the bed.

The guests feast and sing for hours in the atrium, the two families celebrating their new bond. The death mask of Amelia's father, Lucius Aemillius Paullus, is brought in for the celebration. It is propped up on a table next to the mask of Publius Cornelius Scipio, so that the two fathers might share their children's joy.

Pomponia is continually in motion, ensuring that all the guests are fed and entertained, pausing only to politic a visiting senator or two for more troops for her son. The food attendants bustle about, refilling goblets and platters. Laelius moves from one group to the next, regaling young and old alike with his stories about the docks of Ostia and the war in Iberia.

Only Marcus sits somberly, sipping a cup of watered wine, carefully watching the guests and attendants. He notices that one unfamiliar slave follows Pomponia with furtive eyes, a dark young man who busily refills wine cups from the large pottery flagons he fetches from the kitchen.

The young man runs into the kitchen and returns with a fresh flagon. He steps next to a distracted Pomponia and gently retrieves her empty cup, filling it with the sweet Alban wine she has ordered for the occasion. As he turns to hand her the cup his free hand flashes over the top of it. He swirls the cup and hands it to Pomponia before he dashes off to serve another celebrant.

Pomponia grabs the cup, laughing as she talks to portly old Senator Gracchus, an uncle of Pomponia's haruspex. He nods agreeably to her troop proposals but his greedy eyes do not leave the fulsome swell of her breasts, barely concealed beneath her diaphanous gown. Pomponia

V. Departure

stares at him until she catches his eyes, and pulls his eyes up to her face.

Pomponia drops two toasted bread crusts into her wine. Smiling seductively, she raises her wine goblet to her lips. "A toast to the happy couple. May the gods bring them long life and many children."

The senator abruptly stumbles into her, dashing the goblet's contents onto her front, almost knocking her from her feet. "Ap ... apologies," stammers the bewildered Gracchus. The flustered senator pulls out a linen kerchief and dabs at Pomponia's now transparent décolletage. Pomponia snatches it from his hands. "I will do that," she snaps.

The senator bobs his head, flush with embarrassment. "Somebody just hit me from behind, I swear. It was like they pitched me into you." Pomponia eyes him dubiously, and looks about her. All she sees are knots of chatting partygoers and the broad back of Marcus Silenus, marching quickly toward the smoky kitchen at the side of the house.

Marcus hurries after the wine attendant. He unwraps his toga and pitches it to the ground. As he passes the family altar, Marcus reaches into his wide tunic belt. *Where are those damned things?* He curses to himself.

The attendant has already merged into the bustling kitchen. He ignores the waiting food and wine and weaves his way toward the rear exit into the side courtyard. The slave hears a tumult behind him and looks over his shoulder to see a grim Marcus Silenus plowing his way through the other attendants, his eyes fixed on him. "Shit!" the slave hisses. He dashes out the open exit, running toward the front wall that parallels the street.

The slave darts to the wall and crouches to spring up to its top. An excruciating pain explodes in the back of his knee, followed by an agonizing pain in his thigh. The assassin crumples to the earth, two stubby Kordofani throwing knives jutting from his leg.

The terrified man scrambles up, grasping at his thigh. A pair of iron hands flings him backwards as effortlessly as a child might pitch a doll.

V. Departure

The slave lands on his back, breathless, and stares up into Marcus Silenus' yellow-green eyes.

Marcus plants a knee in the slave's chest and puts the last of his knives against the man's throat. "Who?" he demands. "Who? Tell me or I carve your bowels!"

The terrified assassin babbles incoherently. Marcus gives him a ringing slap and shakes him. "Talk or you die!"

"You will not harm me if I tell?" he manages to stammer.

"You can lose your hand or your life, the choice is yours," Marcus says flatly, as if proffering a choice of fruit.

The slave swallows. "He was a tall, lanky, man, robed in black. He rubbed his ass while he talked about her," he blurts, "and that is all I know."

Marcus leans back. "Flaccus!" he mutters to himself.

Without another word, Marcus slides his leaf shaped blade deep into the side of the man's throat and carves a deep gaping gash across it. "I do not make pacts with assassins," he says, watching the light fade from the killer's eyes.

Marcus rises from the lifeless body and pulls it into the back of Pomponia's thick rose bushes, scrabbling earth over it. He turns his tunic inside out to hide the blood spots, and calmly walks back toward the reception. He weaves his way through the kitchen tumult, dons his toga, and returns to the wedding party.

The legate walks over to stand near Pomponia, watching her as carefully if she were some rare animal that might escape. She notices Marcus' gaze and walks over to him, affectionately squeezing his rock-hard shoulder.

"Are you fine?" she asks, looking concerned. "You have a strange look about you."

V. Departure

Marcus grins at his beloved friend, but his burning eyes contradict his lips. "Just a spot of bad wine I had to get rid of," he remarks. "Not worth talking about now. Today is a day of joy, after all."

* * * * *

SABINA HILLS. As his roosters welcome the rising sun, Flaccus rises from his ornately decorated sleeping pallet. He pads into his villa's expansive indoor gardens to visit the stone toilets he had built next to the peristylium, eschewing the clay pots his neighbors use. After sponging off his private parts, Flaccus pulls up his subligalculum and pulls his tunic over it, humming a feasting song. He steps into the garden and basks in the low morning sun, enjoying the twittering of his caged finches. *By now she should be dead*, he smiles to himself. *That should divert Scipio's attention for a while. Then we can move to limit his troop allotments in Sicily.*

Flaccus sits on his favorite stone bench, watching the partridges peck about the thyme and mint bushes. *It will be a wonderful day.*

"You are pleased by the morning?" asks a voice from behind him.

Marcus Silenus steps out from the shadow of a chestnut oak. "Or perhaps you are enjoying the thought of some other event. One that would be a misfortune for another. That is your favorite kind, is it not?"

Flaccus leaps up to shout for help but Marcus already has a throwing knife cocked at him. "You will be dead before you finish!"

Flaccus says nothing, but his eyes turn to his villa.

"Your guards will not come. I have seen to that."

Flaccus sees the knife shining in the morning light, the thin line of its nocked and razored edge gleaming from a fresh sharpening. He sits down, watching Marcus as a mouse would watch a cat.

"Your assassin is dead, Flaccus."

V. Departure

Flaccus shakes his head. "What are you talking about?"

Marcus slaps the patrician's face, the sound ringing off the garden walls. Flaccus' eyes glaze over, and he staggers sideways. Marcus grabs the patrician's chin. "Do not waste your breath on denials. I know it was you."

Marcus pushes his knife into his belt. "The only reason you are not holding your bowels in your hands is because she begged me to spare you, lest the scandal affect her sons."

Flaccus slumps over, relieved. "At least she has some sense," he mutters.

Marcus smiles grimly. "But I must give you a strong memory of retribution, else you try this mischief again."

Marcus' left hand darts out and clamps over Flaccus windpipe. His right hand sticks a knife into the senator's stringy shoulder, cutting into the join of shoulder to chest. Flaccus' eyes bulge and his lips flap soundlessly. Marcus twists the knife and withdraws it. He pushes Flaccus to the ground, still choking him to silence. When he is assured Flaccus will not cry out he releases his throat. Flaccus curls into a ball and clutches his shoulder, whimpering piteously.

The veteran legionnaire stands over the wounded senator, his fists clenched. "When we leave for Sicily, you will become her protector. Because if anything happens to her, or to Amelia, I will strike your family down. All of them."

Marcus cups the senator's chin, forcing him to look him into his steely eyes. "And you, you I will save for last. I will skin you on a cross. Upside down, so you cannot pass out. Strip by strip."

Marcus uncoils a thick string from his belt. He deftly knots Flaccus' hands behind his back, ripping strips off his tunic to muffle him. He rolls his captive into the back bushes.

"Dare to report this, and the Scipios will testify against you for attempted murder. We will see who the people believe." The army

V. Departure

commander walks out through the side garden entrance. He takes his time, savoring the chirping of the multicolored warblers that skip about the oak tree branches. *It looks to be a good day.*

* * * * *

PORT OF OSTIA, 205 BCE. The late summer sun arcs its long morning shadows across the bobbing fleet of newly built warships. Scipio stands at the edge of the Ostia docks, smiling at the sight of his newly-built fleet arrayed before him. *Praise Jupiter, they met my impossible demands. It is time to go to Sicily.*

With Scipio pushing the shipwrights night and day, the craftsmen have built a fleet of twenty quinqueremes and ten quadriremes, all within the allotted forty four days. The quinqueremes are massive ships that will carry a hundred marines, rowed by three hundred free men that Scipio will use as land infantry in Africa. The smaller and lighter quadriremes will first be used to patrol the coastal waters of Sicily, but Scipio plans to eventually use them as plundering African raiders, led by the bold Laelius.[lxv]

As Consul Scipio, his primary duty is to oversee the protection of Sicily. As General Scipio, he has his mind on Carthage. Sicily is but a way station to his African campaign.

The deep-bellied supply transports form a semicircle about the harbor warships. The transports float low in the water, loaded with supplies for tomorrow's trip to Sicily. Most are filled with the necessities for an army campaign: wheat, barley, beans, wine, cheese, dried fruit, cookpots, packs, spare sandals and tunics, repair tools, and ship's sealing wax. Other ships carry thousands of newly minted swords, spears, and weapons.

Scipio has left the weapons' accounting to Marcus' and Laelius' critical eyes, but he personally monitors the quantity and quality of food and supplies loaded onto his ships. He is determined not to be another cautionary tale about a powerful army undone by poor logistics.

V. Departure

Scipio is satisfied with his preparations—for the time being. As is his custom, he has sifted his fingers through the grain, and bent his newly forged sword blades to test their resiliency. On horseback, he and Laelius have practiced attacks with his new two-pronged cavalry lances. The spears now have a lizarder on their end, a long spike that allows his cavalry to reverse their lances if the heads are lost. It is an old Greek style used by the hoplite warriors past centuries.

Scipio has had thousands of the spears forged, ignoring the veterans' protests about mimicking the despised Greeks. *If they only knew I copied Hannibal's ambush tactics*, he laughs to himself.

A half-dozen troop transports are moored at the docks. The last of Scipio's volunteer army marches in formation up the gangplanks, under Scipio's watchful eye. *Their lines are even*, he notes. *There is hope for them yet.*

Scipio has insisted the men march in formation even when boarding, trying to instill the unwavering self-discipline that is part of a legionnaire's nature. Scipio has decided that every one of the recruits' waking hours will be a training hour, every one of their actions will be guided by Roman discipline. In return for their compliance, he will provide lavish feasts as a reward. Scipio has finally learned that morale is as important as discipline.

Yesterday, Scipio finished his preparations with a morale-boosting show for his men. He sacrificed a score of oxen and watched the state augurists examine a dozen sheep's' entrails. When they told Scipio the portents were all favorable—their decision boosted by a surreptitious purse—he quickly relayed the priests' judgment to his men, knowing they would be loathe to sail without good news. *That should boost morale*, he thinks. *I must remind them of the portents when things become difficult.*

When everyone is on the ships Scipio marches onboard, head high and steps measured. He wears his purple toga picta and a newly forged gladius hispaniesis, his brow wreathed with a circlet of olive branches. He is determined to look the part of an Imperator and hero, so that the men will follow him blindly into any battle.

V. Departure

Scipio's stern Honor Guard follows him, including the three gladiators and three patricians he rescued from the games. They have been assigned to protect the two large oak chests that contain Scipio's history scrolls and maps.

"Why are we guarding moldy old scrolls?" asks Praxis, the senior gladiator.

"The General thinks these are more precious than gold," a patrician guard replies. "He says they are his secret weapon."

Praxis looks at his fellow gladiators. They shake their heads, mystified. "Well, it is better than fighting in the ring," he says with a shrug.

Scipio takes his fleet south for the Strait of Messina between Italia and Sicily. He plans to arrive in Syracuse, his headquarters, by morning of the next day. It is a brief journey but he is uncharacteristically anxious. He knows he has less than nine months to complete the recruitment, training, and equipping of his entire African force for a spring campaign. He cannot wait another year, risking his campaign to the whims of the Senate

As he watches Ostia's low hills fade from sight, he racks his brain to see if he has overlooked anything. *I have checked everything, from the plumes on the officers' helmets to the biscuits in the soldiers' bellies. What have I forgotten?* Scipio reaches into his belt purse and fingers his Nike figurine. He feels reassured that everything is under control.

But the capricious goddess Fortuna laughs at those who think they can control their destiny by careful planning. The goddess has favored the brash and inventive Scipio so far, but this time she will not make an exception for him. Fortuna has some surprises in store for him, from the men he counts as friends.

VI. SICILY

SYRACUSE, SICILY, 205 BCE. "Curse those new exploratores, I can hardly read this chart! And where are the outlines of the coastal hills? I should crucify both of those pumpkins!"

Scipio is looking over his new map of Northern Africa, trying to decipher its rude outlines and details. He is perched over his enormous map table inside his expansive headquarters in the port city of Syracuse, the capital of this island nation near the tip of Italia.

As soon as he arrived in Syracuse, Scipio converted his tapestry-filled quarters into a war room, replacing its elegant dining furniture with bins of his ubiquitous maps and scrolls. Recently he has added piles of his newly designed swords, spears, and pack biscuits, so can test them at his leisure.

Laelius and Marcus Silenus stand patiently behind him, amused by the irritable fussiness Scipio displays in private, accustomed to his insatiable attention to detail.

"There!" says Scipio. "This little town on the coast near Carthage. That's Hippo Acra. That's where you will meet him." Scipio leans back from the goatskin map of Northern Africa, and looks at Laelius. "Masinissa should be there at the next full moon. I already sent messengers to notify him."

"If they can find him," growls Marcus. "Our exploratores say Syphax has run Masinissa out of his own kingdom." He shrugs. "Perhaps they are just rumors."

Laelius blinks incredulously at Scipio, and smiles. "Meet him at the next full moon? Gods below, you are in a bit of a hurry, aren't you?"

Marcus Silenus stares curiously at Scipio. "That leaves Laelius less

VI. Sicily

than a week to organize and sail," he notes.

"We have less than eight months before spring is in full flower," replies Scipio. "By then we must all be on Africa's northern shores. Laelius, you must arrive as soon as possible so you can ease our fleet's passage to Africa. I need you to raid and plunder the coastal areas about Carthage, to raise fear and alarm. That will drive the Carthaginians to collect their forces about their city. And draw them away from us."

"Certainly, Laelius' marauding will prompt Carthage to bring more of their warships back to Africa," notes Marcus, puzzled. "But then they will be out in force by the time we arrive."

Scipio nods. "Yes, and likely guarding the coastal towns that Laelius plunders." He smiles. "But I have another landing spot for us." He sees them both looking at him. "I will tell you another time," he says mischievously.

Laelius wrinkles his nose. "Did you say 'plundered'? I take it this is not just an intelligence mission."

Scipio sighs. "More like propaganda. Most of our volunteers have never experienced battle, and the old legionnaires are a bit jaded. We have to inspire them to fight. When you return with a shipload of plunder, we'll show them what treasures can be theirs. That will motivate them."

"Admiral Laelius, now Laelius the pirate," blurts Laelius. "Would Mother were alive to see me attain such elevated status!"

Scipio winks at him. "You might prefer the term 'raider,' it does not sound as criminal. Mother would favor that, would she not?"

Laelius laughs. "I don't know about my real mother, whoever she was. But Mother Pomponia would certainly approve of either term, since they both bear the tinge of rebelliousness!"

Scipio nods. "Yes, she is a bit of a raider herself. Can you do it, Admiral Fancy Toga?"

VI. Sicily

Marcus turns his head slightly toward Laelius, his face stern. "Why ask? He will do it because it is necessary."

Laelius rolls his eyes at Scipio. "As the old goat bleats, I will do it because we need Masinissa's men. Let me take three quadriremes with me, and fill them with my best marines. That will give me eighty soldiers per ship."

Scipio nods. "Accepted. Whatever ships you find vulnerable, attack them. Raid some of the merchant towns on the coast. Enough to raise the alarm."

Marcus shakes his head. "Instead of us making a sneak attack, you want the Carthaginian nation armed and ready for us." He smirks. "Unconventional, to say the least."

"Yes, I do," says Scipio. "Armed and ready for us, where we won't be. Now, what of the Cannenses, Marcus? Have you talked to them?"

"I have." Marcus nods his head toward the massive front doors. "Decimus Agrippa is waiting outside. He is First Tribune of their Sixth Legion." Marcus' lips manage a tight smile. "He is one of the few surviving officers from that massacre."

Laelius grimaces. "That was eleven years ago. He must be near fifty! Likely he is doubled over with age!"

Marcus stares balefully at Laelius. "He is about my age."

Laelius suddenly becomes avidly interested in a ceiling fresco, studying it at length.

Scipio grins. "Well, 'old man,' why don't you summon him?"

Marcus marches to the studded oak doors and swings one open, motioning for Agrippa to come inside. When the tribune enters, Scipio smiles in admiration.

The gray-haired tribune is as tall and thick as a Gaul, his visage stern and his back straight. Though his armor is beaten and weathered, it

VI. Sicily

gleams with a fresh polishing. He marches up to Scipio and bows his head. "Salus, Consul Scipio, I am greatly honored to meet you. All of Sicily has heard of your conquest of the Three Generals."

"Salve, Decimus Agrippa. The honor is mine."

Decimus studies him for a moment, searching for signs of sarcasm. "You are honored to meet one of the Cannenses?" he booms, his tone biting. "To meet one of the legionnaires exiled here because we ran from Hannibal?"

Scipio bares his palm at him. "I meant no sarcasm, Tribune. I was at Cannae, too, as a junior officer. I know your legion did not run. They left certain death to fight another day." Scipio looks at Marcus. "What say you to that, Marcus?"

"The fault was not yours, Agrippa. Your men fought until your commander ordered you away, only when all hope of victory was gone." Marcus looks steadily at Decimus. "Though I myself would welcome an honorable death in battle, I would have done the same as you did—for my men."

Decimus' eyes moisten, but his voice is steady. "I will pass on your words to the Fifth and Sixth Legion survivors. You cannot imagine the solace in what you say. Rome has maligned us for years."

"Are those men ready to fight?" asks Scipio. The Tribune's chin raises a notch. "Every day we train and drill, waiting for the chance to redeem ourselves. They await your bidding, though you send them to fight the gods themselves."

Scipio glances at Marcus and Laelius, who nod their heads in silent agreement. "Decimus Agrippa, I request that you and the Cannenses join me in defending Rome. And that you bring along the survivors of Marcellus' legions, the ones Hannibal destroyed at Herdonia. They have been unjustly slandered, too."

The Tribune nods, but he looks skeptically at Scipio. "Rome has approved our transfers to you?"

VI. Sicily

Scipio snorts. "We don't have time to wait the Senate to fuss about this. We must prepare for a campaign. Troop selection begins three days hence."

Decimus swallows, pausing to find his voice. "Gratitude, General. We are ready to die for you. And for Rome." He grimaces. "But time has taken its toll. There are not enough men for two legions, I fear. Perhaps five thousand who are suitable."

"Your legions will be filled with thousands of new recruits I have brought from Rome."

He sees Decimus' face fall. "Yes, I know, untested men. Most of them have never been in a battle. We will need the Cannenses to mentor them. And to stand beside them in conflict, to help them maintain intention."

"And there are thousands of Marcellus' younger legionnaires still stationed here," adds Laelius. "We can use them and still have men enough to guard Sicily when we depart."

Decimus nods. "Then that should more than enough men, with ours and the Herdonia exiles, to form four legions."

Scipio shakes his head. "Barely enough, I fear. For these legions will be the largest you have ever seen. We will have sixty-two hundred in each legion, [lxvi] not forty-six hundred."

The old tribune's eyes widen. "So large? That would make them difficult to maneuver."

Scipio holds his arms out and joins his hands. "Remember, I was at Cannae, too. The larger legions can withstand the shock of an attack by overwhelming numbers." He looks apologetically at Decimus. "And better resist attacks to their flanks, which proved your undoing at Cannae. They will be very mobile because my cohorts will move rapidly and independently, within the legion." He grins. "As the old saying goes, we will divide and conquer."

"That is quite an adjustment," Decimus muses. "Rome's legions

VI. Sicily

depend on maniples, and smaller legions."

"Rome must learn that an effective army adjusts to the tactics of its enemy," Scipio snaps. "With our new legions, we can more easily adjust to the Carthaginians' tricks. We will not be victims any more."

Decimus nods slowly, not completely convinced. "As you say, Imperator. How shall we select the ablest men? I can review them ahead of time for you, if you will."

"Let us start with a number," Scipio replies. "We are at war, so a man's commission can be extended until he is fifty. [lxvii] Bring everyone who is below fifty-one. That will be our starting point. Then, each must pass the eye test."

Agrippa scratches his head "Eye test, General?"

Scipio nods. "The test of my eye. I will meet each one of these men, face to face. Then I can decide who is ready for battle."

Decimus blinks. "Each one?"

Laelius laughs. "You have not seen the like of this crazy man, Tribune. He might inspect each man's anus before he is done, so have them all take a bath!"

Scipio glances at Laelius and sighs. "Admiral Laelius here is the embodiment of old Marcellus, the Sword of Rome. Laughter in the midst of danger, humor masking a will of iron." He grins at Laelius. "Although a good deal crazier than noble Marcellus."

"This is a task that is serious enough to be taken lightly," counters Laelius. "Humor loosens the mind's imagination!"

Marcus nods. "Certainly, it loosens the mind, as you are evidence of that."

Decimus finally manages a smile. "You will be an interesting group to work with." He snaps to attention. "It will be as you say, General. When shall I muster them for you?"

VI. Sicily

"Three days hence, outside the city gates at dawn. We will have our army at the end of the day. Training on the new cohort maneuvers begins the day after."

Decimus Agrippa extends his arm straight out, fingers pressed together, and closes it about his heart, completing his salute. Scipio returns the gesture. Decimus strides out with his chin set, his spirit again suffused with purpose.

Scipio looks to Laelius and Marcus. Laelius laughs. "If they are all like him, we might as well take over Macedonia while we are at it!"

Marcus Silenus stirs uneasily. "I must return to the recruits now," he says, avoiding Scipio's eyes. "Your brother Lucius is training them while I am gone. I do not want them in his hands for too long."

Laelius nods knowingly as Marcus continues. "The recruits are doing weighted sword training on the posts." He wrinkles his lips in disgust. "Right now, they could not defeat the Vestal Virgins, much less a Libyan phalanx."

Scipio waves toward the door. "Proceed, then. Laelius and I can deal with the cavalry issue." Relieved to be free of a meeting, Marcus leaves quickly.

Laelius turns to Scipio. "So, now we have all our infantry but only one cavalry troop of three hundred recruits, is that correct?"

Scipio holds up two fingers. "We have one troop of three hundred equites who brought their own horses and armor, but we have another three hundred sturdy young riders who were too poor to bring horse or armament. All they brought were plow horses and farm tools!" He laughs. "They care not that equites are supposed to be patricians. They have ridden farm horses and mules, and they think they are ready for the Numidians!'

"They all need equipment, eh?" says Laelius, with a sly grin. "I have a brilliant solution. Remember, years ago, when I needed armor to join your father's turmae of cavalry?" [lxviii]

VI. Sicily

Scipio rubs his chin, then smiles in remembrance. "Oh gods, yes. That was a trick I borrowed from the history book by the great Xenophon of Athens. We tricked that poor Camillus!"

Laelius laughs. "Yes! I went to that fat patrician boy and told him your father was going to recruit him for the cavalry unless he had someone to go in his stead. He begged me to do it!"

"Ah, he almost soiled himself in his terror." Scipio chuckles. "And what an outfit he gave you to go in his place. Your horse and armor were better than mine!"

"And there you have it," replies Laelius. "A bit of harmless but productive mischief. All we need are three hundred gullible men such as Camillus, and we can play the prank again!"

* * * * *

BAU SALEM, GREAT PLAINS OF AFRICA. Try as he might, Masinissa cannot extricate his lance from the chieftain's breastbone. He tugs furiously at the corpse as he leans down from his Numidian pony, kicking desperately at the dead man's head. Panic creeps into the prince's heart; he is painfully conscious of the three indigo-robed Bau Salem warriors running across the village square towards him, their curved blades at the ready.

After a final, fruitless, jerk, Masinissa drops the lance and pulls out his falcata, the Iberian sword he adopted while fighting for the Three Generals. He gallops at the middle warrior and tramples him down. He cleaves his heavy blade deep into the shoulder of the one on the right, rendering the man's sword arm useless.

Even as Masinissa mortally wounds the warrior, his horse screams from the third soldier's stab into its chest. The horse pitches sideways and collapses on top of Masinissa. The tall prince scrambles out from under his dying mount but the last warrior is already upon him, his black eyes shining with fury.

The man swings his blade at Masinissa's head. Masinissa clashes his falcata into the blade, but the force of the blow knocks him off his feet.

VI. Sicily

The warrior hastily bends over and thrusts at Masinissa's heart. The prince scrabbles backwards and the blade hisses into the sand between his legs. Masinissa pushes himself upright, just as the warrior swings his slender blade sideways at Masinissa, aiming to cleave his stomach. Summoning all his strength, the Numidian swings his steel falcata into the warrior's iron sword. There is a ringing, bell-like clash of metals.

The man's sword falls from his numbed hand, broken into a half-dozen shards. He spins to flee but the swift prince is already upon him, thrusting his double-edged blade through the base of his enemy's skull. The falcata's curved point juts out from beneath his opponent's beaked nose. The warrior crumples to the earth, his death-cry drowned in the blood that vomits from his mouth. He pitches forward, pulling his head from Masinissa's sword.

Masinissa bends over to catch his breath, watching his enemy's final death throes. *Thank the gods for Iberian steel,* he reflects. The Numidian prince wipes his blade on the dead man's robe, giving the corpse a final kick.

I've got to get out of here before the rest of them find me. Masinissa tramps about the village square, searching among the smoldering huts for a free horse. The ghostly silhouettes of riders dash all about him in the dense smoke, gathering to pursue Masinissa's elusive raiders.

"There he is! That's their leader!" yells a voice behind Masinissa. He spins around to find a half-dozen militia dashing towards him, curved swords bared. Masinissa rushes back to the soldier dying from his shoulder wound. The prince kicks him over and grabs the warrior's sword off the ground, pausing only to wipe the urine and blood off its handle.

The prince steps away from the groaning man. He spreads his legs apart and faces his onrushing enemies. Masinissa grips a blade in each hand. *If I kill most of them, perhaps Sophonisba will hear the song of my passing.* He raises his blades, preparing to attack with one and defend with the other.

The leader is upon him first. Masinissa blocks the warrior's stab with

VI. Sicily

his enemy sword, even as he dances back from a second attacker. Two other warriors circle him warily, having seen the three corpses of their fellows. The other three flank their leader. The leader barks an order, and the men form a rude circle around Masinissa. He turns slowly, waiting to see who will charge him first.

There is a chorus of heavy thuds to Masinissa's right. He whirls to defend himself from this new threat, only to find Gala bursting out from between two burning huts, leading a dozen of Masinissa's Massylii cavalry. The Massylii trample into the hapless foot soldiers, thrusting their javelins from all directions as they swirl around their outnumbered foe. Within minutes, five of the enemy warriors are groveling upon the ground, bleeding from multiple stab wounds. The leader lies headless, a victim of Masinissa's vengeful falcata.

Gala reaches over and grabs Masinissa's arm, pulling him onto the back of his horse. "We have to run!" he bellows over the villager's screams and curses, "Syphax's men are coming!"

Masinissa looks north. "To the hills."

The Numidian raiding party dashes out, their fellows joining them as they thunder past the broken town gates and out into the open plains, heading toward the northern coastal hills. A Numidian horseman gallops up to the side of Gala's horse, leading a riderless pony. In one fluid motion, Masinissa springs from the back of Gala's mount and onto the racing pony, grasping its knotted rope bridle. He pulls away from the two riders and glances over his shoulder. Hundreds of Syphax's Masaesyli Numidians are pouring into the back of the town. They gallop through the streets and dash into every hut, searching for the rebel prince.

Masinissa can see the white stallions of Syphax and his guards, surrounded by forty Carthaginian cavalry. *What are the Carthaginians doing here? Must I fight both nations, with naught but my rebel band? This is becoming hopeless.*

"We will head back to one of the villages that is still loyal to my father," Masinissa tells Gala. "We can get a few more recruits there. It

VI. Sicily

appears we will need every one we can get."

Within the hour, Masinissa and his band are riding into the thick pines of the foothills, heading up a switchback trail to their camp in the back meadows.

"Masinissa! There's a rider coming!" yells Gala, pointing to a lone figure riding in from the east. Masinissa immediately halts his men. This interloper cannot be allowed to follow them to their hideout. They must kill him or take him prisoner.

The rider slows to a trot, knowing a dozen lances will pierce him if he gallops towards the prince. As he nears Masinissa he drops his javelin and sword belt, riding in with hands upraised. The African wears the humble garb of a local villager, but his upright bearing and penetrating eyes indicate his is much more than that.

"Honor and greetings, Prince. I come from General Scipio. He has a message for you." shouts the man.

Masinissa signals for him to approach. His warriors surround the envoy, spears at the ready. The native speculatore glances nervously at the grim tribesmen. He hands Masinissa a papyrus scroll, sealed with the wax owl emblem of the Scipios. Masinissa unrolls it and is pleasantly surprised to find it written in his native language.

The rider bows his head. "Prince Masinissa, General Scipio requests you appear at Hippo Acra at the next full moon," he announces. "Admiral Laelius will be there. He wants to discuss an alliance with Rome against Carthage." The speculatore looks pointedly at Masinissa. "King Syphax will also be requested to appear." Masinissa stares at the messenger. *Scipio does not know of Syphax's treachery*, he realizes.

In a blink, Masinissa updates Scipio's spy about Gisgo's offer of Sophonisba to Syphax, of Syphax's alliance with Carthage and his subsequent overthrow of Masinissa. "If you value your head," Masinissa concludes, "you will not seek out Syphax."

As the messenger listens, his eyes grow ever wider, his face grim. "This is daunting news. General Scipio will want to hear it at once. I

VI. Sicily

will leave for Sicily and relay what you told me by tomorrow night."

Masinissa nods toward the northeast. "Fare you well. I will be there to meet Laelius, should he arrive."

The rider dashes off. Masinissa watches the dust clouds for a minute, then turns to his men. "Onward, into the hills. Syphax's men may soon arrive." As they ramble up a looping switchback, Masinissa mulls over the tumultuous turn of events that has left him with a skeleton army allied with his former enemy, and his life's love in thrall to his former ally. *My heart and kingdom are in the Romans' hands. Gods help me if the Romans force me choose one over the other.*

Masinissa turns to Gala. "We will head for the north coast in the next week. The Roman captain Laelius will meet us there. If he survives the trip."

* * * * *

NORTH CENTRAL AFRICA COAST, 205 BCE. Flying under full sail, three Roman quadriremes plow through the waist-high Mediterranean waves, pursuing a Carthaginian convoy of three quadriremes and ten supply ships. Laelius stands in the prow of his new flagship, yelling for the oarsmen to increase their pace. *They can only do this for a bit, they will need their energy for fighting*, he reminds himself.

The Roman ships close in on their prey. The Carthaginian warships turn about to face their enemy, but Laelius' ships are upon them too quickly for them to fully come about. Each Roman warship plunges towards one of the Carthaginian quinqueremes. As his ship closes in on his opponent, Laelius walks to mid deck and faces his eighty armored marines.

"All right men, it's time to conquer and plunder! One more load and we'll head for home. First man to board their ship gets a golden crown for his flea-ridden head. Second man gets a silver. And the rest of you get shit!"

"You can keep your fucking crowns. You go first!" rings out a voice.

VI. Sicily

The marines laugh.

"Yea to that, we'll stay here and watch!" pipes up another, and the laughter grows louder. The marines are in a good mood. Laelius' veterans have sunk four enemy ships and ransacked five towns, with very few casualties.

"I will go first, just to shame you pussies," replies Laelius. "And I'll give the crowns to your wives when I'm in bed with them!" He waves down the jeers and turns toward the prow. "Enough! Prepare for boarding, we'll catch their asses in a moment!"

The Roman oarsmen stroke as one, cutting deep into the waves. Laelius' ship eases next to the Carthaginian one. Laelius can see that its decks are bristling with Libyan and Carthaginian fighters. "Get the hooks ready!" he screams. "Get ready to give them a good pitch!"

No sooner has he finished these words than the Carthaginians hurl a wave of javelins at the marines, closely followed by another. The marines form a protective shell with their shields, but not before four of them fall wounded.

"You African bastards will pay for that!" shouts Laelius from the prow. His marines yell out their agreement.

Laelius leaps down from the prow of the boat and grabs one of the grappling hooks. He whirls it around his head like a hammer thrower. "Come on, you sheep-fuckers, let's give them some thunderbolts!"

Laelius flings the four-pronged iron hook onto the side of the adjoining enemy ship. He yanks on the rope and the hook bites deep into the stout railing timbers. A dozen hooks follow it, each one yanked firm by three marines. The brawny Romans pull the hook ropes for all they are worth, dragging the Carthaginian ship toward them as the enemy sailors hack at the ropes. The two warships ease closer toward each other.

"Loose!" Laelius shouts, and the marines hurl scores of javelins upon the Carthaginians, spearing the backs of those who are cutting at the grappling hooks. The Romans grin when they hear the scattered

VI. Sicily

screams, and eagerly grab more javelins from the wicker railing baskets. "Once more!" Laelius yells, and the spears fly again.

The marines pitch out a third volley, forcing their enemy to huddle together. "Prepare to board," commands Laelius. The sturdy warriors draw their swords and crowd up to the ship's railing. The Romans yank furiously on their grappling ropes. The two ships thump together.

"For Rome and victory!" Laelius shouts. He runs to the railing and vaults over to the Carthaginian ship. With a mighty shout, the marines jump over the railing and down onto the decks. The unarmored Carthaginian sailors charge the marines, armed with round shields and curved swords.

"Take the deck!" shouts Laelius, as he fights his way to mid deck. The marines spread out across the deck, and the battle becomes a swirling melee. The battle-wise marines fight in small groups, back to back and side to side. Moving together, step by step, they relentlessly stab and slash their way through the sailors, leaving a trail of blood and bodies. "We've got them, Admiral!" yells out a seamed old marine.

The ship's front hatch opens, and dozens of armored Libyan infantry pour out from the ship's hold. *Shit!* Laelius thinks. *What were they doing down there?* "Get our men after them," he yells to his captain. "I'll go get the oarsmen!"

The Carthaginian sailors are easy prey, but the stern Libyans fight methodically and coldly, undaunted by the many shipmates that lay dying at their feet. The Libyans stand toe to toe, using their long shields to block the Roman's frontal assault, creating an impenetrable shield wall.

Laelius jumps back to his ship and races to the hatch. He flings open the door and sticks his head inside. "All men on deck!" he bellows, and races back to the Carthaginian ship.

The Roman oarsmen boil up from below the quadrireme's decks, sixty well-muscled free men who are well trained to use the swords and shields they carry. Without the burden of helmet or armor they spring

VI. Sicily

easily onto the enemy ship and rush to cut down the remaining sailors.

"The Libyans!" Laelius shouts at the oarsmen, waving his sword toward the armored Africans. The oarsmen attack the left side and rear of the Libyans, cutting into their arms and legs before they can turn to face them. Beset on three sides, the Libyans are pushed closer together, then pushed to their right, towards the ship's railing.

With a lightning-quick stab, Laelius pierces the chest of a burly Carthaginian sailor and shoves the dying man off his blade. He marches towards the front of the Libyan lines, swinging his Iberian falcata. Laelius rams his shield into a front line Libyan and knocks him backwards, gashing open the man's forearm as he falls. Laelius looks back at his men. "Push, curse you, push!" he screams. "All at once!"

The marines and oarsmen join their shields together and lean into them, pushing against the staunch African shield wall. Grunting and cursing, the Romans shove the Libyans back a step, and then two. They slowly move their enemy toward the railing, where the tumultuous sea waits below.

The Africans chop desperately at the Roman shields, but the shield wall holds. "Push!" Laelius yells again, and Romans shove the first of the Libyans over the ship's railings. The armored warriors plummet into the turbulent seas, sinking like a stone.

Crazed with fear, dozens near the railing hurl themselves at the Romans, grabbing onto the edges of their shields. Some cry out "I surrender!" Others grovel at the Romans' feet, begging for mercy.

The Romans kill them all. They step over the quivering bodies and push forward again. A dozen Libyans scream their way into the sea.

Soon, the last of the ship defenders are killed or driven overboard, and the ship is taken. Laelius leaves a cordon of marines to guard the ship and the slave oarsmen who are chained below decks. "We go at that warship behind us," Laelius says to his captain.

Laelius' quadrireme rushes to the aid of the only Roman ship still engaged with the enemy. The two Roman ships grapple onto opposite

VI. Sicily

sides of the enemy ship, and the marines flood onto the Carthaginian deck. After a half hour of furious deck fighting, the marines have sheathed their blades and begin dumping Carthaginian bodies into the sea. With all the enemy quadriremes eliminated, the Roman warships open their sails and plunge after the slow moving supply ships. The Carthaginian transports are boarded and captured without a fight, their crews bound and imprisoned.

Laelius leans over the railing of his ship, watching his sailors tie up the last of the transport's crew. He waves over a rangy older marine with a black patch over his eye socket. "Sextus, I want you to take all of these vessels back to Syracuse," he says to his second in command. "General Scipio will be delighted with all the treasure."

Sextus wrinkles his brow. "You go on alone?"

Laelius smiles. "Well, as alone as I can be with my marines and oarsmen. I have a mission that is best done with one ship, to attract less attention."

As the Roman warships guide their prizes toward Syracuse, Laelius orders his ship turned to the southeast, to sail under cover of night toward Hippo Acra. *Time to change from Laelius the pirate to Laelius the diplomat. I wonder if Syphax and Masinissa will both be there?*

* * * * *

CARTHAGE HARBOR 204 BCE. As Laelius' ship draws close to Hippo Acra, two figures stand beneath the base of the sky-clawing watchtower inside Carthage's vast military harbor, unaware of the enemy ship nearby.

Durro, the tall and stately emissary of Carthage's powerful Council of Elders, is finalizing details with the Roman defector known as Calidus. The man was so nicknamed by his fellow legionnaires because he was hot-headed, a temper that led him to murder his centurion and flee to Gisgo's army in Iberia.

Seeing his intelligence value, Gisgo brought Calidus back to Carthage, trained him in the ways of spying, and sent him back to

VI. Sicily

report on the Roman Senate's actions. Calidus has become one of Carthage's most valuable—and wealthiest—agents, a man only loyal to himself. Now he sets out on a mission to Syracuse, one that will bring him great reward if he can accomplish it.

"You do know the two men we are talking about?" asks Durro for the third time. "Yes, the two gladiators," replies Calidus peevishly. "They are Aulus and Cassius, the Samnites in Scipio's honor guard. They have little love for Romans."

"Good, see that you contact them immediately. Our terms for them are simple. If Scipio dies before he leaves for Africa, they each receive a thousand pounds of silver."

Calidus shakes his head, smiling. "A thousand pounds? Why don't you just give them Carthage?"

Durro scowls. "We would save a thousand times that in mercenary pay, fool. His death ends the war."

"When Scipio dies, do I get what I want?" asks Calidus. "All of it?"

The elder official nods, his lips pursed sourly. He reaches into his robe and drops a bulging purple purse into Durro's hands. "My word of honor. The governorship of Utica. Lifetime protection by your own Sacred Band guards."

Calidus' face becomes predatory, his eyes gleaming with desire. "And?"

Durro looks up at the blazing torches lighting the ten-story watchtower, as if searching for patience. "And Sophonisba," he says to the tower, his voice disgusted. "With Syphax's shade in the Land of Mot."

Calidus grins. "Be it so, then. I sail for Sicily tomorrow." He points his finger at Durro. "Keep your ears open for news of Scipio's demise. I will expect recompense shortly afterwards."

Durro bows. "I certainly will." Patience, he tells himself.

VI. Sicily

Another month and you can kill this fool. By Mot's axe, I do hate traitors!

* * * * *

HIPPO ACRA. Laelius stands atop the grassy hill that overlooks this ancient costal town, studying the shadowy outlines of two cruising Carthaginian quinqueremes. *If they find my little boat on the beach, I'll be swimming back to my quinquereme* he thinks ruefully. He glances over at his Numidian scout. "He said he would be here. Where is he?"

"Masinissa is man of his word," says the young scout in broken Latin. "He will be here if he is still alive."

Laelius looks around the undulating grassy plains beneath him. "Well, I don't see any sign of him."

"And well you did not," comes a deep voice behind him. "Else Syphax would have killed me by now."

Laelius' guards grab for their swords but Laelius calls them off, smiling at the familiar voice. "I am lucky you did not become an assassin for Carthage," he says. "You could get me any time."

Masinissa steps into the moonlit space about Laelius, raising his hand in salute. The two former opponents embrace warmly. "Will you sit with me?" Laelius asks. "My new sandals are vexing my feet."

They plop onto the hillside facing the sea, eyeing the two Carthaginian warships that ply the shimmering indigo waters. Laelius looks south, out toward the faint lights of Carthage's harbor thirty miles away. *There it is. If it falls to us, all is victory.*

"It is good to see you, Prince," says Laelius, pitching a stone down the hillside. "General Scipio is massing his forces to come to Africa, and we will sorely need your men." He shrugs apologetically. "And those of Syphax, unfortunately."

Masinissa sighs. "Ah, friend Laelius, I sent word to Sicily via Scipio's scout. Syphax has joined forces with Gisgo. Together they have ousted

VI. Sicily

me from my kingdom." He looks at Laelius' disappointed face. "I must tell you, I only have two hundred men with me. But all are warriors born. And more men join me every day."

Laelius' shoulders slump. "So the rumors are true. Syphax has betrayed our alliance. He has given Carthage forty thousand warriors." He rubs his eyes wearily. "Why would he do that? Syphax admired Scipio. Did the Council of Elders offer him more money that we could?"

Masinissa laughs bitterly. "Ai, ai, would that it were only money! Gisgo offered him the one thing none of us could. His daughter, Sophonisba the Fairest."

Laelius stares at him, fumbling for the proper words. "I, I had heard that you—that she—you two were to..."

Masinissa cuts him off with a violent shake of his head. "No. Now there is nothing. Nothing for me, until Syphax dies."

Laelius blows out his cheeks. "Well, this will certainly change our campaign plans! We might have to wait another year, so we can amass more allies. Perhaps we should recruit some of the Iberians..."

Masinissa grabs his arm. "No! If you wait another year, my entire kingdom will be forfeit to Syphax. He is taking over all the Massylii tribes and forcing the men into his army. Next year, his force may be doubled. Scipio cannot wait. I will help him. I may not rule my tribes right now, but I will provide him with infantry and cavalry." [lxix] Masinissa pushes himself up and stalks up the hill.

Laelius follows and stands next to him. "I hear you, Prince," he says soothingly. "Scipio should hurry so he can help you regain your throne and your woman. Or at least one of them. Is that not right?"

Masinissa nods. "It is, though gods help me if I have to choose one over the other."

The Numidian dabs at a corner of his eyes. "I go now. I suggest you do the same." He walks back into the shadows, but his voice lingers

VI. Sicily

with a parting word. "He must come soon. Or all is lost for both of us."

* * * * *

SYRACUSE, 205 BCE. Scipio stares out the window of his stone-walled headquarters, popping handfuls of the local almonds into his mouth. He looks beyond the fort walls to study late fall beauty of the rolling hillside vineyards, their leaves ablaze with deep oranges, reds, and holly greens. He takes a deep breath, blows it out, and grimaces. *Curse it all, will I ever have my own vineyards? Even that bastard Cato has a farm. And Marcus, too!*

He tugs moodily at his purple toga, bundling it closer about him. *By Priapus' cock, winter is upon us. March will soon be here, and I must be gone to Africa by then. Syphax has given fifty thousand men to Carthage and here I sit, preparing to play pranks just to get a few horses to fight them. Shit!*

His moody reverie is interrupted by a toga-clad Laelius, who struts in with Praxis, Aulus, Cassius, and several more of the Honor Guard. The guards all wear glistening new armor, aimed at impressing Scipio's visitors, the Syracuse nobility.

Laelius takes a seat to the right of Scipio's silver-inlaid wooden throne. "Do you think this will work?" asks Laelius, looking a little nervous as he picks a thread off the embroidery. "Do I look officious enough?"

"It had best work," says Scipio. "We have three hundred able riders without horse or armor, that's a full legion's complement that is totally unarmed." Scipio smirks at Laelius "Besides, how could it go wrong, it was your idea! When have you ever had a bad idea?"

Laelius sniffs. "You still hold it against me that I thought we should trim the hair on your old mastiff Boltar that summer. I was only ten!"

Scipio rolls his eyes. "It was stupid at any age, and me the stupider for following you. Poor Boltar, he hid under my sleeping platform for a week!"

VI. Sicily

"The families are here," announces Scipio's chief attendant. Scipio motions for him to admit them.

Four elegantly dressed pairs of parents shuffle in, looking worried. Scipio rises and steps down from his dais to clasp forearms with the well-groomed man who stands in front of the group, his face shining with freshly applied olive oil.

"You are Bruno?" queries Scipio, smiling as they shake arms.

The portly middle-aged man bows deeply. "I am. It is an honor to meet the conqueror of Iberia, the Bane of the Barcas, the..."

Scipio cuts him off with a wave of his hand. "Yes, yes, I have had some luck over there. But now it is a new game we play here in Sicily, with a new destination. Wild Africa itself!"

Scipio reaches out theatrically toward Laelius, who struts over to plunk a thick papyrus scroll in Scipio's outstretched hand. With a flourish, Scipio hands it to a bewildered Bruno.

"There is great news in there for you," chirps Scipio. "My council has selected three hundred young men from Sicily's finest families to join my cavalry. They will go with us fight against Carthage." Scipio smiles fatuously. "And your sons are among those receiving the honor! Think of it, they will have the glory of war and death in far-off Africa!"

The families stare at each other, alarmed. Several of the women cry out in dread and hug each other.

Scipio continues. "Three days hence, I want every one of the boys on this list to show up outside the main gate, where I will personally welcome them into our cavalry!"

Bruno moves his lips wordlessly, and raises a trembling hand to query Scipio. Scipio silences him with a stern look. "If any one of these young men do not appear, and I find out they are in the city, Marcus Silenus and his men will drag them before me. Those boys will join the oarsmen in Laelius' flagship!" Laelius nods his affirmation, fighting to control a grin.

VI. Sicily

Bruno finally finds his voice. "Ah, it, it is an honor, of course, General Consul—ah, Consul General, or ..."

Scipio glowers at him.

"Buh-but, some of our boys are needed at home. My son Gratius, for example, he..."

Scipio waves his hand across his face, as if wiping the group from his sight. "Pfah! No excuses. They will be at the city gates in three days, or they will be in the city prison in four! And woe to the family whose son has suddenly disappeared!" He looks over their heads, his eyes distant. "You are dismissed."

The guards move in and usher the sobbing, shuffling group from the room. The doors boom shut.

Laelius slumps with relief and laughs. "Goodness, Scippy, I did not know you capable of playing such an arrogant ass! Perhaps I have misjudged your acting talents. Or your true nature."

Scipio raises his middle finger and jabs it at Laelius, imitating a phallus thrusting. [lxx]

"Ah, that's about the size of it on you, isn't it?" snips Laelius.

Scipio grins wearily. "I need to have a reputation for being cruel, whether I have earned it or not." He glances uneasily at the door. "I only hope our little play bears fruit. We need those horses!"

Three days later, three hundred of Sicily's finest nobility are milling uneasily about the field outside the main gates. The young men glumly watch the open gates, waiting for their fate. They do not have to wait long.

There is a loud tramping sound. Scipio and Laelius march out from the gates, flanked by their honor guard. Three hundred sturdy young men follow them, clad in simple gray wool tunics, the rustic volunteers from Italia. Without any preamble, Scipio steps onto the wide wooden platform that he will use as a rostra. He stares down at the nervous

VI. Sicily

Sicilians.

"I am excited to welcome you to my army, men of Sicily. The fifth and sixth legions have a long history of accomplishment—and sacrifice—for Rome. Many are gone now, of course, as casualties of war. But you will replace them in our glorious quest to conquer the unconquerable: mighty Carthage and the invincible Hannibal!" The young nobles mutter among themselves, looking sidelong at Scipio as if he were mad.

Scipio stands quietly, allowing the dissent and alarm to circulate, and then he continues. "Now, I have heard that a number of you young worthies have complained about this assignment, regarding it as demanding and onerous.[lxxi] He looks at the crowd, seeing many nod their heads in mute agreement. "Well, if such is the case I would ask you to have the courage to speak up now, and you will get a fair hearing." Scipio looks into the eyes of all the recruits. "Is there no one? Was this rumor, or a lie?"

A doughy young man steps forward. His face is sweaty, though it is a cool day. "Illustrious General Scipio, I regret I cannot join you, however sorely I desire it." At these words, several Sicilian youths roll their eyes. The portly youth continues, his voice rising with emotion. "My parents are ill, you see, and I must forsake my own ambitions for their welfare. I must make the sacrifice!"

Several boys snigger, but Scipio raises his voice encouragingly. "Well, there is an honest young man! And I respect your ... 'sacrifice' for your parents. You should not go, if you do not want to. Why would I want a reluctant soldier?" The boy heaves a sigh of relief.

"Of course, I shall have to find you a replacement for you," says Scipio. "You will to transfer your weapons, horse, and all the other military equipment to your replacement. You are to take him home and ascertain that he is trained in horsemanship and armed combat.[lxxii] Would you agree to that?"

The young man bobs his head furiously. Scipio gestures for one of his three hundred Italia volunteers to come forward and stand with the

VI. Sicily

Sicilian boy. "Go now, the both of you." He glowers at the Sicilian noble. "In two months I will test your student, to see if he is worthy to be your replacement. If he is not, you will replace him yourself! You have my leave to go." The boy hurries off with the volunteer.

Scipio turns back to the rest of the youths. "Anyone else?" he asks quietly.

Two more step forward, and Scipio repeats the same pairing. Then ten step forward, then a dozen. Eventually, all the young Sicilians ask to be excused, and all are given replacements.[lxxiii] Finally, the field is empty.

"Well send me to Hades, it worked," blurts Laelius. "We are geniuses! Now we have three hundred more cavalry, ones that can stomach a fight!"

Scipio gestures for his friend to follow him, commanding his guard to follow at a distance. The two stroll around the perimeter of the town walls. Occasionally they pause to pick up rocks and pitch them off the walls, listening to them crack off the massive limestone blocks.

"I suppose I should get back to work," Scipio says. "There is still much for me to do today."

Scipio flings a flat rock high off the wall. It cracks against the wall beneath a sleepy sentry. The guard jumps awake and grabs his spear, staring frantically over the parapet. The two commanders hoot with laughter.

Still chuckling, Laelius wags his finger at Scipio. "Look, genius. You just provided horse, armor, and training for an entire legion's worth of cavalry. I think that is enough work for one morning!"

Scipio sighs. "Perhaps you are right. And I value time for play." He looks at Laelius, a bittersweet smile on his face. He touches the gray hair that tufts about his temples. "I so fear I am losing that capacity. Forever."

Laelius abruptly turns away and looks at the rainbow autumn fields, stifling the sob that rises to his throat. He turns back, a forced smile on

VI. Sicily

his face. "I am curious, mighty general. Do you think we could raise a legion with that trick? We can try it!"

Scipio laughs, shaking his head regretfully. "With the numbers we face in Africa, I would wish that we could, my friend. Would that we could."

* * * * *

CURIA HOSTILIA, ROME, 204 BCE. "We are going to lose our slaves, senators!" grates Flaccus, stalking along the front Senate row. "If these slave assignment limitations take effect, we won't have the resources to maintain our farms! The farms that feed Rome! Food prices will rise to the heavens! Is that what you want?"

"You mean you will lack the resources to maintain the obscene profits you have come to expect," rejoins Senator Severus of the Hellenic Party. "All you have to do is hire citizens instead of slaves. There are plenty available, now that you have brought in all those slaves to do their work. By Jupiter, man, we have mobs of unemployed roaming the Aventine Hill, hundreds of them lying about on the three temples' steps. Rome is one step away from another Conflict of the Orders!" [lxxiv]

"Let them try another labor strike," sniffs Flaccus, "I'll just buy more slaves." He opens his arms toward the senators, facing the Latin Party. "As businessmen, we have a right to our profits, don't we?" he pleads.

"Not at the expense of our city, of our own people!" cries Senator Amelius, shaking his fist at Flaccus.

In the back row, the two Tribunes of the Plebs nod approvingly at Amelius' words. Using their powers of office, the Tribunes convened this Senate session. They proposed the legislation that will limit the use of slaves for work that citizens can do. The Tribunes have seen the lines of proud Romans waiting dolefully for their daily allotment of bread, with no place to go and nothing to do—unless they join the army, which has also become the province of slaves.

Several of the homines novi senators, the men who have just attained patrician status, listen with conflicted emotions. They were small

VI. Sicily

farmers who owned a few field slaves themselves. Yet they have seen villa owners such as Flaccus buy up the small farms and give all the people's work to slaves.[lxxv] And they, too, have seen the long bread lines, filled with hollow-eyed men who once fought selflessly for Rome.

The presiding Senate magistrate finally calls a vote for or against the proposal. Those supporting Severus cluster around him on the left portion of the Senate floor, while those supporting Flaccus stand next to him on the right. Even as the last of the senators shuffle to their groups the outcome is clear: the slave limitations bill has passed. Flaccus stamps out from the Senate chambers.

Later that afternoon, a livid Flaccus downs cup after cup of wine at an open air wine bar near the Forum. "It's that bitch Pomponia," he fumes. "She pushed the Tribunes of the Plebs to make that proposal, I saw her conspiring with them!" The lanky senator moodily bites into a roasted mouse, wagging its butt end at Fabius. "She has the morals of a commoner, always wanting something free from us!"

"I thought you were going to ... reduce her effectiveness, Flaccus," mutters Fabius, staring into his goblet. Flaccus looks aghast at his old companion. This is the first time Fabius has indicated his suspicions of Flaccus' murderous intent toward Scipio's mother. And now Fabius is encouraging it.

Recently, Fabius has become more vicious. With age, the legendary Cunctuator has become too feeble to orate in the Senate, but his resentment toward the Scipios has grown in strength—as well as his desire for revenge. And Scipio's victories in the Senate have only exacerbated the old general's ire. Once he thought Scipio was a brash young boy who would follow military traditions when he grew older. Now Fabius sees him as an arrogant risk taker without respect for Roman strategy or tactic—a reckless man who ignores Fabius' urgings to use attrition and delaying stratagems to defeat Hannibal.

Flaccus shakes his head, refusing to meet Fabius' anxious watery eyes. "That would not be in my—in our—best interests right now. She is safe from me. In fact, I think we should keep an eye out for her

VI. Sicily

safety, so we are not suspected of foul play."

Fabius gapes at Flaccus. "Then what is left to us, now that the Hellenics have the upper hand?" He flaps his arms in frustration. "What future lies for the Party?"

With the Senate defeat, the Latin Party's morale and power is at its lowest ebb. Rome's citizens avidly attend to reports of Scipio's every move in Sicily, waiting to see if he will leave for Africa. When Marcus Claudius Marcellus died fighting Hannibal, most Romans had lost hope that there was anyone left who could defeat the Carthaginian. But Scipio has conquered the Three Generals, and he has become the new hope of Rome. Those who once freely criticized him now do so at peril of a public pummeling.

Realizing their advantage, Pomponia and Amelia circulate at every patrician gathering they can force their way into. They use the patricians' avid inquiries about Scipio as a doorway to introduce their proposals for citizen employment and public education. They read their letters from Scipio at a speaker's platform in the Forum Square, attracting so many plebeians that the other speakers step down and join to crowd to hear them.

The Latin Party fights back. Led by a vengeful Flaccus, the Latin senators generate several proposals for reducing land taxes, and they win the approval of the senators. The Tribunes of the Plebs, however, veto the proposals ostensibly because money is needed to support the war effort. Realistically, it is because the bills primarily benefit the wealthiest landowners. And so, while the Scipios gather strength in Rome and Sicily the war within Rome continues, with the Latin Party becoming more toothless and voiceless.

But that is before Locri.

* * * * *

SYRACUSE, SICILY, 205 BCE. "I tell you, General, Locri is yours for the taking," exclaims the lead delegate of the Locrian exiles. "We have talked to some of our tradesmen who are working inside the city.

VI. Sicily

They are ready to help Rome retake Locri, when we give them the prearranged signal."

The delegate steps back from the dais, joining the rest of the finely togaed nobility who have come to see Scipio. The young general looks at Laelius and Marcus, who flank his throne on the dais. Scipio raises his right hand. "Thanks for your surprising news, Spurius. Your retinue will await my decision on the morrow."

When the delegation has left, Scipio slumps over and rubs his eyes. "Gods above, what importunate timing!"

"We should never have lost that town," growls Marcus. "Those cowardly city elders ran to the Carthaginians as soon as Hannibal got near them. If Crassus would have marched in there and crucified some of those elders, the garrison would still be ours."

"I just don't know about this," replies Scipio wearily. Scipio has been deeply mired in his final tasks for the African campaign, still worrying over the loss of Syphax's troops. Then this august delegation appears before him as if out of nowhere, with the news that Locri can be readily taken from Hamilcar, its Carthaginian commander.

Laelius leans into Scipio's ear. "You know that Locri is in south Italia. That makes it part of the Consul Crassus' domain, not yours."

Scipio frowns at him. "Yes, of course it is. But the Pontifex could not take a calf from its mother, much less win back the twin citadels of the Locri garrison. Need I remind you, Locri is a strategic stronghold for Carthage."

"It's also near Hannibal's encampment," counters Laelius. "You start a fight there and you might have Old One-Eye knocking on your door!" Laelius pantomimes a boxer. "You could fight it out with him right there, and end this thing!"

Scipio sighs. "Ah, and that would be the regret about beating him there. It would not 'end this thing.' Rome would think we are safe and they'd make peace with Carthage, leaving our enemy's native power intact. We need a more severe and strategic treaty, one that they will

VI. Sicily

only agree to out of desperation, a treaty so severe that it reduces their threat forever."

"Mmmph," muses Marcus. "There was a time you would have welcomed the chance to make peace so you could go home." He looks hard at Scipio. "So we could go home."

Scipio nods his head, smiling forlornly. "That was when I thought I could make Rome safe by winning the right battles. Now I see, it's all about winning the right peace. We need Locri."

Two hours later, the three men meet with the tribunes in a hastily called war conference, to decide if they should attack Locri. There is a heated discussion about whether Locri distracts them from their central mission of preparing for Africa. Scipio mitigates this by promising that he will not send the Sicily troops to Locri.

By the end of the evening Scipio has inked out his orders for Locri and gives them to two of his senior tribunes, Marcus Sergius and Publius Matienus. The tribunes are to travel to Rhegium, the nearest allied city to Locri, and join with praetor Quintus Pleminius. The written orders specify that the two men are to act as Pleminius' advisors and help him retake Locri. Their unwritten orders are to monitor his activities and keep him out of trouble.

Scipio is blowing some sealing dust off the final papyrus scroll when Laelius sticks his head into Scipio's quarters. "You aren't done yet? I thought we'd have a game of latrunculi. I might permit you to beat me this time."

Scipio waves his hand airily, distracted. "Soon, let me finish this," He turns to Laelius. "What have you heard about the praetor in Rhegium, this Quintus Pleminius?"

Laelius shrugs. "The few tribunes who know him speak in paradoxes. They say Pleminius is an ambitious and loyal soldier, driven to conquer and command. He has won several skirmishes with Hamilcar's men. But they say he has a brittle character He is quick to take offense and becomes quite angry and vengeful with those who disagree with him.

VI. Sicily

He sounds very unpredictable to me."

"Hmmph," Scipio mutters, as he stamps his seal on the rolled up scroll. "Thick of will but thin of skin." He bites his lower lip. "That could be a dangerous combination."

Laelius smirks. "Dangerous for whom, us or the Carthaginians?"

"For either, depending on the circumstance. Let us hope Sergius and Matienus will be a tempering influence."

* * * * *

BRUTTIUM REGION, SOUTH ITALIA. The legionnaires crunch through the sheaves of dried stalks that have blown across the road between the wheat fields, heedless of the crackling. They have ventured far from Consul Crassus' encampment, and have seen no signs of enemy, not even a forager. And so they march on, heedless of the hundreds of eyes that follow them.

For a month, Hannibal and his men have watched Crassus' scout troops venture ever farther out from their base near Kroton as Crassus seeks to expand Rome's small sphere of influence in South Italia. Day after day, hundreds of Numidians and Bruttians keep watch within the shadows of the surrounding mountain forests. The Romans march under their very noses, but so far Hannibal's men have held back from assaulting them.

Hannibal has given stern orders that the Romans are not to be attacked. He seeks to cultivate a false sense confidence and security in Crassus' troops, leaving them vulnerable to a surprise attack. Hannibal has aided his deception by inventing false reports about his own whereabouts. He gives the reports to his three spies that masquerade as informants for the Romans. The Romans pay the informants, and the informants relay news of the Romans to Hannibal, who also pays them. It is a good time to be a spy.

Now the time is propitious for an ambush. Hannibal and Commander Maharbal have come from his new camp near Scylletium,[lxxvi] ready to spring his trap. Today, the Romans are out in force in a cohort of four

VI. Sicily

hundred eighty men. They march past the same wheat fields that smaller maniples have negotiated a dozen times before. The cohort is heading over to garrison a town that steadfastly supports Rome, a wealthy merchant town that is close to Carthaginian-occupied Locri. Crassus has decided it must be reinforced so that it does not capitulate to Hannibal, as Locri has done.

Scores of legionnaires scout out the thick wheat fields around the advancing cohort. They weave through the tall stalks, spears at the ready, poking into every heaped pile of grasses. Crassus knows of Hannibal's old trick of hiding men within the crops, and he will not fall victim to it.

As always, the scouts find no hidden enemies. The cohort enters a gateway to the valley they must traverse to get to town. The cavalry scouts dash ahead, galloping past the lush olive groves that roll up into the feet of the low lying hills about the gateway. They plunge through the hillsides in search of enemy, but none are found.

Geminus Servilius, the battle-seasoned legate in charge of the cohort, is a very cautious man. He waits at the mouth of the valley until the scouts return and report that the way is clear. Even then, he sends them out for a second reconnoiter before he leads his men through the valley. He rides his white stallion next to the wolfskin-capped standard bearer, ready to move his men into defensive positions. Several scouts return, reaffirming their reports of no enemy presence. Servilius finally waves his men ahead.

As the cohort moves through the valley, Geminus looks about the countryside, admiring the bountiful fruit on the hillside orange trees. He savors the rows of lush, mushroom shaped olive trees that stand sentry along each side of their path. *I could live here,* Geminus considers. *Land would be much cheaper than Rome. I could get a couple slaves and have my own villa.* His eyes linger on the fat green olives that explode from the dense green leaves, fruit as thick as a man's thumb. *What oil I could make with those olives!*

Geminus rides over to a nearby tree and plucks an olive. He bites into it to sample its bitter, grassy, flavor. *Yes, these would fetch a fine price*

VI. Sicily

in Rome. He spits it out and plucks another, looking around as he chews. As he reaches for a third fruit, a glint of metal catches his eye. Curious, he stares into the tree's upper branches. He sees another set of eyes staring back at him, eyes burning with malevolence.

Geminus gapes in surprise and turns to shout the alarm. A gleaming blade flashes down and chops off his hand, the olive it held tumbling to the earth. As the legate screams in anguish, a leaf-covered Bruttian drops down from the tree and tumbles Geminus from his horse.

Geminus batters at the warrior's face with his bloody hand stump. He frantically reaches across his belt with his remaining hand, trying to pull out his sword. In one swift movement, the Bruttian kicks him flat and twists his eight-inch dagger into Geminus' windpipe, ending his cries and his life. His death screams have already alerted the legionnaires, and the battle horns blare the alarm.

Hundreds of leaf-camouflaged Bruttians drop down from the olive trees. Each carries a green-sheathed short sword and a small round shield painted olive green. Hannibal himself commissioned the sheaths and shields for this venture, their color making it easy for the Bruttians to hide within the leafy groves. The Bruttians are lightly armored; they do not plan to fight the Romans for any length of time, only to hold them at bay.

The Bruttians rush at the milling Romans. The legionnaires hastily throw up a shield wall. When the Bruttians close on them the Romans thrust out their pila from between their shields, puncturing the chests and bowels of dozens of foolhardy attackers. But more Bruttians arrive, clustering next to one another as they stab and batter at the Roman shields. The disciplined legionnaires hold their position. The men in the center quickly replace the fallen in front, but they cannot break through the front line Bruttians, who are held in place by the wall of men behind them.

At the top of the surrounding hills, several Numidian scouts stand alongside their horses, watching the Bruttian attack. When their allies crash into the Roman shields, the Africans blow their signal horns. The signal is relayed into the deep hills. The forest begins to rumble with

VI. Sicily

hoofbeats.

Fighting with unbending discipline and structure, the Romans methodically hack down scores of Bruttians. Their hearts grow hopeful that they can escape this ambush.

The sound of thundering hooves penetrates the din of the battle. Many legionnaires look back hopefully, praying it is their equites coming to reinforce them. Others who are more realistic make a silent prayer to the gods and charge maniacally into their enemy, fearing their time to kill them is growing short.

Scant minutes later, both ends of the valley road fill with hundreds of Numidian cavalry, each carrying a Numidian ground fighter on the back of his horse.

The African riders close in on each end of the cohort. Their infantry jump off the horses and fling their javelins into the dwindling Roman center, felling dozens of legionnaires. The Numidian cavalry crash through the front and back of the Roman formation. They gallop about in the Roman center, lancing the backs of the battling Romans.

Hannibal and Maharbal ride in from the road leading out of the valley. They calmly watch the slaughter unfold, discussing the progress of the carnage. As veterans of a dozen battles, they are content to oversee the fighting in this one-sided conquest.

Within the hour the battle has dwindled to dozens of individual mob fights. Handfuls of unyielding Romans stave off the circle of Bruttians and Numidians that presses in on them, cutting down any that are bold enough to charge them. But the javelins and swords come at the Romans from every direction, and their numbers slowly dwindle. By the end of the next hour Hannibal's men are picking through corpses for valuables, their day's work done.

As is his habit now, Hannibal orders that the Roman dead be stacked in orderly rows near his own perished soldiers. It is his tribute to the men he has fought these past fourteen years—he has come to respect Rome's soldiers far more than their leaders. Their grisly task

VI. Sicily

completed, Hannibal beckons for his men to ride south toward the valley exit, where he addresses them.

"You have done well today, my allies," Hannibal shouts from atop his Numidian pony. "Now you will return to Castra Hannibalis[lxxvii] for a victory feast. And to divide up the plunder!"

As the men cheer, Hannibal beckons over Maharbal. "You are ready for tonight's assignment?" Hannibal asks.

His scarred old commander nods, his face wearing a grim smile. "It will be done by dawn, outside the main gates of Crassus' camp."

Hannibal nods and points back toward the sheltering hills. "There are six men up by the horse camp, they have packed all that you need to take."

Maharbal grimaces. "Won't this be messy? We can't leave a blood trail, the Romans will track us down."

"The blood has been drained from them," Hannibal says, "so there will be no dripping trail to follow you." Maharbal turns to leave. Hannibal grabs his shoulder.

"It must be done tonight, before this slaughter is discovered. Otherwise the Romans won't understand the message I'm going to send to them. They will think it has to do with this battle, instead of with their men's criminal activities."

Maharbal grunts his assent. "It is a disgusting message, if you ask me." He jumps onto his horse and gallops back toward the hills. He soon joins the six riders. They gallop north for Crassus' encampment near Kroton, their packsaddles bulging.

The next morning, Crassus is shaken awake by the captain his sentries. "Forgiveness, Consul, you must come to the east gates. There is a horrible thing out there in the wheat fields!"

"In the wheat fields? Jupiter curse you, couldn't you wait an hour?" grouses the old patrician. "I told you not to wake me unless we are

254

VI. Sicily

under attack!"

The Pontifex levers his heavy body from his thickly padded sleeping couch. He drowses while his slave dresses him in a fine linen tunic and pulls on Crassus' silver-studded belt and sandals. The priest pads through camp toward the main gates, rubbing the sleep from his eyes.

Crassus clambers up the rude stone stairway to the walkway that lines the ten-foot wall surrounding the castra. Two wide-eyed guards lead him toward the east wall. He peers over the wall, stares, and draws back in disgust.

There, backlit by the rising sun, grows a grisly crop of thirty human heads. Each one is mounted on a twelve-foot Carthaginian sarissa. The thick spears sprout up from the drying sheaves of wheat beneath them, as if some new crop were rising from the dying one beneath. Each of the heads wears a crawling beard and scalp of bottle-green flies, the cavernous eye sockets staring sightlessly at Crassus. A wooden plaque hangs beneath each head, dangling from a loop of string tied behind the rotting ears.

Crassus blinks his eyes, discomfited. He squints at the dangling wooden rectangles. "Who are they? What do the signs say?" he asks the nearby guard. The guard shrugs his ignorance. Crassus' face reddens with frustration. "Well, get someone out there!" he blurts, and turns away from the grisly scene.

The sentries shove open the camp gates and a maniple of legionnaires stalks out toward the heads, their swords clenched in their fists. Crassus stands by the gates with his guard, his pudgy arms crossed over his gold-trimmed tunic. He offers a silent prayer to Mars and Jupiter, urging their protection from evil spirits.

The maniple soon trots back to camp, the men's faces disturbed. The tribune marches over to Crassus and salutes. "Yes, yes, what news?" says Crassus, jerking out a return salute.

"Those are the legionnaires from the missing scout parties," replies the tribune. "The ones that have been missing for the past week."

VI. Sicily

The Pontifex wrinkles his nose. "How unfortunate," he says emotionlessly. "We shall offer sacrifices for their safe journey to Hades. What did the signs say?"

The tribune's mouth tightens into a grim line. "Three words. *Raptor, homicida, latro* (rapist, murderer, bandit)."

Crassus' eyes widen, but the tribune continues, looking pointedly at the man who is the High Priest of Rome. "They are not all Romans. Five of them are Carthaginians."

Crassus closes his eyes and takes several breaths: he knows the import of the message: these heads belong to men who became marauders. They raided and pillaged the local farmlands while out on patrol,[lxxviii] as restless soldiers from both sides have been wont to do in the absence of a battle to engage them. These Romans and Carthaginians became criminals in uniform, raping and pillaging under the protection of their army.

The placards are Hannibal's message that such crimes will no longer be tolerated. The man the Romans regard as a barbarian will not allow any more atrocities upon the innocents of southern Italia. With Crassus refusing to engage him in battle, Hannibal the general has become Hannibal the censor, defending the innocents and punishing the perpetrators, whatever their allegiance.

Hmm, thinks Crassus. *The man has a sense of honor. For a Carthaginian.*

Crassus does not send out any more raiding parties. Absent any large-scale Roman opposition to contend with, Hannibal's veteran army confines itself to minor skirmishes and foraging.

But Scipio is soon to change that.

VII. LOCRI

RHEGIUM, FAR SOUTH ITALIA. 205 BCE. The Roman legion tramps steadily down the wide dirt road from Rhegium to Locri, but not fast enough for its impatient commander.

"Double the marching time, Julius! We must get to Locri before midnight tomorrow!" Quintus Pleminius, the rangy and sharp-faced praetor of Rhegium, barks the order to his legate. The two ride out front of the legion's vanguard, joined by Scipio's two tribunes, Sergius and Matienus.

"That is a fast pace for the men," observes Sergius, looking at the soldiers behind him. "We still have a ways to go."

"I don't give a shit if they have to run!" snaps Pleminius. "We will get to Locri under cover of darkness or I'll put them all on barley rations!"

"They will be in no condition to fight when they get there," observes Matienus. "If you take another hour or two, it will still be dark enough for the attack."

Pleminius whirls to face Matienus and Sergius, his face flush with anger. "This is not your army to command, Tribunes. I do not welcome your meddling." The two tribunes glower at Pleminius. Sergius leans to the side of his horse and spits.

"As you command, Praetor," replies Julius. "We will be at Locri by midnight." He turns his horse around and trots off to find his tribunes.

Minutes later, the buccinators blare out a change of pace. Pleminius' three thousand legionnaires tread rapidly down the fifty-mile road to the fortress town perched high in the east coast hills, lugging their packs over their shoulders. Watching his legion hurry forward, Pleminius smiles. *We will get there and surprise those bastards while they're sleeping. Locri will be mine by morning. I'll command all of south Italia.*

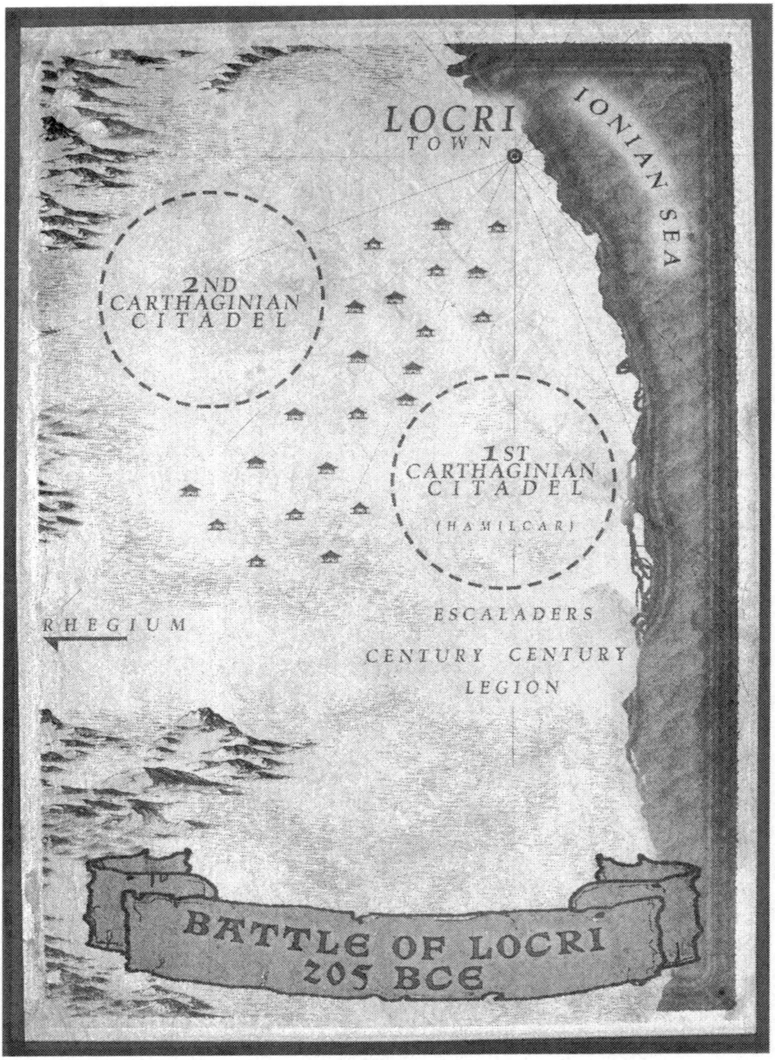
LOCRI
TOWN
IONIAN SEA
2ND
CARTHAGINIAN
CITADEL
1ST
CARTHAGINIAN
CITADEL
(HAMILCAR)
RHEGIUM
ESCALADERS
CENTURY CENTURY
LEGION
BATTLE OF LOCRI
205 BCE

The volatile young commander has shown surprising creativity by marching at night, a maneuver more characteristic of the wily Carthaginians than the tradition bound Romans. It is a wise move on his part: his garrison at Rhegium is the last Roman held town in the

VII. Locri

region. Pleminius must minimize the time his legion is seen in broad daylight, to prevent a counterattack on Rhegium by Hamilcar's forces at Locri.

"I am going to see to the escaladers," Pleminius tells Sergius. "Lead the vanguard until I return." He stares at Sergius. "At the present pace."

Pleminius rides to the rear to check on his laddermen. He finds them slogging along with the pack train, leading the pairs of mules that carry the thirty-foot ladders he had commissioned for the assault on Locri's twin fortresses. "Is all in order here?" Pleminius asks the lead escalader.

The centurion turns his sword-scarred face up to his commander, and raises his thumb stub. "We will be ready, Praetor. We can be up those walls in a blink."

Pleminius grins in acknowledgement, but his heart races with fear. *Unless they can scale those walls we can't get in. Hamilcar will just sit inside and wait for us to leave.* "Mars grant me success," he says softly, flinging out some salt from his belt pouch.

Later that night the Romans march into Locri province. They tread quietly toward the flickering firelights of the town, its twin citadels flanking the huts and houses that flow across the undulating grounds at their feet. Pleminius and his tribunes carefully watch the walls of the main citadel, but they see little movement from any sentries. The Romans are not surprised: who would expect an attack on a redoubtable tower in the heart of Hannibal's domain?

I would bet half their guards are asleep or drunk, Pleminius muses. "Julius!" he hisses over his shoulder. The young legate appears from out of the dark, his face tense with the anticipation of his first battle.

"The time is ripe," Pleminius says. "Give the signal." Julius lights a small torch and waves it sideways three times. He quickly shoves it into the earth. The Roman commanders watch, expectant. Soon a torch waves back twice from the eastern stronghold. Minutes later, the signal is repeated.

VII. Locri

"Send out the laddermen," Pleminius orders. The escaladers trot out toward the tower's walls. Each pair of laddermen lugs along a long, charcoal-blackened scaling ladder, barely visible in the half moon light. A maniple of a hundred and twenty legionnaires follows behind them, their only sound is the jingle of their sword belts and armor.

When the Romans are within two spear casts of the front gates, the lead tribune halts the attack party. He waves his hand to the right, and then to the left. The escaladers split up and dash to the east and west of the circular wall, disappearing into the night. The maniple divides into two centuries of sixty and spreads out along the encircling walls.

Watching the assault, Pleminius can see the flickering shadows of his men's ladders being eased against the walls. At the same time, some loyal Locrians ease down a half-dozen ladders from within. Pleminius sees the Locrians' ladders falling into place and smiles. *Good. Our sympathizers have killed the sentries, just as they promised.*

The escaladers prop their ladders against the parapets and nimbly scramble up the ladders. The legionnaires soon follow them on the ladders provided by the Locrians. The Romans skulk along the winding citadel walkway in both directions, with the laddermen in the lead. The escaladers pad along in bare feet, without arms or armor save for a soot-blackened gladius. They step over the bodies of several guards killed by the Locrians, their throats still oozing blood.

A lead escalader spies a sentry leaning against the rear wall. He signals for the others to pause. Crouching down, the wiry little Roman scuttles forward, blade at the ready, his dark gray tunic blending into the night. As he closes on the Carthaginian he hears the sentry's rasping snores. [lxxix]

The escalader laughs softly. He straightens up and creeps toward the sleeping guard. In one quick motion, he clamps his forearm about the guard's neck and thrusts his sword into his back, twisting his blade into the Carthaginian's heart. The guard's eyes fly open and his mouth gapes, but the escalader's iron forearm throttles his outcry. A minute later, the ladderman gently lays the quivering corpse down and steps over it, signaling for his men to follow him to the next victim.

VII. Locri

The Romans encircle the walkway, methodically eliminating the unwary guards. But one sentry fights his way out from a Roman's chokehold as a dagger enters his back. His dying screams cut through the night.[lxxx]

The Carthaginian ground sentries rush out from their posts, frantically searching for the source of the outcry. They gape at the scores of Romans scampering across the walkway steps. "Romans!" the chief guard bellows into the darkness. "The Romans are inside!"

Dozens of Carthaginians vault from their sleeping pallets and shake their counterparts awake. Groups of half-naked Libyans and Carthaginians rush into the square by the main gates of the citadel, colliding with each other as they rush to organize against their unseen enemy. Some Carthaginians carry only a sword and shield, others a mere fistful of spears. None are in full battle dress.

"Form up in front of the gates!" orders the Carthaginian infantry captain. The men group up into a roughshod phalanx.

The Romans scuttle down the walkway and regroup into their two centuries. The centuries move through two adjoining back streets, heading for the garrison entry.

The torch-carrying Romans step silently through the narrow dirt streets of the darkened fortress, their blackened blades at the ready. Handfuls of Hamilcar's men hurry out from the street side barracks only to stumble right into the Romans. The legionnaires quickly surround them, choking off their cries as they impale them with their dark blades. Grasping their victims' twitching legs, they pull their bodies into the alleyways before they move on.

The centuries burst into the town square at almost the same time. Both centuries halt when they see the enemy phalanx that surrounds the fortress gates. At first sight of the Romans, the Carthaginians and Libyans close ranks and raise their weapons. Handfuls of arriving soldiers scramble into their rear lines, adding to their numbers.

Sophus Pollonius, Pleminius' First Centurion, steps out from one

VII. Locri

century and faces the Romans. "Triangle formation," he shouts. The centuries tramp forward to merge into a wedge maniple,[lxxxi] guided by their centurions.

The muscular old veteran strides toward the gates, drawing out his sword. "Quickly now, before they all get here!" he commands. The wedge maniple tramps forward, shields locked together, with Sophus at the point.

"Follow me in," Sophus yells. "No one stops moving!"

The savvy veteran spies a shieldless man in the center of the front line and marches straight towards him. He batters his shield against the man in the center and knocks him backwards, even as he stabs his gladius into the ribs of a Libyan next to him.

With Sophus' two enemies fallen, a gap opens in the Carthaginian phalanx. The legionnaires push into it and spread the enemy lines apart, using their conjoined shields to fend off side attacks. Pushing and thrusting, the wedge maniple fights its way to the barred gates.

Sophus ducks under the spear thrust of a gate defender and stabs through his calf, bringing the man to his knees. He grasps one of the iron handles of the cross timber that bars the gates. "Come on, boys, help me get this cursed thing open!" he shouts.

Four soldiers leap to the gate and grasp the handles, their faces straining with the effort. A legionnaire falls with a spear in his back, but another fights his way to the gate and replaces him. The cross timber slowly scrapes past the braces that hold it, and tumbles to the ground.

The Romans fling open the main gates. Pleminius and his cavalry barge through the portal and into the citadel's main square. They gallop through the phalanx of gate defenders, breaking them apart.

"Into the back streets!" Pleminius shouts to his riders. The cavalry gallop off in pursuit of the enemy. The praetor turns to watch his infantry enter the gates.

VII. Locri

Sergius and Matienus march in with the front line legionnaires. The infantry cut into the rear of the enemy phalanx protecting the gates, as Sophus' maniple attacks it from the front. Scores of the gate defenders fall to the double-edged Roman attack. The Romans spread their lines and encircle the survivors.

"Surrender or you die," shouts Sophus, "I will not say it again!" The Carthaginians and Libyans throw down their weapons and kneel beside their dead comrades.

Pleminius calls over Sergius and Matienus. "Send the maniples into the east and west barracks," he barks. "Do it!"

The two tribunes glare at him, but they spring into action. Sergius and Matienus confer with the maniples' senior tribunes, who quickly lead their men toward the barracks. Screams soon erupt from the side buildings, as the Romans flood into the confused soldiers' barracks and cut down all they face.

The Carthaginians outnumber Pleminius' army by over a thousand, but the defenders are unaware of their numerical superiority. They only know that there are Romans inside their walls, running about and killing them.

Hamilcar is at the far end of the stronghold, gathering his troops about him near the stables. Clad only in a linen nightshirt, he rides about his men, organizing them for an assault at the gates. "Our citadel has fallen!" he yells to his captains. "We have to move out to the other one, to keep the Romans from taking it." The officers race back to the nearby barracks and bring what men they can find to join them. Hamilcar's Carthaginians nervously clench their weapons, listening to the growing sounds of the street fights.

Hamilcar rides out in front of his men. "On to the gates," he shouts. "We escape or die!" Hamilcar's confused Carthaginians and Libyans finally find a purpose to their movements—to escape death. Led by their captains, they mass into rude phalanxes and stalk through town toward the main gates, beating back the Romans that block their way. They battle to the town square and find three Roman maniples blocking

VII. Locri

the gates.

Hamilcar halts his men. "Prepare to charge," he tells his infantry captains. "We do not stop, we do not turn back." He waves over his cavalry. "You will follow me through those gates."

As Hamilcar's men form up to attack, Matienus breaks from the infantry front line and runs to the far side of the town square, where Pleminius stands with his guard. "They're going to attack the gate, Praetor!" he yells. "We need more men!"

"Get back there and fight, Tribune." Pleminius barks, shoving his sword toward the gates. "Don't whine to me about help!"

"Fool!" barks Matienus. Before Pleminius can reply, he runs back to rejoin Sergius.

"Now!" Hamilcar shouts. He plunges forward, leading scores of his cavalry toward the gate. The riders bash into the front line legionnaires, stabbing a half dozen down with their twelve-foot sarissas. Before the fallen Romans can be replaced, the Carthaginian riders crash their horses through the gaps, fighting their way toward the exit.

Seeing the Romans give way before their riders, the Carthaginian and Libyan phalanxes hurl themselves at the Romans who block their way, fighting demonically as they eye the open portal in front of them, their gateway to salvation.

Beset on three sides, scores of legionnaires fall beneath the frenzied onslaught. The enemy finally breaks through the last line of the determined gate defenders, leaving a trail of bodies behind them.

Hamilcar's men stampede out from the fortress and dash through the town. Hundreds more soldiers flee from the buildings, too many for the Romans to catch.

The sleepy Locrians peer out from their windows and doors as the Carthaginians run through their streets.

"What is going on?" shout several townspeople.

VII. Locri

"Romans!" comes the reply. At these words, some townspeople slam shut their windows and doors, hiding from vengeance for their treachery. Others fling them open and await their saviors, their faith in Rome affirmed.

Within an hour, all the surviving Carthaginians are massed about the base of the second citadel. They scream up at the sentries along the walkway and bang their sword pommels on the doors, staring over their shoulders for oncoming Romans. The gates creak open and the Carthaginians pile inside.

While the second citadel receives the Carthaginian fugitives, Pleminius stands in the central square of the first one. His bloodied bronze armor flickers with firelight from the ring of torches around him. He looks about the square and sees his soldiers dragging enemy bodies into mounds, piling them next to the prisoners. Looking into the streets behind the square, he sees no enemies and hears no fights. *It is ours*, he muses with satisfaction. *It is mine.*

Sergius and Matienus walk in from the front gates, their faces flush with anger. Matienus limps noticeably, his leg bandaged from thigh to calf.

"We lost almost half the men by the gates," Sergius says accusingly. "There were too many of them and too few of us."

Matienus nods. "I told you we needed more maniples up there, Pleminius."

"Your quackings are pointless," replies Pleminius. "We have taken their stronghold, that is all that matters. And the Carthaginians shall pay dearly for the men they killed."

Pleminius waves over his First Tribune. "Close the gates!" He bellows. "Secure the village. Go house to house, door to door."

Carrying fresh torches, groups of Romans carefully stalk through the halls and buildings of the large fort, like wolf packs searching for prey. They coolly dispatch any enemy soldiers who are wounded or hiding, dragging their bodies into the piles by the gates. Tomorrow the fields

VII. Locri

outside the fortress will be ablaze with enormous pyres, charnel flames that will light up the sky.

As his men finish their grisly task, Pleminius stands at the top walkway over the gates, watching the second fortress flare to life with the light of a hundred torches. *I've conquered the largest citadel. Now begins the work of keeping it.*

Over the next week, Roman and Carthaginian squadrons venture forth from their fortresses and skirmish with one another, fighting for control of the town. Most of the fights take place in the neighborhoods of the terrified townspeople. The Locrians hide behind their doors, waiting for a victor, any victor, that they may resume their life.

At the end of the week, two night sentries drag a father and son carpenter duo before Pleminius. The praetor sits on a large throne he ordered built after his victory. The throne is decorated with eagles fashioned from the gold and silver he has plundered from the citadel. Pleminius loves his throne; he has always wanted to be a king.

"Well?" Pleminius intones, looking down at the two raggedy workers. "Do you have something to say?"

The father bobs his head nervously and kneels. He reaches over and tugs at the gauzy worn tunic of his son, pulling him down next to him. "Yes, yes, commander ... esteemed Praetor Pleminius," he says. "We have been loyal Roman subjects, sir. Even when our council men betrayed the town to Hamilcar, we refused to bend the knee to him."

Pleminius picks up an olive from a nearby platter and rolls it in his fingers, studying it. "Commendable," he mutters, still staring at the olive. He pops it into his mouth, chews on it, and spits the pit near the two carpenters. "Is that all?"

"Oh, no, no, no," says the teen aged son. "We have news. We were forced to help build the armory in the other citadel. We've been building the wood frames for Hamilcar's new battering rams."

Pleminius lifts his head up. "Rams? Battering rams?"

VII. Locri

The older carpenter nods. "Yes, commander. I overhead two of Hamilcar's Sacred Band guards say they were preparing to attack you. As soon as Hannibal arrives to help them."

Pleminius vaults from his seat, scattering olives across the floor. "Hannibal? Hannibal is coming here?" he blurts.

The two carpenters nod mutely, their eyes wide with alarm. "That is what they said," the father finally manages to say.

The tribunes in the room stare at each other. "The gods have cursed us!" declares one. "We have to get out of here!" whispers another.

Pleminius' mouth works like a fish out of water. He looks at his officers, but their faces only mirror his own confusion and alarm. *Steady now. You have to be in charge.*

Pleminius' jaw tightens. His face grows stern. "Get all our men from Rhegium," he says to his First Tribune. The officer is already stalking toward the door when Pleminius yells at him. "And get word to General Scipio in Sicily!"

As the tribune closes the door, Pleminius collapses back into his throne. He steeples his fingers together and looks at them, bending them back and forth. He turns to his officers and smiles. "We will prepare a welcoming party for Hannibal. And Hannibal will not welcome what he gets!" The tribunes nod, but they look dubiously at one another.

Within the space of an hour, two riders dash out from the Locri citadel, racing to fulfill their dire missions. One rides southwest to Pleminius' headquarters in Rhegium, bearing his order to bring all available troops and equipment to Locri.

The other messenger rides west to the port town of Messana. Arriving there, he commandeers a small bireme and sails across the Strait of Messana, urging its hundred oarsmen to maximum speed. When he lands, the messenger vaults from the ship and rushes to the port stables. Throwing a bag of coins to the stable master, he takes the reins of a rangy black stallion and plummets toward Syracuse, determined to

VII. Locri

reach Scipio before the next day.

* * * * *

SYRACUSE, SICILY, 204 BCE. "Spread your arms out wider, General. A little more ... there, that's it!" The portly young barber smears more olive oil on Scipio's outstretched arms. He grabs his curved horn blade and scrapes the oil from Scipio's right arm, then the left. "Now for the chest," the barber says, as he flicks the scrapes into a polished marble basin next to him.

"Just get it done, Prostus," grouses Scipio. "I feel vulnerable. And stupid."

Scipio stands naked in the center of his capacious city headquarters, his legs and arms spread wide. One of Sicily's famed barbers scrapes the cleansing olive oil off Scipio's glistening body. Having shaved and trimmed Scipio, the barber is completing the last of his grooming tasks.

Prostus runs his blade over Scipio's chest, and gently scrapes his groin. The barber grabs a heavy felt cloth and wipes off the last of the oil. "There. We are done, General."

"Gratitude, Prostus. I don't look like such a beast any more." Scipio wraps a linen sheet about his waist as the barber dabs the last drops of olive oil from his neck. He reaches into a pottery bowl of coins and gives Prostus a handful of denarii. "Out with you now," Scipio orders.

Scipio walks barefoot to his twenty-foot map table, the same one used by the Carthaginian general Epicydes before Marcus Claudius Marcellus took over Syracuse.

"Now for some breakfast," Scipio says, plunking himself down on one of the chestnut wood benches. He is breaking apart a flatbread when Praxis pushes open the thick doors.

"Apologies, General," says the old gladiator. "A messenger has arrived from Locri. He appears in great distress."

Locri again! Just when I have my hands full planning for Africa.

VII. Locri

"Curse the gods, send him in," Scipio replies.

The exhausted young legionnaire stumbles into Scipio's tent and relays his news about the taking of the main Locri garrison, and about its impending assault by Hamilcar and Hannibal. Scipio chews on his bread as he listens to the news. At mention of Hannibal's name, he places his bread on the table and leans back.

"You say Hannibal is coming to Locri? You are sure of that?" The messenger shrugs. "That is what the two informants told Pleminius. The praetor begs your help in defending Locri, and Rhegium."

"Take sustenance and rest, messenger. You shall have your reply by day's end." Scipio turns to Praxis. "Find Laelius and Marcus Silenus. Bring them immediately."

When Scipio's two commanders arrive he is still at table, dipping a wheat pancake into olive oil. He chews thoughtfully, his mind adrift on Africa's shores.

"Come sit down, take bread with me." He waves them to the table and offers them a platter of breads and fruits. Marcus shakes his head and stares at Scipio, waiting.

"Aah, dates!" exclaims Laelius. He pops several dates into his mouth and stretches out on a bench seat, yawning theatrically.

"Are we here to just share breakfast with you?" asks Laelius at last. "Have you become that lonely?"

Scipio shakes his head. "Would that were all I required. Pleminius has taken one of the citadels of Locri. Hamilcar occupies the other, and Hannibal coming to reinforce him."

"Hannibal?" says Marcus, excited in spite of himself. "Why would he come to that town?"

"Perhaps he's bored," Laelius says. "Perhaps he is desperate to keep us from establishing another allied garrison near him." He laughs. "Then again, it might be a fiction to scare us. Locri is a pisspot little

VII. Locri

city, not worth his time."

Scipio frowns. "If Hannibal comes, Pleminius could not escape without a grievous loss of men. That includes the soldiers I sent him."

"Pleminius was likely seeking the glory of an easy conquest," says Laelius. "And now he has Hannibal to contend with." He pours himself a glass of wine. "We should leave him to his fate; we have larger objectives."

Scipio tosses his pancake scrap back onto the platter. "We cannot afford the loss of men or reputation. And I cannot countenance sending our men to their death." He sighs resignedly. "I am going there."

"What a way to celebrate the new year," says Laelius acidly. "Getting into a battle with Old One Eye himself."

"A battle that we cannot afford to lose, but I would hate to win," muses Scipio, "if we want a permanent peace."

"We cannot afford to lose you. You are Rome's only hope," intones Marcus. "Going to Locri is an act of folly. Don't be a fool."

Scipio blinks in surprise. Marcus Silenus has always been blunt and honest with him, but rarely insulting. He can feel a flush creeping into his cheeks, along with an urge to have Marcus slapped into chains. But he remembers the love this killer of men has had for him. He is a man who would sacrifice his life for the Scipios without a second thought.

"Perhaps you speak the truth, Marcus. My rational self is telling me to send a legion there under someone else." He smiles forlornly. "But my spirit tells me that no one would fare better against Hannibal than I, and I might be sacrificing them all if I were not leading Locri's defense."

"Pish," sniffs Laelius. "You have an overweening concept of yourself." He grins sideways at Scipio, raising his eyebrows. "Which is not to say it is false. Go then. But do not tarry, General Scipio. Remember your words to the men: 'Africa awaits us.' "

* * * * *

VII. Locri

GENOVA, NORTH ITALIA, 205 BCE. "By Baal's balls, what is out there?" fusses Mago, as he looks at the fleet of new quinqueremes and transports filling the Genova harbor.

Durro smiles his dry smile, his gaunt hands folded inside his thick indigo cloak. "Reinforcements, General. Paid for by the citizens of Carthage. The Senate created a new war levy to prevent Scipio from attacking Carthage. Our citizens were most glad to pay it." Durro shakes his head, as if discussing a silly child. "Admiral Laelius' raids on our coast have them all terrified, they thought Scipio himself had come to get them!"

"So what did you bring me?" Mago says. He has already noticed that the ships are floating low in the water, obviously laden with supplies.

Durro pulls out a sealed scroll and hands it to Mago. "Here is the list, along with your marching orders. We brought you twenty-five warships, six thousand African infantry, eight hundred cavalry, and seven elephants. Plus money for more Gallic mercenaries." [lxxxii]

Like a child with a present, Mago eagerly snatches the document from Durro and breaks the seal. He eagerly scans the list of resources. And he smiles.

Durro reaches out and gently pulls the list from Mago's hands, recapturing the general's attention.

"This is all for one purpose, you know," says Durro.

Mago bobs his head impatiently. "Of course. I am to march south to join Hannibal. Merge forces with him and attack Rome." He furrows his brows at Durro. "It is not a complex plan."

"Then you had best commence it, General," says Durro. "We want Rome's troops and resources diverted from attacking Africa to defending their homeland. You and Hannibal will create that diversion."

"And what of my brother?" asks Mago. "Have you finally given him the resources to do something? Finally?"

VII. Locri

Durro ignores the sarcasm. He sighs. "We sent him eighty ships laden with grain and weapons, but Baal saw fit to blow them off course into Sardinia. The Romans captured the ones that survived." [lxxxiii]

"When will he receive more?" asks Mago.

Durro shakes his head. "We cannot give him any more. The last of our war funds went to Philip of Macedon. A bribe for him to renew his war with Rome. He will be another diversion."

"It would have been better spent on Hannibal," says Mago. "But I will march south, regardless. When I depart from my camp in Liguria, I will have thirty thousand men, counting the Gauls I will pay to join me."

Durro hands the scroll back to Mago. "Then by all the gods we hold dear, I entreat you to march on Rome as soon as possible."

"By the next full moon we will head south along the coast, toward Rome. No one can stop us."

"Perhaps, perhaps not," replies Durro. "Our spies tell us that Rome has sent six legions north to guard against an attack from you. Three of them are stationed on the east coast, near Ariminum. But there are several legions of slave volunteers in Arretium under Marcus Livius.[lxxxiv] They will block your way south to Rome."

Mago snorts. "Slaves? They send slaves against me?" He looks at Durro, incredulous. "And you would have me worry about them?"

Durro purses his lips. "Many of them were trained by Marcus Silenus himself, I have heard. I would not take them lightly."

Mago laughs. "Yes, trained slaves. Just like trained dogs. And a trained dog is still a dog." He waves the scroll under Durro's nose. "I will tell you this. While I finish my recruiting up in Gaul, I will send my best men out to test these slaves. We will see how fiercely these little dogs bite!"

* * * * *

VII. Locri

LOCRI, BRUTTIUM REGION, 205 BCE. Scipio's four troop transports ease into the shallow waters of an unnamed bay near Locri, and crunch into its rocky shore. The gangplanks are lowered and the first legionnaires step down into the shallow waters.

Within two hours, Scipio is leading two thousand legionnaires down the back roads to Locri, traveling with the light pack and armament that his army employed in their lightning marches through Iberia.

As they near Locri that afternoon, Scipio steers the men off the road to a nearby farm. After confining the farmer's family to their house, Scipio directs his men to spread out into the wheat fields and groves of the farm, hidden from any who pass by the far road.

Scipio sits at the table with the awestruck family, happily chatting with them about the progress of their crops in this late fall season. He graciously drinks their raw wine and eats the pistachios and olives given him, extolling the virtues of each humble food. He winks at the farmer's little girl as she peers out from behind the knee-length tunic of her mother, and hands her a shiny silver coin.

Scipio gives the nervous farmer a bulging bag of coins as payment for his meager supper. "It has been a pleasure staying with you, citizen. I regret I must leave, but my old friend Nightfall approaches."

When night is full upon the land, Scipio musters his men for the short march to Locri. Scipio's scouts ride to Pleminius' citadel and alert him to the general's arrival. At midnight, Scipio walks out from the farm on foot, leading the first narrow columns of soldiers down the farm road. The legionnaires thread their way from the adjoining fields and march down to the main road.

Scipio is soon marching up to the torchlit gates of Locri. Pleminius is standing at the fortress gates when the revered commander arrives, grinning broadly.

"I am most honored at your presence, Imperator," Pleminius exclaims. The praetor impulsively embraces Scipio and kisses him on both cheeks.

VII. Locri

Scipio gently pushes him away. *Gods above, the man is more emotional than a woman. And he is in charge of south Italia?*

"Please, General, come to my headquarters," urges Pleminius. "I have prepared a celebratory feast." Scipio shakes his head. "I will wait here until all my men have safely entered the fortress. But I could use a chair for my weary bones." A large chair is fetched, and Scipio sits in the citadel's public square for the next hour, watching his centuries trickle in.

When all men are accounted for, the main doors ease shut. Pleminius turns to Scipio. "Now that your legion is all inside, General, may I ask you what you are doing here?"

Scipio looks about the thick stone walls of the fortress. "Well, in some ways my decision to send men to you has put you into this trap, so I thought it only fair to help extricate you!"

Pleminius sighs. "I welcome your assistance, certainly I do. But we are still outnumbered. Hannibal is camped over by the River Bulotus with thousands of his own men. [lxxxv] I fear he will storm the city below us tomorrow, and then join forces with Hamilcar to besiege our citadel."

"Well, for once Hannibal does not know everything!" Scipio says jovially, taking Pleminius aback. "Hannibal is not aware that I have arrived here, isn't that true?"

"Oh yes, even I did not know you were coming until your scouts came to me."

"Well, the best kept secrets are the ones no one knows! I decided to surprise you, in case you had an infiltrator in your midst. Hannibal is famous for his spy network"

Scipio rubs his hands together, glad to be back in the intrigue of battle. "Now it is our turn to surprise the Carthaginians. We will let them attack. And if we are lucky, they will try to storm the fortress!"

Pleminius stares at Scipio, and swallows. "General, I know you have a

VII. Locri

reputation for, uh, unconventional ideas. But my apologies, I do not see the sense of what you say."

Scipio grins. "Do you remember Aesop's fable, The One-Eyed Doe?" Pleminius looks at him blankly.

Scipio waggles a finger at the praetor. "You should study the classics," he says. "They are the source of all my strategy! The one-eyed doe was undone by a sailor who shot her from the seashore, while her good eye was trained on the land, looking for huntsmen. She was surprised by an attack from the least likely place!"

Pleminius blinks at him. Scipio closes his eyes in frustration, and continues. "Hannibal will be our one-eyed doe, we have to keep his attention trained on one spot, while we come in from another."

Scipio walks over to a nearby table and sifts through the map scrolls piled there. "Ah, here we are, a map of the region!" Scipio pulls up a chair and points to an empty one next to him. "Sit down. We shall plan this trick together, Praetor." A bewildered Pleminius sits down next to Scipio.

"Now, in the next day or two, the Carthaginians will attack, and when they do, we shall place our men here by the gates," says Scipio, pointing to the entry of the stronghold. "That's when we will spring our little deception."

"What deception?" asks Pleminius.

"Why, we are going to kick up a little dust!" says Scipio wryly. "Here, let me show you an old Spartan trick..."

As Scipio and Pleminius commune about tomorrow's engagement, Hamilcar is reading a message scroll from Hannibal. The Bane of Roma has ordered Hamilcar's troops to attack the citadel at daybreak, and Hannibal will bring in his army to join him. Hamilcar signs the message and gives it back to the messenger. He begins his preparations.

At dawn, Hamilcar's citadel opens its doors. The Carthaginians march out into the streets of Locri, blaring their battle horns. Several

VII. Locri

skirmishes erupt through the town, as knots of Romans and Carthaginians battle among the town's streets and buildings. The outnumbered Romans soon retreat to their citadel.

Hannibal and his men arrive with Hamilcar's attack in full sway, his men standing thick around the garrison walls. The Carthaginians catapult rocks and firepots at the Romans, who return fire with their ballistae and scorpios.

Hannibal takes one look at the towering walls of the occupied citadel and curses. *Hamilcar didn't tell me how tall it is. We'll have to build new ladders. His men are in the way, regardless. I can't mount an attack.*

Hannibal summons Maharbal to his side. "We have to delay the attack until tomorrow. We'll camp here." Hannibal orders his men to pile up their trunks, barrels and baggage into an improvised wall,[lxxxvi] as if they intend to lay siege to Pleminius' fortress. Seeing Hannibal's army prepare to camp, Hamilcar ceases his attack and returns his men to the safety of his citadel.

With the battlefield empty, Hannibal rides around the Roman citadel with a squad of his Numidian cavalry. He assesses the length and type of ladders he will need to scale the stronghold, and the best points of attack. Lacumaza, a lusty young Numidian captain, rides next to Hannibal, his teeth gleaming in his sunburnt brown face.

Lacumaza chatters energetically about attacking the citadel, obviously eager for killing and plunder. "Maybe they know you are the great Hannibal down here, so maybe they will surrender." He says. "Me, I would rather kill them. But I bet they give up!"

As Hannibal ponders a reply, he is distracted by a whooshing sound. There is a loud *Thunk!* Lacumaza flies off the back of his horse, impaled by a finger-thick, arrow-headed iron bolt from a Roman scorpion.[lxxxvii] Hannibal gapes in surprise for a moment, then looks down at the still-twitching corpse of his erstwhile captain. "No, I do not think they'll surrender," he says to the dead Numidian, as he trots out of range.

VII. Locri

After two hours of inspecting the fortress, Hannibal is satisfied with his assessment of the citadel's defenses. He returns to camp and begins planning his attack. Hannibal's carpenters work furiously through the night to construct scores of tall scaling ladders, while Hannibal draws out his plans for his army's mass assault on the citadel, bolstered by Hamilcar's ground forces.

Hannibal calls together his officers, his face eager with anticipation. "Tomorrow we will take Locri and that cursed citadel," he says. "Even if we have to fight all day to do it." After the officers depart, Hannibal brings Hamilcar into his tent.

"I need you to stay in the garrison tomorrow. There isn't room for both armies, we'd get in each other's way."

Hamilcar blushes. "Is there something I have done wrong?" he asks. Hannibal shakes his head. "No, it is best that I do this myself, with my own men. You would only be an obstruction."

Hamilcar bows in acquiescence. *Fuck you*, he thinks.

Dawn finds Hannibal mustering his men for the assault. He rides out from camp and soon appears in the plains below Pleminius' fortress. Hannibal rides atop a black stallion covered in red ring mail, the horse looking like a bloodied beast from hell. He leads his ladder-bearers toward the citadel, followed by his Libyans, Numidians, and Carthaginians. *One full assault,* he thinks. *They cannot adequately cover every wall with their few men*

Hannibal draws within two spear casts of the gate and calls for his laddermen to encircle the fortress. Trios of lightly armored Libyans dash forward with their tall ladders, looping toward the rear walls of Pleminius' redoubt.

Hannibal sees the Romans lining the top walls, ready to fend off the attack, and he orders his men into a full-scale assault upon the walls. Twenty sets of laddermen run in toward the front walls of the citadel. Hordes of warriors slowly follow them, clashing their spears onto their shields. Hannibal's battle horns sound the attack and the infantry

VII. Locri

hurries forward, eager to destroy the Roman sanctuary.

Without warning, the citadel's front gates burst open. Thousands of Romans stride out from the gates, eight abreast, marching rapidly toward Hannibal and his scattered troops. The Carthaginians halt in surprise at the heavy frontal assault, wondering where all the soldiers have come from. The Carthaginian officers scream for a recall but it is too late, the Romans are upon them.

Scipio rides behind the first wave of his men, surrounded by his Honor Guard. He directs the infantry's attack maneuvers from his vantage point, studying the effect of his surprise tactics. Scipio has ordered the legionnaires to shuffle their feet as they march, stirring up dust clouds that make it difficult to determine the size of the Roman attack force.

The Romans arrive at the open land in front of Hannibal. The legionnaires rapidly rearrange themselves into four cohorts of 480 infantry, four lines to a cohort. Fighting shield to shield in dense rows of hastati, principes, and triarii, the methodical veterans quickly cut down two hundred of their enemy.[lxxxviii]

Hannibal charges about on his horse, organizing his men to counter the surprise attack, but it is to no avail. Pleminius' men soon follow Scipio's out into the battlefield, giving the impression there is a never-ending stream of Romans coming from the citadel.

Pleminius' defenders hurry toward the flanks of their disorganized enemy, intending to encircle them. Hannibal's men begin to panic, all they can see are Romans materializing from everywhere in the dust. Many turn and run from the front lines, dropping sword and shield in their haste to escape.

Hannibal sees scores of weaponless men rush past him. He also sees an imminent Roman victory, and the chance he may be captured or killed. *I could lose the war fighting over this little shitpile*, he curses to himself. *Because of one surprise attack.*

Hannibal calls over Maharbal. "How many of them are out there?"

VII. Locri

demands Hannibal.

Maharbal shakes his head vigorously, his frustration evident. "With all that dust and confusion, I just do not know, General. They are still coming out of the gates. Our men are running away!"

"We are losing, Maharbal" growls Hannibal.

"I will get the Numidians to come in on our flanks, so they can counterattack," Maharbal says. Hannibal shakes his head.

"No, we don't have enough of them," He looks back at the unfolding carnage, and sighs heavily. "Sound the retreat, get our men out of here before more of them are slaughtered. We will return to our river camp."

Maharbal curses in frustration, but he nods his acknowledgement. "But what about Hamilcar?"

Hannibal grimaces. "He will be safe in his fortress for now. Tell him he is to wait until the Romans retire and then he can join us. Now let's get out of here." Hannibal turns his back on Locri and rides toward his camp, slumped dispiritedly in his saddle.

Maharbal immediately follows Hannibal's directive. The Carthaginian battle horns blow a retreat and Hannibal's troops hasten back to their main camp. Hannibal's heavy infantry of Libyans fight gamely as they withdraw from the battle. They maintain their phalanxes formations, covering the retreat of the rest of the troops. The Romans harass the retreating Libyans, but they cannot break their lines.

Scipio and Pleminius ride at the vanguard of the advancing troops, excited at the prospect of Hannibal's army in full retreat.

Pleminius turns to Scipio, his face flushed. "Let's chase them back to their camp and destroy it," he shouts. "We can get Hannibal himself! Think of the glory!"

Scipio reaches over and grabs Pleminius, almost pulling him from his horse. "Fool! Have you thought of the men who would be killed?" he says angrily, pulling Pleminius' face next to his. "You would march

VII. Locri

our men into that wily fox's den? Attack an army that outnumbers us? We will content ourselves with driving Hannibal out. Tomorrow we will take the other fort."

Scipio orders a return to the citadel. He rides at the head of his weary but happy army, passing by dozens of Locrian sympathizers that have ventured forth to loot the field of battle. And to vengefully kill any wounded Carthaginians they find. *At least Pleminius will have the townspeople behind him*, Scipio thinks. *The dolt will need all the help he can get.*

That night, as the army feasts in celebration and mourning, the guards summon Scipio and Pleminius to the battlements. There they see the enemy fortress ablaze, it's walls crumbling upon themselves.[lxxxix] A stream of torches trickles out from the gates, flowing down towards Locri town. Pleminius gasps. "Hamilcar's men are assaulting the town!"

He looks to Scipio for orders, but Scipio merely smirks. "Those are not soldiers. They are Carthaginian sympathizers who have fled the fortress. I would wager Hamilcar has already sneaked out under cover of darkness. The blaze was set to distract us."

"I can get our cavalry after them," says Pleminius. "We can finish off that bastard before he reaches Hannibal."

Scipio fixes him with a look. "You would rush out for a night fight with our few cavalry, against an enemy of unknown force, near one with superior numbers?" He puts his hand on Pleminius' shoulder. "You will not be taking my men on such a folly."

Scipio gives him a gentle push, his face grim. "Go have a cup of wine, relax for the few hours we have for such things. Tomorrow we root out the town traitors."

The next afternoon, as the day nears dusk, Scipio sits at a feasting table in Pleminius' headquarters, accompanied by Pleminius, Sergius, and Matienus. Six notable Locrians join them. The group is acting as judge and jury for the Locrians who are being tried, men convicted of

VII. Locri

betraying Locri to the Carthaginians.

Four town magistrates have already been before them, begging and pleading for their lives, denying they ever spoke against Rome or advocated for Carthage. In each instance Scipio allows the defendant to plead his case without interruption for five minutes. When the person is finished Scipio turns to his table of Locrian loyalists. "Is that true?" Scipio asks them. If any say the man is lying, the captive is summarily dragged off by the guards. And Scipio calmly calls for the next defendant.

The final Locrian is brought in while Scipio slowly rubs his eyes, weary of the day's adjudications. He takes a deep breath and looks up, enthused that he will finally be done for the day. His face falls when he sees the person before him. He is an old and portly man, his spindly arms dangling from his thick white toga. A man who grins anxiously at Scipio.

"Titus?" Scipio says wonderingly, staring hard into the old man's lined face. "Is that truly you?"

The elderly man's smile broadens, belying his glassy stare of fear. "Ah, young Scipio! You have grown to be such an impressive man! Your mother Pomponia must be so proud of you." He bows his head. "My regrets about your father. He was a good friend to me. I always had a bed at your domus when I came to see the Senate."

Those seated at the table turn and look curiously at Scipio. He grins self-consciously. "Titus was ... is a member of the Senate of Locri. He came to Rome when my father was consul." Scipio sees the doubt on their faces. "Whatever happens, I tell you he was a good man!" he says defiantly. Titus looks at every person at the table, searching for his fate. What he sees there makes his head droop.

"Your 'friend' was one of the ringleaders of the revolt," says a young Locrian noble, his eyes smoldering. "He ordered the deaths of those who resisted him."

Hearing these words, Scipio looks back at Titus, boring into the old

VII. Locri

man's eyes, even as he feels his heart pound with the dread of what he may have to do. *Say it is a lie*, he prays. *Give me a reason for what you did. Please.*

Titus' head rises, as his pride conquers his fear. Scipio can see the truth of Titus' betrayal before he opens his mouth: without a doubt, the man is preparing his final words. Titus speaks to Scipio, but it is as if Scipio is a symbol more than a person.

"Rome, you abandoned these lands when Hannibal drove you from them. And ignored those who were loyal to you." He looks at the table attendees, then sweeps his arm behind him, taking in the southlands of Italia. "Look about you. All but Rhegium is in Hannibal's hands, we were alone!"

The old man stares at Scipio, his eyes moist with fearful tears, his voice pleading. "If I did not turn Locri over to Carthage, there would be no Locri. Who would help us? Doddering old Fabius? Marcellus, long dead on the fields of Herdonia? You?" He swallows. "We would all have been dead." He sneers at the Locrians "Would you deny that, too?"

"He is responsible for the death of the dissenters," says an older Locrian. The younger man who first spoke nods his agreement.

Scipio's eyes dart about, as he thinks frantically for a way to resolve this without killing Titus. He knows the news of his decision will race faster than Mercury to Rome. And faster to his men. *If you show favoritism, you show you cannot be trusted.*

Scipio looks back at his childhood friend. He bites his lower lip and shakes his downcast head. "My heart breaks to say this, noble friend, but you are guilty."

"No!" blurts Titus, before Scipio can speak, pushing against the guards who have grabbed his arms. "I did what I did to save my people, not to kill them!" The old man summons himself and stands upright, again raising his head high. "And I would do it again."

Scipio faces his guards, his voice quavering in spite of himself. "You

VII. Locri

know what to do. Do it now."

At those words Titus' will breaks, and he collapses into the guards' cold arms. They drag the old man into the courtyard as Scipio sits immobile, his gaze at a distant place. There is a long silence, and the attendees shift about uncomfortably.

Matienus leans to Scipio's ear. "General, it would be best if you witnessed the sentence, as you know. It tells the people you are willing to accept the consequences of your decision."

Scipio glares at Matienus, but his look softens when he sees the honest concern on his face. "I am out there in a minute," he replies, as he heads to his chambers in the rear rooms.

Scipio goes to his washbasin and douses his face, rubbing it vigorously, as if removing some grime from it. He towels off and stretches out on his sleeping platform. "Leave me," he commands. Scipio lies there, staring at the ceiling, taking deep breaths. A racking sob escapes him, then another. He rolls over and buries his face into his sleeping pads, pounding his fist.

After a few minutes Scipio swallows and pushes himself upright. He walks stiffly from the room, passing through the now-empty meeting hall and out into the courtyard. He strides through the open gates, forcing himself to walk toward the screams.

There, outside the city gates, are five crosses. One of the Locri ringleaders is impaled on each one of them. The men hang from the finger-thick spikes driven into their wrists, their overlapping feet nailed to the bottom.

One of Pleminius' centurions orders the soldiers to strip Titus down to his subligalculum. "Drive 'em deep," the centurion shouts to his men, raising his voice to be heard over the wailings of the others. "We don't want 'em slippin' away in the night, do we now?" The centurion gives Scipio a gap toothed grin, which quickly disappears when he sees the General's face.

A trembling Titus is straddled across the two intersecting timbers and

VII. Locri

rudely pushed onto them. Two soldiers pin down his left hand. The third raises his hammer and drives a thick spike into the old man's leathery palm. Titus' eyes start from his head, his scream drowning those of the other lost men. He catches sight of Scipio. "I did love your father," he shouts desperately. "I did it for Italia! For Rome!"

Scipio does not reply. His jaw is so clenched that his neck veins are purple. His eyes are fixed on some distant place, far beyond the field of torture. *Jupiter help me get through this, that is all I ask.*

The soldiers complete their grim spiking task. The four move to the head of Titus' cross. They lift it up and let it plummet into the deep hole dug for it. It lands with a thud, yanking the old man downward. Titus wails in anguish.

With all the men impaled on their crosses, Scipio faces the wide-eyed crowd of Locrians and soldiers. He starts to speak but the words choke in his mouth. *Come on. Just a minute more, then you are done.*

Scipio swallows hard, and raises his head to face the crowd. "This is the fate for those who betray Rome!" he fumbles out. "Heed your commander Pleminius, that you do not suffer the same fate!"

He turns to Pleminius, and speaks loudly, that all may hear. "Praetor, you are to turn these men's property over to the ones who accused them, in recognition for their loyalty.[xc] Sell their families into slavery, and give the money to the same loyalists." Scipio flips his hand dismissively at the awestruck onlookers. "We are done here." He swallows. "I am done."

As the soldiers post torches about the dying men, Scipio marches back through the gates. Pleminius follows at his heels.

"You gave them a memorable lesson, General," says Pleminius with a grin. "Nothing like seeing traitors hanging from a cross to give people some respect for loyalty!"

Scipio whirls on Pleminius. "I just ordered the death of one of the finest men in Italia, and ruined his family," he snarls, the spit flying from his mouth. "A man who sacrificed himself for the greater good. If

VII. Locri

you had half his character and courage, I would not have had to come here and pull you out of this mess!" Scipio shoves Pleminius. "Away from me, I cannot bear your visage!"

Pleminius watches Scipio stalk back to his quarters, his face flaming red. "Who needed you? I could have taken the fortress myself," he says petulantly, to no one in particular.

Back in his room, Scipio quickly undresses and pitches himself on his sleeping pallet, listening to the muted sounds of the legionnaires' revelry, men celebrating conquest and another day of life. *At least they are not screaming. Screaming at me. Screaming because of me.*

Scipio lies on his side, refusing his attendant's food offerings, content to sip from his goblet of watered wine. He can feel the fever start to rise within himself, and he pulls a wool cover over his naked body. He wills himself to sleep, intending to rise early and return to Sicily. *Go to sleep, boy, the real war yet awaits you.*

But Febris has chosen this night to visit him, after years of being gone. Scipio's mind whirls with the scenes and sounds of the battles he has fought, fleeting images of retreating enemies, dying compatriots, tortured captives, and fearful duels.

He is suddenly back at Carthago Nova, standing at the foot of the citadel tower in which General Magon hides. He sees Magon sneering down at him. "I will not surrender to you, boy! Come up and get me!" Magon says, as his soldiers laugh around him.

He thinks I won't come after him. But we'll lose hundreds if we try to take that tower. I have to show him that I'm willing to do it.

"No matter what you do, people will die," comes Marcus Silenus' voice behind him. "You decide if it will be ours or theirs."

Scipio feels the familiar dread as he again raises his hand to order the murder of the townspeople. He can feel his right hand twitching, the queasiness in his stomach, the desperation to think of some alternative to killing innocents.

VII. Locri

"Marcus Silenus had it right," booms a deep voice behind him. "People will die by your decision. You must serve the greater good for your people. As Titus did."

Scipio turns to see his dead father standing behind him, a kindly smile on his craggy face. Publius Scipio is arrayed in his battered battle armor. His breastplate is gashed open where the merciless swords and javelins took his life in Iberia.

"Titus betrayed his oath to Rome," Scipio says to his father.

The older man nods slowly. "He did. He thought Hannibal would destroy Locri if the councilmen did not capitulate. You gave him what he deserved by our laws, but that makes him no less an honorable man." He smiles at his son. "Nor you."

Publius walks up and squeezes his son's shoulder. "You will have to make a similar decision, soon. A decision on who will die and who will live—and which of your principles you will sacrifice to your other ones."

"I never wanted any this!" Scipio retorts petulantly. "You took me from my life as a scholar, making me swear to be a soldier and protect Rome."

Publius looks up at the tower, then back at his son. "I love you. But I could not act out of love. To deny Rome your talents, with Carthage threatening us, it would have put us all at peril. I made the decision I had to make, as you will have to do."

Scipio's father walks toward a dark doorway that appears nearby. He pauses at the entry and turns to his son. "The haruspex was right. Those you love will die because of your enterprise. But you must not abandon it."

Publius enters the doorway just before the legionnaires again rush into it with drawn swords, murdering the townspeople as General Magon watches in terror. And the screams begin. Again.

Scipio pitches from his pallet and tumbles to the floor, crashing onto

VII. Locri

his back. "Get away from me!" he shouts, kicking off his wool coverlet. He pushes himself to a sitting position, blinking groggily. Sweat pours down his body.

Scipio stumbles out the main door, seeking the coolness of the cavernous stone hallway. Peering through the bars of a narrow window, he sees the first fingers of sunrise clawing across the battle-tilled fields of yesterday. A cock crows his challenge to the daylight.

"Pontius!" Scipio shouts. His chief attendant materializes as if from thin air. "Call in the tribunes after breakfast. Tell them we must be at Rhegium by dusk."

Pontius scurries off, as Scipio stares out the window. He watches a brown-winged eagle soar on the air currents, slowly circling and dipping around the citadel's parapets before it glides away to parts unknown. *Fly free and long, noble bird. You are blessed to be able to follow your nature.*

VIII. JUDGMENT

SYRACUSE. "Again, lift!" shouts Marcus Silenus, glowering at the recruits. "Use your legs, not your back!" At his command, hundreds of recruits lift up their boulders and begin marching spraddle-legged with them. Scipio's sweaty volunteers resume the rock training they started in Rome, lifting, carrying, and pitching the heavy stones.

Scipio's army commander has already grown bored with his inaction in Sicily, and has reassumed his role as trainer of legionary recruits. The short, blocky man is ruthlessly conditioning the volunteers from Rome, determined to give them a legionnaire's body before they alight on the plains of Africa.

Marcus knows that a soldier's deadliness is in his legs as much as his arms, that even the most skillful fighter can be bested by a fresher opponent if his legs weaken. It is a strength he cultivated within himself after watching Rome's best boxers train their legs for their deadly fights. He would watch as the lighter man would dodge his larger opponent, who eventually tired from chasing him and became easy prey.

Marcus will ensure that each man will have legs strong enough to battle for hours, or to complete one of Scipio's twenty-mile speed marches with a laden pack. The legate has vowed that no recruit will die because he was too easy on him.

Aulus, one of Scipio's Honor Guard, strides up to Marcus. "Salve, Marcus Silenus. I have come from Scipio's headquarters in Messana. You are to ride north immediately to meet him there." Seeing Marcus' puzzled look, he adds, "The General says he requires your advice."

Marcus thumps down the large boulder he was lifting and faces the former gladiator. Aulus looks away from Marcus' probing stare, refusing to meet his yellow-green eyes.

VIII. Judgment

"I will be there on the morrow," Marcus replies, carefully watching Aulus' face. Aulus hastily salutes and whirls away. *That man is hiding something*, Marcus considers, wiping the sweat off his torso. *But what would an Honor Guard have to hide?*

Marcus shrugs off his concern. "Pentius!" Marcus shouts, summoning the legion's praefectus castrorum. The one-armed military trainer limps over on his two scarred legs, hefting his training shield with his iron arm fashioned to hold it.[xci] "I must leave immediately. Take the men over to the dummies to practice their thrusting."

The old tribune nods, raises his thickly muscled right arm in the air and waves his gladius toward the east training field. "Time to fight the wooden Carthaginians, puppies," he bellows. "And this time you had better win!"

By late evening the next day Marcus is riding through the gates of the Messana garrison, the fort captained by Scipio's brother Lucius. Marcus dismounts at the stone cottage that is Scipio's temporary headquarters. He pushes past the protesting sentries poised at the entrance and shoves open the thick studded doors of the banquet hall on the right. He finds Scipio, Laelius, Lucius, and the tribunes huddled around the banquet table, with an obviously distressed Scipio standing at the head. Scipio clenches a crumpled message scroll in his right hand. He waves it at Marcus as he marches into the room. "It is good to see you, Legate, I will need your voice in my ear. We have been discussing Locri."

Marcus takes off his helmet and swordbelt. He carefully places them on a stool. "What has developed there?"

"Chaos!" Scipio growls. "This message came from the Locri magistrates this morning. It says that the city is in chaos!"

Marcus blinks at him. "You recently left Pleminius in charge of the garrison there, did you not?"

"That is part of the problem!" fumes Scipio. "The message says that Pleminius and his men have gone wild. His men plundered the temple

VIII. Judgment

of Proserpina. His soldiers were seen dragging women, girls, and boys from their homes and raping them." [xcii]

"I cannot believe that Sergius and Matienus would allow that to happen," comments Crassus Pollus, a veteran tribune.

"That is the other half of the ram," says Scipio. "Sergius and Matienus scourged one of Pleminius' men for looting a house." Scipio face reddens. "And this Pleminius, he had the two tribunes whipped in the town square!"

"It is hard to believe our legionnaires would have allowed that to happen," says Marcus.

"That is just it," says Lucius. "They didn't. Our men became outraged. They attacked Pleminius and cut up his face. A fight broke out between both sides, with many wounded."

Scipio pitches down the scroll. "There were Romans fighting Romans. That is all I know so far, but it is more than enough."

"By Jupiter, it sounds like Sucro," says Laelius. "Our own soldiers warring with each other as soon as you turn your back."

"This cannot be countenanced," says Scipio. "What should we do?"

"Send our quaestor to investigate," says one tribune. "He will identify the guilty parties."

Scipio stares at him incredulously. "Cato? You want me to send Cato to investigate my men? Cato has been complaining to the Senate about my leadership and misuse of funds. He would use this as more fuel for his fire."

"The legate Pleminius is your hand-picked man, correct?" says Marcus "The one you appointed to Locri?" He looks steadily at Scipio, his face flat.

Scipio looks at the other officers, then at Lucius, and sees the same unspoken agreement. He sighs. "Yes, this is my pack to carry. I must

VIII. Judgment

investigate this matter myself."

Marcus smirks. "I agree. I thought it stupid for you to go there in the first place. But since you did, you should investigate what your actions have wrought."

Laelius smirks. "Given Cato's sharp eyes and ears, you'd best settle the matter quickly. Or the Senate will hear about it."

"Ha!" cackles Crassus Pollus. "They'll hear about it anyway! The Senate would know if our General here has a runny nose, given the Latin spies that are all about."

This prompts a round of nervous laughter, and Marcus notices that several of the officers seem to be laughing self-consciously. *I must watch what I say among our officers.*

"We can talk more about it tomorrow," proposes a young officer. "I know several men who served under Pleminius. Perhaps they can give us more insight."

Scipio shakes his head. "*Acta non verba*. Deeds, not words, as Marcus has often reminded me," says Scipio. "I leave on the morrow, and will return three days hence." Scipio glances at the door, and the tribunes rise to return to their duties.

The officers file out, muttering and arguing among themselves. Marcus ostensibly watches them go, but his eyes glance back to Scipio's guards, where Aulus and Cassius stand along the wall. He sees that the other guards stand silently, their eyes fixed at attention. But Aulus and Cassius' eyes follow Scipio's every movement. Their heads tilt toward each other as they mutter to one other. *Those two are about something with Scipio. Mars help them if they mean him harm.*

Marcus walks outside the building and summons a horse for his return trip. Laelius soon appears, having a final word with Scipio. Marcus waves over Laelius. "I leave now. But I ask you this: incline your eye to Aulus and Cassius. I trust them not."

"Go with peace of mind, Marcus." Laelius says. "He is my beloved. It

VIII. Judgment

will be my life before his, if it comes to it."

Marcus grunts. "I know. That is your one redeeming feature." An equite rides up, towing Marcus' fresh horse. The stocky little man effortlessly vaults into the saddle and sets off at a brisk pace.

"Old bastard," says Laelius fondly as he watches Marcus ride away.

* * * * *

LOCRI, 205 BCE. "Open the gates!" shouts Pleminius' sentry captain. "Romans are coming!"

Scipio and his retinue gallop up to Locri's open citadel doors and dismount, handing their horses' reins to the stable slaves. The general marches quickly toward Pleminius' quarters, his face grim. Scipio is determined to mete out the proper punishment and depart, that he may promptly return to Sicily. The new year approaches, and he must finalize his spring campaign plans. *Marcus was right, I should have never come here in the first place.*

Scipio barges through the doors of the headquarters. He finds Pleminius bent over a table, busily signing orders for the daily administration of Locri. His quaestor stands behind him.

Pleminius looks up and Scipio freezes in midstep, transfixed with dismay. He is looking into the face of a man with a ragged stub of a nose and short clumps of ears, scabby proturbances where his aquiline nose and large ears once were. Pleminius blinks rapidly at Scipio, his black eyes shining with rage and shame. He points at the place where his nose was, and his ears.

"This is what your men did to me! They took a sword to my face!" He stands up and faces Scipio, his hands pushing against the table as if he were trying to shove it through the floor. "This is the doing of Sergius' and Matienus' men. They attacked me and my lictors while I was having the two beaten,[xciii] and left us almost dead!"

"Where are they?" is all Scipio can think to say. "Where are my tribunes?"

VIII. Judgment

Pleminius spits derisively. "They are in the cells below the armory. I would have crucified them both, if it wouldn't precipitate a mutiny."

"You are to do nothing to my men without my permission," Scipio commands. "Is that understood?" His eyes lock with Pleminius' resentful stare, and there is a silence.

After several heartbeats, Pleminius looks away. "As you say."

Scipio turns to the attending tribune. "Fetch Sergius and Matienus, we will have this hearing now!"

Within minutes, the two bedraggled officers are pulled into the general's presence. Scipio sits at the head table. A surly Pleminius sits on a nearby bench.

"I want your story of this affair," Scipio orders. "Swear by Veritas, goddess of truth, that what you say will be accurate."

The tribunes glower at Pleminius. "It will be our pleasure," replies Matienus.

Sergius begins. "You have but to know that Pleminius has treated our loyal Locrians like dogs, beating them and pillaging their belongings."

"Aye," adds Matienus, "Several of the town magistrates have already left for Rome to plead for Pleminius' dismissal."

By Jupiter's cock, now the Latins will hear all about this! Scipio fumes. "I am truly sorry to hear that," He says.

Pleminius jumps up. "These men exceeded their authority by punishing my own man. They fomented their assault by their blatant disregard of authority!" He runs his hand across his disfigured face. "Look at what their men did to me. They are responsible for this!"

"I would do myself if I had the chance," says Matienus. "No decent Roman would treat the Locrians as you have done. No commander would allow his men to perpetrate such infamy!"

Scipio listens impassively to each side of the case, but his mind is a

VIII. Judgment

whirl of argument and doubt. He knows his tribunes to be honorable men, devoted to preventing the abuse of military power upon the powerless. But if he does not punish his two tribunes he tacitly endorses rebellion against military authority, however misplaced that authority may be.

On the other hand, if he punishes Pleminius, he shows he does not support the actions of the men he places in command. And Pleminius is a Latin Party favorite; any sanctions against him may be reflected in a lack of support from the Senate, just when his entire campaign is in danger of being undermined from lack of support. As with Carthago Nova, he is faced with a decision where someone will unavoidably suffer.

His mind races. His right arm begins to twitch. *Punishing Pleminius could usurp my campaign. For the greater good, I must spare him. But I have to protect my tribunes from his abuse.*

"Pleminius, you are absolved of any blame for your actions," Scipio pronounces, eliciting howls of unbelieving protest from his tribunes. Scipio turns to face them, his face set. "As for you, Sergius and Matienus, you will be led in irons to Rome. There you will await further judgment by a tribunal." He looks sternly at Pleminius. "These men are to be taken to Rome unharmed, do you understand?"

There is an angry silence from Pleminius, who has been dreaming of their death. "I understand," he finally replies.

"It is done, then," pronounces Scipio. "Pleminius, you will make it so."

The next morning Scipio rides out from the Locri gates, intent on returning to Syracuse. Pleminius stands inside the open portal, watching his commander ride out toward Rhegium.

As the dust settles on the road, Pleminius calls over one of his scouts. "Follow them. Let me know when General Scipio is on his ship for Messana." The scout hurries off to find his horse.

Pleminius watches the fading outlines of Scipio's company, and

VIII. Judgment

scratches the scabby stub of his nose. "Take them to Rome? Hmph!"

The next morning, the scout returns to Pleminius. He finds the praetor in the spacious feasting room, perched on his improvised throne, adjudicating the Locrians' petitions and complaints.

"Scipio has boarded his ship for Messana," the scout affirms. Pleminius rises from his chair, eyes bright with malevolence.

"The audiences are over for today!" he tells his attendant. Pleminius waits impatiently as the remaining Locrians file from his presence. When they are gone he summons his jailers. "Fetch Sergius and Matienus. Bring them to the courtyard in one hour. In chains."

The two tribunes are soon dragged into the courtyard. Pleminius stands in the middle of the courtyard, wearing only a belted gray tunic, flanked by the two crosses that his guards have laid beside two empty postholes. A large brazier burns brightly with fresh coals. The mutilated praetor stands next to it, humming softly as he stirs the coals with a branding iron in the shape of a Roman double-eagle.

"Ah, there you are!" he says brightly to his captives. He points to the crosses. "Put them up."

Sergius and Matienus are pulled over to the crosses. Pleminius fingers the hilt of the gleaming pugio attached to his broad leather belt, a leaf-shaped army dagger he has often used in battle. His hand wanders down to lovingly stroke the top of its keen blade. *Soon, old friend, I will have some work for you.*

"Strip them," Pleminius orders. The two frightened men are disrobed, their ragged tunics cut from their unwashed bodies.

"What are you doing, fiend?" shouts Matienus, his voice quivering with outrage. "You have no jurisdiction over us, we are Scipio's men!"

Pleminius snorts, an unwise action that streams mucus above his lip, angering him all the more. "Your Greek-loving General is gone, asshole." He holds the dagger in front of Matienus' eyes. "Your fate is mine now, and woe to you for it."

VIII. Judgment

"Give them a traitor's punishment," Pleminius commands. He smiles with sickly humor. "But no nails, we are not beasts, after all."

The two guards grab the tribunes and push them down onto the crosses. They splay out the tribunes' arms and pull their feet together. The guards tug heavy ropes across Sergius' and Matienus' arms and feet, biting into their flesh.

"By the honor of Rome, and the gods above, cease what you are doing!" wails Matienus. "We retaliated in the heat of anger, just as you did. We have all suffered enough!"

Just before the crosses are lifted into place, Pleminius steps over to Matienus, and gently strokes his stubbled face. "Dear tribune, I would disagree. Some of us have not suffered enough." He fingers the stumps on his face. "You made me a monster for life. I have suffered—will suffer—more than enough. But you two..."

Pleminius whirls about and grabs the branding iron. With one sword-like thrust, he presses it down into the middle of Sergius' chest. The tribune's tortured cry echoes off the walls of the courtyard.

"You are the dog of a savage," snarls Matienus, gaping at Sergius' agonized face. "The gods will repay you for this."

Pleminius holds up the branding iron, smoking swirling up from the burned flesh on it. "This is the gods repaying you for what you have done. I am but their vehicle." He plunges the red iron into the Matienus' chest, eliciting fresh screams of anguish. In his pain and terror, the staunch legionnaire voids his bowels.

Pleminius covers his nose pit, but his eyes twinkle malevolently. "Ooh, what a foul odor! Flesh and shit, shit and flesh, what a terrible stink they make!" He pitches the smoldering iron to the ground. A soldier bends over and retches. Then another.

Pleminius stalks off from the two writhing men. "Put them up," he mutters. The guards reach behind the crosses and push them into their holes. They land with thump, provoking agonized groans from the tribunes.

VIII. Judgment

Pleminius looks at the vomit beneath his soldiers' feet. "Apologies men, I did not mean to make it so unpleasant for you. Let us try something less irritating to us." He looks at his two victims. "But not for them."

Pleminius unsheathes his pugio and looks at the stunned soldiers. "Let us have a contest, men. How many stabs can a man endure before he dies? Place your guesses, the winner receives a hundred denarii!" He grins at his sobbing victims before he turns back to his men. "But I should warn you, I am very skilled at this. Guessing starts at a minimum of twenty-five stabs on each!" As his men watch dumbfounded, Pleminius tromps exultantly toward his two victims.

Then Pleminius pauses, eyes rolling as if a new thought has occurred to him. "And, oh yes, we shall have a beauty contest after it." He mugs his ravaged face at the horrified legionnaires. "We shall see which of them looks most like me, when I am done with them..."

* * * * *

KROTON, 204 BCE. "You cannot fight them, Hannibal, it would be suicide," says Maharbal, turning his horse toward Hannibal's good eye.

"Baal's balls, we have to take them now, while they are vulnerable!" Hannibal fumes. "That doughy old Crassus, he could not lead a horse to water, much less two legions in battle. If we take them down we can control all of Bruttium before winter sets in."

Maharbal shakes his head, and points down the hillside, towards General Crassus' garrison. The two can see that scores of legionnaires are busy outside the town walls. Most are building massive funeral pyres. Others are pulling oxcarts of bodies to the pyre sites. When the oxcarts stop by a pyre, the legionnaires throw bodies onto the top of the woodpile and cover them with wood.

"See all those pyres?" says Maharbal. "You know what they mean."

Hannibal blows out his cheeks and grimaces with disappointment. "Plague. There is plague in the area." [xciv]

VIII. Judgment

Maharbal nods. "Yes, and we will catch it if we come in contact with them." He places his hand on Hannibal's shoulder. "Crassus' diseased soldiers could do the one thing no Roman army has been able to do: wipe you out."

"Curse the luck!" Hannibal grouses. "That is why we saw all those cohorts leaving Kroton. They were leaving before they became sick."

"All is not bad news," says Maharbal encouragingly. "The garrison is indisposed. We could march past them and go north to join Mago."

Hannibal barks a laugh. "And leave a Roman army here among our allies? It would be like leaving a wolf among the chickens. Especially if Crassus obtains reinforcements."

"Very well," replies Maharbal. "Then what can we do?"

Hannibal turns around and looks behind him. Twelve thousand warriors are arrayed on the high plain behind the hill, awaiting his orders. His shoulders droop with disappointment.

"It is time to go to winter quarters. We can prepare for the spring campaign. At the first blush of spring we will advance to meet Mago, and end this thing."

* * * * *

CURIA HOSTILIA, ROME, 204 BCE. "You have heard the Locrian delegation," fumes red-faced Fabius, his gaunt frame shaking with anger. "General Scipio has perpetrated an atrocity upon the good people of Locri!"

"Their main complaint was with Pleminius," counters portly Senator Ovidius, a Hellenic leader. "The Praetor committed the improprieties, not Scipio."

"Improprieties?" Fabius cries. "You heard what their chief delegate said, that Pleminius is human only in shape and appearance![xcv] He is a monster who has committed monstrous acts! But that does not absolve Scipio, no. Scipio did not control him, he was derelict in his duty."

VIII. Judgment

Flaccus holds up a scroll bearing the seal of Rome. He walks to the Senate floor. "Thank you, noble general," Flaccus says, gesturing for Fabius to sit down. Flaccus points the scroll at Senator Ovidius.

"You think Scipio is without fault, Ovidius? I have here quaestor Cato's report about Scipio's escapades in Sicily, the one we reviewed it last week. Do you remember what Cato wrote?" He unrolls the scroll. "Cato reports that Scipio parades around in Greek finery, wasting money on lavish parties? [xcvi] He says the men waste their time practicing on Scipio's bizarre weapons and tactics."

Flaccus spreads his gaunt arms wide. "Why, Scipio even hosted a welcome celebration for the cowardly Cannenses! He wants to take them to Africa with him!"

"I am outraged," says Fabius, his lips trembling. "This 'general' is naturally disposed to ruin the discipline of his men.[xcvii] I daresay his men have grown fat and lazy. They will be no match for Carthage's Libyans and Numidians, no they won't!"

Fabius faces the two Tribunes of the Plebs who have attended the meeting. "You Tribunes have the power to revoke this scoundrel's imperium. I propose we do that right now!" [xcviii]

The Senators burst into a cacophony of arguments, the Hellenics and Latins shouting across the aisle at each other. The Senate leader vainly stamps his staff to gain order.

Flaccus loudly declaims Scipio. His face a mask of anger, but he is secretly pleased at the turn of events. He can see the tide of battle turning for his Latins. *We'll run him out of the army*, he gloats.

A sturdy middle-aged man limps to the Senate floor, leaning on a stout oak crutch that replaces his missing leg. He gently pushes Flaccus to the side. "I would have the floor," he says to Flaccus. With a grimace, Flaccus stalks back to his seat. The man raises his hands over his head and spreads his arms, requesting silence.

Glabius, the Senate Leader, steps next to the man and booms his staff onto the stone floor. "Let Quintus Metelius speak," the old senator

VIII. Judgment

shouts, his voice quavering with the effort.

The Senators resume their seats and wait. Senator Metelius is a respected former legate and praetor. He is known as an intellectually courageous man, prone to go where the truth takes him, whatever the consequences.

"I agree with honored Fabius that the Locrians have suffered terrible indignities at Pleminius' hands. And that this loathsome man should be brought to Rome in shackles." Senators on both sides shout their agreement. Metelius pauses and waits for them to quiet.

"But I cannot agree with Fabius Maximus about his proposed treatment of Scipio. This is the man that stepped forward to go to Iberia and face the Three Generals, when no one else would go. Then, when he defeated them, we made him consul with the express mission of ending the war forever." [xcix]

Metelius walks to the front row of the senators, looking slowly across the rows of his many friends and colleagues. "My honored peers," he says softly, although his voice is edged with rare sarcasm. "Would you treat this brilliant General, a young man who has never lost a battle, like a coward or incompetent? Would you judge him without any evidence from our own eyes?" He sweeps his arm toward the door. "You heard the Locrians yesterday. They said Scipio was not even there when these atrocities were perpetrated."

"This atrocity requires that all responsible for it be punished," Fabius retorts. "This is an abuse of our allies, and insult to Roman law and justice! Scipio had his chance to prevent it!"

"Nor will it go unpunished!" Metelius shouts above the groundswell of angry voices. "But we will investigate the matter ourselves! Let us send a delegation down to Locri and Sicily, one that will act as judge and jury. If Pleminius is chiefly at fault, let us arrest him and drag him back to Rome."

Metelius looks to his left, staring at the Hellenic Party senators. "And if Consul Scipio is truly derelict in his command, or he ordered the foul

VIII. Judgment

treatment of the Locrians, we will drag *him* back to Rome as well!"

Before the Senate can erupt into chaos again, Glabius steps in front of Metelius. "Quiet! Every man shall speak to this issue, as is our custom. Then we will vote on the proposal." Glabius looks at the most senior senator after himself. "Tratius, you shall be first..."

The next several hours are spent in declamations and supports of Metelius' proposal. Scores of senators disagree with the idea, wanting to revoke Scipio's command immediately. Most support the proposal, however, with a few emendations.

A number of senators offer proposals about the number and type of investigators that will join the delegation. They insist that the Tribunes of the Plebs be part of the group, so that the citizens of Rome will have a voice in the matter—and so they will not rebel if Scipio is arrested.

The Senate finally agrees upon the specifics. Ten senators will accompany the two Tribunes of the Plebs, the praetor of Sicily, and an aedile. The Latin Party senators insist an aedile join the group, because his sacred office allows him to arrest any Roman on the spot who is judged guilty of malfeasance—including Scipio himself.

The weary politicians pour out of the Senate chambers, eager for a late afternoon cup of wine or a visit to the baths. Metelius stays until almost everyone has left the chambers. He converses with several of the other senior senators, men who either praise Scipio's brilliance or condemn his wastrel habits.

One new senator lags behind, waiting for his chance to confer with his honored associate. Metelius waves goodbye to the dozing Glabius and walks from the hall. The young senator rushes to catch up to him.

"May I accompany you, Senator Metelius?"

Metelius grins at the young man. "Of course, Agricola ... excuse me, *Senator* Agricola!" They walk down the Curia stairs together, watching the Forum vendors lighting the night torches on their stalls.

"Do you think our General Scipio is at fault?" Agricola asks.

VIII. Judgment

"Just a minute, Metelius replies. He stops to purchase a hefty slice of roasted wild boar. "Put some garum sauce on it and wrap it up," he tells the vendor, before he turns back to Agricola.

"Well, I don't think him being at fault is the question. Here we have a man with one foot already in Africa, the only one brave enough to march on Carthage itself. A man who is Rome's best hope to end this war soon—and save tens of thousands of lives by doing it. And we would yank him back for some stupidities committed in some flyspeck allied town?"

Metelius sighs. "This is not a time for to consider what is just... that is a luxury we cannot afford. It is time to consider what is wise."

Agricola scratches the back of his head. "We knew him to be an honorable man, but time and events change people. Is he the same young genius who left for Iberia, believing he could conquer the world?"

"I would hope not," replies Metelius. "Genius will only get you so far when ethics get in the way. We can only hope he has become more pragmatic." He looks away from the young senator's trusting face. "That he has become a bit more ruthless."

As the two senators converse, a rider hurtles out from the main gates of Rome, heading for Ostia. A swift bireme awaits him there, one that will take him to Sicily with fateful news for Scipio.

* * * * *

SYRACUSE, 204 BCE. "I want you to throw Pleminius into chains," Scipio orders, pushing his legate toward the door. Scipio shoves a scroll into his hand, the wax still cooling from his owl's head seal on it. "Take thirty equites with you to Rhegium, ones from the noblest families in Rome.[c] They will bear witness to what I have ordered."

"Hurry, Quintus," enjoins Laelius. "Pleminius must be in prison by the time that delegation gets here." The legate raises his right arm in salute and strides out the main doors of the headquarters.

VIII. Judgment

"You have made the right decision, Scippy," says Laelius. "The delegation may not come here at all, once they see that Pleminius has been punished. They can take him back to Rome for trial. That should placate the Locrians." He makes a disgusted face. "And maybe the Latins, too!"

"It will not placate the Senate," Marcus says. "There are those who want you to lose your head, or your command." He frowns. "No, the delegation will come here, regardless."

Scipio stalks about the room, his fists clenched. "They would come here to investigate me, just as I am completing our preparations for Africa! The Carthaginians themselves could not have prepared a better delaying tactic!"

"We cannot stop them from coming, but you can resolve their concerns," Marcus replies. "Your speculatores in the Senate have told you about their accusations: lax discipline, excessive spending, poorly conditioned troops." He eyes Scipio's lavish Greek toga. "Excessive finery."

Scipio fingers his toga and grimaces. "I conquer Iberia for them, and they are concerned about what I wear?" He looks at his two commanders' faces. "Yes, yes, I am ranting when I should be planning."

"You know how you handle an investigative committee?" says Laelius. "You give them a show! A show of force."

Marcus nods. "It sounds superficial, but Laelius has the right of it."

Scipio's eyes light up. "Very well, we will give them a show! Muster all our men. Drill them mercilessly; every man must be in peak condition. Every maneuver must be impeccably executed. Everyone's armor must be gleaming and spotless, do you hear me?"

Laelius and Marcus blink in surprise, taken aback by Scipio's stern anger.

"You will prepare our army for war," says Scipio. "We war against

VIII. Judgment

the delegation, though we will receive them most graciously. Right now they are a bigger threat than Hannibal."

Laelius steps forward and grasps the sleeve of Scipio's toga. "As you say. But General, may I make a suggestion? Much as it pains me to sound like that dimwit Cato, I think you should dress a bit more 'Roman' when they arrive."

Laelius looks down at his own purple and gold toga. "I will certainly do the same." He rolls his eyes heavenward. "I will wear something ... plain."

"The gods take me, I cannot believe what I hear," blurts Marcus.

Laelius grins self-consciously. "I know, I know. But in times of war, we must all make sacrifices."

* * * * *

LIGURIA, NORTHWEST ITALIA, 204 BCE. He has been watching the Romans all day, waiting for them to drop their guard before he strikes.

Two maniples move carefully through this high winter valley, their scouts riding ahead of them to probe for enemy. Korbis and his Balearics are safely hidden among the craggy outcroppings in the forest hillsides, although they are close enough to see the breath clouds streaming from the Roman horses' noses.

Korbis drapes his fur cloak over his elephantine shoulders, ready to shed it when the battle begins. He spits onto the frozen ground. *This place is too fuckin' cold, I need to get back to the Islands.* He grasps the pommel of his weighty falcata. *I'll have Mago's balls on a plate for sending me here!*

From his winter headquarters near Genova, Mago has sent the Balearic infantry and Ligurian cavalry on a joint mission. He hopes to forge fighting bonds between the divergent mercenary groups, as his brother Hannibal has done with his mercenaries. But this is more than a communal exercise. Mago has heard that a Roman army has moved

VIII. Judgment

northwest from Central Italia and draws closer to his region, ostensibly to block his path to Rome.

With Spurius Lucretius' legions already camped northeast of him, Mago must find out if these rumors are true. His directive to Korbis and the Ligurian chieftain was quite simple: do not return until you find the Romans. Come back with Roman heads, or do not come back at all.

Korbis will gladly fight anything that moves, but in this frosty northern clime this bear of a man only feels like hibernating. When Mago ordered the Balearics on an extended march north with the Ligurians Korbis forcibly demurred, proposing that he and his Balearics stay inside with the rest of the army, to prepare for next month's campaign—inside where the fires burn night and day.

Korbis can still remember Mago's angry reply, as he pointed toward the Alps. "My brother Hannibal took an entire army across those mountain passes in the dead of winter. You can at least venture out into the valley bottoms with a few hundred men!" And that was the end of the discussion.

At least I will fight today. Take somebody's head, even if it's not Mago's. The Balearic chieftain fingers the bronze battle horn at his belt, feeling his heart pound with the anticipatory thrill of battle. He knows his slingers are ready, they have sidled up into the last line of trees by the plain, waiting for the signal to loose their missiles. The slingers have pulled dark green winter blankets over their heads and bodies, making them virtually invisible within the chill shadows of the forest.

A Ligurian appears next to Korbis, leading his horse through the trees. The stocky brunette warrior wears only a blue shirt and leather breastplate with his threadbare brown plaid pants. *These Ligurians are crazy*, Korbis thinks. *They must have bear blood in them.*

"We are ready," the Ligurian signals, raising his hand-axe over his head. Korbis gestures his acknowledgement, and the Ligurian melts back into the trees, returning to his two dozen compatriots.

VIII. Judgment

The Ligurian cavalry have eased themselves to the front and rear of the Romans, determined to prevent any riders from galloping back to their camp. Korbis grins as he watches the cavalry seal off the escape passages. *Good. No prisoners to drag back. Kill all.*

Minutes later, Korbis finally sees what he has been waiting for. The last Roman scout has returned, and now all six equites are gathered about the lead tribune. Korbis snatches the horn off his belt and blasts two brassy notes, an attack order that is echoed by the slingers' and cavalry's horns.

The slingers trot out from the tree line on both sides of the Romans. As they run they adeptly fling stone after stone at the legionnaires. The first round catches the Romans while they are moving into formation, cracking the bones and skulls of several soldiers and bruising a dozen more. By the release of the second round, the well-disciplined maniples have joined together to form a turtle shell of shields, and the deadly missiles thud off harmlessly. Eight brave soldiers scuttle out from the sheltering shield wall. They dash out into the field and grab the legs of the scattered wounded. As the stones whistle past their heads, they pull their comrades back inside the shell.

The slingers wreak no more casualties, but they continue their onslaught and the Romans are forced to stay within their shell. Korbis and his Balearics rush down from the left side of the hill, following the covering fire of the slingers. "Kill them all," Korbis roars, circling his battle axe over his head.

Dozens of bold Romans stand up from their shield shell and hurtle their pila at Korbis and his horde. The slingers direct their missiles at the spearmen, and a half dozen are stoned to the ground before the rest duck under the shields. A few minutes later the Balearic infantry crash into the Roman shield-wall, hammering at it with swords and axes.

The Romans plant their feet and raise their shields high against their attackers, stabbing out with their short swords. They cut into dozens of unwary Balearics, killing any who fall wounded at their feet. The islanders' initial attack stalls. The outnumbered Romans push forward, one coordinated step at a time, driving their opponents backward.

VIII. Judgment

The Romans take heart and quicken their attack pace, flinging the last of their javelins into the backs of any who turn to flee. "Onward!" shouts the lead tribune. "We have them beaten!"

With a roar of defiance, Korbis whirls about and rushes at his attackers. "Come on, women. You follow me!"

The giant Balearic batters into the shield wall. He wields his heavy falcata like an avenging hammer of the gods, hacking out chunks of any Roman shield that faces him. A Roman in the front line falls to Korbis' heavy sword, his helmet chiseled into his skull. Another screams out his life as Korbis' blade pierces his armor and chest. A third collapses screaming to the earth, his knee hacked open.

The chieftain pushes his way inside the shield wall, flailing back and forth at any within reach. Two spears stab into his torso, penetrating the gaps in his Gallic ring mail, but the pain only serves to madden him. A dozen of Korbis' bravest men barge into the gap he made, following their leader. The Balearics fight back to back within the center of the Roman maniple as the rest of the islanders press in from outside.

A dozen more Balearics fall to the Roman gladii, and Korbis' circle of defenders shrinks about him. *Where are those fuckin' Ligurians?* Korbis fumes. He pulls out his battle horn and blows three mighty blasts, then three more. *Get out here, you stupid crazy bastards* he curses, as he batters a centurion's shield and knocks him off his feet.

Korbis hears a distant horn sound twice, and he smiles. The Ligurian cavalry thunder in from the north and south of the Romans, their bloody swords testifying that their attack on the scouts has been successful. Screaming their tribal battle calls, the Ligurians hurtle into the Romans, chopping at them with their thick-headed battle axes, stabbing at their necks with their long bladed swords.

The Romans fight back furiously, but now they fight for a noble death, not a victory, as the legionnaires become almost invisible beneath the welter of infantry and cavalry that mill about them.

A gore-spattered centurion stands on top of a hillock of his own men's

VIII. Judgment

corpses. He shouts "Gloria Romam" (glory to Rome) as he shoves his sword into the spine of a Ligurian who crawls beneath him. The centurion plants his feet and yanks his blade out, so tired he stumbles backward.

Korbis stalks over to the solitary centurion and stops, staring at the man's blood covered face. With a respectful nod at the Roman's valiance, the giant jumps upon him.

Korbis batters the weary defender down to his knees and hammers the butt of his sword onto the Roman's helmet, stunning him. He jerks the centurion's helmet off and grabs his curly raven hair. With one effortless swipe, he severs the man's head from his body. Korbis steps back from the spurting corpse and looks admiringly at the dripping head. *Good trophy. He was brave man.*

Within an hour the Balearics are finishing the battle, administering death cuts to the few remaining Romans who lie moaning on the field. Korbis picks his way through the scattered field of bodies, searching for another life to take.

Tulio, Korbis' captain, pulls a dead Roman's head up by its hair, and attempts to cut the head off in one fell stroke of his cleaver blade. After four attempts a disgusted Korbis pushes him aside and sends the Roman's skull flying.

"Put the heads in a sack," Korbis orders, "We bring a present for fuckin' Mago." After wiping and sheathing his blade, Korbis steps back up the hill and surveys the carnage he has wrought. *Good day's work. Get drunk tonight.*

He blinks in surprise at some the bodies he sees, at features he did not notice in the heat of battle. There are black men here, and Gauls. And red-haired Thracians, their bodies snaked with multicolored tattoos. He motions Tulio over to him and points at the corpses. "These are not Romans," he says to Tulio.

"They are slaves," Tulio notes, pulling the bandana off a dead Gaul's forehead. "Look, this one has Roman letters tattooed on his forehead.

VIII. Judgment

They are part of that slave army we heard about."

"We report this to Mago," Korbis says. "Go strip the bodies, we divide the plunder tonight." He rubs his bloody hands together and blows on them. "Now we get out of here and back to a big fire, before my balls freeze off!"

At camp that night, Korbis and the Ligurian chieftain confer about their slave soldier discovery. The next morning two Ligurian scouts ride back the way the Romans came. They have orders not to return until they find the legion's main camp.

A week later the scouts return to Mago's winter camp, a day after Korbis and the Ligurians' arrival. The scouts bear the news that Mago has feared: the Romans have fielded a slave army of two legions, and they have built a permanent camp at Ariminum, near Mago's pathway to Rome.

Mago receives the news with equanimity. "My spies were correct, then. Rome has mounted two armies to block my way to Hannibal." He turns to his chief officer, a Carthaginian of many campaigns. "How many men do we have now, Sakarbal?"

"About twenty thousand infantry, and three thousand cavalry," he replies.

Mago makes a face. "More. We need more men to destroy them." He slumps back in his chair and looks at Sakarbal, a sad smile on his face. "Well, old friend. It looks like this year will be spent recruiting, not fighting. We must raise an army that can defeat their combined forces."

Mago drinks deeply from his wine cup. He belches loudly. "Slave legions. Hah!"

* * * * *

SYRACUSE, 204 BCE. "Get us on the dock, we have no time to waste!" shouts the praetor.

Marcus Pomponius, Praetor of Sicily, has landed with his

VIII. Judgment

investigative retinue from Rome. The gangplank has no sooner touched the dock than he is heading down it for Scipio's headquarters. The senators, tribunes of the plebs, and aedile follow behind him, staring at the hundreds of warships and transports that carpet the deep blue Ionian Sea.

The delegation is in a grim mood. They have just come from Rhegium, where they slapped Pleminius and his co-conspirators into irons and sent them back to Rome. The delegation has heard Pleminius' case, in which he blamed Scipio for letting his tribunes exercise excessive power in Locri. The senators and tribunes were unconvinced of Pleminius' innocence, and immediately sent him away for trial.

After hearing Pleminius' condemnation of Scipio, however, most of them wonder if Cato's accusations about frivolity and lax discipline are true. They wonder if it is time to revoke Scipio's imperium, as Fabius has demanded, and pull him back to Rome. Marcus Pomponius is determined to stay in Sicily until his party can make a decision about Scipio.

The delegation moves down the dock walkway and comes to the main harbor street at the end of the docks. Scipio, Laelius, and Marcus Silenus are waiting there for them, each clad in snow-white togas of simple design. The trio stands next to a large carriage, a troop carrier with four oak benches inside.

Scipio waves as Pomponius walks toward him. He stands patiently, waiting for the praetor to acknowledge him.

"Salus, General Scipio. It is good to see you are well," says Pomponius. The praetor shifts about uncomfortably for a moment, then stares into Scipio's eyes. "Consul, you have received a message about the purpose of our delegation, I take it?"

"Salve, Salve to all of you," Scipio exclaims, as if he did not hear. "I am honored that you have come here, whatever your purpose."

Scipio embraces each delegate if they were visiting family, smiling broadly at each. "I am always delighted to show my army to my fellow

VIII. Judgment

Romans, and to answer any questions you may have about it. But I must say, you have arrived at a very busy time. We are preparing to depart for Africa soon. Spring is dawning down here, you know."

He sweeps his arm toward the carriage. "Please, let me lead you into town. This wagon is not very fancy, but it has served us well. And that is all that matters, eh?" The delegates clamber onto the plank seats and endure a short rumbling journey to Scipio's headquarters in the heart of town.

That night, Scipio holds a feast for his guests. The delegation dines on several types of meats and cheeses, accompanied by plenty of good Sicilian wine and a bounty of local fruits and vegetables. The feast is tastefully done, with only the freshest foods, but it is simple by Roman feasting standards. Pomponia has informed her son of Cato's accusations of spending excess, and he is determined he will do nothing to corroborate such allegations.

The next morning Scipio leads the delegation to the parade grounds outside the Syracuse walls. The delegates take their seats on top of a large open platform ten feet above the ground, facing the wide expanse of chalk-marked training fields. Two of Scipio's legions stand before them in a mile-wide line. Each legion is arranged in ten cohorts of infantry, their polished armor blazing in the early spring sun.

Scipio stands in front of his guests and waves toward his legions. "I thought you would want to see how well my volunteers from Rome have adapted to military life," he says. "They have joined with the Cannenses to form two new legions."

One of the elder senators peers at the troop rows of each legionary rectangle. "Those legions look rather large, I would say."

Scipio nods enthusiastically. "Yes they are! I have increased the legion size from 4800 to 6200 soldiers.[ci] They are formed of ten large cohorts, rather than maniples."

Questus, one of the Tribunes of the Plebs, scratches his head. "Why would you change our legions? They were good enough for Fabius, and

VIII. Judgment

Marcellus ... and for your father."

At mention of his father, Scipio flushes. "These larger legions can better withstand the shock of attack by superior numbers. They will not collapse under pressure, as happened at Cannae."

Opiter, one of the Tribunes of the Plebs, looks quizzically at Scipio. "Wouldn't that size limit their mobility?"

Scipio grins. "I shall let you be the judge of that." He waves his hand at his nearby trumpeter. The man blows three short notes on his cornu.

The two legions immediately break apart into ten cohorts moving independently of each other. Some move forward as if attacking, others dash behind them in a flanking maneuver, heading to the sides of the infantry front lines. The cohorts march quickly and in unison. The army's formation changes entirely, as the cohorts encircle an imaginary foe in the center. The trumpeter blasts three notes again and the legions halt in place, the maneuver completed in a matter of minutes.

Scipio turns to his amazed hosts. "Of course, I would send out the velites first in a regular battle, but I wanted you to see the mobility of our heavy infantry. We can quickly adapt to any terrain we fight upon, without losing formation. If needed, the cohorts can divide into smaller maniples, or even centuries, in the midst of battle. That should solve some of the problems we encountered against Hannibal at Trebia, Trasimene, and Cannae."

Pomponius nods his head appreciatively. "They seem very mobile, General. Very mobile. You have trained them well."

Scipio bows his head slightly. "They not only move well, they have learned some new fighting tactics. Please come with me."

The delegation walks over to a field where two centuries of muscular young legionnaires face each other. The men wear protective quilted vests over their grey wool tunics, and weathered bronze greaves on their shins. They each wield a battered wooden sword and shield. The youths stamp about, eager for action. Marcus Silenus and Praxis stand at attention in front of the men, waiting for the delegation to settle in

VIII. Judgment

about them.

"Now, delegates, we will see a demonstration of some new legionary fighting tactics," explains Scipio. "They are intended to make our men more deadly in single combat."

"Romans fight together, in formation," growls an older Latin senator. "Our tactics have sufficed for centuries."

Scipio waggles his finger. "Ah, but they have not sufficed, Senator, particularly against the wily Carthaginians. Particularly when formation breaks down." Scipio nods at Marcus, and the stolid little commander stalks to the middle of his waiting trainees.

"Commence," he orders.

The men begin a fluid sequence of cut, thrust, parry, and block, looking more like dancers than warriors. One row of men thrust forward with their swords while their opponents block their thrusts and shove their shields at them. Their opponents react by whirling sideways and administering a side slash. The delegates notice that the men kick, duck, and dodge—that they fight like gladiators, using their feet and legs as much as their arms. The men's style is flexible, spontaneous, and adaptable, characteristics the delegation just saw in the legions' maneuvers.

Scipio raises his right arm, and Marcus halts the foray. The young men stand panting, their eyes agleam with excitement and effort, grinning proudly at the delegation.

"Mmm, most pretty," mutters the Latin senator. "But will it work in the open field?"

Praxis looks at Scipio, who nods him permission to speak. "Honored Senator, I used to be a gladiator. Those are the combat moves that I used for a score of bouts, with over a dozen kills to my credit. If they did not work, I would not be here."

The senator huffs several times, but he says nothing. Scipio reaches up and vigorously scratches his nose, his hand hiding his grin.

VIII. Judgment

After demonstrations of pilum throwing and cavalry maneuvers, Scipio takes the delegation back to his headquarters for a brief afternoon repast. The men sit about and pick at plates of roasted fish and olives, peppering Scipio with questions about his plans for Africa.

Several senators voice their doubts about the Cannenses' capabilities to fight under duress, but Scipio gives them all the same answer. "I would stake my life on their bravery." He laughs as he swishes about his goblet of watered wine. "In fact, I have staked my life, because I'll be dead if I'm wrong!"

After the meal, the delegation rides down to the harbor. They take seats on the edge of the dock that juts farthest into the sea. The officials watch Laelius leading the army's thirty warships on graceful maneuvers against each other in a mock battle.[cii] The quadriremes and triremes execute speedy turns, assaults, rams, and blockades, gliding within feet of each other without mishap. Laelius has planned the maneuvers to illustrate that the navy is fully prepared to defend and supply Scipio's army during its land campaign.

The maneuvers conclude, and the flagship eases into the dock next to the delegates. Admiral Laelius descends and joins the dignitaries, ready to chat with them about the drill they witnessed. He explains how his men can quickly board Carthaginian vessels without the use of the traditional but unwieldy corvus boarding-plank, and how his rope-hooks worked so well on his recent raids on the African coast. "We'd throw a handful of hook lines over to their ship and pull them in like a big fish. Then we'd clean the fish and take it home," he says cheerily.

With dusk approaching, the party returns to their rooms for several hours. They emerge to participate in an evening feast with the officers of Scipio's army and the town dignitaries. "Ask these men anything you like," Scipio tells the delegation. "I have no secrets."

The delegation gathers the next morning for a private meeting. Scipio moves about his daily business as if they were not there, inspecting grain shipments, testing the newly made gladii, conversing with the armorers and cooks. He is busy with army details, but always his mind is on the closed doors of the delegation. *They have my fate in their*

VIII. Judgment

hands. Fortuna be kind, I just want a chance at Africa.

By midday the doors open and the delegation emerges. Pomponius walks into Scipio's headquarters, where he interrupts Scipio's meeting with Cato, his irascible quaestor.

"May I speak to you alone?" queries Pomponius.

"Certainly!" replies Scipio, glad to be rid of Cato. "Our business can wait, can it not?" he says to Cato, implying a command.

Cato frowns at him. "Saving money cannot wait! You still waste coin on feasts and finery!"

As Cato stalks off, Scipio turns to Pomponius, a mournful smile on his face. "You see how he is?"

Pomponius shrugs, noncommittal. "I came to notify you of our decision, General. The rest of the party prepares to return to Rome."

The praetor approaches Scipio, his lips pressed into a thin line, his eyes averted from Scipio's expectant face.

Then he smiles. "It was a brilliant display," says Pomponius, shaking Scipio's forearm, enjoying his little joke. "That crabby old General Tadius, he wants to go with you to Africa!" He laughs. "And the legates, the tribunes, everybody, they praised your work with the fleet and the army." [ciii]

Scipio exhales loudly. "Gratitude for your kind words. My trainers worked night and day with the recruits, to get them ready for this—and for battle. Now they heft a gladius as well as the veterans."

Pomponius nods. "Ah, to that matter of soldiers. We have voted to allow you your pick of the soldiers here in Sicily." He grins. "But from what I have heard, you have already completed your preparation anyway!"

"This is good news. It means that Marcellus' men can legally become part of my army." He grins embarrassedly. "I admit I had already

VIII. Judgment

incorporated them into our drills. You saw all our new maneuvers and fighting tactics—I just could not wait until Rome took a vote to approve them. I hope you understand."

"I do," replies Pomponius, "Politicians should not make decisions about an army, much less lead one into battle, as we Romans often do." He looks back toward the training fields. "How many men do you have now?"

Scipio rattles off the numbers, figures he reviews every day. "At the moment with have four legions of infantry. Two are the veteran Cannenses, blended with my volunteers from Rome—the veterans can mentor the recruits next to them. Two are men from Marcellus' legions that have been stationed here these several years—they are ready to fight anyone to get rid of the boredom. There are Laelius' forty-eight hundred marines. And, let's see, we now have three hundred cavalry for each legion. My army is close to thirty thousand men." [civ]

Pomponius looks skeptically at his Scipio. "That is not a very large force for Africa. Hundreds of thousands await to fight you."

Scipio taps his index finger on the Praetor's chest. "Ah yes, but many of my men are veterans, men with years of fighting the Carthaginians in Iberia, Italia, and Sicily. This is a professional army, Praetor, just like Hannibal's army. But *we* have Romans, and he doesn't!"

Pomponius raises his hands in mock defense, smiling. "Cease, General, you have made your point! You think can take Africa with your little army, and I believe you!" He pauses, as if remembering a triviality. "Oh, and the Locri thing, we absolve you of any blame for that horror."

"I am pleased to hear that I can put that behind me and concentrate on Africa," responds Scipio. "We are as ready as we can be. We only require Syphax's cavalry support to complete our forces."

"I had heard you sailed over to Siga and made a treaty with him," Pomponius says. "He will most be valuable. To that point, I should tell you: the delegation unanimously voted for you to cross to Africa and

VIII. Judgment

begin your campaign at the earliest possible moment.[cv] I daresay the Senate will follow our recommendations." He claps Scipio on the shoulder. "Go in peace, and end this war."

"Thank you, my cousin," [cvi] Scipio says. "I am certainly glad you were picked to lead the delegation."

Pomponius laughs. "Do not thank me, thank your mother Pomponia. She was the one that engineered my being 'nominated' by Metelius over there. And she secured the votes with a few lavish bribes!" He laughs. "I don't know where she gets all the money!"

Scipio looks down, smiling mysteriously. "Our family has always been good at managing the money we acquire, whatever its source."

Pomponius nods, and heads over to the delegation's carriage. He stops walks back to Scipio "What happened at Locri, anyway?" he asks softly, his eyes searching Scipio's.

"I behaved like a fool," Scipio replies. "I picked the wrong man and backed him when I should have clapped him in irons." He shakes his head, talking to himself. "I was an idiot, for true."

Pomponius nods solemnly. "Then I hope you have purged your system of all idiocy, young General. It is a luxury you cannot afford when you are alone in the Carthaginian Empire."

Scipio nods silently. Pomponius gives him a playful shove on his shoulder. "Do not be so abashed! Even a genius is human."

Pomponius starts to walk off. "We must hurry on our way," he shouts back. "We have to return to Rhegium and Locri before we go to Rome." The praetor clambers onto a bench next to Metelius and waves goodbye as the wagon driver snaps his whip.

Scipio watches the delegation trundle off and breathes a sigh of relief. Laelius walks to his side as the wagon disappears out the front gates.

"Do you think they will sway the Senate?" asks Laelius.

VIII. Judgment

"I'm not sure," answers Scipio. "Old Fabius would like nothing better than to end 'this African nonsense,' as he calls it."

Laelius laughs. "Well, I think the Senate will do what they say. The delegation was formed by the Senate, I would think they have no choice." He throws up his hands. "By Jupiter's cock, who could dissuade them from following the delegation's recommendations?"

"Only one," says Scipio.

Laelius looks curiously at him, then nods. "Oh. Yes."

Scipio grins ruefully. "My old friend Pleminius."

IX. SCIPIO'S DREAM

CARTHAGE, 204 BCE. "Masinissa's men have raided another of my villages, Gisgo. If we are to demolish Scipio's African force, we should get rid of Masinissa first." Syphax stalks about Gisgo's private meeting room, his sandaled feet clacking on the marble floors. "Let's get rid of him now!"

Gisgo leans back in his plushly stuffed oak chair, rubbing his hands over its gold-inlaid arms. He sighs irritably, as one would do with a recalcitrant child. "Yes, yes, of course. I'll give you a thousand more cavalry, our finest Libyans. You can build a net about the area he's hiding and close in on him. Or something such as that."

Gisgo quaffs deeply of his wine. "Just give me several weeks to deliver the men to you. This Scipio occupies my mind." He looks suspiciously at Syphax. "I have heard your old friend Scipio will be in Africa by summer."

"You know he is not my friend any more," Syphax retorts.

"Do I?" says Gisgo. "I still remember you made a treaty with him at Siga. And you have not revoked it."

Sophonisba reclines on an elephant tusk couchlet backed against a tapestried wall. She watches her father and husband argue over Syphax's loyalty to Scipio, but her mind is on her heart's treasure, Masinissa. *He needs Scipio to help him take back his throne from this pig,* she reflects. Syphax glances her way, and she forces a pleasing smile for him. *That cursed Roman has ignored him. Scipio needs to be goaded into coming here.*

A faint smile comes to her face. She reaches for a large peach and bites into it. *If those Latin senators found out that Syphax had married me and joined Gisgo, they would try to end Scipio's campaign right now. Scipio must come here before they try to stop him.*

IX. Scipio's Dream

Sophonisba casts the peach onto the floor. As her slave rushes to pick it up, the Numidian queen rises to stand next to Syphax, gazing adoringly at him.

"You are a man of honor, my king. Dalliance does not become you," purrs Sophonisba, her hand on his bare bicep. "It would be honorable for you to formally declare your divorce from Scipio."

Gisgo smiles broadly at his daughter. He fixes Syphax with a stern look. "She has the right of it, Syphax. You must be clear about your loyalties. Carthage will look very favorably upon you, if you do."

Syphax's eyes wander from Sophonisba to Gisgo, as he tries to think of a way of avoiding the declaration. He would, after all, much prefer to keep all his options open, should the war tides turn. His mind races for a solution, but none comes to him.

"Of course, I should have thought of it earlier," Syphax blusters. "I will make it clear to all that I am your ally."

"That is good," says Gisgo, suddenly much friendlier. "This may even daunt that brash Roman fool from coming over here."

"Any man would be daunted by the might of Syphax!" declares Sophonisba. "Your renunciation will be a display of your strength. Men will flock to join your army."

Syphax looks at his wife, then back at Gisgo. They watch him expectantly. He sighs. "Would I were as sure as you two! But it will be done..."

Three days later, Scipio is startled to learn that a Numidian quinquereme is docking in the harbor. "Get Laelius and Marcus here," he says to Praxis. "Bring the Honor Guard. We must go to Harbor Street immediately."

Scipio's party is soon marching toward the docks. *Syphax must have sent them*, Scipio thinks. *He will want to know when and where we will land. He must have fifty thousand men by now.*

IX. Scipio's Dream

As they arrive at the docks they see forty regal Numidian warriors marching out from the purple-trimmed vessel, dressed in the flowing indigo robes of Syphax's tribe. The men carry six-foot ceremonial spears and wear ivory handled silver swords on their belts, looking like a delegation of kings.

Their leader is a ropy man well over six feet tall, ebony eyes staring from under his bushy black brows and beard. He points toward Scipio, and the procession moves slowly toward the general and his men. A crowd begins to line the main thoroughfare along the docks. Word quickly spreads of the Africans' arrival, and the crowd swells.

When the Numidians draw near to Scipio's party the Numidian chief raises his arm over his head. The Numidians halt and become statues. The chief walks forward, trailed by a bent old man clutching a scroll. When he is within speaking distance from Scipio, the tall warrior bows.

"Well wishes to you, General Scipio," the leader says via his interpreter. "I am Nasamone, the King's Messenger. I bring news from Syphax, rightful ruler of all Numidia."

Scipio glances at Laelius and Marcus. "I wonder what Masinissa would say about that 'rightful ruler' title?" he remarks in Latin.

"I wonder what Masinissa would do to this errand boy, were he here to hear that," rejoins Laelius.

Scipio turns back to Nasamone. "What news have you, Messenger?"

Nasamone extends his hand to his assistant. The man hands him the scroll and looks up at Scipio, ready to deliver Nasamone's words. Nasamone solemnly hands the document to Scipio.

"With this message our mighty King Syphax does give you notice, oh great General," Nasamone declares. "He does encourage you to fight your war with Carthage apart from African soil. If you come to Africa and bring your army up to Carthage, he will be obliged to fight you for the sake of Africa." [cvii] He crosses his arms. "That is all."

Scipio unties the scroll and scans it. A scowl creases his face. He

IX. Scipio's Dream

hands the document to one of his tribunes. "Put this in my meeting room," he says curtly. "No one is to see it."

The Messenger looks at Scipio's guards. "I beg your permission to stay safely in Syracuse tonight. We will leave on the morrow."

"You will stay near my headquarters, honored Messenger. A repast will be provided you." Scipio turns to a guard. "Direct them to the granary rooms near my quarters."

Nasamone bows and starts to leave. Scipio raises his hand peremptorily. "I ask one thing of you, Nasamone." Scipio says. He points his finger in the Messenger's face. "Tell Syphax I deeply regret his betrayal of our treaty," he growls. "And that I fear he will soon regret the loss of our alliance. Very, very, soon."

The Messenger's eyes blaze at the affront to his king, but his face is a mask. "I will tell him the same, Roman," says Nasamone curtly. He turns his back on Scipio.

Marcus takes a step toward the African, his fist on his sword, but Scipio looks at him and shakes his head.

"Praxis will lead you to your quarters," says Scipio, pointing to his Honor Guard. "You will be ably guarded with his men."

With Praxis in the lead, the Africans stroll toward Syracuse, chatting as casually as if they were in a familiar village.

Laelius steps next to Scipio. "Well, in one hour all of Syracuse will know that Syphax's Numidians were here to visit you. By tomorrow Rome will probably know it, too."

Scipio looks back to ensure his guards cannot hear him. "We are cursed!" he spits. "If the Senate finds out that Syphax has withdrawn his alliance, we are undone. They will dictate that I remain in Sicily, regardless of Pomponius' recommendations."

"No one heard what the Numidians said," notes Laelius.

IX. Scipio's Dream

"Do we truly know that?" says Scipio. "Suppose some loose-mouthed guard heard them? Or one of those boys that were dashing around the Numidians? Our secret would be out in a trice. Shit!"

"What do you plan to do about it?" asks Marcus, a hint of demand in his tone.

Laelius laughs. "You know what we should do, Marcus. Acta non verba!"

"Yes, it is a time for deeds, not words," says Scipio. "We have to sail for Africa as soon as possible. And get out of Syracuse before someone stops us!"

Scipio's right hand begins to twitch, and he grabs it. "I want our war council in my headquarters, every one of them. We are taking every man and ship to Lilybaeum."[cviii]

"You want to take our entire army to that little port city?" asks Laelius. "That seems a bit crazy—even for you."

"That is our quickest route to Africa," Scipio says. "When our army lands in Africa, the ram will have touched the wall. No one can recall us, because we will be warring against the enemy."

Marcus bends over and picks up an egg-sized rock. He flings it at the Numidian ship. It bonks loudly against the hull. "We just lost Syphax's entire army, and Gisgo has likely gained it. Is it wise to take them on?"

"It is not wise, it is more than that," replies Scipio, suddenly weary. "It is necessary."

* * * * *

TEMPLE OF APOLLO, ROME. "Did you hear, Flaccus? A delegation of Numidians met with Scipio, for some reason or the other. But King Syphax was not with them."

Fabius plants his walking stick onto the marble step below him as he totters his way down the temple entrance, with Flaccus holding his

IX. Scipio's Dream

elbow. The two have attended a March sacrifice at the Temple of Apollo to welcome this first month of the year. The city is alive with festivals and merriment but the two senators' minds are elsewhere, occupied with plans to halt Scipio's expedition to Africa.

"Well, what of it?" shrugs Flaccus. "I remember his boasting about his treaty with Syphax, how it would give him tens of thousands of soldiers. The Numidians could have been there to renew their alliance with him."

Fabius shoves his bony elbow into Flaccus' side, irritated. "No, it was not like that! The citizens said Scipio was very angry with the Numidian leader, and the Numidian was angry, too. He stalked off into the town and left the next day. Perhaps something is amiss between them."

Flaccus' eyes light up. "Now that would be good news. Without Syphax's Numidians, he has only half the army he boasted he would have there. Some of our senators would certainly reconsider their support for the campaign! How can we find out what really happened?"

"We could ask Scipio. He is a Consul, after all," Fabius mutters, absently picking at a scab on his arm.

Flaccus shakes his head. "Would you believe him? This is the fellow we suspect of hoarding Iberian plunder for his own purposes."

"We do not know that, no we don't," Fabius retorts.

Flaccus shakes his head. "Yes we do. Pomponia has been spending entirely too much money on those land reform and salt tax campaigns. The family is not that wealthy, General."

Fabius purses his lips, thinking. "I tell you what, I will send two of my cousins there. They know several of Marcellus' old tribunes who are still down there in Syracuse. If there is trouble between Scipio and Syphax, they will find out. Then we might block this African campaign foolishness." Fabius grins. "Make him languish in Sicily until his consulship is done. That would teach him to disrespect me in the Senate!"

IX. Scipio's Dream

Flaccus hears a loud piping and clanging. He looks down the temple path, and frowns. "Jupiter's cock! Here come those Leaping Priests," he says, shouting over the rising music. "We will talk more when it quiets down."

Flaccus guides Fabius to a bench and eases him onto it. The two sit quietly as the noisy procession of the Twelve Salii pass by, young men cavorting joyously in ancient bronze battle armor, celebrating Mars, the god of war.

When the pipers and dancers have passed, Flaccus leans to Fabius' ear. "Send your cousins to Syracuse. In the meantime we will go to prison and meet with Pleminius. He will implicate Scipio in that Locri mess." Flaccus winks at Fabius. "Especially if he has a little inducement."

Fabius bobs his head. "Yes, he should testify, I say testify, against this foolish Scipio boy. Africa, my ass!"

He is becoming so querulous, muses Flaccus. *I need new allies.* "You had best send you cousins tomorrow. Scipio might leave any time now, Senate approval or not!"

*   *   *   *   *

SYRACUSE. The spring rains have come early, and they have come heavy. Syracuse is quiescent this afternoon, as its residents take shelter from the thundering downpour that envelops the bustling port city. Even the fishermen have stayed inside, mending their nets and tying their lines, dreaming of catching a large tuna or hauling in a magnificent swordfish. The farmers have followed suit, gazing happily from their cottage windows at the drizzling sustenance for their parched fields, groves, and vines.

It is a dark and gloomy day, but it well suits Scipio's task this morning: passing judgment on the men who just tried to kill him.

Aulus and Cassius sit before him, trussed up into two stout wooden chairs. Their faces are swollen and discolored, mute testament to the beating the two endured by the man who captured them.

IX. Scipio's Dream

Marcus Silenus' lips are also swollen. One eye is blackened from the fist that entered it, but his face is otherwise unscathed. His arms, however, are stitched with the claw marks that Aulus and Cassius inflicted as he beat them down with his bare hands.

For weeks, Marcus has spent his spare time spying on the two guards. He has watched Aulus and Cassius eye Scipio as though he were prospective prey. He became alarmed for his general's safety, knowing he could not be near Scipio all the time. And so Marcus followed the lead of his beloved general, and created his own network of speculatores.

Marcus' spies were boys, a half dozen of the crafty youths who infiltrated the Roman camp every day. The boys are known for begging food and money, running errands, and pilfering anything they can get their hands on. So many of the scruffy boys run about the camp that they are virtually invisible to the soldiers. Marcus needed that invisibility for his intelligence work.

He hired the boys to follow the Aulus and Cassius, with different "spies" rotating on different days. The boys reported back to him in the evening, before he assumed his own evening watch on the two former gladiators. One day, a boy reported that Aulus and Cassius were burying some serrated cutting knives near their tent. Marcus immediately became Scipio's shadow, drifting in the background as Scipio moved about his daily activates.

Last night brought the moment Marcus had anticipated. Scipio was staying at his command tent in the center of camp, unattended save for a few visits by his guards. One of Marcus' boys came to him, saying he had seen the two Samnites circling about Scipio's tent at dusk, looking at the tent walls.

Marcus dismissed his spies and posted himself inside a nearby legionnaires' tent, his eyes fixed Scipio's headquarters. After midnight, two shadows appeared outside Scipio's tent, outlined by the torchlight inside. Peering out from behind one of the eight-man tents, Marcus watched Aulus and Cassius take out their cutting knives and open a slit in Scipio's tent.

IX. Scipio's Dream

It was a simple matter for the legate to pad up behind the two with a small cudgel in hand. Marcus clubbed Cassius above the ear, but the tough old gladiator twisted around grappled with Marcus as Aulus rushed in with his knife.

Marcus ducked Aulus' killing lunge and tripped him to the ground. A quick fist put down the woozy Cassius, and Marcus jumped onto Aulus. With two strokes of his cudgel, Marcus beat the man unconscious, ignoring Aulus' stabs and scratches. It took all Marcus' willpower not to kill them on the spot, but he was duty bound to turn them in.

"What say you to the fate of these two dead men?" asks Scipio angrily. *Careful. You are letting your emotions take the reins.* "Should I show them mercy?" he adds.

Laelius snorts derisively. "Mercy? All in Syracuse have heard about the allegations of laxity and lenience that brought Pomponius' delegation here," says Laelius. "You must deal with these betrayers harshly, and deal with them in front of the men."

"For once he makes sense," adds Marcus. "The men respect you. But they do not fear you. They do not fear your justice."

Scipio shrugs. "And what if they do not? I am in command, regardless. Why not sell those two into slavery and get back to our preparations?" He throws up his hands. "I just want to be done with this!" he says peevishly.

"Respect is the reason they will march confidently into battle for you," Marcus replies "Fear is what will keep them there when things become difficult. They must fear retribution for retreat, or cowardice."

He looks sternly at Scipio, but his voice is soft. "You cannot treat Aulus and Cassius as you treated Pleminius. Many of the men think that your leniency toward him brought death to Sergius and Matienus."

Scipio's face reddens. He sits silently, looking at his two surly victims. "You think the men need an example."

IX. Scipio's Dream

Marcus shakes his head. "Not old Marcellus' men, they are true veterans. And men such the Cannenses, they fear further dishonor more than they fear death.[cix] But both legions are filled with recruits that have not tasted battle. They need an example of your wrath."

"We are leaving soon, Scippy," says Laelius gently. "This is your final chance before we start battle." He puts his hand on Scipio's shoulder. "Remember Carthago Nova? The killing of the citizens? That onerous act saved so many of us that would have been lost."

Laelius smiles wanly. "Yes, I fear a lesson is in order. Do something dramatic, give them something to talk about."

Scipio sits quietly for a minute. The room is still except for the nervous shuffling of the captives' feet.

"Who paid you to kill me?" asks Scipio suddenly, studying their eyes. The two merely stare back at him. "If you tell me, I will grant you a death worthy of a gladiator," adds Scipio. There is still no response.

"He may crucify you if you don't tell," adds Laelius, but the two remain quiet.

Scipio sees that his tribunes are watching him. *You have to get this resolved now!* He turns back to his captives. "Tell me who ordered it, and I will grant you a bout between the two of you. To the death. The winner becomes a slave in Sicily."

There is no reply. Then Cassius speaks up. "No work in the mines?" he asks. Scipio nods. "I promise, you will not work in the mines."

"Calidus," spits Aulus, as if it were a bitter taste in his mouth. "A Roman spy for the Carthaginians. He bribed us to slay you." Cassius sneers at his companion, but he nods his agreement.

Scipio takes a deep breath. "Very well. Two days hence you will fight to the death." *Fear. Your men must fear your judgment.* "You will fight as boxers against each other. Both of you will use the myrmex, the face piercers that gladiators have used in the arena."

IX. Scipio's Dream

Aulus looks at his friend Cassius. Cassius manages a grim smile at his co-conspirator, and then looks up to face Scipio. "Gratitude for a warrior's death, General. It is all a gladiator asks."

Two days later, thousands of Scipio's soldiers pour into the shallow bowl next to the training fields. They seat themselves around the thirty-foot wide dirt circle in the center, basking in the warm morning sun. Cassius and Aulus are led in chains to the center of the ring. The legionnaires and allies buzz with excitement. The new recruits are especially captivated: they have not seen a boxing bout before.

A centurion unlocks Aulus and Cassius from their chains and pushes them toward a waiting attendant. The two Samnites extend their arms and spread their hands, staring blankly into space. A muscular old slave carefully wraps each of their hands in iron-studded straps, tying the ends about their wrists. Aulus and Cassius swing their fists about, testing their weapons' weight and balance. The inch-long spikes protrude from the top of their knuckles and wrists, each point sharpened for maximum penetration.

Aulus and Cassius walk to opposite sides of the circle and face one another. Aulus looks into Cassius eyes. "Forgiveness, brother, for what I must do."

Cassius' eyes flare. "Apologies for what I will do to *you*, that I may live." Aulus nods. He runs his sandaled toe across the earth, testing its traction.

Scipio steps into the ring, wearing polished battle armor and a blood red cape. He slowly turns and stares intently at his men's faces, as if he is assessing their individual mettle. The soldiers quiet, watching their general. When he has completed the circle he pulls out his gladius and points it at Aulus, then at Cassius.

"Aulus and Cassius served me honorably for months, guarding my life with their own." He shakes his head ruefully. "Then I find they have plotted to kill me. The same men that I rescued from the arena, to become part of my Honor Guard." Scipio glares at them. "Murder was how they would repay me for that."

IX. Scipio's Dream

Scipio raises his head. "Let all know this before we depart for Africa: treachery, cowardice, or betrayal will meet a similar fate as theirs, however honorably you have served me before."

Scipio steps to the side of the circle. He draws his gladius and points it at the two prisoners. "Begin!" he shouts. "If either stay your hand, I will burn the both of you alive!"

Aulus steps toward Cassius. Cassius begins circling the perimeter of the wall formed by the legionnaires' bodies, keeping his distance from Aulus. Aulus watches' his opponent's eyes, as gladiators are taught to do, looking for clues to his next move. Slowly, the two draw nearer to each other.

Cassius lunges forward and snakes a blow at Aulus' face, seeking to blind him for the kill. Aulus reflexively raises his shield arm to block the blow. Cassius' steel spikes dig deep into Aulus' thick forearm, which blooms with blood.

Bellowing with pain, Aulus strikes back at the underside of Cassius' outstretched arm, cutting shallow furrows into its tender flesh. Both step back, blood streaming at their feet, sizing up their opponent for the next attack. They both know that they will soon grow weak from loss of blood.

Aulus strides forward with his right arm extended, almost as if he were coming to greet Cassius. When he closes he swings his right arm at Cassius' neck. Cassius' iron fist clacks into Aulus' spikes, knocking his fist sideways. But that blow was a feint, as Aulus spins on his left foot and kicks Cassius in the midsection, knocking him breathless to the ground.

Aulus leaps upon him, but Cassius has already turned on his side. Pushing himself up with one hand, Cassius shoves his other fist into Aulus' chest. The spikes bite deep into his breast. Aulus jerks his head back and yells in anguish, but the old warrior grips Cassius' fist against his chest. With a roar of effort, Aulus jams his studded fist into Cassius' throat.

IX. Scipio's Dream

Cassius grasps his neck with both hands, He gasps for breath as he spits up blood, his shocked eyes bulging from his face. Aulus clambers on top of him, ignoring the flailing blows that scourge his back and sides. He hammers his spiked fist into Cassius' eyes, again and again, blinding him forever.

Aulus pushes off from his opponent and steps back. Wailing in agony, Cassius ineffectually flails about, rolling from side to side on the ground. But he strikes only air, as Aulus stands apace from Cassius' throes, sadly watching his brother in arms die.

The legionnaires cheer wildly. "He's had it," they chant, repeating the gladiatorial phrase as they thrust their thumbs down.

Cassius raises himself up on one elbow. He lifts his blind eyes to the sky. "Aulus!" he gurgles from his mouth, swallowing blood so he can form his words. "End it! End it!"

Aulus takes a deep breath. "Apologies, brother," he mutters through clenched teeth. He stalks toward Cassius and raises his fists. With a despairing scream, Aulus batters into Cassius' forehead, trying to kill him as quickly as possible. With a deep groan Cassius, slumps to the earth. His body lies lifeless but Aulus continues to beat his face, tears streaming down his cheeks. The cheering crowd quiets.

"Pull him off!" Scipio orders. Two guards rush in and grasp Aulus' arms, pulling him from Cassius' butchered corpse. They drag Aulus to the edge of the circle and clap him back in chains. A Greek slave bandages the sobbing man's wounds, then two guards drag him away.

Scipio walks to the middle of the ring. "Aulus is the victor. He has won a life of slavery instead of instant death. Who can say which of the two is more fortunate? But justice has been meted to both."

Scipio looks up the rise to a spot behind the troops. He draws his sword and waves it back toward the ring, beckoning someone to come down to it. There is a loud rumbling sound behind the men. Scipio turns back to them, an excited expression on his face.

"You have seen the fate of those who do not do their duty, my men.

IX. Scipio's Dream

Now, let me show you the rewards for those who do." The crowd parts as a mule-drawn wagon barges its way through the soldiers and into the dirt circle, even as Cassius' body is dragged out of it.

The two beasts pull in a small wagon loaded with a treasure of gold and silver. Precious crowns, statues, metalware and jewelry are piled atop a hill of coins. The soldiers goggle at the wealth before them.

"Yes, this is all yours," Scipio says, sweeping his arm across the wagon. "But this is not all!"

Another cart trundles into the ring, laden with the same trove of treasure. The two wagons stop inside the circle. Scipio employs the same motivational ploy he used on the men before the distraction of Locri took them all from their purpose. He is showing them Laelius' plunder from the coasts of Africa.[cx]

"These riches are but a potful compared to what awaits you. Carthage alone has a thousand times this wealth, yea, and more besides!"

He holds up a scroll with a shining gold seal attached to it. By every appearance it is an important document. "You know that Syphax's men visited me a few days ago. And you may wonder why they came." Scipio swallows, and his hand begins to bob nervously. *Veritas forgive me.* He looks toward Marcus Silenus but the old centurion looks away from him: he knows what Scipio will say.

"Our Numidian allies bid us to come to Africa as soon as we can," Scipio lies. He looks above his men's heads to avoid their eyes. "The Numidians you saw, they want to know why we delay." [cxi]

Scipio points toward the harbor. "I told them we will not delay any longer, because King Syphax, our friend, he badly needs our help. And so I tell you now, we will march to Lilybaeum three days hence, and from there we sail for Thapsus in far eastern Africa. And then we march on Carthage itself!"

Before the crowd can react, he spreads his arms wide, as if entreating them. "In Africa you will find wealth for the taking, plunder beyond your dreams. But that is not the truest reward, men."

IX. Scipio's Dream

Scipio motions for two of his guards to approach. When they are standing next to him, he spreads his arms across their shoulders, as if the three of them were dear comrades. "You have the chance to devote your mind, body and spirit to the noblest purpose of all—preserving your homeland. The richest men on earth cannot purchase the feeling of fighting side by side with brothers of like mind, for the glorious cause of Rome."

"You men of Italia will have the immortal honor of saving Rome from the Carthaginian scourge; you will attain the deathless glory of ending this war forever. And so I ask you: are you ready to go there and take it?"

It has been said that a black cloud of birds darkened the sky at that moment, because the men's cheers were so loud they put every nearby bird to flight.

Standing in the maelstrom of his men's enthusiasm, Scipio raises his shining gladius skyward, as if challenging Olympus itself. He smiles triumphantly. *Our time is here. Gods above, do not let Rome stop me now.*

* * * * *

ROME, 204 BCE. "Up, murderer. You have a visitor!"

Pleminius raises himself from his soggy straw pallet. He turns his scarred face toward the churlish jailer, and spits at the man's feet.

"I am Praetor Quintus Pleminius, Labeo!" It would behoove you to remember that, or I'll have you scourged when I get out of here!"

The jailer bares his scraggly yellow teeth. "Oh, Apologies, 'Praetor' Pleminius," he chortles. "I should show you *much* more respect, shouldn't I? And perhaps you will do the same for me, should you want your shit bucket changed more often, as your illustrious self has requested!"

Chuckling at his humor, the bent old man pulls a ring of iron keys from his greasy leather belt. He turns the lock in Pleminius' cell,

IX. Scipio's Dream

creaking back the thickly barred door.

The jailer looks to his side, attending to someone Pleminius cannot see, and bows obsequiously. "Yes, of course, madam," he says. "Whatever you wish! Just tell me."

A long, graceful arm appears, reaching toward the stooped jailer, and drops a bulging little purse into his palm. Then a finger points upward.

The jailer glares at Pleminius. "You try anything and I'll kill you!" he snarls in his raspy voice. The jailer bows deeply to the hidden figure and crabs up the mossy stone stairsteps, scraping the door closed behind him.

Pomponia Scipio eases her way into Pleminius' fetid cell, walking as regally as if she were coming to sit at a throne. The queenly matron wears a gown of aquamarine, her flaming red hair piled like a burning torch. She studies the mossy walls and flat pallet of the cell, ignoring its odor.

"Come out here, Praetor," Pomponia commands. "We have business to discuss." Pleminius steps from his darkened cell and out into the light.

Pomponia barely suppresses a gasp. She has heard about the praetor's appearance but she is still taken aback at the scabbed stubs of his nose and ears, at the burning hostility in his eyes.

"Apologies for this unannounced visit. Do you know who I am?" she manages to say.

Pleminius snorts wheezily. "You are the mother of the bastard that had me arrested. Who let those two tribunes do this to me. Yes, I know who you are."

Pomponia bows her head slightly in acknowledgement. "Tomorrow you go before the plebs, to be tried before the people." She paces about, avoiding Pleminius' eyes, speaking as if she were talking to herself. "My son is at a sensitive time in his campaign, the Senate will soon meet with the Locri delegation to decide his fate." She faces Pleminius.

IX. Scipio's Dream

"What you say tomorrow could affect the Senate's attitudes, noble Praetor. And their vote."

Pleminius barks a laugh. "Well, I should certainly hope it would have some effect on them," he snaps. "Truth be known, I hope to see your son down here in my place!" He runs his fingers across his scarred face. "This is what his two dogs did. Would they were both here, so I could kill them again!"

Pomponia calmly endures his spitting diatribe. She smiles into his angry eyes. "You may blame the two tribunes all you want, Praetor. They are dead by your hand, and beyond further harm. But I would ask that you refrain from impeaching my son." She stares levelly at him. "Do that, and you will find the people of Rome most sympathetic to your plight. I guarantee they will plead for your acquittal."

Pleminius shakes his head. "As you say, the two bastards are beyond my reach. But their commander is not, and I will have my revenge." He smiles gloatingly. "Besides, noble Flaccus has offered me a goodly sum if I implicate Scipio."

The room is silent for several heartbeats, as the two eye one another.

"You cannot spend that money if you are in prison. I can promise you your freedom." She steps closer to the sneering praetor. "And I can promise you one other thing."

There is a bright flash. Pleminius is startled to find a knife at his throat, its gleaming blade cutting into his jugular just enough to loose a trickle of blood. Pomponia pushes the knife further against his throat. Pleminius cranes his head backwards. He reaches out to grasp her hand.

"Don't!" Pomponia barks. Her eyes glare into his, her face transformed with demonic anger. She shoves the blade farther to emphasize her point, and Pleminius' hands drop to his sides.

"I promise you, you will be dead before you can enjoy any rewards from that piece of pig shit you call Flaccus, if you do manage release." She flips her wrist, and the throwing knife disappears into her gown sleeve. "You can only hope that I will do it myself, because my

IX. Scipio's Dream

assistants will scrape the skin from your body. Do you understand me?"

Pleminius rubs his throat, looks at his bloody fingers, and swallows. "Freedom? You can promise me that?" he says challengingly, trying to salvage his dignity.

Pomponia puts her hand over her womb. "On my children's lives, I promise you that the plebs will become sympathetic to your cause and that you will be found innocent."

"How can you promise that?" Pleminius insists, his hope rising. Pomponia shakes her head. "I have my ways. You consort with cursed Flaccus, so you will not hear of them. You have only to enjoy their effect."

Pleminius looks about his musty cell. "I can plead my case for my own innocence?"

Pomponia nods. "Of course, just do it without implicating your General, which is a cowardly thing to do, regardless."

Pleminius bites his lower lip. He touches his throat again, and nods silently.

Pomponia leans her head toward him. "Say it."

Pleminius inhales her spicy perfume. His eyes wander over her curved form. *What a bitch goddess*! He sighs. "I will not blame your son."

"Excellent! See that you do not, and your safety is assured." She lifts up the hem of her gown and carefully steps her way from the filthy cell, pausing at the entrance. "And if you do slander him, whatever protection Flaccus may promise you, it will not be enough."

Pomponia mounts the steps to the jail entrance, motioning for the jailer to return to his post. Exiting the prison, she meets her waiting attendants and walks back to the Scipio domus, where Amelia anxiously waits for her.

"All is well," Pomponia says as she sees her daughter in law. She

IX. Scipio's Dream

walks past Amelia, heading for her chambers. "Wait for me please. I must wash the stink off me."

An hour later, Pomponia and Amelia stand in the atrium garden, sipping honeyed wine as they walk among the famed Scipio rosebushes. Pomponia cups a fist-sized red bloom in her hand and inhales deeply, savoring its heavy perfume.

"Will Pleminius accuse him?" asks Amelia anxiously. "Should I mount a slander campaign against him, or call for his conviction?"

Pomponia waves her hand. "Let us leave well enough alone for now, daughter. We will see what he says during his public appearances in the Forum. As a praetor, he is granted leave to take his case to the people."

Pleminius makes several appearances before the people. He pleads his case by indicting the two tribunes and their men for the atrocities perpetrated upon him. The Roman citizens see his disfigured face, and his speeches are met with resounding applause.

With each appearance, Pleminius' tale grows more colorful and the plebians' cheers for him grow louder. He can see the attending senators nodding their heads in agreement with the crowd. *I have become a favorite*, he thinks, as the prison guards lead him down from the Forum's speaking platform. *If Pomponia were to try anything, I could speak out against her and her precious Hellenic party. I'll tell the bitch that, then we'll see how tough she is!*

The guards lead Flaccus to a new prison cell, a spacious one with a padded bed and a bench toilet connected to the Cloaca Maxima, Rome's sewer system. Pleminius looks about the well-lit cell. One of the guards shoves him inside and clangs shut the iron barred door. "This is a gift from Senator Flaccus," says the guard. "He will be in to see you."

That evening the jailer brings Pleminius a dinner with roast pork and fresh bread. "This is from Senator Flaccus," says the kitchen slave. An hour later the jailer opens the cell door and Flaccus walks in.

"You have quite a following out there," Flaccus says. "In fact, you are

IX. Scipio's Dream

becoming one of the people's favorites." He smiles. "I would think you could run for office if you were released from here. You could become a consul!"

"Gratitude, Senator," replies Pleminius, as he nibbles on a last crust of bread he has hoarded from the meal. "Perhaps I will do just that."

"You have not said anything about Scipio's role in this sordid affair," Flaccus says. "Remember our discussion? No Scipio, no freedom."

Pleminius shakes his head. "I cannot speak those words. Pomponia will have me killed if I do."

Flaccus looks back up the prison steps to affirm no one is near. He steps close to Pleminius, and leans to his ear. "I am certain that Pomponia is not long upon this earth. Do you understand what I say? And if anyone should raise a hand or blade against you, I will personally have that person dragged off to jail and crucified."

"Those are strong words, Senator. I want to believe you, but it is my life at stake, not yours."

Flaccus frowns at him. "Do not be such a mouse! You have fame and fortune ahead of you if you will but take it! There is a man, a very special man, who waits for a word from someone you know. When that word is given, Pomponia ceases to exist. Speak against Scipio and you will find the truth of it, *Consul* Pleminius." Flaccus stalks out of the cell, leaving Pleminius to ponder his words.

The next day, Pleminius gives his final public defense speech in the Forum Square. "You have heard that Sergius and Matienus did this to me," shouts Pleminius, running his hand over his ravaged visage. "But now I must tell you, had Publius Cornelius Scipio exercised proper control over his men, this would never have happened!"

He spreads his hands beseechingly. "I do not lie. Scipio's own quaestor, the honorable Marcus Porcius Cato, did report the same to the Senate. And Cato's veracity is beyond doubt. I am a victim of lax discipline, General Scipio is responsible for it!"

IX. Scipio's Dream

Scattered jeers break out at the end of Pleminius' speech. Scipio is the people's favorite, and his words are not well received. "I am innocent!" Pleminius blurts to them before he steps down from the speaker's platform. This time Flaccus and Fabius stand next to his guards, their presence a mute endorsement of Pleminius' innocence.

Early that evening a sumptuous platter is brought to Pleminius in his cell, a plate lined with slices of pheasant and pork. The jailer hands the platter to a grinning Pleminius, and gives him a bronze flagon of wine. "This is Falernian, the finest," adds the jailer, a young Roman Pleminius has not seen before.

Pleminius grasps the platter with a broad smile. He raises the flagon to his cracked lips and sips the wine. His smile broadens. *Flaccus is not a man to spare money on food*, Pleminius thinks. *Or bribes.*

"Gratitude for the repast, I shall do it justice," says Pleminius, as he lays the platter on the floor and sits in front of it. He looks over the jailer's shoulder. "Where is old Labeo? He brought the last meal."

The young man grins. "He is likely sitting over a hole at one the public latrines, cursing the tainted chickpeas he ate last night." The jailer points at the food. "You had best get to it, Praetor, before we are discovered." He locks Pleminius' door and clacks up the mossy stone steps.

Pleminius hears him step up to the next flight and close the prison door. "To Flaccus," he says loudly, raising his flagon to the empty cells. *I think I'll join the Latin Party when I get out of here,* he muses, smacking his lips. *Consul Pleminius, ruler of Africa!*

Minutes later, as Pleminius pulls a pheasant bone from his mouth, he hears a rattling of keys. The upper jail door creaks open, and a pair of feet pad down the old stone steps. *Those aren't that jailer's footsteps*, Pleminius thinks. *Someone is coming to visit. Maybe Flaccus has come back.* Pleminius stands up and brushes the breadcrumbs from his tunic, ready to receive his guest.

The old jailer shuffles in to the front of Pleminius' cell, carrying a

IX. Scipio's Dream

bucket of porridge. Pleminius blinks. "Labeo! What are you doing here? Your replacement told me you were sick."

"What in Hades are you talking about?" Labeo growls. He peers into Pleminius' cell. "Where did you get all that food? And wine?"

Pleminius eyes widen with dawning realization. He bends over and jams his fingers down his throat until he vomits onto the cell floor. Even as he jams his fingers back down his gorge, he feels his arms and legs grow heavy. His vision blurs, and he begins to teeter.

"It's that bitch," he mutters to the uncomprehending Labeo. Pleminius topples to the floor. His legs kick once, and he is still...

The next day, Fabius intercepts Flaccus in the Forum square, just as Flaccus steps up to the Curia Hostilia. "Have you heard?" Fabius wheezes. "A misfortune struck Pleminius last night. He died in his cell, of causes unknown." [cxii]

Flaccus whirls about. "What! He's dead? We were to discuss his case today! That's all that's keeping our indictment of Scipio alive!"

"Ah, but misfortune comes to many when they least expect it, especially those who deserve it," comes a sultry voice from behind him.

Flaccus turns to see Pomponia smiling at him, her red hair cascading down to the emerald green gown she wears. She pulls her carmine-tinted lips back and bites deeply into the ripe peach she is holding, chewing it sensuously as she smiles into Flaccus' angry eyes.

"I heard about poor Pleminius." She says, her lips pouting. "You just can't trust prison food, can you?"

"I will see your son upon a cross," splutters Flaccus. "Both of them, curse you!"

Fabius tugs at Flaccus' toga. "Come, now, come! People can hear you!"

Pomponia puts the rest of the peach into her mouth. She chews and

IX. Scipio's Dream

swallows, and spits the pit at Flaccus' feet. "Don't you have a meeting to go to?" she says to him, smiling radiantly at several passersby. "You wouldn't want to be late. It would create the impression that you were unreliable. Someone who could not deliver what they promise."

Hips swaying, Pomponia rejoins her waiting attendants and walks over to visit a Persian spice merchant's stall.

As Flaccus stomps up the Curia steps, he listens to Pomponia and her retinue laughing and chatting. *Marcus Silenus be damned, I'll kill her.*

That day, the Senate drops any further consideration of Pleminius' case and with it any further consideration of Scipio's involvement. A disheartened Flaccus summons the Latin Party membership to consider a new proposal at the next meeting—that Scipio's consulship be restricted to Sicily, and he be forbidden to journey to Africa.

"We've got to stop him before he leaves for Sicily!" Flaccus says to the Senators.

There is an awkward silence. Fabius shuffles out to face Flaccus. He puts his withered hand on his arm. "I tell you as a friend, forget it! As the old saying goes, that ship has sailed..."

* * * * *

PORT OF LILYBAEUM, SOUTH ITALIA, 204 BCE. "This place is as rowdy as the Plebian Games," remarks Laelius, as he looks about the port of Lilybaeum. "Listen to them hoot and cheer over there. You'd think we were going to ride out on elephants and bring them jugglers!"

"We are heroes to them and we need their support. So wave, you pumpkinhead, wave!" Scipio grins as he waves energetically at the cheering Sicilians thronged along Lilybaeum's harbor walls. *This is just like running for office*, he muses, as he bends to kiss a woman's baby. Scipio walks inside a wedge of his Honor Guard, leading the last cohort of his men down the thoroughfare that leads to his tethered flagship.

Laelius trots back to lead the hundreds of marines who are marching behind Scipio's men. The young admiral rides on a snow-white stallion

IX. Scipio's Dream

he has borrowed for the short trip to his flagship quinquereme. It is no accident that the horse matches the dazzling chalked tunic he sports beneath his mirrored armor. With the Locri delegation departed, Laelius has happily returned to his decorative ways.

Laelius waves enthusiastically to the crowd, taking time to wink at the attractive young men he sees, casting roses to the women and children in the back rows. *Might as well enjoy it, this may be my last time on Roman soil for several years—or forever.*

Scipio moves his men slowly to his ship, no longer feeling hurried now that his ships are loaded with men and supplies—now that Rome is too late to stop him. He lingers to grasp the hundreds of hands that reach out to touch his shoulder, his leg—any part of this man who communes with the gods.

"Ave, Savior of Rome, Ave!" a man shouts out. Scipio winces at the title, but he smiles benignly at him. *Savior of Rome? Minerva give me the wisdom to fulfill their hopes.* His left hand reaches into his belt pouch and withdraws his smudged and worn figurine of Nike, Greek goddess of victory. *I'll not disappoint you, Amelia. Or you, Father.*

Scipio peers out toward the choppy waters of the deep blue Mediterranean, out beyond Lilybaeum's sheltered harbor waters. He looks at his fleet awaiting him there, warships and freighters bobbing on the swell as far as the eye can see. A chill runs up his spine. *It is going to happen. Africa is really happening.*

Suddenly nervous, Scipio summons Laelius to his side. "Are all the supply carriers ready?" he asks. Laelius rolls his eyes. "No, I forgot. But who cares, we can buy what we need over there, can't we?" He playfully shoves Scipio's shoulder. "Of course they are ready, grandmother! As per your command, the carriers are loaded with food and water for a forty-five day land campaign." [cxiii]

"Good," Scipio mutters. "That will give us time to take over an African region and become self-sufficient—or die trying." He inhales deeply of the salt sea air, willing his heart to cease its hammering.

IX. Scipio's Dream

Laelius studies Scipio's drawn face. "You know, the African coast is only seventy miles away," Laelius says.

"I know, but it feels as if we are leaving for a far distant land. It's not the distance, it's the importance. When we are done there, Rome or Carthage will rule the world."

"Psh! You put too much pressure on yourself." Laelius waves over Marcus Silenus, who leads the troop vanguard. "Marcus, our general thinks the fate of the world hangs on his shoulders. That Rome perishes if we lose!"

Marcus shrugs noncommittally, but there is a twinkle in his eye. "He likely has the right of it, pretty boy. We have an army of untested recruits and old men, with a paucity of resources and political support. If Hannibal comes to engage us, we fight a general who has not been defeated, with an army of battle-tested veterans. It is not a pleasant prospect."

"Mmph," grunts Scipio. "I heard that same story when we faced the Three Generals, Marcus. And I triumphed."

"Yes you did, General" Marcus says pointedly. "You certainly did." He snaps the reins of his horse and trots back to his men.

The Romans halt at the walkway to the main dock. Scipio's guards wedge their way through one side of the crowd, allowing Scipio to ascend the twelve-foot high platform that he has built for this occasion. Scipio stands before the thousands who fill the streets and byways of the harbor, the dock waters gently lapping behind him. He looks at the sea of hopeful faces and a fist of dread suddenly clutches his heart. *They expect me to save them from Carthage. Oh Mars guide me, I am but a quiet scholar, chained to a soldier's life by my promise.*

Scipio feels his eyes moisten. He bites hard on his lip, the pain rousing him from self-pity. He takes several sharp breaths, as if preparing to lift a heavy weight, and begins his invocation.

"O Gods and Goddesses of the seas and lands, I pray and beseech you that whatsoever things have been done under my authority, are being

IX. Scipio's Dream

done, and will be done, may prosper for me and for the people and commons of Rome, for our allies ... I pray that you bring the victors home again safe and sound, enriched with spoils and laden with plunder to share my triumph when the enemy has been defeated, that you grant us the power of vengeance upon those whom we hate and our country's enemies, and give to me and to the Roman people means to inflict upon the Carthaginian state the same sufferings which the Carthaginians have labored to inflict on ours." [cxiv]

His short speech done, Scipio raises his arms in blessing to the crowd. He descends to a deafening tumult of cheers.

The Sicilians follow the Romans as they march out onto the long, wide dockway, watching as they board the two waiting command ships. As Scipio's cohort marches past the nearest flagship, a familiar face glares at him from atop the gangplank.

"Dispense with the rest of this wasteful ceremony, General," grouses Cato. "We are past time for departure!"

Marcus looks at Scipio's pained expression and grins. "Why you made him a co-commander of your fleet's right wing is beyond me. He is more trouble than the Carthaginians!"

"That wing has twenty warships, so Laelius needed help. As quaestor, Cato was the next highest ranking officer." Scipio grins. "You should have seen Laelius' face when I told him Cato was going to help him command the wing![cxv] He was ready to kill me!"

Marcus looks back toward Cato's ship and grins. "I would not blame him for trying."

Scipio shrugs. "Perhaps it will help my relations with the Senate to have a Latin Party member as part of my command. We can get more money from them."

Marcus chuckles. "Gods above, you are as much a politician as a soldier, and as much a scholar as a politician. We might have a chance, after all."

IX. Scipio's Dream

Laelius and his marines board Cato's waiting ship, while Scipio embraces Lucius on the gangplank of the other one. The ships' sailors scramble about the dockway, untying the arm-thick ropes that hold the mighty quinqueremes to the timbers. As the two ships edge from the dockside, the sailors trot up the gangplanks and pull them up after them.

The two flagships ease their way out of the harbor, moving gracefully under slow and steady oar strokes, gliding among the fleet ships all about them. The horns sound from Scipio's ship and it opens its sails to embrace the lively spring breeze. The other ships soon follow suit, and Scipio's armada is under way for Africa. Thirty thousand Romans and allies stand in the holds, wondering what Fortuna will bring them in this foreign land.

The ships' navigator stands next to Scipio in the ship's prow. The two stare out toward the African coast, looking across the endless sea. "So, we aim for Thapsus on the southeast coast," says the captain, "and then on to Carthage!"

Scipio turns to his captain, his mischievous smile returning. "Thapsus? Carthage? Oh that, that was just a ruse.[cxvi] Another little fable for the Carthaginian spies."

He grins with excitement and arrows his arm to the right of the prow. "We sail to Cape Bon, my man. And thence on to Utica. We'll have another little surprise for Carthage when we get there..."

About the Author

Martin Tessmer is a retired professor of instructional design and technology, and a former training design consultant to the Navy and Air Force.

The author of eleven nonfiction and fiction books, his most current endeavor is the Scipio Africanus Saga, which includes *Scipio Rising*, *The Three Generals*, and *Scipio's Dream*. A fourth book, *Scipio Risen*, is due out at the end of April 2016.

He lives in Denver, Colorado.

END NOTES

[i] Gabriel, p. 128.

[ii] Gabriel, p. 129.

[iii] http://en.wikipedia.org/wiki/Masinissa

[iv] Livy, 28, 18, 472.

[v] Ibid.

[vi] Livy, 28, p. 472.

[vii] http://en.wikipedia.org/wiki/Marcus_Livius_Salinator

[viii] Gabriel, pp. 138-39.

[ix] Livy, 28, 19, 473.

[x] Livy, 28, 19, 474.

[xi] Livy, 28, 20, 474.

[xii] Ibid, 28, 20, 475.

[xiii] Livy, 28, 36, 495.

[xiv] Livy, 22, 477.

[xv] Livy, 22, 477.

[xvi] Livy, 28, 22, 478.

[xvii] Livy, 28, 21, 476.

[xviii] Gabriel, page 132.

END NOTES

[xx] Livy, 28, 26. 483.

[xxi] Polybius, The Histories, Book 11, Section 28. http://penelope.uchicago.edu/Thayer/E/Roman/Texts/Polybius/11*.htm

[xxii] Liddell-Hart, B. H. *Scipio Africanus: Greater Than Napoleon.* Cambridge, MA: Da Capo Press, p. 76.

[xxiii] Livy, 28, 29, 487.

[xxiv] Ibid.

[xxv] Polybius. *The Complete Histories of Polybius.* Translated by W.R. Paton. 2014. Digireads.com. P. 343.

[xxvi] *Scipio Rising*, p. 177.

[xxvii] Livy, 28, 33, 492.

[xxviii] Gabriel, p. 137.

[xxix] Livy, 28, 33, 492.

[xxx] http://en.wikipedia.org/wiki/Fabius_Maximus

[xxxi] http://en.wikipedia.org/wiki/Fabius_Maximus

[xxxii] Ibid, 28, 38, 497.

[xxxiii] Ibid, 28, 38, 497.

[xxxiv] http://penelope.uchicago.edu/Thayer/E/Roman/Texts/secondary/SMIGRA*/Triumphus.html

[xxxv] Livy, 28, 38, 497.

[xxxvi] Ibid, 28, 46, 512.

[xxxvii] Livy, 28, 46, 512

END NOTES

[xxxviii] http://www.italythisway.com/places/articles/Kroton-history.php

[xxxix] Livy, 28, 38, 497.

[xl] Livy, 28, 38, 497.

[xli] http://en.wikipedia.org/wiki/Publius_Licinius_Crassus_Dives_%28consul_205_BC%29

[xlii] http://penelope.uchicago.edu/~grout/encyclopaedia_romana/gladiators/gladiators.html

[xliii] Livy, 28, 39, 499.

[xliv] Livy, 28, 40, 500.

[xlv] Livy, 28, 41, 502.

[xlvi] Livy, 44, 509.

[xlvii] Livy, 28, 45, 511.

[xlviii] Livy, 28, 45, 510.

[xlix] Livy, 28, 42, 503.

[l] Livy, 28, 44, 509.

[li] Gabriel, p. 144

[lii] Plutarch. *Lives: Cato the Elder. Page 12.*

[liii] Livy, 28, 45, 510.

[liv] Ibid.

[lv] Livy, 28, 45, 511.

[lvi] Livy, 28, 46, 512.

END NOTES

[lvii] Gabriel, p. 140.

[lviii] Livy, 28, 46, 511.

[lix] Peddle, John. *Hannibal's War*, Gloustershire, England: Stroud. 1997, p. 223.

[lx] Gabriel, p. 143.

[lxi] http://en.wikipedia.org/wiki/De_Divinatione

[lxii] http://penelope.uchicago.edu/Thayer/E/Roman/Texts/secondary/SMIGRA*/Caput_Extorum.html

[lxiii] https://en.wikipedia.org/wiki/Nexum

[lxiv] Gabriel, p. 144.

[lxv] Peddle, John. *Hannibal's War*, p. 222.

[lxvi] O'Connell, Robert. *The Ghosts of Cannae: Hannibal and the Darkest Hour of the Roman Republic*. New York: Random House, 2010, p. 228.

[lxvii] Polybius, 19, 385.

[lxviii] Tessmer, Martin, *Scipio Rising: Book One of the Scipio Africanus Trilogy*. Denver, CO: Dancing in Chains Productions, 2013, p. 50.

[lxix] Livy, 29, 4, 520.

[lxx] http://en.wikipedia.org/wiki/The_finger

[lxxi] Livy, 29, 1, 514.

[lxxii] Ibid.

[lxxiii] Ibid.

END NOTES

[lxxiv] http://en.wikipedia.org/wiki/Conflict_of_the_Orders

[lxxv] http://www.unrv.com/culture/roman-slavery.php

[lxxvi] http://en.wikipedia.org/wiki/Scylletium

[lxxvii] http://en.wikipedia.org/wiki/Scylletium

[lxxviii] Livy, 29, 6, 521.

[lxxix] Ibid, 522. According to Livy, a number of guards had fallen asleep while on watch.

[lxxx] Livy, 29, 6, 522.

[lxxxi] https://en.wikipedia.org/wiki/Maniple_(military_unit)

[lxxxii] Gabriel, p. 146.

[lxxxiii] Gabriel, 147.

[lxxxiv] Livy, p. 521.

[lxxxv] Livy, 29, 7, 523.

[lxxxvi] Ibid.

[lxxxvii] *Ibid*

[lxxxviii] Ibid.

[lxxxix] Livy, 29, 7, 522.

[xc] Livy, 29, 8, 524.

[xci] http://www.amputee-coalition.org/inmotion/nov_dec_07/history_prosthetics.html

[xcii] Bagnall, p. 274.

[xciii] Livy, 29, 9, 525.

END NOTES

[xcv] 29, 17, p. 535.

[xcvi] Livy, 29, 19, 539

[xcvii] Ibid, 19, 538.

[xcviii] Ibid, 539

[xcix] Ibid,

[c] Ibid, 541.

[ci] Gabriel, p. 238. Marius is given credit for the formation of larger cohorts and legions, but Gabriel indicates that Scipio may have used both, although they were not systematized throughout the Roman army.

[cii] Ibid, 29, 22, 542.

[ciii] Ibid, 29, 22, 543.

[civ] Gabriel, p. 144.

[cv] Ibid, 29, 22, 542.

[cvi] Livy, p. 695.

[cvii] Livy, 29, 23, 544.

[cviii] http://en.wikipedia.org/wiki/Marsala

[cix] Livy, 29, 545.

[cx] Livy, 29, 6, 521

[cxi] Livy, 29, 23, 545

END NOTES

[cxii] Ibid.

[cxiii] Livy, 29, 25, 546.

[cxiv] Peddle, pp. 225-6.

[cxv] Livy, 29, 25, 546.

[cxvi] Gabriel, 156.

Made in the USA
Middletown, DE
03 May 2016